*The*

# OTHER
# VALLEY

# The
# OTHER
# VALLEY

~ A NOVEL ~

## Scott Alexander Howard

**ATRIA** BOOKS

New York   London   Toronto   Sydney   New Delhi

ATRIA
BOOKS

An Imprint of Simon & Schuster, LLC
1230 Avenue of the Americas
New York, NY 10020

First Atria Books hardcover edition February 2024

**ATRIA** B O O K S and colophon are trademarks of Simon & Schuster, LLC

Simon & Schuster: Celebrating 100 Years of Publishing in 2024.

For information about special discounts for bulk purchases, please contact Simon & Schuster Special Sales at 1-866-506-1949 or business@simonandschuster.com.

The Simon & Schuster Speakers Bureau can bring authors to your live event. For more information or to book an event, contact the Simon & Schuster Speakers Bureau at 1-866-248-3049 or visit our website at www.simonspeakers.com.

Interior design by Jill Putorti

Manufactured in the United States of America

1  3  5  7  9  10  8  6  4  2

Library of Congress Cataloging-in-Publication Data
Names: Howard, Scott Alexander, author.
Title: The other valley : a novel / Scott Alexander Howard.
Description: First Atria Books hardcover edition. | New York : Atria Books, 2024.
Identifiers: LCCN 2023004270 (print) | LCCN 2023004271 (ebook) |
ISBN 9781668015476 (hardcover) | ISBN 9781668015483 (paperback) |
ISBN 9781668015490 (ebook)
Subjects: LCGFT: Magic realist fiction. | Novels.
Classification: LCC PR9199.4.H678 O84 2024  (print) | LCC PR9199.4.H678 (ebook) |
DDC 813/.6--dc23/eng/20230426
LC record available at https://lccn.loc.gov/2023004270
LC ebook record available at https://lccn.loc.gov/2023004271

ISBN 978-1-6680-1547-6
ISBN 978-1-6680-1549-0 (ebook)

# Part I

I used to stand alone by the cloakroom door. In the morning before school, and again when the lunch bell rang and the others ran out to the field, I walked to the same spot and rested my head on the sharp crags of stucco. An outcrop of shadow protected the wall from the autumn heat. With folded hands I stood in the shade, gazing at the backwoods and waiting out the day.

I took up my station at the rear of the school after Clare's parents moved downtown, leaving me friendless in the neighborhood. I sometimes ran into her at the store or on the boulevard, but as our mothers chatted, our scant talk revealed that our common ground had been only literal, the adjoining area between our yards. The new neighbors were old and seemed to wear housecoats all day. And so, at school, I became the girl by the door: Odile who stands by herself. Never spoken to and seldom spoken of. Staring at nothing with eyes like carved wood, as motionless as an effigy.

Before the bell called everyone in, I liked to slip inside the classroom a minute early. Six empty rows faced an immaculate blackboard. The dusty odor of chalk blended with a pungent oil. My teacher, M. Pichegru, habitually rubbed his desk with a wet black rag. When I was younger the oily smell had made my nostrils curl.

Then the bell would ring, the cloakroom door would open behind me, and the room would rush with noise. In the storm of laughter and gossip,

I remained alone. But when Pichegru strode in with his books and his switch, everybody hushed. We stood in our uniforms until he motioned us to sit, and for the next hours of lectures and tests I was glad to have company in my silence.

That fall I was sixteen and the course of my life was ready to be determined. My class had reached the apprenticeship level, and most people were excited about the impending transition out of school. At the end of September we were to hand in our applications and wait to see who chose us; later on, once the decisions were made, we would split our time between Pichegru's lessons and training for our vocations around town. Some people knew the work they wanted, and others were scrambling to figure it out. All month there were visits scheduled from clerks and artisans explaining their trades, as well as field trips to the farms, the orchards, the mill, and the border.

That, at least, was the regular way of things. My mother, however, thought that I was destined for the Conseil. She had always believed this, or wanted to.

The Conseil's process was different from other apprenticeships. I could not simply apply at the end of the month and hope to be picked. Before that, they had a special vetting program, and gaining admittance to that program was difficult in itself. Pichegru would have to nominate me, and he could send just two students, unlike the downtown school, which got to send more. If you managed to get accepted into vetting, you had to get through September without being cut. Those who succeeded were offered apprenticeships in the Hôtel de Ville. Only a few candidates made it each year; some years no one did.

My mother worked in the Hôtel de Ville, but in the basement archives. I see the apprentices they get, she told me. They're smart, but you're smarter. She had tried out for the Conseil when she was my age and made it to the end of the second week. When I said I might be too shy for a career in politics, she scoffed.

She didn't know how I acted at school. The idea of me on the Conseil was ludicrous. I had no desire to be a conseiller, and no illusions about the likelihood of my becoming one. The prospect of competing against others mortified me, let alone the prospect of prevailing and having such a public job. But my mother's job seemed not so bad, despite her frequent gripes: filing petitions in a tucked-away room, collating reports with blacked-out names and ages. Underneath the Hôtel de Ville was somewhere I could see myself. And the fact that all such positions went to students cut from the Conseil's vetting program had helped prepare me for the shame of asking Pichegru, on the first day of school, whether he would consider nominating me. My mother had dropped me off that morning and confidently wished me luck.

School began on the final Friday of August, an encroachment on the summer that never ceased to feel cruel. For the younger children it was a half day, but Pichegru treated it like any other, directing us to open our fresh textbooks without welcoming us back. I saw that some girls in the room had new haircuts, and there were discernible shifts in the social landscape—people who'd traded desks to get closer to each other. Alliances and flirtations I imagined developing during long afternoons at the beach.

I took care to look engaged in the lessons, and when class let out I ventured up to the lectern. Pichegru was erasing the blackboard. He was barely taller than me, but he was muscular and rapid, destroying block letters in vigorous swirls. The overhead light gleamed off his bald skull. I stammered that I was interested in a Conseil apprenticeship.

He finished cleaning the whole board before responding. Through the window I heard muffled shouts on the playground. Pichegru tossed his cloth on the chalk ledge and turned to me.

I'm surprised to hear that, Odile. You know the vetting program requires you to speak.

A blush climbed my face, but the next thing he said was matter-of-fact.

Write me something over the weekend and give it to me Monday. I nominate next week.

He told me that his recommendations were based on a personal essay— the shorter the better, but well considered. The downtown school nominated according to nepotism, but his essay method was based solely on merit. If I could write a paper that demonstrated a suitable intellect and, more importantly, a suitable temperament for the Conseil, he would be willing to give them my name.

I asked what I was supposed to write about. Pichegru said that he gave the same question every year: If you had permission to travel outside the valley, which direction would you go?

I walked home from school on the neighborhood's one real road, notched into the mountain's edge. On the uphill side of the chemin des Pins, houses peered from the tops of steep driveways. Across the road the slope continued downward, clumped with balsamroot and weeds. You could see the whole valley beyond the faded grey roofs of the lower homes: the calm lake, the arid mountains rising from the opposite shore.

Our house was a small one below the chemin des Pins. I walked down the laneway and let myself in. My mother was still at work. She'd been reorganizing the books in the living room, and precarious towers had sprouted around the floor. I sat cross-legged and picked up a vellum-bound collection.

It was the only art book she owned. It contained woodcuts done in red ink, compact square landscapes that made the valley look like a fairy tale. Each illustration was protected by a glassine page that had to be turned delicately. I opened to a picture of a hillside apple orchard, a rolling murmuration of trees. On the next page was the downtown park. It was a perspective from out on the lake, maybe from the summer swim dock. Little bathers stood on the beach. The crimson water in the foreground swayed with lines as thin as hair.

The most interesting picture was at the end of the book. It assumed a vantage point in the sky, looking at the valley from above. Our small town in the middle was nestled against the lake, which stretched like a finger up and down the page. The mountains surrounding us were tall and empty.

To the left of the mountains was an identical small town, on the shore of an identical lake. To the right, it was the same: the mountains, the lake, the town again. After each valley came another. The towns repeated in both directions, east and west. Dark lakes slid up the page in parallel.

My fingers paced the mountains as I considered Pichegru's fantasy exercise. In addition to the valleys' natural borders, each town was encircled by a fence—something not shown on this particular woodcut, but something everyone knew. The fence followed the ridge above my school, high in the backwoods and mostly out of view. Where it came down out of the mountains, it tracked across the wide yellow swath of plainsland on the eastern outskirts of town. It curved toward the lakeshore and then continued across the water, reaching the other side to claim the narrow slice of land inhabited by the western guards.

I had never seen the border up close. I sat on the floor and imagined how it would feel to cross it.

When I described my exchange with Pichegru to my mother, she didn't ask whether I was actually more interested in visiting the east or the west. She said to prioritize what the Conseil wanted to hear.

It's a trick question, Odile. Think about what you're applying for. They don't want apprentices who are curious what it's like over there. A conseiller mostly tells people they can't go.

We were on the back patio in our mismatched iron chairs, sipping cold soup for dinner. The soup was tangy and red. It was still daylight but there were some early stars. Our backyard was shaded by trees that blocked our view of the lake. I asked what she thought I should say in my paper if Pichegru's prompt was a trap.

Be honest and say you don't want to see those places. Say you're content where you are.

*

I worked at my father's old desk in my bedroom. The desk was so tight over my legs that I couldn't picture a grown man using it, but it gave me an idea for making my essay more personal. This helped me feel better about not technically answering the question. After all, I had to write something. I picked up my pencil.

*Given the chance to visit another valley, I would not take it.*

I scratched this out:

*Would respectfully decline.*

The only legitimate reason for requesting passage, we'd been told, was consolation. To lay eyes on a person you would never otherwise live to meet, or a person you would never see again at home. In fact, for me, there was someone like this whom I could write about. When I was four years old, my father died in the old garage next to my grandparents' orchard. If I were to go west, I could find him, and watch him for a bit. He'd be in his early twenties on the other side of the mountains, and would have met my mother only recently, hanging out by the fountain in the Place du Bâtisseur. I knew the story: she'd wished on a coin and refused to tell him, an inquisitive stranger, what her wish was. He threw a coin of his own and wished to take her out. She said he'd nullified his wish by sharing it, but she went out with him anyway. It would be tempting to go there and look. To feel like I knew him better, or like I knew him at all.

But, I wrote to Pichegru, seeing him would not console me. I might not even recognize which man he was. What good would it do, to have him pointed out from afar and be told I was looking at my father? The truth was that he was not so much a vivid loss in my life as an abstract deficit, the explanation for why our house was quieter than Clare's. The real loss belonged to my mother, and she always swore that she'd never petition for a viewing. She said she remembered enough: how he started sleeping all day, how he started seeming asleep even when he wasn't. She said her memories were what helped her not to miss him.

I concluded my essay by vowing that, as a future conseiller, I would advise petitioners to seek whatever closure they needed here in their own valley, which is to say, in the safer pastures of ordinary grief. If that was enough for my mother, then it was enough for me, and so it ought to be for anyone. Reading it back under my breath, my answer struck me as reasonably good. Moreover, it seemed like the kind of writing that might impress Pichegru. The only checkmarks he ever scrawled on my homework, regardless of the subject, were next to the toughest-minded statements that crept from my pencil. Perhaps he would see this as another one of my small severities, and approve.

It was late when I transcribed my final draft. My mother was reading in bed. She placed my essay on her book and tilted it to the lamp, her shadowy eyes scanning the page. I was nervous and looked away, finding my distorted face in her magnified makeup mirror: my jumble of curls, my too-long jaw. The paper fluttered when she handed it back.

Very clever, she said.

We hadn't talked about him in a long time. He had worked in the little grocery store on the rue de Laiche. He did everything there, but his specialty was fruit, which made sense given his upbringing. It was a sore spot between him and my grandparents that he didn't want to run the orchard when they retired. They had to sell the land to the neighbors instead, and the two orchards were merged. But the Nancys were always kind to me, and when we visited my grandparents, I was still allowed to wander through the cherry trees that used to be ours.

One of the few memories I have of him is from that orchard in the summer. Although the sunshine was splitting hot, under the leaves the air felt lush and languid. My father held my hand as we walked barefoot up the row. I took big steps through the tall grass, squishing overripe cherries between my toes, feeling like a giant in a slow green land. When we reached the orchard's edge, he lifted me onto the stone wall that formed the property line. Before me was a barren vista, a field of wild mustard climbing toward rounded foothills. The sun had gone white in the clouds.

What I felt was a kind of thrilling sadness, something I have since experienced when looking out over other open spaces and lonely boundaries: an emotion that lives on the desolate edge of the known.

As important as this memory is to me, the next part contains too much hindsight to be genuine. Still holding my father's hand, I glance back into the trees. They are all the very same height, and through their branches I see the white-walled garage, crouching. The moment has the air of a premonition: instead of a parent, you will have this haunted place. Yet apart from avoiding the garage where he'd done it, I really didn't think of him often. When he left us, I had been too young to understand, and so the disavowal in my essay came easily.

On Monday morning I left my nomination essay on Pichegru's desk and hurried to my seat before he came in. More students filed to the front to do the same. I soon regretted leaving my paper face-up, because I noticed Henri Swain and Jo Verdier pausing to skim it before putting theirs on top. Henri gave me a smirk on the way to his desk. When Pichegru entered the room he stuck the essays in a drawer.

Lumped into our normal lessons that morning was a short visit from the druggist's assistant, who was there to answer apprenticeship questions. A few people eagerly raised their hands. It seemed like it would be all right working at the counter and pouring tinctures, but the main druggist was Lucien's father and one of the available spots was bound to go to him. I tuned out the assistant. As little as the vetting program appealed to me, I had no idea what I would do if Pichegru turned me down. I'd prepared no alternatives because of my mother's insistence on the Conseil. Her ambition for me was vicarious, I knew. Anything else I might do with my life would fall short of the life she'd wanted for herself.

\*

I was standing against the wall, eating my sandwich outside, when a crack went off near my head. Stucco granules sprayed into my collar. I flinched and looked around.

Out on the lawn, Henri and Tom were stifling laughter. A rubber ball, dusted white, landed in the grass.

Sorry about that, Odile—I missed. Henri gave an exaggerated shrug.

I reddened, stepping away from where the ball had left its mark. The shoulder of my navy blazer was speckled with grit. I brushed it off and pulled a fragment out of my hair. There was a sandwich lying on the pavement, and darkly I recognized my lunch. I was deciding whether or not it was salvageable when the ball struck a second time.

You missed again, said Tom, dissolving into giggles.

This time I hadn't startled as much. I stayed with my back to the wall and took a second small step to the right, but as I did, I felt my mistake. There was something too automatic about the way I'd moved, too much like a clock figurine. Henri's laughter trailed off and he regarded me oddly. He scooped up the ball.

I shut my eyes to the next shot, winced, and took another side-step.

That's so funny, Henri remarked.

Sensing an event, other kids started to watch. Each time he threw the ball, I dodged from the waist up, but only shuffled a bit farther down the wall. The laughs around the lawn grew louder. Some of the spectators were younger but some were in my class. I saw Justine Cefai looking disgusted; beside her, Jo wore an incredulous grin. Sitting under a tree at the far edge of the grass, Edme Pira and Alain Rosso were watching too. A teacher squinted from the playing field but didn't come over.

I'm not sure why I kept stepping along the wall when that was the whole problem. I could have dashed for cover in the backwoods, in fact I longed to run for the trees, but running felt like the greater humiliation. Sickeningly, I began affecting a distant smile as they hooted at me, as though I was in on the joke.

Then Henri let out a curse. I looked up and saw Edme and Alain marching across the lawn toward him. They'd untucked the fronts of their uniform shirts to use as pouches, and the pouches were full of sticks.

Hey, Henri! Edme called in a cheerful voice. He whipped a stick over the grass and hit Henri in the shin. Alain threw another, this time striking his shoulder. Swearing and covering his head, Henri retreated and Tom followed. Edme and Alain chucked their remaining sticks after them, a fusillade that fell well short. They wiped their hands and strolled back to their tree.

I cleaned my uniform in the bathroom and spent the rest of the lunch hour indoors. My blazer and pinafore were damp from the sink, and my head hurt, not from the ball, which never actually hit me, but from clenching my teeth, the afterache of shame.

It was hardly the first time I'd been harassed, and usually the worst of it happened at the start of the school year, before Henri and the others got bored and turned to other games. But my dejection made me realize that I'd been hoping things would have finally changed. Apparently, I was still what I was.

Edme's desk was ahead of mine in the next row over. That afternoon Pichegru was teaching geology. Slate, schist, gneiss. There was a leather case sitting at Edme's feet. He played violin in the humble school orchestra. His neck was the color of sand in the shade, and his hair was blacker than shale.

Edme and Alain didn't talk to me, but they didn't tease me either. The two of them were a pair, friends since before school began. Alain's house was a little ways down from mine. He was a ruddy-cheeked loudmouth, red-haired like me, though more orange than my ruby frizz. Years ago, before I went quiet, Clare and I had sometimes played with him in the neighborhood. He'd been eager to throw apples at cars, and I'd been too scared to do it. He seemed the same now as he was then: hyper, irreverent, hard to predict. Alain's antics earned him the switch from Pichegru more often than most, which was part of why people liked him.

Edme lived past the school. His parents worked at the packing house, crating apples and peaches in the harvest months. In the winter I would see them shoveling snow and salting sidewalks downtown, always together. People never referred to M. and Mme Pira individually; they were, fondly, the Piras. My mother and I sometimes passed them doing their odd jobs, and they invariably said hello.

Their son was soft-spoken and sharp-boned, with a haircut that hung in his face. I didn't see Edme around the neighborhood much, except for with Alain. Their friendship might have been surprising if it hadn't always been there. Where Alain was blustering, Edme seemed thoughtful, with slender, dancing eyes. On the other hand, he wasn't really shy: if Alain did something outrageous, Edme would join in with an abstract smile, like it was the only thing to be done. One morning in our second year, when we were eight or nine, Alain shimmied up a birch tree in front of the school. The tree wasn't any good for climbing and wobbled from his weight. But he got near the top, pulled out his flute, and began mangling one of the Cherishment hymns that we had to learn in music class. Poised at the base of the tree, Edme raised his violin. Eyes closed, he came in screeching and off-key, which had to be on purpose, since everyone knew how well he could play. I hid a smile and walked to my wall, but I could still hear the dreadfulness echoing, and eventually a teacher yelling at them to stop. They got beaten for it, but not badly, because Pichegru didn't know quite what to think.

After school I delayed going home to avoid walking near Henri and Tom. I stayed in my desk long enough that Pichegru noticed. He addressed me from the front of the room.

I've read your essay. I'm not going to nominate you.

My teacher slid his books into his leather bag. It seemed like all he intended to say.

Why not?

It was effrontery to ask; in the swiftness of my failure I'd forgotten my place. Pichegru looked irritated, as if I shouldn't need to be told.

I asked you a question—east or west—and you didn't answer it. All you did was add some pity.

He flipped off the overhead on his way out, leaving just the depleted light from the window. I blinked at the playground and field and pond, all blurring together and threatening to flood, but I tightened my jaw and didn't let myself cry.

I yanked my bookbag from my cloakroom peg and went outside. Everyone else had left the schoolgrounds. At my house, all that awaited me were hours of fear before my mother got home and asked how things had gone with Pichegru. I tried not to imagine how she would react. Across the sunny lawn was the forest where I'd wished I could escape at lunch. I shouldered my bag and crossed the grass, leaving the school behind, letting the pine trees swallow me.

The backwoods had an amber smell, a tang of warm earth and resin. The ground was a motley mix of reddish anthills, fir sheddings, and stumps decomposing into soil. The path felt spongy and hollow underfoot. Creaking branches replied to the sound of my breath, and slowly my breathing settled.

It was a while since I'd been in the backwoods. I didn't remember my way around. If I went far enough I knew I'd hit the border fence, but that was at least another mile up the mountain. Down here, the trees were still dense and the incline was mild. I followed the trail in the pine stubble. The soil was the soft grey of a cat's belly.

After several minutes the slope above the path became barer, dotted with sedge and loose stones. Farther up was a rocky ridge where I could see a thin wall of brush positioned on the edge. Something about it seemed too isolated to be an accident, so I stepped off the path to explore. The hill bristled with tiny coral lichens that crunched as I climbed. Without many trees to filter the sun I had to shield my eyes with my hand. I walked along the crest of the ridge toward what looked like a small fort.

It was children's work, either half-finished or half-ruined. There was a big log forming the base of a single wall, and on top of it a sagging heap of branches like a dam or a bird's nest. Protruding from that heap was the vertical brush that I'd spotted: dead copper bushes rustling in the breeze, circular leaves spinning like paper coins.

The abandoned fort was peaceful. Its dirt floor had some prickly moss

and sparkles of quartz. I sat down, grateful for the shade and my hidden-
ness from the path below. It would be possible to clean this place up, I
thought. Haul in fresh foliage, thicken up the branch barrier. The bark had
peeled off the log and the wood's flesh was inscribed with shallow lines,
worms that had traveled at weird angles. As I reclined against the log, it
took more and more effort to keep my eyes from closing. I lay my head on
my bookbag and listened to the light wind slipping through the wall.

\*

My eyelids opened to the sound of footsteps. People were passing on the
path.

I heard them speaking, but their voices floated up the ridge and away,
revealing nothing but the sure presence of others. Soon they were gone.
They'd sounded like adults, which was unusual for the woods behind the
school.

Even though I'd napped for only an hour, the day's memories felt harder,
like sore muscles that were worse upon waking. Henri's jeers, Pichegru's
snide rejection. I got to my feet and brushed off my uniform. The daylight
leaned sharply behind the wall of the fort. The sun was already low in the
west, the valley sighing in the heat's afterlife. I walked back down the slope
and rejoined the path.

The school's playing field was freshly mowed. The custodian was locking up the utility room. It was almost four-thirty; soon my mother would
be getting home. Stalling, I kicked around the playground's perimeter,
watching the custodian start his car and drive away. On the far side of the
school I heard music, a distant rehearsal bending slightly out of tune.

I looked at the swings. Normally they were the little kids' domain, but
sometimes my classmates took over and stood on them, swinging until
they were level with the crossbar, then leaping like cliff divers into the
sawdust.

I wiped a shoeprint off the black rubber seat and sat with a squeak of
the chains. At first I rocked listlessly, but when I felt the tug of momentum,

I lifted up my heels. A couple of short pumps and I began rising without effort. It surprised me, the force that could be released by the limpest of actions, and in spite of the day's troubles, I pointed my toes.

Soon I was nearing the crossbar and the wind was in my ears. Through watery eyes I looked out past the field. The pond rose into view and became sky. As I reached the swing's highest arc, I strained for that perfect stillness at the outer limit of gravity. My swing plunged down and the pond disappeared. But when I rose again, I was startled by the sight of something past the bulrushes.

Three people stood on the surface of the pond, or so it seemed to me. All had black masks on their faces. It was two men and a woman—none young from their postures. One of the men wore the green uniform of the gendarmerie, and the others wore formless visitors' tunics. I watched the man in green lean toward the woman. She began taking her mask off to answer, but the gendarme reached out and pulled it back on so abruptly that she stumbled. I saw, now, that they were balancing on a jetty of reeds extending from the pond's shore. The man in the tunic caught the woman's arm before she fell into the water. Then, clinging together, the two visitors stared directly at me.

Dread poured through my body. On the downswing I dragged my heels hard against the playground's mulch. I jumped off the swing too fast and staggered to the corner of the school, but when I got there, I looked back. From the ground, I could still make them out across the field.

I had seen masks before, but never when I was the only one around. I tried to reason breath by breath. They had to be the same people I'd heard on the backwoods path, so they'd come from the eastern fence. They'd waited by the school, so they were probably somebody's parents— but there were two of them, so they couldn't be mine. As I hurried past the empty classroom windows I clutched at this thought, that they weren't here for me. But their stare was not the stare of strangers either. I'd just passed our cloakroom door when Edme rounded the corner carrying his violin case.

Instantly I knew.

It was Mme Pira's lips when she'd raised the mask. It was M. Pira's hasty bearing when he steadied her. My heart lifted. The visitors were the Piras, it was the Piras, it wasn't about me at all.

Ahead, their son raised his hand in a mild wave.

Hi, Odile.

My voice vanished. I stopped a few steps away and hugged my arms across my stomach. We were face-to-face. I was the only thing between him and the pond.

Edme scanned my expression under curious brows. Are you okay?

Oh, yeah—I'm fine.

My body stayed where it was with a solidity I didn't understand. I saw Edme notice too—the moment we should have parted, but didn't—and he chuckled.

Fine is good, he said, unbothered by the awkwardness, and somehow my laugh in response was easy and light, like a streamer in the sun.

What are you up to? he asked.

Just heading home.

I usually don't see you here after school.

I went for a walk in the backwoods.

Nice. I like it up there.

I glanced at the trees, nodding in agreement. In the corner of my eye I thought he shifted his weight.

Actually, I added, I might've found something. There's kind of a fort.

Really?

Yeah. Probably some kids made it. It's not much, just part of a wall. It's a little off the path.

I began to blush: surely it was a childish thing to mention. But Edme replied that he'd like to see it sometime. I didn't know if he meant with me, so I didn't answer, and he didn't elaborate. He switched his instrument case to his other hand and smiled again.

If you're going home, do you mind if I walk with you? Rehearsal let out early, maybe I'll head to Alain's.

I must have said yes, because he turned around and paused for me to join him. And I must have gone to him, because we left the schoolgrounds together, without passing the playground or the pond.

He walked on the gravel at the side of the road, the sun silhouetting his face. Behind him the lake shone with light.

My house was only ten minutes away. I could suppress the implications of what I'd seen for ten minutes. With him beside me it felt wrong to think about, indecent, so I tried to act unfazed.

Edme was saying it was hard to believe this was our apprenticeship year. He asked what I was applying for.

There wasn't a way around telling him. As soon as I uttered the word 'Conseil,' before I got to the part about botching it, he whistled.

The Conseil, that makes sense. We always figured you were, you know—wise.

I felt embarrassed and gratified at the same time. We who?

Just me and Alain. But everyone else too, I bet. You're very serious. Sorry, is that annoying for me to say?

I managed to smile at my feet and shake my head, wishing the subject would change. What about your apprenticeship? I asked.

Well, now, that's a matter of controversy. I want to try out for the conservatory. They're starting a combined composition and performance stream. But my parents want me to do something more useful, like the butcher shop. With one hand Edme lifted his violin case in the air, and with the other he made a gesture of futility.

That wouldn't be so bad, I offered. My father was a grocer.

I've heard that.

They were simple things, but felt intimate to say. Edme's footsteps kicked the gravel in comfortable silence. The sinking sun touched the far ridge.

So what are you going to do? I asked.

He hopped ahead of me, swinging his case, his movements boyish and quick. No clue. We'll see. It'd be nice if I could go over there and find out. He cocked his head at the mountain.

My stomach tightened, but he went on. They're letting me do the audition, at least. I think if I get in, they'll give up on the whole butcher thing. Which means I've got a couple weeks to perfect my repertoire.

I wanted to reply that he was obviously good already, but I worried that the compliment might sound like false reassurance in spite of being true, so I said nothing. We reached the top of my laneway.

Thanks for the walk, said Edme.

Okay, I replied.

His dark eyes were lively. See you tomorrow! He tapped a little drum-roll on his case, and continued down the hill.

R ight away she asked if I'd submitted my essay to Pichegru. I began
     mumbling that I had. But she must have assumed it would take him
longer to decide, because she didn't ask for my result. Instead she praised my
strategy again: my essay showcased my unique perspective, levelheadedness
in the face of personal tragedy. With an encouraging look she went back to
chopping onions. Soon the house smelled good and I realized I was hungry.
I hadn't had anything since I dropped my sandwich at lunch. At the dining table, I avoided conversation about the vetting program by eating. My
mother was going on about a colleague in the archives who'd been sick for
a week, so she had more work to do at home. Nothing else was said about
the Conseil, but I still felt nervous that she would return to the topic while
I finished the dishes. I rinsed and dried with such efficiency that I almost
dropped a plate on the floor. As soon as I could, I went to my bedroom and
shut the door.

I knew what it meant that his parents had come. In reality—not in a hypo-
thetical essay prompt—permission to leave one valley and enter another
was only ever granted due to a loss. On their side of the mountains, twenty
years from here, Edme must be gone.

I'd felt relieved when I realized it was the Piras. Now I felt guilty. I hadn't even thanked Edme for what he did, fending off Henri and Tom. If he ever talked to me again I needed to do that.

The black masks were larger than normal faces, which made them look uncanny from a distance, sinister even, but it was simply to prevent recognition. That was one of the few things Pichegru had taught us in our geography lessons when we were young and in need of coddling: nothing about the masks was designed to frighten. Behind them were regular people. Still, they had a disquieting effect.

There were places around town that served as unofficial viewpoints for visitors. Gendarmes from the neighboring valleys would escort them there. Typically these spots were at a remove, close but not too close. The outsiders would hang back behind a pair of cottonwood trees at the far end of the park. From there, they had a view of both the pavilion and the open green, where people had picnics and played football or pétanque. I once noticed a mask in a guildhall window overlooking the town square, waiting for someone to pass by. I watched surreptitiously, although you weren't supposed to, and others who saw the visitor looked away. Their presence was unsettling: the swim of daily life interrupted by looming, expressionless faces against the glass. Inevitably you worried that it boded ill for you.

He didn't seem sick. I thought, too, of the relaxed way he'd mentioned his disagreement with his parents over the conservatory—not the manner of someone about to do something dramatic.

A year ago a girl from the downtown school, Yvette Cressy, died. She'd had some kind of disease, so no one was surprised when it happened. I'd seen her once or twice, moving weakly on her mother's arm, so emaciated that she seemed not to touch the ground.

Masks had visited that time. I didn't see them myself, but I heard Marie Valenti talking about it: two older people and a gendarme, in the park, by the cottonwoods. The word spread in whispers. If Yvette noticed them watching, she must have put it together too. But you were not meant to know who they were or who they'd come for. Usually, if they were somewhere they could be seen, it was busy enough that you couldn't tell who they were looking at. And since they all dressed the same, you couldn't tell if they were from the east or the west—unless you'd overheard them in the woods, close to the eastern fence, so you knew they were here for bereavement.

I lay in my school clothes on top of my bed. I rolled over to close my curtains. A tiny moth roamed the quilt, wings folded into a lost arrow.

Marie Valenti had seen the masks in late autumn; Yvette had not passed away till the spring. Whatever would befall Edme, he had some time. Yet a knot had formed in my abdomen. I lifted my shirt to rub it, but the sensation of my fingers on my skin only added a second detail to the discomfort. My body buzzed with nameless agitation, something distinct from simple pity.

I tried to distract myself with homework. Although it was the second day of the year, Pichegru had already assigned us a set of logic problems. I trudged through the proofs, crossing out my wrong turns, then idly darkening the strikethroughs with my pencil instead of correcting the errors. Every few minutes I found myself staring at the ceiling. Finally I gathered my papers to work in the kitchen.

It was past nine o'clock. My mother was still hunched at the table with a box of files. I moved a placemat and dropped my homework across from her. She leaned back in her chair.

Look at us, she sighed. I need more wine.

She opened a new bottle and poured herself a glass, then set another one down by my homework, as she sometimes did. Tonight I frowned and muttered that I had to be able to think straight.

My mother looked bemused. You're right.

I did my proofs deliberately, feeling her watching as she sipped her wine.

Things will work out for you, she murmured.

I paused before glancing up. Her eyes were tired and her glass was stained purple at the bottom. You'll see, Odile, once you show them what you're made of, the conseillers will eat you up. It turned out she was not gazing at me, but at her box of files.

I could have told her then what Pichegru had said, but she was seldom this tender with me. I reached for my wine glass and raised it to her.

Soon after, my mother went to bed, taking her files but leaving the rest of the bottle. My pencil plodded to the end of the proofs. When I was done I carefully tore out the pages I would hand in tomorrow and wrote my name. Because I thought it was homely, it was my habit to scribble it small: Odile Ozanne, the letters bunched together as if trying to hide. It sounded better the way Edme said it: Hi, Odile.

I finished the glass of wine and decided to pour another. His was a nice name, Edme Pira. If you said it aloud, each word ended with parted lips, as if promising something more. I dismissed a strange temptation to write it in my notebook just for myself. He was the first person to be nice to me in years—setting aside childhood, the first ever. But something was going to happen to him, and only I knew. Bleakly I wondered how I was supposed to look at him now. What if he saw it in my eyes.

My essay had cautioned against visiting the other valleys. Pichegru said I hadn't given him a proper answer. But now I saw I was more right than I'd known. Visitation *should* be discouraged—not just because the viewers themselves might find it unconsoling, as I'd argued already, but also because the viewings could place unfair burdens on nearby onlookers. It was too easy to glance the wrong way and see a mask lift up for a moment, or notice a posture that looked familiar. That was all it took to have a terrible secret about your neighbor—something that might gnaw on your mind until every thought you had was wet with its teeth. It was a grim thing to live with, and not everyone would have the prudence or discipline to keep it to themselves.

The hanging light above the table flickered. I splashed the rest of the wine into my glass. The feeling coming over me, like a brushfire up my scalp, was more than reproach or indignation: it was contempt for

Pichegru, for his casual no, for accusing me of weaseling out of his question when I *had* answered it and gotten it right. I picked up my pencil and dug it into a blank notebook page, denouncing his rejection and arguing more stridently against leaving the valley. I would not apologize for my position, or, for that matter, for getting in the way of the Piras' viewing—it was not my choice to see them. With zealous disdain I drew heavy circles around words like 'risk,' 'danger,' and 'foreknowledge.' Now I wrote down Edme's name.

I dreamed of the school playground. It was as if I'd gone back at night to swing again. I couldn't see the masks, but knew they were around. The clouds were too bright, almost yellow, hissing like oil in a pan.

In the morning my bedsheets were sweaty and coiled. My mouth was parched with wine, my tongue a dead slab. When I made myself move there was pain behind my eyes. I had woozy memories of finishing the bottle. I walked to school squinting through daggers of sunlight, then slumped against the outside wall and closed my eyes until the bell.

Alain was loitering at Edme's desk, his butt leaning into the aisle. Edme hadn't acknowledged me after our walk yesterday, but with my headache I was grateful to be catatonic before class started. It was only when Lucien brushed by with a sheaf of paper that I remembered my homework.

At Pichegru's desk I opened my notebook to the assignment. I was about to leave it on the pile when I noticed the drunken screed underneath. It was my righteous attack on Pichegru, complete with a scarlet stain in the shape of a glass. I'd torn the page out but not yet destroyed it. Hastily I covered it with my logic proofs. Then someone poked my shoulder.

How are you feeling about this? Confidence level on a scale of one to ten?

Alain was looking at me eagerly. It took me a second to realize he was talking about the homework.

Confidence level, I repeated. Um. Six and a half.

Six and a half, mused Alain. That's semi-respectable, do you mind if I crib? Any friend of Pira's is a friend of mine. Just a friendly little cribbing . . .

I didn't react fast enough, and suddenly he'd plucked the homework out of my hand. He darted around me and began copying my proofs at the big oak desk. I stood helplessly as I heard Pichegru coming down the hall.

Well shit, Alain sighed, glancing at the door. He shoved the pages into the submission pile and patted it straight just as Pichegru walked in. Both of us lowered our eyes and went to our desks. Edme was laughing silently as I passed him.

*

Where the playing field ended in marshy weeds, I took the path that circled the pond. The shoreline was overhung with dead branches that reminded me of claws. The sounds of the lunch hour grew distant.

It didn't take long to reach the spot where the visitors had stood. A few steps down the embankment, a section of reeds had broken sideways into the water, forming a natural dock. I nudged it with my toe and put my weight on it. Mud leaked up through the reeds. There were no footprints, no cigarette ends, no indications of anyone. Orange tadpoles, fat and bright, swarmed slowly in the shallows.

When I came back from the pond I found Edme and Alain on the edge of the field. Alain had a leather ball at his feet.

If it isn't Mlle Ozanne, who went out of her way to lend me a hand, he said. Alain talked in that way where you didn't know if he was being sarcastic or not.

Edme rolled his eyes at me. Never help him. Once you do it's hopeless. I'm not sure if he knows how to read or write. He might just be copying the shapes I make.

You could take advantage of that, I said.

Fuck you, and you, Alain said pleasantly, pointing to us in turn. He lifted the ball with his foot and kicked it in the air.

Edme ignored him. We were wondering. You know that fort you found? Would you mind showing us where it is?

Sure. I blushed. I mean, it's nothing.

The bell rang across the field. Alain booted the ball into the weeds.

How about after school? asked Edme.

Today? Sure, okay.

In the classroom I opened my notebook to a fresh sheet. I had just written the date when I realized that the wine-stained page wasn't there. I remembered Alain snatching my homework, then thrusting a heap of papers onto Pichegru's desk.

I looked to the front of the room. The papers were gone.

I searched my notebook, the inside of my desk, my notebook again. I couldn't piece together everything I'd written, but isolated phrases came back with nauseating clarity. The page had been dark with scorn. I'd asserted the superiority of my judgment over Pichegru's. Worse, I'd identified the Piras—Pichegru would blame me for exposing him to information neither of us was supposed to have. I would be beaten, without a doubt. After that, I had no idea what further punishment would be dispensed for defiance on this scale. Pichegru used the switch for regular discipline; I had never seen his reaction to something so grave.

For the rest of the day I stared down at my desk. Only once, after finishing a quiz early, did I risk looking up. Edme was writing with his head low, his cheek nearly touching the page. In the far corner of my eye it seemed as if Pichegru might be watching him, but I didn't dare confirm it. Instead I made the mistake of glancing at Henri, who was rolling his rubber ball under his palm. He raised his eyebrows at me in boredom.

The clock dragged out the day: half one, half two. I'd thought my hangover was done with me, but it moved from my head to my guts, where it congealed together with my fear. I squirmed miserably in my seat.

Finally the bell sounded. I tried to exit with everyone else, but Pichegru yelled my name.

There was no escaping him. Against the current of students, I angled
my way to the front. Pichegru planted both hands on his desk as though
about to lunge at me. But instead he yelled past: Verdier!

Confused, I looked back. I saw Jo making an amazed face at Justine.
She rushed up, smoothing her shiny black hair and shooting me an anxious smile. I couldn't put together what was happening.

Both of you expressed interest in the Conseil, said Pichegru. The vetting program starts tomorrow.

He gave Jo a piece of paper, then held one out to me.

We're the nominees? Jo said excitedly.

Yes.

Outside the cloakroom, Edme and Alain were waiting for me, and Justine
was waiting for Jo, so they had drifted together. When I came out Alain
was talking to Justine. She had sunny brown hair and freckly brown skin,
and when she giggled she tucked her hair behind the tips of her ears, which
were prone to reddening. Her miniature blushes seemed endearing instead
of embarrassing. Jo flew past me and threw herself into Justine's arms.

I got it! she cried. They jumped around together in a circle.

This is for the Conseil? Edme asked, looking amused.

Yeah! Me—and Odile. Jo paused her celebration to size me up. I never
knew you were so ambitious.

I managed a shrug.

That's great! Edme enthused. Congratulations.

Hey, and Odile did it without a rich dad in the mix, Alain quipped.

Jo scowled. Watch your mouth. Remember her dad?

Ah, shit, sorry.

Everyone looked at me. That's okay, I said quietly. Then I added, like it
was an afterthought: But fuck you, Alain.

For a worried beat I thought I'd misjudged, but they were only surprised:
Alain laughed along with Edme and Justine, and Jo cracked an apprecia-
tive grin. My stiff reputation, it seemed, was possible to play with. Alain

gave me a low bow of deference, and as he came back up, he waggled his middle fingers at the others. It's these little gestures, it's these classy things you do, remarked Edme.

It was natural to invite Jo and Justine along to the fort, although I kept downplaying the interest of the find. The five of us walked on the back-woods path. The forest hummed with insects.

I pointed up the slope where the trees were sparse and the sun streamed down. The boys took off their blazers, and their white shirts were blinding. Jo and Justine loosened their ties and unbuttoned their collars, so I did the same. As I followed them up the hill I wiped my forehead and smeared a tiny fly with my thumb.

This is it? Jo said, surveying the log wall with a hand on her hip.

I know, I apologized. Like I said, it's really not much.

Not much? exclaimed Alain. Are you kidding? This spot's ideal. He stepped up on the log and balanced on the brush heap. You've got bounti-ful building material. You've got a panoramic view. You've got the crucial advantage of height.

Are you preparing for battle or something? asked Justine.

No, just a place to hang out, said Alain. Although if a battle comes our way . . .

He aimed a stick down the ridge like a spear. It hit the path and sent up a puff of dirt.

Well, said Jo, on the topic of battles, Henri's pissed that you attacked him yesterday.

Edme laughed. Henri's such a piece of shit. So's Tom.

Tom is a slightly smaller piece of shit, Alain said. What some might call a turd.

They can be shitty, Jo agreed. She and Henri were childhood friends: the Verdiers and the Swains were the only wealthy families with connec-tions to the north end.

I fidgeted with the pleats of my pinafore. I wanted to thank Edme and

Alain for how they'd chased Henri and Tom away, but it felt impossible to do in front of Jo after I'd seen her laughing. Instead I waited for the conversation to change, and soon enough it did. Alain walked around the wall and began retrieving some of the slag brush that had fallen over the side. Edme followed suit, then I went, stepping with care down the steepest part of the slope. Jo and Justine stayed near the top. I was still worried that they thought the fort was silly, but they gamely accepted the stones and branches I passed, depositing them as we sent them up the ridge.

For nights afterward I would return to this memory, in which nothing special occurred. Alain and Edme are below, ferrying things into my hands. I'm balancing on shale fragments, keeping my feet light, trying not to trigger a rockslide. Edme passes me a bulky grey stone that's pocked with air holes and damp on the bottom. He makes sure I've got a good hold on it before he lets go. I give it to Justine, who scrunches her freckles at the wetness. It's wondrous to be here, in the center of the chain.

When we'd finished hauling for the day, we sat on the lichens above the fort and looked over our work.

Justine asked me what I'd written in my application essay for the Conseil. She'd submitted her own but hadn't been picked.

Odile totally dodged Pichegru's question, Jo interrupted. Sorry, I peeked.

What do you mean? Justine asked.

Jo looked over at me, wry and admiring.

All she wrote was: 'I wouldn't go anywhere—not there *or* there.' I thought it was brilliant. Well, to be honest, I thought it was crazy, but it worked! I mean, it seemed like you gave a bunch of reasons. I never would've thought of that, though.

Edme widened his eyes, impressed. What was the question?

He made us say which direction we'd go in, Jo explained. If the Conseil let you visit somewhere.

What did you write? I asked.

Jo stuck her hand in the air, swiveled her wrist around, and pointed to the mountain behind us. They say going east is safer for people here, so I went with that. My parents are keen on me getting in.

I bet you'll make it, said Justine. I mean, I bet you both will.

Well, it's super competitive, said Jo. In the long run you'll definitely be happier with your second choice. The veterinarian's, she added for our benefit.

Nice, said Alain, I hear Émilie's applying for that too.

Justine groaned. Would it be out of line if I begged her not to?

You should just come work at the mill with me, said Alain.

Or the butcher shop with me, said Edme.

Basically, we're saying you should get into the chopping business one way or another. What you chop doesn't matter, chopping's a whole lifestyle.

Justine sigh-laughed at Alain and flopped back on the ground.

Why on earth would you want to be a butcher? Jo frowned at Edme. I assumed you'd do music.

Yeah. It depends who wins the argument.

You should at least audition, she said.

He's going to, I put in.

Both of them looked at me. Edme nodded.

When is it? asked Jo.

A few weeks.

You know what I wrote for Pichegru? Justine said to the sky. I would walk west until I got to a valley where they didn't have modern veterinary medicine yet, and I'd give it to them. How stupid is that?


In front of the school we lingered while Alain unlocked his bike. He was saying that we could get the fort's wall higher in no time, his mother had chicken wire we could use as lattice. He proposed meeting at the same time tomorrow.

I should practice, said Edme.

And vetting starts tomorrow, said Jo, smiling at me. Sunlight glanced off her eyes, green aventurine.

What about lunch? I suggested, thinking of how I'd slipped off to the pond without any teachers noticing.

Edme pulled a haggard face. I should practice then too.

Ahh, practice at the fort in the open air, Alain scoffed. Serenade us as we build.

We said goodbye with a vague plan to reconvene soon. I walked home on the chemin des Pins as the sun was setting. I watched my shadow get taller, stretching up the scrubby hill until it touched the trees, seeming to mark the expansion of my life.

\*

The expression on my mother's face when I told her I'd been nominated was something I'd never seen before: I realized it was pride. I surrendered to her radiance and let myself feel warmed. She poured us wine, the fancier kind, as she began reminiscing about her own time in the program. My eyes followed the calligraphic flourishes of the name *Verdier* on the side of the bottle. Jo's family owned the winery down by the lake; her house looked enormous even from the road.

Mindful of the day's hangover, I drank less, leaving my mother to finish the bottle as I gradually withdrew. In my bedroom, my thoughts returned to Pichegru.

What to make of his change of heart? Why did he choose me? Running the memory forward and back, I tried to find some hint of respect in his eyes, grudging humor on his lips. Despite his temper, it wasn't impossible to imagine Pichegru as a man who could admire a certain type of brazenness if it was intelligent. Even a man who could admit, upon reading an insolent diatribe, that the argument had merit. Yet although I could picture both of these reactions, they were missing from the memory of that moment, which refused to divulge his motivation. He had rejected me; I denounced the decision; the decision was reversed.

But, of course, what I'd written was more than just a denunciation. My second essay, if it could be called that, had revealed what I saw on the playground, identifying the masked visitors by name. The more I looked at it, the more obvious was the conclusion: Pichegru nominated me because I'd recognized the Piras. I did not know enough about the Conseil's operations to understand why this would commend me to their attention, but it was the only explanation that made any sense.

The night before I began the vetting program, it took me a long time to get to sleep. My pupils widened to the size of my ceiling until at last my thoughts became weightless and started to rise. Edme held the wet stone and passed it up. Our eyes met. What is the thing that's coming for you.

T he next afternoon I waited under the rust-chewed sign with the old charabanc painted on it. The bus stop was in a cul-de-sac across the road from the school. A stout white bus made the trip downtown and back a few times a day. In practice, nobody from town ever came up here, so the bus was mostly used by north end kids and elderly people who didn't drive anymore. No one else was waiting at the stop after school. I dug my toe into the gravel and twisted juniper tips off a hedge, flicking them down the long stairway that led from the cul-de-sac to the pebbly cove below—the closest thing our neighborhood had to a beach. The torn bits of juniper pinged lightly against the metal handrail and spun into the brush.

That day Pichegru had continued acting normally, which is to say he paid me no mind. At lunch I'd stood in my spot against the wall trying not to feel anxious about the Conseil. It was hot out. I saw Jo in a big group of people on the field, and when they came closer I noticed Alain with them, hanging around Justine again. Henri and Tom were in the group too, but they were talking to Marie and some other girls. Spontaneously I picked up my things and moved around the corner.

I usually never went to that side of the building. Fleeing from the masks was an exception. The lawn disappeared and the forest crowded the school, pine trees dropping pincer-like needles all over the cement. The window of the music room was propped open with a piece of wood. At the sound of the solo violin I stopped walking.

Other than his prank with Alain in second year, I'd only ever heard Edme playing with the orchestra. The piece was unknown to me, but it had what I thought of as an olden sound. Its pace was measured, like a boat's prow moving through still water. The melody glided on the cusp of sadness. For the rest of the hour I listened outside the window. When it ended, there was silence for a few seconds, and it would start again.

The bus trundled through the residential mile of the chemin des Pins, then through the part of the north end that was too steep and densely wooded for houses. At the hairpin turn the sun reemerged, and the bus eased down off the mountain. I cracked my window open to feel the breeze and breathe out my nerves. Near the lake, Jo's house stood amid the blanket of green rows. The bus drove past the vineyards. She must have gotten a separate ride.

The shacks and warehouses on the edge of town gave way to leafy streets with redbrick homes and flat rectangular lawns. The buildings downtown were pretty, but I had a certain distaste for clean land, shorn of the wilderness that entangled my neighborhood. The park helped, however, and I was glad of the broad maidenhair trees when I stepped off the bus. Beyond the archway at the head of the beach promenade, a blue-and-white kite was diving at the lake and soaring out over the sky.

I glanced once more at the paper from Pichegru. He'd written the place and time. The vetting program was held on weekdays in the Grande École, which, despite its name, was a fairly narrow building located on the north side of the Place du Bâtisseur between two guildhalls. I walked past the vendors at the park's entrance, where the smell of fried food wafted from various stands, and joined the bustle of the square.

In the square's center stood the monumental fountain. Water shot from hidden spouts and cascaded off its pedestals. At the top, the great conseiller statue gazed at the mountains across the lake, his hand resting on the shoulders of a family who clung to the iron folds of his robe. Behind the statue, the granite façade of the Hôtel de Ville spanned the whole east side of the square. Its grey colonnade was imposing, but the building's long steps doubled as public benches. Earlier in the day, gendarmes and staff ate and smoked there, and the steps were now strewn with students from the downtown school. A girl was playing a guitar, and I wondered if she was preparing for an audition too; the conservatory was across the square.

Fountain spray grazed my face as I approached the Grande École. I had never been in the building, but from the outside I'd always thought it seemed more like a house. I looked up at the single upstairs window. It was large and shaped like an eye. I straightened my school uniform and went inside.

The foyer was cool and funereal. The rug on the floor was oddly soft. There was a vase of pink flowers with petals like animal tongues. A handwritten sign directed candidates to go upstairs, where I could hear low murmuring voices—the sound of being early. I touched the wooden banister, which was worn shiny and smooth. Reluctantly, I followed the sign.

The stairway narrowed as it curved upward to the second floor. From a sunlit landing, I saw a classroom that seemed to have been fashioned out of an old parlor or sitting room, though I could never quite say what gave me that impression. The entire far wall was taken up by the oval window I'd seen from the square, and the rich wainscoting on either side gleamed with afternoon light. A dozen school desks were arranged close together. Resting on each was a pencil and a leather notebook imprinted with the cryptic, angular icon of the Conseil.

Six or seven students stood clustered in the corner, all wearing the burgundy blazers of the downtown school. They looked at me and resumed their conversation. I crossed the room and stood waiting on the far side of the window, not wanting to sit yet in case seating was assigned.

At the front of the parlor was a chalkboard, murky green like lakewater. On the wall beside me was a large topographic map of the valleys. It covered much more terrain than the engraving in my mother's book: here I counted a dozen lakes in each direction, with intricate details in the mountains. The map showed the border fences, represented as raised silver lines enclosing the towns and some surrounding land. The enclosures formed loose circles, crossing the lakes to capture a crescent of each western shore.

The town in the middle of the map was unlabeled, but the foreign valleys to the left and right bore their proper names, written in neat type and accompanied by what I realized were temporal designations:

| Ouest 3 | Ouest 2 | Ouest 1 | | Est 1 | Est 2 | Est 3 |
|---------|---------|---------|---|-------|-------|-------|
| (-60) | (-40) | (-20) | | (+20) | (+40) | (+60) |

Studying the series, it occurred to me that although the valley where I lived was in the center, that was only relative. In the eyes of the others, theirs would be centered, and mine would be off to the side—somebody's future, somebody's past. Therefore, however different everything else must be in those distant places, the map on this wall would look exactly the same.

I shaded my eyes and peered out the window. Below, Jo was arriving with her father. He hugged her goodbye, she slipped out of view, and I heard light footsteps on the curving stairway. When she saw me she gave a quick wave and went straight to the others, absorbed into their circle despite her north end uniform. The last few students arrived and joined the group, until there were eleven chatting at one end of the window, and me standing at the other.

A side door opened and the room went quiet in a single hitch of breath. A small woman entered. She was middle-aged and sharp-nosed, and wore her hair in a long braid. She was dressed in the formal obsidian robe of the Conseil, and announced herself as Mme Ivret in a voice as trim as a paring blade.

Everyone hastened to stand beside a desk. I ended up in the back corner next to the wall map, Jo in the middle of the room.

We stood still as the conseillère looked us over. The light from the window made her face appear cast in amber. She told us to sit, and held up one of the notebooks.

The things we will be discussing in this room are not to be discussed with others. This notebook is for you to use until you are dismissed, at which point you will return it and any other notes to me. As for dismissals: a minimum of three of you will be eliminated each Friday. After three weeks, the candidates who remain, if any, will begin apprenticeships at the Conseil, and may one day become conseillers.

The girl seated in front of me, mussy-haired, raised her hand. Ivret paused, her features impassive.

Madame, it's already Wednesday, so do dismissals start this week?

Ivret stared at her. Did I say every Friday?

Yes.

Do you anticipate a Friday this week?

The girl's shoulders sank. Chastened, she opened her notebook and the rest of us did the same, glue cracking in a dozen nervous spines.

Write your name on the inside cover, said Ivret. As we did, she walked behind us and drew the curtains to block the light.

She lectured for two hours without a break, and unlike Pichegru, she paced freely without notes. The only noise in the room was her voice, conducting our busy hush of pencils. No one raised their hand again. Elaborating on points in the margins, sometimes steering scribbles around the sides of the page, I wrote all that I could:

That the Conseil's sole purpose is preservation.

That conseillers are the safekeepers of the life that we know.

That the fences have always existed, and the Conseil has always protected the border.

That the Conseil and gendarmerie may be thought of as a single protector.

That, in this metaphor, the Conseil is the protector's head, the gendarmerie his hands.

That there has always been visitation between the valleys.

That the Conseil ensures that visits are carried out with minimal inherent risk.

That approved visitors from the immediate family may observe the subject in the foreign valley, anonymously, at an appropriate distance.

That the Conseil balances the protection of the many with the legitimate needs of the few.

That risk is asymmetric and depends on the direction of movement.

That in every case, the overriding principle is the safety of our township and our people, just as the principle of each foreign valley, we must assume, is the safety of theirs.

Casuistry, pronounced Ivret, spelling the word on the board. In our time together, what will engage us is the weighing of cases.

She drew an envelope from the pocket of her gown, and from the envelope, a stack of beige cards.

These are mock petition briefs. Each week, you will consider a visitation request—either to or from our valley, as the case may be. Give it some thought. On Friday you will declare your verdict along with your reasoning: Should the Conseil permit this visit? Why or why not? If you demonstrate satisfactory reasoning, you will stay; if not, you will go. I will hand out the first case now. Your decision will take place in two days' time.

The mussy-haired girl passed me my card. The stiff paper was covered with blue-grey typewriting on both sides. I wanted to read it immediately, but I saw that Mme Ivret was packing up for the day and other students were putting away their notebooks, so I stuck the card in my bookbag. As I did, the girl beside me, whose chestnut hair was done in a crown of lace braids, gave me a shy smile of solidarity. Startled, I forgot to smile back, and then Jo came and stood in the way.

Have you looked yet? she said. It's called *Case of L.M.*

Not yet.

Well, let's talk it over tomorrow, she replied. I must have looked confused, because she added: Remember, at lunchtime, in the woods, with those boys?

Oh, right. Sure, that sounds good.

Until then, then! Jo wrinkled her nose at the repeated word, which was something I noticed about her—she liked to react to things she'd said as though someone else had said them. She flashed me a smile, cinched up her bag, and dashed after the candidates who were heading downstairs.

Too late, I realized that only Mme Ivret and I were left in the parlor classroom. I hurried to clear my desk.

Stay a minute, she said.

Her tone was not cross, but firm. Wordlessly I went to her. Ivret's robe had a faintly earthy smell, like chrysanthemum water. She was smaller than me, but I shrank my body inward until I was almost looking up at her.

She thumbed through a folder and stopped.

'Yesterday I wrote that I would not leave the valley. Tonight I *more than* stand by that judgment.'

She raised her eyes. I was lanced with recognition. Somehow, until then, it had not occurred to me that she would have personally read what I'd given Pichegru.

Who else have you told about what you saw?

No one, I whispered.

Speak up.

I'm sorry. I haven't told anyone else.

She studied me. Her irises were blue with black flakes, ashes floating on water.

You'll continue keeping this to yourself, she said. You'll say nothing more to your schoolteacher. You'll say nothing to your family, your friends, or your fellow aspirants here. You will not imply that you possess any sort of secret.

I understand.

This goes double for the boy and his parents. Repeat that for me, please.

I won't say anything to them.

Why won't you?

Because it's forbidden.

Yes. Why do you think that is?

I blinked. Because if they found out they'd try to change it.

Ivret looked at me for a long moment, then inclined her head. A favor, she added, almost in passing. Watch him. If something strikes you as unusual, make a note of it and tell me. Can you do that?

She paused for my answer, but her inflection was not that of a question.

Of course, I said.

The conseillère went back to her things. I gave a goodbye halfway between gratitude and apology, and descended the stairs as quickly as I could without running. Outside the Grande École, my pulse recovered in the early twilight.

Holding the beige card by my bedside lamp, I read the account of a widower who was asking to come to our valley to view his wife. The basis of his petition was acute, incurable grief. His pain had refused to break down over all the intervening years, neither crumbling away nor hardening into bedrock. *Attends her tomb each day*, the card noted. *Admits planning petition from time of passing. Advanced age a factor.*

The detail about the tomb made me see him. In my imagination, L.M.'s elderly head was shaded by a wide-brimmed hat made of fraying straw. He limped down the cemetery path, where the sun was hot on the headstones.

My mother had been careful not to ask directly about my first day of vetting, but in the car on the way home she'd nodded and clucked at everything I mentioned, so out of annoyance I'd stopped talking. I was preoccupied anyway.

Of course Pichegru would give Ivret what I'd written, probably it was protocol, and from there, the only sensible thing would be to make sure I knew the rules about recognition. So everything was to be expected. What gave me a strange feeling was her parting request that I supply her with information about Edme. I realized that the feeling was a small, guilty thrill of importance.

I looked from the card to my notebook page. What was there to say about L.M.? The story was piteous. My arrogant vitriol against Pichegru

circled back into my consciousness, riding a slow carousel of chagrin. I'd
declared to him, and so in a sense to Ivret, that if I were on the Conseil, I
would dissuade applicants from going through with their requests. But it
was another thing to make such arguments about somebody like L.M. He
had been grieving for longer than I had even been alive.

*

In contrast with my mother, Alain began peppering Jo and me with questions about vetting as soon as we were on the backwoods path. How many
other candidates were there? What were the conseillers like up close? Had
we found out anything juicy so far? Jo made eye contact with me and
shook her head.

You know we're not supposed to talk about Conseil stuff, she said.

Whatever, it's not like you signed a contract in blood. Unless?

No.

Hmph.

He thinks all contracts are void without blood, Edme explained.

That's true, Alain replied, swinging a stick at some brush. No deal.

It was a fifteen-minute walk between the school and the fort, so we had
less than half an hour there before we had to turn back. Still, it felt good
being off the schoolgrounds. When we arrived I continued higher up the
slope to gather some leafy branches for the wall, and Jo came to join me.
She wore a candy-red beret.

What was Ivret saying to you yesterday?

When I didn't answer, Jo made a sardonic face.

She asked you to come talk to her, I heard her from the stairs.

I turned away, concentrating on bending a stem out of the ground.
The stem was stubborn, with fresh green tendons straining where the skin
split. My hand started burning and I gave up. Jo looked at me, expectant.

She was asking after my mother, I said. She works in the Hôtel de Ville.

Jo's face lit up. Oh, that's right! She's a secretary.

Archivist.

Archivist, sorry—so was she in vetting too? I've heard they give those jobs to the other people.

I affirmed that my mother had been one of the other people, and from the subject of dismissals, we moved on to the case of L.M. Jo said she wanted to approve the visit. It just seems cruel not to, don't you think?

Yeah, I said.

What's it to me if he comes here, the sad old bastard?

I shrugged and wiped my hands on my stockings, and we trotted back down the mountain. Edme was fitting sticks into the top of the wall. The barrier had already grown to chest height.

Alain lounged on the ground listing off more things that could be added to the fort: a picnic table, lawn chairs, a garbage can for fires. We could put a grill over the can and cook, he insisted. Edme listened with a wry smile. Alain took a pen knife from his pocket and said we should carve our names in the main log.

We took turns cutting our initials. I could not manage to make two Os, so mine looked like deranged pyramids in the wood. I wondered if Jo, too, was thinking of L.M.'s initials as she perfected hers. By the time she passed the knife to Edme, he demurred and said we had to get going. He pretended to offer Alain his knife back, then snatched it away again, escaping down the hill. Alain bellowed threats and bounded after Edme, pinwheeling his arms. Jo and Justine and I laughed. We collected our school bags from the ground, but my eye caught the cluster of names with Edme's missing, and I felt my smile dissolve, like a wave thinning over sand.

On the path below, Alain had managed to tackle Edme. Straddling him, he ripped handfuls of goldenweed flowers from the dirt and pelted them one by one at Edme's chest. When Edme surrendered the pen knife, Alain helped him to his feet. Edme's school shirt was stained yellow from the flowers.

Let's trade, said Alain. I'll wear yours, you wear mine. Otherwise Pichegru'll have your ass.

Ah, that's okay, said Edme. I can hide it with my blazer.

Alain looked skeptical, then inspired. He uprooted more flowers and rubbed them against his own chest until the blotches were much worse. This way I'll draw your fire, he said, tucking a mangled flower behind his ear for effect. I expected Edme to roll his eyes like he often did, but he grinned and put his arm around Alain's shoulders. I watched them walk that way for the rest of the path, and when class resumed, Pichegru indeed administered Alain the switch. Bent over the oak desk, Alain tried to wink at us between winces, but it worked: Pichegru chose to overlook Edme's shirt.

*

It was a cloudy afternoon and the parlor classroom felt more drab than the day before. The early candidates congregated again by the window, Jo already among them. I noticed that since school had let out, she'd taken off the beret and done her hair in a single braid like Ivret's.

Even though the first dismissals were tomorrow, Ivret did not straight-forwardly explain the principles of visitation or the rules that determined a petition's success or failure. Instead, she walked back and forth at the front of the room giving us questions to consider, some more clearly applicable to L.M. than others. I tried writing as rapidly as she talked:

Is the petitioner eligible?

What reason is given for the request?

Is the reason credible?

Is there an ulterior motive?

Is there a safer option?

Is visiting 'right' for this person? Will it satisfy them, or make things worse?

Is this their first request? Or an appeal?

If the petition were approved: what risk of interference during the trip?

If the petition were denied: what risk of an escape attempt?

If escape were attempted: what chance of success?

On it went. At last a boy raised his hand to ask for a clarification, which Ivret allowed. The girl in front of me kept writing fervently, but I put my pencil down in the fold of the notebook and shook out my wrist, cracking my neck from side to side. The land on the large wall map was rusty brown and forest green, and the lakes gained color from top to bottom, light frost flowing into teal. I realized that I found the map pretty.

Ivret never so much as mentioned L.M.'s case, despite the whole room trying to deduce the right verdict from her remarks. She kept asking us things without answering, and the only elaborations she offered were more contours of the questions. The implications for tomorrow's test were left to us.

When the lecture ended I made sure to get out of the room before Ivret could corner me again. It was superstitious in a way, since I knew she would summon me if she wanted, but she didn't. I heard Jo talking with another candidate as I was leaving. It felt good to hurry off before her, as though I had somewhere to be.

Instead, I waited in the colonnade of the Hôtel de Ville for my mother to get off work. The fountain lamps were on for the evening, and the water's glow underlit the statue of the conseiller and huddled family. I pictured my mother sitting on the fountain's stone bench, tossing a coin and leaning closer to my father. Counting through the years, using what I knew, I wondered when that day would also become the past in Ouest 1. A parent's early life was a hazy thing.

I heard clacking feet on the flagstones and saw a group of men enter the square. I moved aside as they approached the Hôtel de Ville, stepping partway behind a column. The men were all gendarmes. Their leader was unmistakable—he was a step ahead of the rest, who fanned out and kept his pace. He looked to be in his forties, with a black beard as short and thick as turf. One of the younger gendarmes shot me a smile as they passed. Maybe because of the shadows, I smiled slightly in return. They disappeared into the building through the heavy door, and a minute later my mother came out.

On the drive home she asked if I was prepared for my first verdict. I said that I needed to think more, but Ivret had given us questions to consider, and they seemed to tell against approving the petition. My mother said that that sounded plausible. When I complained that Ivret had mentioned many factors but not how to weigh them against each other, my mother said that candidates were taught more after each round of dismissals. At first they're just testing your sensibility, she said. They don't give out anything sensitive to people who'll be gone after a couple days. She'll teach you more next week.

If I'm still there next week, I replied, watching indigo trees slide past the car window.

My mother gave a mirthless laugh. Don't say that.

Sorry.

She glanced over. What's the matter? You're nervous?

I shook my head.

Being nervous is normal, but as long as you pay attention and give each case serious thought, I don't see you getting cut. You belong on the Conseil.

Why?

I'd never asked her directly, never challenged her certainty, but now that I was in vetting, I felt I had the license. My mother made an impatient noise.

Because you're well suited to it. Like I was.

Her words bled into the silence as we drove. The car's darkness tempted me to honesty.

Would it be so bad, tomorrow, if I got cut? I asked. The clerical jobs in the Hôtel de Ville . . . not that they're easy, but maybe I'm more suited to something like that? I could even take over for you in the archives one day—or not, I'm not presuming, I'm just trying to think ahead.

I could feel my mother's mood brewing, but she didn't say anything until we parked in our driveway, by which point her upset was obvious. Instead of opening the door, she turned to me.

Fine, Odile, let's think ahead. If you're cut in the first week you won't be any sort of clerk in the Hôtel de Ville. Your progress in vetting puts a cap on your clearance level. So: Do you feel like pushing a broom for the rest of your life? Or pouring coffee in the conseillers' chambers? Maybe that appeals to you. If not, you should hang on until week two to be dismissed. Then you'll be eligible for the second-tier clerical positions. Lucky you. You see how glamorous my job is.

I tried to object; she spoke over me.

What you *haven't* seen is how I take orders from the same people I was in vetting with. My equals, once upon a time. Some of them less than that. Now they pop their heads into the archives and tell me to do something, and I say 'Yes, right away,' even if it's five minutes before closing and it'll take hours—I say 'Yes, thank you,' and god knows I never forget to use their formal title. And that is my career. So at the Grande École tomorrow, look around at your fellow candidates and imagine who you'd like to serve. Or maybe you'll reconsider how hard you feel like trying on your verdict.

I'm *going* to try. I didn't say I wasn't going to try.

She was still glaring and made no move to get out of the car. I'd never heard her speak so harshly about work. Unable to bear the silence, I asked:

Was Mme Ivret in vetting with you? I mean, was she one of the other candidates, back then?

After a beat, my mother let out an incredulous bark. Ivret? How old do you think I am?

She shook her head and laughed again, to my relief. Even though I wanted to know more, like how she was eliminated from vetting, I asked instead why she'd wanted to try out for the Conseil when she was my age.

Oh, I fell in love with their houses, she sighed. My girlfriends and I used to bike up to the gates. Sometimes the guards would let us look through. I could stand there for hours. We fantasized about living in houses like that.

Oh.

My mother glanced at me tiredly.

It's not bad to want comfort, or respect from others. It matters more than you think. She reached between us to retrieve a banker's box from the back seat, and we went inside.

Up until then I'd felt fairly calm about the test. My secret hope had been to fall short of a Conseil apprenticeship and settle into a quiet job like hers. I hadn't realized that my opportunities would be more limited the sooner I was cut, and so, for the rest of the evening, I was robbed of the soothing prospect of failure.

E dme left the classroom as soon as the lunch bell rang. Alain made a groan and gestured at us. From his desk, Pichegru watched me follow the others into the hall.

Pira! cried Alain as we entered the music room with its garish orange walls. What the hell is this?

Edme unclasped his case. My pieces aren't ready yet.

So practice on your own time, Alain said. The building hour's upon us!

If he needs to practice, let him practice, said Justine, and she tugged on Alain's sleeve. My eyes caught Jo's, and she smirked.

Fine, fine. Come along, keepers of the faith. Alain stopped at the door, sizing up the timpani set. Say, would M. Gruillot mind if we rolled these up the mountain and turned them into wading pools or tubs of some sort?

Yes, he'd like that, Edme said without looking up.

Jo announced airily that she'd actually meant to eat with Marie that day, so we should go to the fort without her. Alain feigned an objection, but I saw Justine send her a look of fizzy appreciation, and I realized that I should make my excuses as well. It didn't turn out to be necessary, since the two of them left without checking if I was coming. I was standing in the middle of the room, halfway between Edme and the door. I could have said goodbye and slunk away, but the thought of being alone on the wall was newly repellant in a way that surprised me.

Do you mind if I stay and watch? I asked him. You can say no . . .

Sure. I have to play in front of the judges, right?

He tuned his violin. In the stillness of the room, the chords formed little glyphs in my imagination, lines steering into perfect parallel.

I'm having a tough time with this one, he warned, but it's too late to rewrite it. There's this part in the middle I've been avoiding—you'll see what I mean. He raised his bow.

It was the same piece from when I'd eavesdropped by the window, but indoors the strings had a closer timbre. With each stroke of the bow I felt the sound graze my skin. Although Edme's eyes were open as he played, they seemed to be focused on something farther than the room. The chords bloomed in distant air.

Then the notes sped up in a burst, the melody scrambled, and Edme slumped with his bow.

There it is.

I thought it was sounding really good until then, I said.

Until then. It's supposed to be even faster there.

To demonstrate, he played it again at satirical speed. The fast part leapt and frenzied for a few seconds before a wrong note sent it spinning. He threw his head back at the ceiling, extravagantly weary.

What was I thinking, Odile? Tell me. I've brought this on myself.

Laughing, I asked if it would help to read the music as he practiced. I know you wrote it, I added, but still?

Edme eyed a portfolio resting on the piano bench. No, I'm well aware what this torturer wants from me.

I was about to change the subject and say it must be nice to have the room to himself at lunch, but before I could, a junior appeared in the doorway and gave us a tentative nod. Edme said hi to the girl, who went to the far corner and began assembling a clarinet.

Edme smiled with resignation and began his piece again. A few seconds in, there was a trill of round clarinet notes behind him. He concentrated and didn't falter, but rueful amusement touched his lips. The girl's clarinet loudened and quickened and the two together sounded terrible. Edme lowered his bow in defeat.

Want to walk around or something?

We left from the door near the junior classrooms, where the drinking fountain had a stepstool tucked underneath. The exit was at the front of the school near the roundabout where people got dropped off in the morning. In the middle of the roundabout was the tree Alain had climbed when they'd deliberately butchered the hymn.

It seems hard to focus when there's someone else there, I said.

Yeah. Aimee's incredible, though. When she's old enough she'll audition and get in like nothing. But she can practice at home too.

What do you mean? You can't practice at home?

Edme was reluctant. I'm actually supposed to stop playing completely.

Why?

My parents made up their minds about the apprenticeship.

They're not letting you audition? I paused. But you're still rehearsing?

He gave me a mischievous look, but the smile seemed for my benefit: the corners of his eyes were sad. Unsure if he wanted to talk about it, I gave a vague sigh of commiseration, and he didn't add anything more.

We turned the corner of the building toward the playground. At the swing set, two girls were rotating a boy, winding his swing until it was too tight to twist further. They shoved him free and cackled as he flew around in a wild ellipse. Out on the field I saw Jo and Marie having lunch on the grass. Edme asked if I'd eaten yet.

No.

Me neither. Shall we?

Instead of joining Jo, we walked to our cloakroom door. The stucco was still scuffed from Henri's ball a few days before. Edme dropped his bag and sat in the place where I usually stood. He gave me a gallant gesture of invitation.

I sat down beside him on the cement. Somehow I had never done this before. The new angle made the pines look taller across the lawn.

Not such a bad spot, Edme reflected.

I wondered if he was making fun of me, but he didn't sound like it. We unpacked our lunches together and ate quietly in the shade. In the corner of my eye, I watched him break individual green grapes off their pedicels. There was an unrealness to his future, a gap between my knowledge and the simple presence of him. Whatever would one day close that gap, it felt unfair. He offered me a grape and said his father grew them. It tasted bright, with tiny bitter seeds.

*

A red car sped into the cul-de-sac and pulled up at the bus stop. Jo's head popped out the passenger window.

Care for a lift?

I nodded.

So, this is her, Jo said as I got in the back. Her father glanced in the rear-view mirror, just sunglasses and silvery hair. I thanked him and he shrugged.

Have you decided what you're going to say? Jo turned as soon as we were driving, poking her face around the headrest and gripping the top of the seat.

You mean about the case?

Yes, obviously! Her tone was one of breathless conspiracy.

I tried to gauge her father's expression, but he didn't seem to be listening. We were barreling downhill toward the vineyards, driving much faster than my mother did. The wind from the windows blew Jo's hair around her face and she spat some from her mouth with a laugh.

I'm going to say yes, she revealed. If L.M.'s healthy enough to make the trip, hooray for L.M. It seems like the right thing to do. Unless you think it's wrong? She studied me intently.

I didn't reply for a moment and watched the rows of grapes zipping by. The lake air smelled briefly sweet.

I think I'm going to say no.

Really! Okay, why?

Because he had a chance to say goodbye. His wife was sick for a long time.

Well, but so was Yvette Cressy. Do you know that I knew her? A little, anyway. And she was sick forever. If her folks didn't get around to saying goodbye, they really dropped the ball. But they were still allowed to visit— Marie was positive it was them.

I know, I said, but I wonder if that might be different because Yvette was so young. *Too* young. Not like L.M.'s wife.

Huh. Jo sucked in her lip and chewed it for a second. Now you've thrown me for a loop. Damn it. Do you think there's even a right or wrong answer with this? Maybe it's more about the presentation than the side we choose?

I have no idea, I said.


I was partly proud and partly uncomfortable getting out of the Verdiers' car. But I was happy that Jo kept chatting with me before class instead of going over to the downtown candidates. She also sat closer to me at the back of the room, displacing a boy with curly blond hair who was the desk's original occupant. When Ivret came in, Jo cast me a jittery look that said: Here goes.

Ivret waited until everyone was seated in silence. Then she walked to the topographic map on the side wall. We watched her insert a pushpin into the middle of Est 1, press another into our valley, and carefully tie a white thread between them. With the thread tight across the mountains, Ivret faced us.

Lower your foreheads to your desks.

I glanced at Jo and saw others looking confused. Ahead of me, the mussy-haired girl dropped her head and adjusted her chair until it bumped the front of my desk. I moved my notebook aside and rested my head on the wood, placing my hands on my knees. Other chairs scraped; clothes rustled around me.

Shut your eyes.

I listened to Ivret walking the aisles, leaning to check everyone's face. When she was close I smelled her scent, a hint of citrus this time, like a lemon in soil. Her steps receded, and when she spoke next it was at her familiar volume from the front.

In the matter of L.M., keeping your head down, raise your hand in the air if you would *approve* this petition. Opening your eyes will result in dismissal.

I heard the shifting of sleeves as arms lifted up. It sounded like the whole room. Nervously, I kept my hands where they were. My forehead was getting a dull pain from the desk, and I became aware of the hardness of my skull.

Hands down, said Ivret.

I felt the small draft of many arms dropping.

Now raise your hand if this is a petition that you would *deny*.

I discovered that my sitting position allowed me to raise my arm only from the elbow up, like a wave, so I had the sensation of giving a tepid hello, or trying to attract a waiter. I spread my fingers wider to compensate.

Keeping your hands where they are, you may all sit up and open your eyes.

Awkwardly, my arm still in the air, I maneuvered myself upright and looked around. Only three other hands were raised. One was Jo's, and her face was now pale.

Those of you with hands up, go to the left side of the room, Ivret said. The rest of you, go to the right. Bring any notes you've prepared.

With Jo and the two other deniers, I stood by the wall map. The eight candidates across the empty desks seemed excited to be in the majority, whispering with hidden smiles. On our side nobody spoke. I looked to Jo again, hoping she didn't blame me for leading her astray. She had fixed her eyes straight ahead in meticulously managed fear.

Ivret stood between the two camps and addressed the room. Because most of you have voted to approve, we'll begin by hearing two arguments from that side; then we'll hear one argument against, and so forth until we've heard from everyone. Take whatever time you believe you need, but please limit yourself to your best argument, not everything under the sun, or I will ask you to stop. To address something many of you will be wondering: don't be concerned if a prior candidate has 'taken' your answer. Novelty is not required. Conversely, if you hear an argument that you're tempted to replicate, remember that your eloquent neighbor might just as well be wrong. Thus, the best course is the simplest: give me the reasons that led *you* to your ruling. Scerri, you begin.

On the opposite side of the room, the curly-haired boy whose seat Jo had stolen stepped forward. In a voice approximating confidence, he listed the reasons why L.M. should be permitted to visit. They were the same basic points Jo had made in the car: L.M.'s personal need was great, the case fit the criteria, the risks to us seemed minimal, so why should he be turned down?

He was done speaking in under a minute and stepped back into the group. The girl next to him gave him a congratulatory nudge.

Brusson is next, said Ivret, her opinion impossible to read. The girl who'd nudged Scerri came forward, and when she spoke, her voice was huskier than I expected. Her reasons were similar, but she went into more detail about why L.M. posed no threat to anyone—his age meant that the escorting gendarme could easily restrain him if he broke protocol. When she finished I thought she'd done well.

Ivret turned to our side of the classroom.

Ozanne, she said in the same bland way.

Unsure if I should step out of our already small cluster, I shuffled a few inches into the room, enough to make me feel awfully exposed. Under my school uniform my back felt moist. I could tell that my face was already reddening: the inescapability of the classroom's eyes.

I cleared my throat and willed my voice to be loud. The result sounded strained.

In the matter of L.M.'s petition, I deny the request.

The word 'deny' came out much sharper than I'd intended, and my skin blazed. Ivret waited. I ignored the other candidates and directed my words at her, trying to wring a glimmer of approval from her countenance.

My reason—my main reason—is this. L.M. is experiencing persistent grief. That satisfies one condition for a request like this, but there are others. Grief isn't everything. L.M. knew that his wife was going to pass away. They could prepare together, they could say goodbye to each other. And one goodbye should be enough. Everybody dies. We can't let everybody visit, though. It should be for exceptional cases. L.M. is not exceptional, at least not in this way, so I reject his petition.

Eyes downcast, I retreated.

Ivret gave no reaction. Erro, she prompted.

The girl who'd tried smiling at me on the first day began the next compassionate argument in L.M.'s favor. I couldn't hear it over my heartbeat. My ears drummed with hot black blood.

By the final arguments, it seemed like everyone was less comfortable with their own position. The mussy-haired girl, whose name I learned was Mouderie, stumbled through her turn, blurting out counterarguments as if she was going to rebut them, only to riffle through her notes and change course without addressing the problems she'd brought up.

Jo was called last. She was more poised than I expected her to be from her worried face beforehand. Her answer resembled mine on the subject of goodbyes, but the way she said it was less blunt, more sympathetic to L.M.'s plight, and more regretful that his request could not be accommodated. She came across as caring, where I'd come across like I didn't understand what grief was. She gave me a relieved look as she stepped back into the group.

Everyone take your seats, said Ivret. The room obeyed, and she wasted no time.

Erro, Grech, and Mouderie: please put your notebooks on your desks and leave us. Thank you for participating in week one.

With a sick feeling I watched the three stand. The girl with the crown of braids cleared out the desk beside mine, her face now pink. Grech was a boy with smudged glasses who'd been on our side, but bogged his case down in flustered irrelevancies. Both left the parlor with their heads hung, but Mouderie clung to her desk.

Can I add one more thing to my answer? she pleaded. I forgot to give my best reason!

Your notebook, Ivret repeated, her look now unsparing.

The mussy-haired girl slapped the book on her desk and let out a sob. Everyone except the conseillère watched in awed embarrassment as she ran for the stairs.

There was still over an hour left in the day's lesson, and what my mother said was true: with the room less full, Ivret became more expansive with details, less chary of saying what the Conseil thought and why. She didn't share the standards by which we had been judged, though the results made it clear that you could pass or fail choosing either verdict. She did reveal that L.M. had been a real person, no longer with us, whose petition had been approved by his local Conseil in Est 1 but denied here. That is not unusual, Ivret commented. She went on to describe how gendarmes relayed communications between the valleys, leaving sealed petitions in a safebox in the mountains and sending verdicts back the same way. Decisions about visits had to be unanimous, so L.M. had never gotten his trip. As the others raised their hands to ask more questions, my mind drifted off, through the oval window and over the square, past the marina to the hospice by the lake. I imagined L.M. keeping vigil at his wife's deathbed, dabbing her brow, listening to her panted breath. Hoarsely vowing that he would see her again in twenty years if he was well enough to make the journey, unaware that this had just been rejected in the neighboring Hôtel de Ville.

J o hugged me on the front steps of the Grande École. She leaned back,
holding me by my shoulders.

Odile! Two out of three dismissals were on the other side—you sure
know how to pick a chicken!

You too, I stuttered, mystified by the phrase. And you added a lot to it,
you were really good.

Oh, I know, I gave my own reasons, but I still wouldn't have thought
to go that way if you hadn't shown me the path of no mercy. At first I was
being too soft.

You were so professional, I said. You made it sound like you cared even
though you were saying no.

Does *this* . . . sound like I care? Jo asked in a gentle way. I had to admit
that it did, until she batted her eyelashes with sugary sarcasm and dropped
her voice back to normal.

Honestly I think part of this job is making people feel better about rejection. Think about it: if you shoot them down, you can't go rubbing it in
their face like you don't give a shit, or they'd be that much more likely to
go climb the fence or whatever.

The other candidates had all left. I told Jo I had to meet my mother for
a ride home.

No, you should come over! Justine's going to be there, and Alain and
Edme are coming afterward for schnapps. Jo noticed my sudden quiet and

added: Sorry I forgot to mention it sooner—inviting them was Justine's idea, she's got a thing for you-know-who.

I wondered when the plan had been made, both wanting and not wanting to know. That's okay, I should head home, I said. My words made the wound obvious.

Nonsense. Jo took my arm. Let's inform your mother you've got plans.

The car slowed down on the private lane, its headlights carving ghostly grapevines out of the dark. The radio was playing a corny song that reminded me of a matinee my mother had taken me to when I was little— tooting horns and crashing cymbals. All I remembered of the play was a fat man toppling over on his rump, and the kids around me screaming with laughter. The song seemed especially frivolous compared to Edme's music. Out the window, Jo tapped her nails on the roof of the car. Then the mansion appeared, three stories high with long windows and a wraparound veranda that glowed with buttery light. It looked like a doll's house, or a cake in the patisserie window, except that the veranda was festooned with giant fronds and vines, which gave it a wilder feeling.

My mother had been surprised when she found me waiting with Jo, but she was happy to let me go to the Verdiers'. It was Jo who broke the news that we had passed the first week. My mother clasped her hands together and gushed, Congratulations, young ladies! When she was gone Jo said, Come along, young lady, to which I said, After you, young lady, and the transient guilt I felt at teasing my mother was cleansed by Jo's laughter as we got in the car.

The house had a huge foyer, its walls and staircase shining white. Jo's mother, her older double in a flowing dress, came out of the dining room with Justine, who'd changed into a chiffon blouse with jeans and a knit cardigan. Mme Verdier gave me a brief puzzled smile, then asked her daughter: Well?

I was grand, said Jo as she stepped out of her shoes. Mom, this is Odile Ozanne, my partner in grandeur.

Of course—Pichegru's other nominee. Welcome. Florine made plenty of food, I hope you like bourride.

At dinner the wine was poured by a domestic. Jo and Justine took it in stride, but I whispered a hesitant thank you to the frail woman as she tilted the bottle into my glass. It had the Verdier label but the paper was black and gold instead of the usual crimson.

Jo's parents asked her questions about the dismissals, and her mother snickered when she heard that the girl named Erro was among the first to be cut.

It's just as well, her parents have a shop that needs her, she said. You know the tailor behind La Fremerie? We tried it once, do you remember, Joelle, they made a mess of my alterations? Maybe a smarty like Lucie will improve the quality.

Jo made a face of pointed boredom. Her mother turned to me unfazed. And Odile, what do your parents . . . oh, excuse me. So sad. What does your mother do?

I swallowed my food and said my mother worked in the Conseil archives. I never knew how to respond to condolences.

That's useful work, said Jo's father from the head of the table, already looking slightly flushed.

She was in the vetting program too, I replied.

Of course, said Mme Verdier. And do you think that's something you would enjoy, the archives?

Um. Maybe.

I heard Jo sigh as I took another bite of stew. It was thick and lemony, with tender chunks of fish and an unfamiliar herb.

Keeping those records is very useful, repeated M. Verdier. Then again, without the Conseil, every record in the archives could change under her nose, and your poor mother'd never be the wiser! The idea seemed to tickle him.

You wouldn't be the wiser either, Jo retorted, before steering the conversation to Justine, asking for the latest gossip from track and field, and who was objectively the weakest link on the relay team. Soon the table was rollicking at the foibles of my classmates, all of whom the Verdiers seemed acquainted with, at least by reputation. I laughed along, trying to forget that only days earlier, my peculiarities might have supplied them with similar amusements.

When dinner was over, the domestic cleared the table and Jo's father vanished to his study. Jo's mother asked what we had planned for the evening.

We've got company coming, Jo said, adding with a saucy drawl: Boys.

Mmm, is that so, who?

Edme Pira and Alain Rosso.

How about that, said Mme Verdier vaguely. No Henri?

Yuck, no. You only see one side of him. At school the other day he was bullying Odile.

Her mother made an astonished face. I can't imagine.

Anyways, said Jo, they'll be here soon, can Florine send them upstairs?

All right, but leave your door open.

Oh, do a head count, Mom—we're not having a sex party!

Joelle, the rule is the rule.

Jo and Justine giggled as we hit the stairs. I was blushing too hard to turn back and thank her for the meal.


Jo's bedroom was bigger than my mother's. I had been expecting something daintier, I realized, but Jo's style was mostly linen white and glossy black, everything of such high quality that it could afford to be spare. Her closet was the kind you could walk into. She emerged from it wearing a cinnamon sweater dress and tossed her school uniform in a hamper. I sat at the bottom of her bed in my pinafore, wondering if I should take off my tie.

The most impressive thing about the room, at least to me, was the cushioned seat in the deep bay window. In the daylight, Jo's view would be of the vineyard and the lake. There was a small pile of books there, and the idea of reading in such a place gave me a twinge of envy.

Since I'd been invited as an afterthought, I felt anxious when the boys' arrival was announced, hoping they wouldn't be disappointed to see me. But Edme and Alain simply said hi as they came in and looked around Jo's room. They, too, had changed out of their uniforms, and wore short sleeves and jeans.

Nice digs, Alain said. He plopped down on the window cushion and theatrically reclined.

A gentleman of leisure, Edme narrated like a radio play. Alain inspected a book, then fake-yawned and curled up to sleep.

Here, we observe him at his repast, Edme continued.

I laughed and said: I think 'repast' is a meal.

In his sleep, Alain pretended to chew.

It was almost eight o'clock, and the sound of the radio echoed up through the foyer and the stairs. Jo proposed that we borrow some bottles from the wine cellar and go for a walk. She said she could filch them easily, but Alain insisted that we all go together, and finally Jo relented. We crept downstairs and through the sparkling kitchen, following her to a small door that led to a tighter staircase. We tried to keep from laughing as our feet squeaked on the steps.

Jo pulled on a chain, and when the bulb awoke we were in a low-ceilinged grotto with wine racks along the walls, a hundred corks aimed at us like gun snouts.

Can we take our pick? asked Alain loudly. Justine shushed him and he switched to a whisper. Seriously, can we clean this place out? Edme looked at me with deadpan tolerance.

I can take about three before they notice, Jo said. But not that stuff—down here. She pulled out a crate containing unlabeled bottles and passed three up to us. Technically there's something wrong with these, but you can't tell the difference.

Edme held up a bottle and turned it around in his hand. The hanging lightbulb shone through the emerald glass. Where should we go?

We'll show you, Justine said. Jo replaced the crate and pulled the chain and we paused for a moment in the subterranean dark, waiting for footsteps above us to clear. I could feel Edme breathing, a small warmth near the nape of my neck, and to maintain the silence I didn't move away.

The blue vineyard descended gently to the lakeshore, where a raised wooden walkway crossed a stony beach. We followed Jo and Justine down a short dock with a gazebo at the end. There were benches along the gazebo's five walls, so we each had one to ourselves. Jo reached under her bench and retrieved a hidden corkscrew. As she opened the wine, I listened to the little waves lapping against the underside of the gazebo. The moon was silver on the water.

Alain demanded the first drink, gulping from a bottle long enough for us to complain.

Trust me, though, this shit is piss, he gasped. Many discordant notes! He guzzled some more.

I thought the wine tasted good. My brain warmed instantly. The bottles were passed around the pentagon, and I handed Edme one just as Jo did the same from the other side. He accepted both and took an obliging swig from each, then crossed his arms to send them on their respective ways. Jo took her new bottle and fixed me in the eye.

To surviving the first week, she said. To the Honorable Conseillères Verdier and Ozanne, as long as they don't blow it.

I tapped her bottle and we both tossed them back, which became an imitation of Alain, each trying to outdrink the other until Justine marveled, Ooooh! We sputtered forward coughing with laughter.

Before long the wine was gone and our talk was giddy and blaring. For some reason, our toast about the Conseil had led to the subject of folklore, the ancient tales about the valleys. Most were fables with an obvious message, and the message was usually the same: never leave, never meddle. It was why the Conseil didn't ban the stories despite their being fanciful. There was even a collection of folklore in the school library, on the shelf reserved for seniors, although by the end of junior year everybody knew the stories, at least the bloodiest ones.

The tale that commanded the most fascination was called The Girl. Like all the legends, it took place in a fictional age without fences, when nothing stopped a person from walking over the mountains to the next valley (though the final story, The Builder, was about the construction of the border, and had lent the town square its name). In the story of the girl, she walked east, and what she saw of her future dismayed her. In one version she stabbed the woman in her kitchen; in another, she entered the bedroom and pressed a pillow down with the weight of her whole body, which, though small, was sufficient. Then this child began to live in the house and sleep in the woman's bed. She had children who were older than she was, and an aged husband who shrank from her and wept. They hated her, but they could not banish her. She was, after all, the same person they mourned.

Sometimes I thought about the family coming home to it: a blood-wet child crouched on the kitchen floor. What would have been the expression on her face? The woodcut in the library book depicted her mostly in shadow, piercing eyes under raven hair. I could imagine her rowing her boat across the lake toward the sleeping town, and I pictured her now with a funny sort of fondness in the dizzy drunken night.

I dare you to ask Ivret about her, I told Jo. My words slurred happily. You should put your hand up and say, "Scuse me . . . but I have a question about . . . The Girl." Jo squeezed her eyes and rocked in silent laughter.

'No one panic,' said Alain in a doltish voice, meant to be a gendarme. 'There's a killer on the loose, four feet tall and wearing pajamas.'

Edme hummed an ominous musical cue. He was lying on the bench with his head propped on his hand, looking at the few stars on the edge of the moonlight. Along the northern path of the floating fence, buoy lanterns poured yellow into the water, reflections bleeding in wavy trails.

I dare *you* to ask her, said Jo lazily. You and Ivret have a special rapport.

I felt my smile fade and I willed it back on, murmuring that we didn't.

Are you saying Ozanne's the conseillère's pet? Alain said. Shocking.

What do you mean?

Nothing, Justine told me, he just means that you're good at school. You are, right?

Nooo, I objected, my genuine incredulity exaggerated by the wine. People only think that because I'm quiet. I'm no good at school. I actually think Pichegru might hate me.

Well he definitely hates me, Alain said proudly.

Wait—does he hate me too? Edme sat up, his voice filled with concern.

Gravely, we nodded. But you're not alone, I reassured him, Pichegru hates us all.

Edme's mock worry turned to mock relief, face lighting up with a serene smile.

Not you, though, said Jo across the gazebo. Pichegru and Ivret both love you. Then she sighed and stretched, her knees showing under her sweater dress. God, it's been hot, I feel like swimming. Let's go to the beach this weekend, don't you think?


The lights were off in the mansion's windows when we teetered back up through the vineyard. Alain had hurled the empty bottles as far as he could into the water, boasting that he could hit the closest lake outpost and get the guard to sound the alarm. The bottles landed with pitiful splashes a short distance from the gazebo, but he swore they'd made it all the way and the guard was just too dense to notice.

When Justine and Jo started discussing their post-sleepover morning, I remembered that I needed to find a way home. My house was a long walk uphill. Alain was stalling, moaning at Jo to let him stay too, what if he crashed in the wine cellar with Justine. Edme and I waited at the end of the lawn until Justine and Jo stage-whispered goodnight and Alain ambled over with a vanquished shrug. He picked his bike up off the grass. Edme did the same and looked at me.

You're on foot, hey?

Yeah. Jo's dad drove us after vetting.

He turned to Alain. What do you think about walking?

Alain made a face. No offense, he explained, I'm just in a state of mild agitation and I'd prefer to, uh, go take care of my ablutions.

Edme laughed and shuddered.

What? No! I have an important beauty regimen . . . Alain grinned.

Yeah, okay, please spare us the details. Odile, I'll walk with you. And I apologize.

No, I'm fascinated, I replied. Alain hopped on his bike and wobbled up the driveway waving goodbye. The wave turned into a fist-rub motion as he disappeared around the corner. Edme laughed again, but in Alain's wake it sounded more pained.

Sorry, he repeated.

I smiled at the ground and started walking. Edme pushed his bike next to me. The spokes clacked placidly. The moon had clouded over and the sky was soft and still.

For a while we didn't say much, but like before, it was all right. The wine helped glide away the thought that silence was perilous, that someone needed to talk. Instead I listened to our footsteps drift into harmony and out.

He asked me what vetting was like, and although we weren't supposed to, I started describing it. I even mentioned, in an offhanded way, that Jo had copied my answer on the first test, which seemed to surprise him; quickly, to avoid making a thing of it, I emphasized how well she'd spoken, and that I wished I could speak with that kind of polish.

He said that I was speaking pretty well right now, and I said maybe I should take up drinking wine on the bus after school, and both of us laughed. Then I added that sometimes my mother sneaked a drink before work in the morning. It was something I'd never told anyone, because I'd had no one to tell.

Edme was quiet for a bit. We were walking in the center of the road that led to the neighborhood, approaching the bottom of the main hill.

Do you think that has to do with your dad? he asked.

I guess maybe. That was a long time ago.

Does it bother you?

I don't know. You'd think it would. It's more about how she hides it, or tries. As if I can't tell. Like one time this summer. We finished breakfast, I left the table, but then I forgot something and came back behind her. She slammed the cupboard and wiped her mouth and acted all cheerful, which—well, you don't know her, but she's not the cheerfullest.

I've seen her around, Edme allowed. You buy fruit at the packing house sometimes, I've seen you both there.

I knew he went to work with his parents, carrying empty bins at the far end where the floor was black from the hose. He wore an apron covered in purple berry stains.

Huh, I can't believe you noticed me, I said.

I didn't know how I'd meant this to sound, but it came out so timidly that I wanted to shut my eyes. But what he replied was:

Of course I noticed you.

I thanked the night my cheeks weren't visible. We were walking up the steepest stretch of the hill, and Edme leaned on his handlebars to push his bike. At the hairpin turn we stopped to rest and look out over the valley. Below us, Jo's dimmed house seemed even more like a toy. On the other side of the lake, the rough line of gendarmerie campfires twinkled in the dark, like a necklace dropped down a well.

After the hairpin turn the forest smothered the chemin des Pins, and the stars and valley disappeared. Although the air was still warm, the odor of dry soil and pine sap was less intense than at the height of the day, when it rose out of the earth and became part of all your feelings. I heard the bike spokes but could hardly see Edme.

Anyway, I went on, I don't think that's the reason my mother drinks. It's not because of him. It's because of her job.

Oh yeah?

She's bitter that she's not a conseiller. She resents being an underling. But she also worships them. She wishes she lived in one of their houses, she told me so last night.

Well, who doesn't, Edme said.

I guess. But I think it explains why she made me go into vetting. I mean the real reason. It's about her status more than mine. If I was a conseiller, she'd be a conseiller's mother, and people would have to be polite to her. Maybe she'd move in with me and get her nice house after all.

I snorted, but I sounded ungenerous, even to myself. Edme's response was gentle.

Sometimes people want things for more than one reason, he offered. You're right, it's prestigious, but it could be more than that for her. You were saying that vetting's about weighing other people's grief . . . if that's your job, maybe it makes you less vulnerable to grief yourself. Like you stand above it. Does that make sense? Your mom could be trying to protect you from going through what she did after your dad. Or, I could be bullshitting. More than likely.

I was ready to point out that my mother had never seemed very vulnerable to me, had never really mourned for my father, but then I remembered a day when I was little, probably in the weeks after it happened: she spilled something in the kitchen and exploded, hurling food and dishes all over the floor. I ran to my room and later everything was clean. The insight of Edme's interpretation surprised me. At first it had seemed too kind to be correct. Quietly, I admitted that he might be right.

Well, he said. Speaking of parents, and jobs. You know how my folks are making me apply at the butcher shop?

Still no luck changing their minds?

The more his silence grew, the more I sensed he had something troubling to tell me.

To be honest, they've been acting a little strange.


Nothing his parents were doing proved that they suspected anything. But as he talked about the way life had been at his house since the school year began, I became unsettled. His mother seemed worried in the mornings before he left, and she had started asking, after years of knowing that he went tramping everywhere with Alain, for accounts of where Edme would be after school. He had pushed back, but she denied that the rules had changed: You're still going out and doing whatever you want, aren't you? But the very way she put this belied her claim that things were the same.

Then there was the apprenticeship. They'd been pressuring him to choose the butcher over the conservatory well before what I'd seen at the pond. But within the last week their position hardened, and what had been a family conversation was treated as settled. Their reasons for making him quit the violin were the usual ones—practicality, stability, the odds of success—yet they'd brandished their case with new impatience. I said what I could to comfort him in the moment, suggesting that it was probably nothing. But it put a coldness in my stomach, and I was only partly relieved when Edme agreed.

He walked me down my laneway. In front of my house we stopped under the old streetlight with moths and mosquitoes filling its halo. I thanked him for the walk.

Actually, that reminds me—I want to apologize. The other day when we walked home together, I think I said something about you being wise.

I frowned as though I didn't remember.

And tonight, you were saying people make assumptions about you because you're shy, like it means you're smart, so I realized that I probably annoyed you when I said that.

I paused. Edme . . . are you trying to tell me I'm stupid?

He blinked, and smiled. I wasn't sure how to break it to you. We've all been waiting for the right moment.

I reached out and pushed him on the shoulder. He felt skinny under his shirt. Goodnight, I said. As I found my key at the bottom of my bookbag, I heard his bike creaking up the hill.

I changed into my daisy nightdress and splashed my face with water. I liked how my eyebrows and lashes looked in the bathroom mirror, bold, shock-wet, well defined. As I stared at myself I fought a smile and lost. You're falling for him, clearly have already fallen.

I spent Saturday indoors with a displeased stomach. My mother made a special dinner to celebrate my success, or my avoidance of failure. I chewed slowly and didn't bother hiding my hangover. She was nice to me, and didn't pour me any wine.

Ivret might want to know what I'd learned. Not wanting to make something out of nothing, I considered how the changes Edme had described in his parents could be unrelated to the visitors. It could just be the apprenticeship deadline making them nervous, or the fear that if he went behind their back and did his conservatory audition, they would be unable to talk him out of going. But the competing prospect that the Piras had somehow heard a rumor about the masks was too plausible to ignore. Perhaps, after I'd stymied their viewing by the pond, they'd gone to another location to wait for Edme; and perhaps someone else saw them there and thought they seemed familiar. So, with my door closed, I separated a page from my Conseil notebook and jotted down the things Edme had told me. Imitating the case of L.M., I wrote only his initials at the top. I folded the paper and addressed it to the Conseil.

On Sunday I was raking the backyard, pushing rolls of pine needles down the hill, when my mother called from the sliding door saying I had guests. I looked down at my attire. I was wearing an oversized plaid shirt that had belonged to my father, which my mother let me keep because it was ratty enough for chores.

The four of them stepped out of my kitchen and looked around the yard. They were prepared for the beach, Jo and Justine in breezy sun dresses, Edme and Alain in tanktops that showed their small muscles and armpit hair. It was the first time they'd seen me not in my school uniform, and I was dressed like this. I wiped my forehead with the back of my gardening glove.

My mother, not used to people coming by, hovered. In a sweet voice, Jo asked her if I could go swimming, and my mother said she supposed the yard would still be here later.

I hurried inside and found my bathing suit, a turquoise one-piece that I hadn't worn in ages but still more or less fit. I threw a loose linen blouse and shorts over it and shoved a towel in a cloth bag. As I slipped from my bedroom to the bathroom, I saw my classmates inspecting a family portrait at the end of the hall, and picked up my pace. In front of the bathroom mirror I jerked my shorts back down and ran a razor up the peachy hair of my legs and thighs, nicking myself, cursing, blotting a bead of blood.

I assumed we would go to the cove near the school, but Jo checked her watch and peered up the road, where, sure enough, the downtown bus was coming. We were far from the bus stop but Jo started flagging it anyway, so the rest of us waved too. Unexpectedly the bus pulled over and the door opened. We showered the driver in thanks, ignoring the unimpressed looks of the other riders as we jostled down the aisle.

Even from the archway we could see the beach was busy. On the promenade, we dodged prams and dog walkers, inspecting the picnicking families and the kites looping over the lake. Where the walkway's planks finally sank into the sand, the beach was thick with towels and parasols, punctuated by tetherball poles, sandcastles, and the red-and-white lifeguard tower with tanned legs hanging over the side. Despite it being September, the air had the delicious summery smell of sunscreen and fried dough. The town was enjoying one of its last nice weekends before the weather changed.

Jo wanted to go to the swim dock anchored offshore. It was actually four long docks assembled into a square, like a window floating on the water. The middle area teemed with kids and parents, but the far end, over deeper water, belonged to teenagers.

We put our things down next to a sunbather and stripped to our swimsuits. I had never gone to the beach with friends, never undressed in front of anyone but the doctor. Edme tossed his tanktop on the sand. As I folded my clothes a breeze came up from the lake and gooseflesh covered my bare legs and arms. But when I saw what Jo and Justine were wearing under their sun dresses, I felt prudish if anything. Their suits were skimpy two-pieces, Jo's racy red, Justine's periwinkle with polka dots. Though they looked like models in the window of Cazelles, they seemed utterly unselfconscious, gabbing away as though they were wearing their blazers and ties.

How pretty was Jo? Until then I hadn't really considered it. Justine was pretty in a simple way, like an artist's depiction of a good-looking girl: doe eyes, a smile with dimples. Even half-naked she still seemed wholesome, smiling attentively at what Jo was saying as she unscrewed her water bottle. Jo was more complicated. She'd looked a little funny when we were younger, her cheeks round like a chipmunk's. Now, though, with her eyes vibrant green and her fingers resting on the curve of her hip, I thought she was truly beautiful. I fidgeted back and forth trying to find a posture to the side of my actual body, somewhere I wouldn't feel so bony and inferior. I noticed a piece of lint on my suit and tried to flick it, only to discover it was a pill in the fabric that wouldn't dislodge. Before Edme and Alain tore off toward the water, I wondered if Edme's eyes had stayed longer on Jo. See you in there, he told us.

As he ran down the beach I realized something. By putting what I felt into words—even an unspoken confession to the mirror—I had changed the shape of every interaction we could have. From now on, I would always be monitoring whether things with Edme were going well or poorly, measuring my distance from an aching, inchoate goal. I watched Jo strut down to the wet sand and scan the lake. The emotion I was experiencing was new in my life, but I recognized it immediately. From books I expected jealousy to be a hot feeling, like anger, but this was hollow and self-punishing, somewhere between nausea and despair. At that point, though, nothing had happened, and I followed her to the shore. Alain and Justine were already swimming away. Edme and Jo and I went to the swim dock and took turns shooting off the slide. Edme's bathing suit was navy blue. His hair was slicked to his forehead and he kept pushing it straight back. Jo marveled at how my hair was so curly that it barely looked different wet. She tousled it and splashed me and said how she wanted it. I said I'd swap her in a heartbeat, and soon the three of us were laughing together.

Among the teenagers on the dock were a girl and an older-looking boy kissing more forcefully than most. The boy was almost all the way on top of her, and others giggled furtively at the display. I didn't know him, but when the girl moved her head I saw she was Lucie Erro, whom Ivret had dismissed from vetting. Her crown of braids now hung loose from the lake. As the older boy moved down her neck, Lucie turned toward me, but instead of registering recognition, she closed her eyelids to the kiss, so I looked away.

Nothing more passed between me and Edme about what he'd told me on our night walk. At the beach, I wondered if I wasn't supposed to mention his parents, and took my cues from him. But on Monday morning I saw him and Alain behind the school before the bell, and Edme was so obviously distracted that I asked if he was okay.

I didn't have permission to go downtown yesterday, he said. Or at least, I forgot to ask, which I haven't had to do for years, so now I'm under house arrest.

What does that mean?

It means they've gone off the deep end, sighed Alain, tossing a pebble in the air and trying to swat it with his tie.

I have to go straight to school and back every day, said Edme. If I go anywhere else, I'm supposed to go with one of them.

Really? For how long?

No idea.

I told him I was sorry; I didn't know what else to say. Soon we went inside. But before Pichegru came into the classroom, I unfolded my note to Ivret and scrawled another sentence at the bottom.

That morning there was some apprenticeship talk. Pichegru said that with the deadline closing in, everyone ought to be nearly settled on where to apply. For those still unsure, there would be visits that week from the shops and guilds that had spots open, and in a few days, we would also have a field trip to the border to learn about gendarmerie recruitment.

The border trip was a regular highlight of senior year, partly because it was an afternoon off, and partly because it was the only time most of us were expected to set foot there. The class buzzed when Pichegru mentioned it. Still, the prospect of joining the gendarmerie was not one to which most people gave serious thought: it was a difficult life, somewhere you ended up rather than somewhere you aimed to go. The majority of gendarmes I'd seen on downtown detail were intimidating types, wordless men with wrinkled scowls. Pichegru eyed certain students when he announced the trip, the boys who did worst in school. He lingered on Alain, who returned the look with smug defiance.

Jo and her father gave me another ride to vetting, and when we got to the parlor classroom she introduced me officially to the downtown candidates. They said hi and were pleasant enough, but mostly I listened to them talk about last week's dismissals and what the next case might be. Out the oval window, the sky's few clouds were rosy wisps already, and pink light brushed the stone walls of the Hôtel de Ville. Some of the treetops on the edge of the square had started looking thinner. Though there would still be hot days, autumn had arrived.

I wondered if the weather was the same in every town. Of course it was the same season, but how far did that go—if it rained here in the morning, was it also raining in Ouest 1? Or, if the weather differed from valley to valley, where did the storm clouds end? Across the room, the wall map was mum on the subject of weather. But it seemed clear that any shift would have to occur over the mountains. Did the clouds just clear up naturally, their shadows giving way to startling brightness, as it sometimes happened on a windy afternoon? Or would there be a seam through the sky, dividing light from dark? It was the sort of thing I would like to ask Ivret but knew would sound naive. The weather was probably the same everywhere.

Ivret began the second week with a different kind of lecture than we were used to. At first, the room seemed to trust that her purpose would be revealed, but the more she spoke, the fewer notes I heard being taken around me. Soon, all of our pencils were resting on our desks, and we stared at her, uncertain and transfixed. There was a change in her voice from her normal clipped tone: it was reverent, almost incantatory.

She was reciting the most basic facts about the town, one after another. Many were things that any child knew: the fact that there were two schools, and that the tallest structure was the chapel spire; that the main orchards and farmlands were east and south of town, while the vineyards lay to the northwest. She stated the locations of businesses, and some of their proprietors. She even told us that the Grande École, the building we were sitting in, was in the town square, and seemed not to notice the glances around the classroom.

Now, said Ivret: Are all of these things true?

After her long monologue, the fresh silence was awkward. Hesitantly we nodded.

Yes, she agreed, just as true as the fact that many of you are curious why I'd begin today with what goes without saying. Who, then, wishes to venture a guess at my purpose?

Immediately a prim-looking girl at the front, whom Jo had earlier introduced me to as Renée Tan, raised her hand.

The point is contingency, she said. All the things you said are things that could be otherwise—if not for the diligence of you and the other conseillers.

Conseillers such as your father, smiled Ivret. Nobody else in the room seemed to react to this; I realized I was the only one who hadn't known. If Renée's father was on the Conseil, surely one of the three possible apprenticeships was already reserved for her.

Indeed, the point is contingency, Ivret continued. Let us use some examples from closer to home. Scerri, you live on the rue des Cerises. Tell me then, is that where you live?

Scerri gave a small, reluctant laugh. Yes, it is.

Ivret nodded seriously and turned to another boy.

Barreau, you have a younger sister. Tell me, are you an only child?

A few people snickered. Barreau answered, as if giving proof, that his sister's name was Carol.

Good, said Ivret. Are you certain?

Without waiting for his perplexed response, she switched her attention to Jo. Verdier, your parents run a winery. What do they do for a living?

They make wine.

Is that so. Ivret then looked at me.

Ozanne, forgive me, but your father is no longer with us. Tell us, then, is he dead?

Yes. I sounded defensive, but Ivret simply nodded and moved on, leaving the skin on my face numb.

This whole time, she'd been pacing the front of the parlor, tapping the wooden pointer in her hand. Now she set the pointer down and picked up a stack of beige cards from the lectern. She handed them to Renée, who took one and passed them back. When Ivret spoke again she sounded more like herself.

Last week's case was about whether to let someone enter from the east. Every visit has its risks, but all things considered, an eastern visitor is capable of doing far more damage to himself and his own valley than he could do to us.

This week, however, you will consider a request to hike west from our valley—a mourning tour into *our* past. In such cases, we are the ones shouldering the disproportionate risk.

Ivret began walking the rows of desks. A moment ago I asked you to confirm some simple facts for me, facts you felt were silly or offensive to repeat. Barreau has a sister named Carol; Verdier's parents make Verdier wine.

But now imagine if I asked my silly question again, and this time, mere minutes later, with just as much confidence in his voice, Barreau answered: *No*, I haven't any siblings, Carol or otherwise.

Or imagine I tested Mlle Verdier's patience by asking again if her family runs a winery, but this time she replied: No, madame, they run a drinking hole on tavern row, and we all live together in the room upstairs.

I watched Jo in the corner of my eye. She sat very still, a blush growing on her neck. Ivret turned back to Barreau.

Why might you not have a sister?

He stared at her a little sullenly. With a wave of her hand, Ivret opened the question to the room.

Maybe there was some kind of accident, a girl offered.

Thank you, Cadieux. Of what sort?

The girl hesitated. It could be anything . . . a fire?

Others around the room raised their hands.

Maybe his sister got sick.

Maybe she was stillborn.

Maybe Barreau's parents learned their lesson after they had him. This was the conseiller's daughter's tart suggestion. There was stifled laughter as Barreau, who had been rigidly enduring the example, shot Renée a look. Ivret held up her palm.

Is any one of these things inconceivable—however morbid, or rude? What is your opinion, Barreau?

No, he muttered.

No, she repeated. All these fates could have befallen sister Carol. The present is a delicate thing.

We picked up our pencils.

Yes, there are much greater risks associated with westward visitation, she said. If something were to go awry, if there was any interference in that valley, we here at home would receive no warning. The result would be instantaneous. A relationship, an occupation, an individual, a family: vanished, eliminated, you'll have heard it referred to in such terms. 'Interference means disappearance.' Well, the slogans are useful enough. But those are crude schoolyard concepts, and from you we expect a deeper understanding. Consider this. Something that vanishes creates an absence, and such an absence, in principle, can be detected. Whereas what we are talking about now is undetectable. Why? Because there was never anything to detect. From the moment of interference in the valley west, that change, whatever it may be, is a twenty-year-old fact to you and me. It is not a 'new' fact entering our lives, to our horror or delight—it's important not to picture it that way. No, it is simply a fact like any other, just as obvious as the taste of a tomato, something you'd have no reason to second guess. At your age, fifteen or sixteen, you will have lived your entire life in a valley where that thing is taken for granted. Thus you might be a person who never had such-and-such a family member; who never fancied such-and-such a relationship; who never did the things which today you'd swear are your most treasured experiences. Those things are not *gone*—they never were. And never-weres leave no trace. No obscure memory, no nagging sense of something amiss, no fleeting shiver, nothing at all.

These are the stakes of interference. This is why the Conseil is so vital. We are the bulwark against nonbeing. Against a replacement so utter and complete that what is lost is never mourned.

We knew much of this, of course: everybody knew, though mostly in the way that Ivret had called crude. But we still listened with amazement, because she was saying out loud what was normally left unsaid. Cherishment services dealt in similar themes but emphasized the positive, drawing the town together every season in ceremonial gratitude, commemorating the life we had. The sermons were celebratory, in content if not always in delivery, and the few references to fragility passed by without pausing over the magnitude of what could be silently swept away.

Ivret answered the class's questions, several of them the kind that I was glad to hear answered and equally glad not to have asked. Someone asked why we should think interference in the west poses thoroughgoing risks to the town. If, for example, an approved visitor were to wrest free of their escorting gendarme and make illegal contact with their family, wouldn't any ramifications be limited to that family, more or less? In response Ivret enumerated the unpredictable consequences of one's actions, the changes that could have direct effects on a few but indirect effects on many more, until hardly anyone remained unaffected. She made a gesture like a stone splashing into water, and rippled her hands outward until they were wide apart. Now, she said, wiggling her fingers, are even the souls at these outer edges, far from the site of interference, *wholly* undone and replaced? Or do they persist into the altered valley, surviving in slightly altered form themselves, however we might conceive of that? I myself favor the totalist school of thought, which is to say, I subscribe to complete replacement over muddled halfwise continuity, but candidates at your stage need not be concerned with matters of philosophy, so take heart. Ivret indulged us with a rare mirthful look.

I noticed this maneuver more than once—gestures toward controversies that only the eventual apprentices would unpack. The bare fact that changes proceeded from the point of interference forward, leaving all of the prior past intact, engendered 'queer hypotheticals' that Ivret passed over without elaboration. At last someone asked her why, given the dangers, visitation to the west was allowed at all. Because, Ivret repeated, visitation has always been allowed. Barring it would be a form of interference, a violation with its own consequences. So we conduct it carefully, as we always have. But bear in mind that there is also a strong personal deterrent against interfering in the west, which greatly helps mitigate the risk. Even a person who is unmoved by the thought of flinging his home valley to the wind—the prospect of blindly squandering an untold number of eastern lives—even he might think twice when he recalls that his act of interference will eliminate *him* as well. Take the example of a visitor from our town breaking free from his gendarme in Ouest 1. The moment he interferes in any matter of significance—which is the only kind people ever attempt—what do you think happens next? He is no more. His action undid the conditions of his very presence. His body, his life for the last twenty years, his reasons for wanting to interfere in the first place: all sprang from a future which will no longer come to pass. The valley he came from does not exist. And visitors from nowhere do not exist either.

But that's impossible! the boy named Scerri exclaimed. He looked animated and perturbed and raised his hand belatedly. To undo your existence you'd have to exist in order to undo it—see what I mean?

Ivret's gaze was almost tender. No, she replied. A person goes west, he interferes, and then new time rolls over him like a wave, leaving nothing behind. It's as simple and ruthless as that.

By the end of the lesson, the room contained a sense of a conseiller's burden, even the burden of an apprentice. The feeling was one of graveness and privilege. The subject of the other valleys was only ever touched upon discreetly in everyday life, including by my mother, who spent her days sorting the Conseil's records. There was an understanding, as tacit as knowing how close to stand when talking to a stranger, that matters of geography were not directly discussed. Instead they were the stuff of glancing remarks, one-off asides that didn't invite further probing. I remembered the week before, when Edme joked that he wanted to peek over the mountains to see which apprenticeship he'd get—comments like that. Likewise, the fence was referred to mostly in the capacity of a landmark, the same as a road or a river, with few allusions to its actual function.

There wasn't any law against talking about visitation, but the taboo did the same work. A person who brought it up too frequently made things uncomfortable, and they tended to take the hint soon enough. The boundaries of conversation were something that most people sensed from an early age, exercising an instinct that I shared without fully knowing where it came from. Maybe, though, it was a product of our single short geography unit in the first year of school.

The day that Pichegru taught us about the valleys it was winter. The radiator ticked in the corner, and the dreary window was soaked with condensation. When he began describing things openly, it felt abrupt and almost profane. As if all our childhood rumors had been simmering in a cauldron for years, and Pichegru plunged in his hairy arm and yanked the truth out, jiggling and wet.

His stern tone as he explained the basics was sufficient for most of us to realize it was nothing to make light of. Still, not everyone picked up on this, and over the next days, the Deguara twins began bringing a game to school that they must have been playing at home. Their game was simple: Giselle pretended that the playground slide was a mountain leading out of the valley. She would find her footing and climb carefully up the metal in her fuzzy boots, where Gail waited at the top pretending to mind her own business. Then Giselle would tap her on the shoulder and say, Hello there, I'm *you*!

Her sister would gush back, Wow, look at me, I'm so young and pretty! And after they'd finished giggling, the older self would tell the younger about her life now, where she lived, the classmate she married (whispered confidentially), those sorts of things. The fact that they looked identical made it funnier, and I laughed along with everyone from the side of the frosty playground. They also pretended to hike in the opposite direction, westward in time, but upon saying hello, the hiker tumbled down the slide again, annihilated.

Pichegru must have heard about it, because soon enough, he announced that the twins had been misbehaving and ordered them to the front of the class. They started crying before he even brought out the switch. He never said the visitation game was why they were being punished, but as we watched him raise the rod and slash it down, nobody had any doubt. The Deguara twins never played the game on the slide after that, and nobody made jokes about visitation either.

As vetting wrapped up for the day I glanced at the beige card: *Case of C.R.* I slipped it into my notebook and checked to make sure Jo was safely on her way out. Then I withdrew my note for Ivret and unfolded it, smoothing the creases with my fist.

I had hoped to pass it to her and leave, but something in Ivret's posture expected me to wait. When she was finished reading she refolded it and looked at me.

You've befriended him.

I hesitated, then nodded.

These observations are all his, she said, which is helpful. But what have you observed yourself? How would you interpret the parents' behavior?

I don't know. I've never been over to their house.

Ah. Ivret's eyes drifted to the far window. I had the feeling that she was not as concerned with the Piras as she was with evaluating me.

I could try getting invited, I suggested. He's grounded right now, but maybe in the next few months?

Ivret's eyes came back to me, and although they didn't change, she smiled.


When I was on my own, I was mostly able to partition my friendship with Edme from what I'd seen at the pond. Later on, I would wonder whether the reason I let myself develop feelings for him was, in fact, my fore-knowledge: that it offered me a secret reserve of confidence, or a sense of liberatory abandon. But while it was happening, I tried to confine the distant future to the darkness where I didn't have to face it yet. What else to do with a certainty that was also unknowable, a sadness about which I was forbidden to speak? Only when Ivret acknowledged it directly did the situation's pain become inescapable, and I was relieved when she said goodnight and let me go. Instead of waiting for my mother outside the Hôtel de Ville, I walked several times around the whole square, sloshing my feet restlessly through the dry maple leaves that were growing into piles at the edges.

I f the case of C.R. was true, then it had to be from long ago, or else everyone would have heard of it. The story was terribly sordid. C.R. was the father of a murdered son. The killer was known: he was C.R.'s own brother, the uncle of the boy. The uncle appeared at school one day, took the child on an innocent-sounding pretext, and neither was seen alive again. The boy's body was found on a remote logging road, run over twice by a car; the uncle was found nearby, having driven himself off a steep embankment.

Now the father was asking to go to Ouest 1 to see his son again. The card mentioned that C.R. and his wife were no longer together, but otherwise the mother didn't figure into the brief. I wondered why this was, but there was no way to know. What was clear, however, was the dilemma of the request. Unlike the elderly L.M., C.R. could not have prepared for this death, so his case had both pathos and eligibility; but, also unlike L.M., here was an obvious risk of interference. If C.R. was allowed to go, he could easily catch sight of his brother while looking for his son.

It also didn't escape me that the case was about a parent trying to visit his only child. On Tuesday, I asked Edme if he wanted to go to the fort at lunch, but his audition was next week and he had to practice when he could. The Piras had evidently not yet informed M. Gruillot that their son was done with the violin, so Edme was squirrelling his instrument away in the music room. At lunch I didn't see Alain and Justine either, and although Jo said hello, she was with other friends and I hung back. After a minute loitering by the cloakroom door, I headed for the fort on my own.

The path was dappled with shade, but it still felt more humid in the forest than it did behind the school, as though the heat, pouring down the mountain, had gotten trapped and angry inside the maze of pines. I was glad to leave the path and climb the open slope, even though I had to hold my collar tight to keep my neck from burning. A breeze picked up and the sight of the glittering lake made the air seem less torrid. The wind was so refreshing that I hiked higher up the mountain than I needed to.

When I turned and looked down at the fort, I saw skin flashing in the sunlight. I untangled the limbs, brown and white: Justine and Alain. Both their tops were off. Alain was lying down and Justine was over him making effortful movements. Alarmed, I retreated down the hill, trying not to crunch the ground as I took refuge behind one of the ridge's only trees. I was about level with the fort now, and they were no more than forty feet away, close enough that I could hear Justine. She giggled *Shut up*, and Alain said something muffled in return. I narrowed myself as much as I could, but couldn't help listening; leaving now would risk them noticing me. Alain would probably jump up and salute, but Justine would be mortified, so I kept myself hidden as her breaths grew airy and high.

The unsought voyeurism with Justine and Alain was the first time sex seemed to me like an actual possibility, instead of an abstract whisper on the edges of adolescence. If they were doing it—people I knew, my friends—it was suddenly conceivable that I might do it too. The idea slipped through my body like warm water. His face swam into my mind. Our complexions would make for a similar contrast. I fought this off with a blush so intense that it sparked my forehead. But even my shame rippled with excitement.

I managed to creep away. Back at the school, I didn't want to have to seem casual when they came off the backwoods path, so I spent the last part of the lunch break indoors, looking at the school pictures in the hall.

I scanned the tiny faces in the morass of blue uniforms. Dabs of oil paint stared back. At the end of the chemin des Pins there was an old gravel logging road: if C.R. had grown up in the north end, he would be represented somewhere on these walls, along with his brother, and elsewhere his son. The school paintings were unlabeled—no names, no dates—so it was a futile exercise trying to find them. I was somewhat surprised that Jo hadn't wanted to talk about the case right away, what with it being sensational. We could search these faces together, looking for someone with a menacing aura. But everyone in the class portraits looked alike. The bell rang and the hallway busied with students. Over the bustle I saw Justine dart to the bathroom. Then Edme's voice startled me.

Guess who got Aimee'd again.

It took me a moment to remember the clarinet girl. Oh no, you mean you couldn't practice?

Edme made a so-so gesture. Maybe Alain's right about doing it outdoors.

I chuckled, then saw that he was actually considering it.

Can I ask you for a favor? he said.

Of course.

I'm supposed to give my pieces to the conservatory in advance. I'd do it myself but I'm grounded, and obviously my parents won't. Vetting's in the square, right? Would it be out of your way to stop by for me? Just tell them it's my audition program.

I replied that it was no problem, I could go today. Edme opened his portfolio and handed me the papers.

Thanks, I mean it.

It's no big deal, I said. Don't mention it.

But I will mention it, at embarrassing length. Odile, I'm forever in your debt.

I rolled my eyes as I folded his compositions. Okay. I hope you remember this big sacrifice, someday—

I stopped.

What?

Someday when you're a famous violinist.

Yes, the famous violinist who didn't practice for his audition. Should I give them a pretentious excuse? I don't believe in preparation, my performances must be fresh?

I laughed nervously, but had a thought.

You know, if you did want to try practicing outside, you could keep your violin at my house. I know a good spot nearby, there's no one there at night.

He looked at me curiously.

But, it's just an idea.

No, that sounds fun, let's try it. Edme gave a pleasant shrug, like there was nothing to lose.

*

I stepped off the bus with Edme's violin case in my hand and his music in my pocket. Autumn leaves were burning somewhere, and the park had a smoky smell.

I walked to the Place du Bâtisseur and crossed the square, pigeons giving me grudging looks as they meandered aside. The conservatory was a newer building. There was an awning above the door made of purposely raw-looking tin. As soon as I entered the lobby I heard the happy racket of several instruments playing at once, dampened behind doors down the hall. At reception a young woman with her hair in a messy bun smiled at my violin and asked if she could help. I presented the sheet music, still warm from my pocket, and immediately apologized for not unfolding it. She read the composer's name.

And, this isn't for your audition—you're not Edme Pira.

No, I'm just dropping it off for him. He isn't feeling well.

All right. You can tell him we've received it and we're looking forward to meeting him. I have him down for—she checked her calendar—next Thursday at four. He should get here a little early.

Okay. I think he knows but I'll tell him.

Will you be attending as well? Some people like to bring their girlfriend or boyfriend. All our auditions are open to the public, but usually it's just parents and someone special, not half the town. I'll make a note if you want to come, so there'll be a chair for you.

Oh. Thank you. I'm Odile Ozanne.

The woman jotted it down. Done! Nice meeting you, Odile, and tell Edme to get well soon.

I left the conservatory. It was still sunny out, and the bright swallowtail pennant whipped and snapped over the Hôtel de Ville. Mist tickled my nose as I passed the fountain. At the Grande École's entrance I bumped into Jo. Without thinking, I rotated the violin case so that his stenciled surname faced inward. She looked at it, then me.

Where were you after school? I was going to drive you. She lowered her voice and widened her eyes. We've got to talk about this *case*.

I agreed and followed her up to the parlor.

That day the tone of Ivret's lesson was back to normal. She didn't talk about C.R.'s petition explicitly, but the pencils around the room quickened whenever she said something that seemed applicable to one side or the other. Once I noticed her looking at the violin under my desk, but she said nothing to me when the session ended. I begged off from Jo, telling her I had to go meet my mother, but promised that we'd talk about C.R. soon. I sat down on the steps of the Hôtel de Ville to wait.

Not many people were around that evening. Music floated across the lamplit square from the conservatory. And it was the muffled music, I think, that pried me open a bit. I felt something at the back of my skull: a buried urge to cry. I remembered to remove my blazer and cover up Edme's violin before my mother came. When she did, I made a flustered smile and brushed my eyes, relieved to find them dry.

P ichegru announced that we were going to the eastern border today. The disruption of our routine sent a flutter of glee through the class. At noon we lined up in the front roundabout, some people munching on their sandwiches. Pichegru warned that anyone acting foolish would be remembered and reprimanded, that Jean-Savile was not a patient man, and that the gendarmerie was the best thing some of us could hope for. Those who were implicated poked each other proudly until Pichegru glowered them into submission. When the bus arrived it was a grey gendarmerie transport, the kind that drove the guards to their patrols along the fence. Somehow I had been expecting the same bus I took to vetting. The driver was a tired-looking specimen with a tobacco-stained beard. Inside the bus it was stifling. I ended up in a window seat next to Justine, with Edme and Alain in front of us and Jo across the aisle.

I hadn't really talked to Justine since seeing her with Alain at the fort, but she seemed more confident, a freshness in the way she smoothed her hair. As the bus left the schoolgrounds, Alain peeked around the seat and she bent forward with a quick kiss. I glanced at Edme's head over the vinyl upholstery, but he was gazing out the window.

We drove down the mountain, past my house and the hairpin turn and the private lane to Jo's estate. On the outskirts of town students craned to catch glimpses of tavern row. Instead of pulling into my usual bus stop at the park's entrance, the gendarmerie transport continued onto the main boulevard, its engine wheezing. A few women were chatting on the side-walk carrying shopping bags from Laurier's and Cazelles, and some truants from the downtown school were slouched on a bench, smoking and watching us.

I feel like an escapee in this thing, Jo complained.

The quaint homes with their square lawns gave way to bigger but more tumbledown houses as we approached the sprawling orchards east of town. We passed the road where my grandparents lived, and I glimpsed the end of their driveway, their grassy ditch and elm tree. I hadn't been out to see them since the school year started.

After my father died, there was a period when my mother and I stopped visiting my grandparents. I was used to going over on Sundays to drink cherry juice and pedal my trike in the driveway; abruptly weekends were spent at home. It was not until I began school that we resumed—on important occasions like Cherishment, we would meet them at their house beforehand. The low tire swing still hung from the elm, but by that time I was too gangly for it. Already growing shy, I read on a blanket on the dewy grass, and later sat in the chapel pew between my mother and grandmother, comparing their perfumes, half listening to the conseiller drone about the town and the harvest and the wisdom of the Conseil. My eyes would wander the stained-glass windows, the incongruous folkloric scenes, some figures recognizable, others mere geometries of light. The services were dull and I envied Clare, whose parents let her and her brother stay home. But afterward my grand-parents would take me to the tea boat at the marina, and the pie and ice cream made up for it.

The paved road ended and the transport entered an orchard, where the road was reduced to tire treads separated by a meridian of weeds. The bus rattled and kicked into an even louder gear. The first fruit trees were apples in politely spaced rows. Then the cherry orchard began, muscular trunks as stout as barrels, their shade closing over the sky. Branches dragged across the bus windows, leaves slapped the glass, and the air smelled cool and green.

We pulled into a clearing. There was a checkpoint there, a hut with a white boom barrier extended across the dirt road. It was the first sign of our proximity to the border. A gendarme came out of the hut, and our driver let the engine idle as he and Pichegru got off and took turns writing on a clipboard. We stayed quiet without being told. I heard sprinklers revolving deeper in the trees. Edme was resting his head on the glass. Pichegru and the driver came back and the white pole lifted. I watched the checkpoint guard aim a volley of spit into the grass as we rumbled through.

The orchard ended and the thin grey sun returned. The road turned to gravel. From here to the border there was only one straight route across the scrubby yellow hills. It was an oddly treeless landscape, the start of the eastern steppe, and the bus got warm again despite the dusty breeze from the windows. When the buildings finally appeared ahead, the desolate complex shimmered in the cloudy heat and looked like a place of exile.

The black-bearded man I'd seen leading gendarmes into the Hôtel de Ville stepped out of a long, single-floor building; he had to be Jean-Savile. He pointed for us to park at the side. We got off the bus and crossed the dirt lot, approaching the commandant, who had not walked over to greet us. When Pichegru talked with him he looked deferential and nodded his bald head more than once, quickly signing another clipboard and handing it back.

Jean-Savile looked us over. His face was as dark as his beard, but in the daylight his eyes were the eerie color of water trapped beneath ice. He spoke in almost a sigh.

Who has been here before?

For a moment no one answered. Then Lucien raised his hand. He said that his stepmother had been allowed to visit Est 1, and when she'd returned the family met her here. I'd never known this about Lucien.

Jean-Savile made no acknowledgment of the anecdote. In his calm voice, he said: Most of you won't come back after today. If you do, most likely it won't be to cross the border, but to take up a post. If you're interested, talk to me at the end and I'll explain the next steps. The rest of you,

I hope not to see. He turned and walked inside. Pichegru motioned us to follow.

The building was a large mess hall with nobody in it except a baby-faced cadet mopping the linoleum. There were rows of wooden tables with benches attached. A ceiling fan rotated so slowly that you could see the individual blades. Jean-Savile led us straight out the back door again, and there, towering over the rear yard, was the fence.

It was mostly made of horizontal wires. I had caught sight of it before—a hard unnatural shine through distant trees. But none of us, with the apparent exception of Lucien, had ever gotten this close. Its height was more imposing than I'd expected, at least twenty feet tall. Our class cowered by the mess hall door.

Go touch it, said Jean-Savile.

No one moved.

Go.

A few people went, including Alain and Edme, so I went too, and soon the whole class was wandering around poking the fence. The rows of steel wire were pulled taut by giant white posts crawling with rust. Every few inches the wires twisted into barbs that tessellated up and down the length of the fence. The sun brightened, and I narrowed my eyes against the metallic glare. When we touched the wires the vibration made brittle alarm bells clank along the fence, jarring and abrasive.

Edme nudged me, and I turned around. Outside the mess hall, more gendarmes had assembled beside Jean-Savile, men of various ages, all with the same bland stare. One held a rifle pointed at the ground. When the rest of the class noticed and the quivering bells died down, Jean-Savile spoke.

See where you're standing.

We looked down. On both sides of the fence were several yards of soft, raked dirt. Our side was now covered in shoeprints.

The gendarme with the rifle shifted it slightly, and everyone's eyes flew to him. His face grew into a smile, but the rifle stayed down. Jean-Savile beckoned us away from the fence.

It was then that I realized the field trip to the border was not actually about recruitment, or not just that. The true purpose was to fix this in our memories: the wall of wires and alarms, the cold men with rifles, the dread atmosphere of inevitable capture. I looked over at Jo, and she looked back—it had struck her too. Conseil candidates got Ivret's discourse on interference and preservation; the rest got this.

In a cursory way, Jean-Savile took us through the duties of a gendarme. I noticed that no one took notes, but Pichegru didn't tell us to, and in any case it was easy to remember. Most of the job amounted to patrolling the border, here at the main gate and between the periodic watchtowers. Delivering the Conseil's mail, escorting viewing parties, hunting escapees: all came after years of service. Jean-Savile added cleaning to the list of tasks. Kitchen, lavatory.

Everyone was a little disappointed. I had been hoping for a closer look at the gate itself, maybe even a tour of the watchtower above it. Both were visible, but a ways from where we stood. A small guard leaned on the tower's high railing, smoking a cigarette under the searing white sky.

On the ride home Edme switched with Justine so she and Alain could sit together, and he sat with me. Everyone kept their voices low until the border was behind us, and then the chatter returned. Jo was laughing with Marie on the other side of the aisle. I tried to think of something to say to Edme, but I wanted to avoid the obvious topic of the border, in case it led to the topic of visitation. After a bit he asked:

Would it be okay if I borrowed the violin tonight?

Borrowed. Yes, I suppose I'd be willing to loan it out.

Thanks, I promise to return it in one piece.

I gave him a nod as though accepting his terms, and with equal solemnity he offered a handshake. His hand was warm and dry. He said he'd sneak out and bike to my house as close to ten o'clock as he could. I told him where to find my window, using my finger to make an invisible map on the vinyl seatback.

*

From outside I looked into my bedroom as if I were him. Partly obscured behind my gauzy ruched curtains, I saw my bed, my father's cramped desk stacked with textbooks, and my one painting, which was askew. All the shapes were vague through the curtain, their outlines blurred, like the idea of my bedroom, half remembered. Experimentally I touched my knuckles to the pane.

I brought in some logs and made a fire while my mother heated yesterday's stew. She listened as I described the border trip, then asked how things were going in vetting. Later on, after my homework, I tidied my desk and straightened the painting. It was a watercolor, the kind they also had at the doctor's, a view of the lake under feathery cirrus clouds. The painting had always been there and I had never questioned it; it might have come with the house. I lifted it off the wall and its wire snagged on the hanger, which sagged loose from the plaster. The picture's absence revealed a paler square of wallpaper that made the rest look dingy, so I replaced it where it had been.

I put his violin case at the foot of my bed, cleaning off the dirt from the basement crawlspace where I'd hidden it from my mother. When Edme showed up, I thought, I could be curled on my bed with a book, or perhaps writing. I took off my uniform and decided on a black shift dress with a rounded white collar. My grandmother had given it to me. It had always been roomy, but in the mirror I thought it was fairly nice.

Ivret had not pressed me on my progress getting invited to the Piras', and vetting had been uneventful. The most notable thing I learned was something I overheard before the lesson began: the downtown school's border field trip wasn't until the end of the month. Jo laughed and said of course they'd prioritize our school for gendarme recruitment. She took my arm when Ivret came in and reminded me that we should talk about Friday's verdict.

*

I heard him before he was at the window: a small scraping sound in the driveway. I straightened up in my desk and pretended to write, even though I had been writing. He tapped on the glass. We waved at each other through the curtain. On my knees on my bedspread, I opened the window and let in the night air. He was wearing a hooded sweater that pressed his hair down on his forehead more than usual, and he spoke in a whisper.

Hi.

Hi.

I produced the violin case and passed it to him. He took it, bemused.

Look what it's come to. You're joining me, right? To show me the spot?

I nodded. I mean, unless you want to be alone, I can just point you there . . .

Edme shrugged. You've already heard me. You can tell me if I'm getting better.

A semi-secret footpath ran behind all the yards on the low side of the chemin des Pins. I led Edme across my back lawn side-stepping the ambient light from the neighbors', and down the hill covered in pine slag. We pushed through an opening in a raspberry thicket and joined the skinny trail.

The trail traveled along the mountainside parallel to the road until eventually winding down toward the lake bluffs. Not far from my house there was a turn in the path that formed a kind of natural amphitheater, where I told Edme he could practice without being heard. It was somewhere I used to go, and once, when I'd pretended to run away from home, a place where I'd hidden, since no adults seemed to know about it.

In the moonlit clearing was a stone retaining wall. The wall was overgrown with weeds, but its staggered tiers gave the sense of raised seating along the bend in the trail. I sat at the top with my ankles crossed.

Edme took out his violin, tested the tuning, and flinched. As he set about adjusting the strings I asked if something was the matter.

Trying for nonchalance, he wondered where I'd stored the violin. When I told him about the crawlspace he gave a strained nod of understanding, so I asked if that was a bad spot.

It's just about the air, he admitted. These things are finicky, I'm sorry. Maybe there's somewhere else . . .

Sure, I said quickly, I'm sorry, I didn't know.

In the pearlish half-light he made an apologetic smile and scrutinized the violin from the top and then both sides. When he was satisfied, he raised his bow.

Ready? This is my, shall we say, dissonant number. His voice was constricted by the violin pressed to his chin.

He stood very still, then lunged. The bow collided with the strings, notes flying everywhere like dirt from a shovel. It was terrifically loud, and around us I heard the thick flap of escaping birds. I laughed but Edme didn't notice; he was racing at each measure and hurling himself forward. The strings seemed to wail and groan as the bow sawed over them. He twisted and lurched extravagantly in front of the trees; his violin ripped the night into ribbons.

When he stopped, the silence rang. I clapped and my palms sounded dull. Edme cracked a sheepish smile. Thanks, he breathed.

That was incredible! I guess we can stop whispering.

Edme laughed in agreement—but it was true, his regular volume still sounded incautious in the quiet woods. I just wanted to respect the neighbors, he explained softly.

We heard tires on the road above, and yellow headlights scanned the tops of the trees. Jagged shadow branches stretched to grotesque lengths across the amphitheater, then the car passed and the night returned.

He practiced the same piece again, this time repeating a part until he felt he'd made progress. After that he played the slower one with the challenging middle section, the elegant song from the music room. It was my favorite of the two. I lay back in the weeds with my arm under my neck and let an ant explore my elbow. The melody rose from the trees.

On the way home I didn't care that the path was narrow: I walked beside him. He said he liked the outdoors better than the music room, and thanked me for showing him the spot. I talked about how, when I was little, Clare and I would put on dances in the amphitheater for make-believe audiences.

What kind of dances are we talking about?

I can't remember. They were choreographed—we'd work them out in the backyard. Then we'd walk into the theater like it was real. Blow kisses at the audience, that kind of stuff.

How old was this?

Six or seven.

I think you still remember your dances.

I don't. Maybe just the gist.

Good enough for me. Next time, then.

No!

It'll be a solo revival. I can prepare a score—fast or slow?

No! I laughed again.

You just watched me make a fool of myself, this is fairness!

I sighed, but he could tell I was smiling. At my bedroom window he gave me his violin, and when he was gone I stashed it under my bed like he'd asked. I turned out the lights and lay on my quilt, still wearing my dress, feeling too happy to sleep.

In the jostle of the cloakroom, Jo proposed that she and I have lunch at the fort. I stole a sidelong glance at Alain and Justine, and she understood. Not to worry, she intoned, I've reserved us the honeymoon suite.

She didn't wait to ask how I planned to vote. I answered that I was undecided, and we began talking through the options on the backwoods path.

Okay, I said. On one hand, nobody would deny that he's got a good case for visiting after what happened to his son.

Hideous, said Jo.

And it happened suddenly, so he couldn't have prepared for it.

Right, she said.

So, C.R. has a better argument than L.M., because he ticks that extra box. We all want to say yes . . .

We *want* to.

But the problem is, he's an interference risk.

Definitely, Jo agreed. So it comes down to how much we can trust C.R. not to take a run at his brother while he's there?

Yeah. I guess that's always sort of going to be an issue in petitions that have to do with preventable losses.

Oh, said Jo, I like that! It sounds smarter to use a principle. She bumped me with her shoulder. Smarty.

We arrived at the fort and sat down on the main log. The dirt really did look like people had been rolling around in it. Jo took it in with a forlorn smile.

My my. No offense to Alain, he's funny, but it's a surprise.

I think I know what you mean, I ventured. I always thought Justine was so . . . and then, Alain's Alain.

You thought she was so what?

I shrugged. Pretty?

Jo angled her toe back and forth in the dirt. She doesn't think so, but that's Justine. And I mean, Alain's not bad for the north end. Who else is there, really?

I paused. Do you want to hear something funny?

You have gossip! Jo exclaimed. She put her hands out like a bowl. Give it!

I mean, it's nothing new, you already know. But . . . I kind of *saw* them. I raised my eyebrows meaningfully at the disturbed ground.

Oh god!

I didn't mean to! I just came up here for somewhere to be, and they were already here.

Ha! Tell me the truth, was it repulsive?

I hardly saw anything. But I heard, you know, everything. I had to hide behind that tree.

Jo, already tipping forward with laughter, let out a loud snort, which got me giggling too. She asked me to demonstrate my hiding technique, so I stood up and became a wide-eyed pencil.

That's too good! Can I tell her?

You can *never* tell her!

Ahh, okay. But who was louder? Never mind, it was him. Was it like this— and here Jo made a low, cowish moan that made us both fall apart again.

After a bit we settled down. An oversized dragonfly flew into the fort and hovered in front of us, then zipped away over the brush wall. Jo stretched her neck as she yawned, and I saw the sparkle of a gold necklace under her collar. Well, good for you, Justine, she sighed. She turned to me with an honest look. How about you, how's your love life?

I gave a scoff that sounded too dismissive and felt the blood catch up to my face.

Because, Jo continued, I have a suspicion, and correct me if I'm wrong, but are you interested in Edme?

The second before my denial was time enough.

You *are*! Odile and Edme, sitting in a tree! Then she made one of her mid-thought frowns, and mused: Remember when he climbed up the tree in junior year and sang a hymn wrong or something? I must say, that was a good one.

No, I corrected involuntarily, he stayed on the ground and played it wrong on his violin.

Youuu! I was right! Jo sang.

I couldn't help it, I was blushing too hard. I buried my face in my hands. She laughed.

Don't worry, it's not that obvious, I just have a sixth sense for these things.

I nodded mutely.

In a breezy way, she added: For what it's worth I can see the two of you together. Then she squinted up at the sky and said we should be heading back.

I couldn't have anticipated the impact of her simple remark. It was because it came from Jo, someone who'd had boyfriends and could probably pick anyone she wanted: if she didn't find the prospect absurd, it meant something. We walked back down the trail talking about C.R. again, but the entire way, my chest was vibrating like the dragonfly's wings. Later, in the back of Jo's father's car, the radio was playing chamber music with a violin. The wind and sun danced on my face, chords arcing through each other like waves.

We had concluded that the best verdict tomorrow would be another rejection. So I was startled when, near the end of the penultimate lesson, Ivret said something that seemed to argue strongly for the opposite. In the midst of talking about the various ways the Conseil calculated the true extent of a petitioner's grief, she remarked, as though it had just occurred to her:

Then again, take a case like our C.R. There, you have unimaginable pain that's hard to quantify. Loss so profound that it's difficult to comprehend, even if you have children of your own. It's certainly impossible for any of you to fathom.

Ivret paused reflectively, then returned to the main lesson without further comment. It was the first time she had mentioned a case by name in the lead-up to the test. After a safe-enough interval, I turned to Jo. She broadcast a worried look and hurriedly scribbled more notes.


Pain we can't even understand! she groaned in the twilight. How is anyone supposed to vote no when she says something like that? She basically warned us that we have no idea what we're talking about if we deny the petition. She never says anything that specific!

I saw my mother talking with a coworker on the Hôtel de Ville's steps, an older woman named Claudette. I replied that I'd think about it more tonight—maybe Ivret was trying to throw us off. Unconvinced, Jo nodded.

My mother needed to stop for groceries before we went home, so we gave Claudette a ride to her place. She worked at the front of the archives, receiving sealed items and doing the preliminary filing. Odile, I hear you're Conseil-bound, she said from the back seat. She had a raspy voice that my mother had a secret knack for imitating.

I'm only in the second week, I said.

Very true. I'm not supposed to say anything. And I don't know anything! But, I do hear some things, and the other day, your teacher mentioned your name to Mme Acroyant.

I didn't respond until my mother gave me a firm smile from the driver's seat. Really, I said.

Really! Claudette rasped. Trust me, I've been around forever: you want the conseillers knowing who you are. She gave my shoulder a squeeze.

We let her out at her little house just off the main boulevard. There was a sleepy creek behind it that I recalled from childhood, with a footbridge where I used to dangle my feet and watch frogs. Claudette waved to me again in the car's headlights.

She means well, my mother said in the dark. But you can't go thinking you've got it sewn up just because the conseillers know your name. There are nine of you, they know all your names.

I walked the harshly lit aisles while my mother went ahead and filled a basket. In the grains section I was leaning against an oversized sack of millet when, through the front window, I noticed two familiar figures getting out of a station wagon. Edme's parents unloaded their brooms and a bucket of cleaning supplies. When they started toward the entrance, I rejoined my mother, and managed to avoid crossing paths with the Piras in the store.

It was after seeing them again that evening, the stark reminder they forced on me, that I first began imagining saying something to Edme. A quiet word of caution. I was anxious not to break the rules or betray Ivret, but my silent acquiescence had started feeling uneasy, like betrayal of a different type. And I had to admit, as selfish as it made me, that this feeling's urgency had increased after Jo gave her offhanded blessing to the idea of me and Edme. If that was possible, then perhaps this was too: devising the perfect remark, informative enough to avert whatever awaited him in the spring, yet subtle enough that the Conseil would judge it unintentional if and when they found out. Striking that balance was daunting: how to craft such a delicate warning without the relevant facts in hand. To say nothing of all the things that couldn't be warned against: diseases lying dormant since birth, allergies revealed in death. I vacillated between helplessness and determination and hoped for an answer to present itself.

He came to my window again that night. We had not arranged it in advance, but I thought that he might. I was at my desk planning tomorrow's argument when I heard the gentle tap. I put down my Conseil notebook and left with him.

His frenetic piece sounded more assured this time, though that may have been because I was learning its spiky stops and starts, making them feel less random. Edme's physical movements were just as wild, jumping and darting like the night before, which now seemed integral to the piece, not a byproduct or an affectation. I wondered if he would do the movements in the actual audition, and partly wished he would.

When the piece was reaching its crescendo, a porch light came on through the trees, denuding the darkness. A man bellowed: It's late, you idiot!

Edme stopped playing, cupped his mouth, and called: Sorry! But something about his reply was too singsong and teetered toward sarcasm. A screen door slapped shut. The neighbor was coming.

Whoops, Edme remarked. Hastily he knelt to pack his violin, a process that seemed agonizingly slow. Just as we heard angry footsteps fumbling into the bushes, Edme stood up and we took off running. We didn't slow until we were well clear of the light.

The forest tapered off and the path grew rugged as it descended toward the bluffs. Where the trees ended, we walked out onto the open rocks, the lake wide before us, the valley brimming with starlight. Together we stood on the rim of the sky. I gave an incredulous laugh. Edme, removing his sweater and reopening his case, grinned over his shoulder.

What?

I swept my arm across the night. I don't know, it's like a painting, it's too much.

On the bluff's edge Edme obliged with a dramatic pose, bending one knee and tilting his violin up from his chin. He raised his bow in the air. I've always wanted to do this, he confessed, then struck a huge, heraldic chord. The sound flew over the lake and seemed to bounce off the western mountains and fill the whole valley. Our eyes met, astonished.

Wow. Want to try?

I waved him off, but he held the violin out to me. He fit the instrument's neck in my hand and it felt warm from his. I raised it to my chin, trying to copy him with a grudging smile.

Am I supposed to know how to play anything?

Absolutely, it's your big audition.

Ah. I mashed my fingers into a few strings and gave a flippant tap of the bow, barely yielding a sound. Edme bobbed his head forcefully.

Nice, nice.

Shut up, I laughed, handing it back.

Here. He positioned his fingers exactly where mine had been and bounced his bow off the strings to demonstrate. My abortive chord was confirmed as ugly. Then Edme improvised a zig-zagging melody around it, a coarse cluster of notes that capered up and chopped back down, coming to rest in the same place.

Well, Ozanne, I like it. What's the name of this composition?

It sounds like a dead bird falling out of the sky, I said.

Concerto for Dead Bird, he pronounced. Bird Theme in the Key of Death.

He turned toward the valley and played the squiggling melody again, gradually adding more to it, smoothing it out, finding prettier and prettier phrases, until it became nice, then overripe. As the final note trailed off, he fashioned a drippy smile and sang in falsetto: *Bird.*

He practiced for a long time, finishing each of his pieces and doing them over again. After a while we stopped making conversation in the gaps. I sat facing the lake, admiring the sky's asymmetry. The stars gathered in the south, flowed northward, and dwindled, as though somewhere in space the blackness overtook everything. With that thought came a tremor of vertiginous excitement. It was the same sort of feeling I had when my father lifted me up at the orchard's end and showed me the barren fields beyond. I rolled my head to one side, taking in the promontory: the bluffs that rose steadily up the lakeshore, culminating in distant cliffs.

Edme stopped practicing when he said his ears were numb to progress and imperfection alike. We went back, our eyes fully acclimated to the shrouded path. In front of my house he gave me the violin case, then made a regretful face.

We forgot about your dance! You were supposed to show me tonight, I was looking forward to it.

Well, they stormed the amphitheater during your concert. All further performances were cancelled.

Postponed, he corrected.

I smiled, and then, before I could second guess my impulse, I hugged him. First I nestled my body into his; then, with my free arm, I tugged him a little closer. I could tell he was surprised, but he put his arms around me too, his hands resting on my shoulder blades, his chin weightless on my hair. We stood like that for a moment. Then I stepped away.

Bye, I whispered, walking down my driveway before he could reply.

M ost of the talk at the fort the next day was about the test Jo and
I had later—Justine and Edme reassuring us, Alain bugging us
for details. Something he'd heard must have tipped him off that the week's
case was lurid.

Just tell me, he whined. I'll give you the right answer. Both of you will
come out looking like champs.

Even if we were allowed to talk about it, you really don't want to know,
Jo repeated. You'll wish you could unhear it.

No I won't, Alain said through a mouthful of apple.

She's right, I said. It's grisly, like folklore or something.

Alain looked exasperated. That stuff's great! Gore, incest!

It's nasty, said Justine.

Whatever, I wish it was still like the stories. They should dismantle
the fences and fire the conseillers and let us all run wild. Alain grinned
at us.

That's good advice, Jo said flatly. I'll say that to Mme Ivret today and
tell you how it goes.

She'll be wowed. She'll surrender the keys to the Hôtel de Ville. She'll
strip off her robe and give it to you on the spot.

Jo ignored him. Alain leaned back, insouciant, but Justine cast me an
awkward glance. I forced a light laugh.

What do you think Ivret would do if we actually said that? I asked Jo.

Who knows. Probably give her speech again. 'It doesn't work like folklore, the second anybody messes around in the west we all get wiped out, the end.'

Wow, is that the best she's got? Alain asked. Then all you have to say is, 'So what!' Right? *I* won't notice the difference, will I? Somebody messes around over there, and a new me pops up here. Voila, I'm still alive!

Voila, echoed Edme. Well, I'd like to hear your teacher refute that.

Jo said nothing, so I slipped Edme a smile, sat up straighter, and issued a theatrical cough.

Aha, is this a conseiller impersonation? exclaimed Alain.

Be quiet, you dolt, I answered in my best Ivret voice. It wasn't anything the real Ivret would say, but Alain slapped his knee and a smirk touched Jo's lips. Encouraged, I continued in the same authoritative tone.

M. Rosso. In your opinion, western interference results in a 'new you popping up here.' Is that correct?

Yes, madame, that's correct. A new me pops right up! Alain took another happy bite of apple.

For a second I toyed with an apple analogy—tossing Alain's lunch out of the fort, offering him a replacement apple that was surely not the same—but I decided it would get me off track. All right, I said. Let's pretend there's been an escape to Ouest 1, there's been interference, and now, as you put it, there's a new you here. In that scenario, what becomes of *you*—this person, sitting in front of us now? I pointed my finger squarely at Alain.

He puffed in disappointment. You're not following. *I'm* the new me. God, is it too late for me to apply for vetting myself? It sounds like I could test out of the first half, even skip straight to the apprenticeship.

Jo rolled her eyes. Hearing him spout off was worsening her nerves about this afternoon. I realized that the best thing to do would be to shut him down, and, as I cocked my head and narrowed my eyes like Ivret, I saw how.

The right kind of example was not a frivolous abstraction about apples. Instead I drew on the memory of Clare's family who used to live next door. The reason they'd moved away was that her father had gotten a new job in town. In my conseiller persona, I bade Alain to posit some small act of interference twenty years ago: a very modest change on the perimeter of his preexistence, it didn't matter what. Among the indirect consequences of that change was a different promotion decision at the mill, a job that now went to Alain's father, and which paid well enough to get the young Rosso family out of the north end. Thus, when Alain was eventually born, he grew up attending the downtown school, with a different teacher and different friends. The odds of him and Edme becoming inseparable were now meager, were they not? When, after all, would the opportunity arise, without both of them living in the same neighborhood? But then, who *was* this other Alain, absent his defining friendship, absent the sensibility the two of them had developed together? Consider who would really exist in your place, I told him. Consider whether you'd credit such a person as being *yourself* at all. The 'new you' could be anyone; the person we know as Alain would be gone.

At this, Edme let out a long wistful sigh, breaking the spell I'd cast. Everybody laughed, and Justine clapped. Amazing! she enthused.

My voice and face were mine again, and I blushed. It's like Jo was saying, it's all about contingency.

This is what you get up to after school? said Alain with a sulky air.

Pretty much, Jo replied. Her eyes smiled at Alain's defeat, but her voice was distant.

Seems like a real hoot, Alain remarked. Give me folklore any day.

The conversation shifted when Edme mentioned how he'd once found a sheaf of old folkloric suites kicking around in the music room—pieces based on stories like The Thieves or The Orchardist that weren't half bad. From there we got to talking about his audition next week, and, over his protestations, how he was sure to ace it. It never came up that he and I were meeting at night to practice in the woods, and I realized that I liked it that way; it would let out the intimacy to mention it in front of the others, reducing the possibility it held when it was secret. The amphitheater had felt less special in the glare of the porch light. So, when everyone was insisting that he had nothing to worry about, I joined in, adding, Yes, you should try to relax, I'm sure you've got your pieces under control. Edme gave me a slightly quizzical look.

She's right, said Jo. Her mood seemed recovered. We should go to the beach this weekend. You need to relax before next week, and after today, Odile and I will either be celebrating or drowning our sorrows. Naturally, the wine's on me.

We agreed on Saturday night, this time at the cove near the school so that Edme could safely sneak there and back during his parents' evening shift. I trailed the rest of them to the schoolgrounds. Jo and Justine sauntered arm-in-arm in front of Edme and Alain, who were chatting about something I couldn't hear. My mind returned to what I'd said at the fort. It *was* hard imagining Alain without Edme. Was that not one more reason, wholly unselfish, to give some sort of warning? Alain scooted forward between Jo and Justine, disrupting their linked elbows. The juniper bushes growing on the backwoods path had a fresh aroma, and sapling firs hid in the blue shade of the pines.


But Jo was still wavering on her verdict, rattled by Ivret's comments the day before. Her father dropped us off on the boulevard and we entered the Place du Bâtisseur from another direction, a diagonal walkway lined with balding trees.

I gave my opinion: We couldn't read Ivret's mind. She might have mentioned C.R.'s anguish as a genuine caution against denying his request, or she might have mentioned it for the opposite reason, a trick to tempt the gullible. Each explanation was possible. But in that case, it seemed best to resist changing our votes on the basis of an ambiguous clue, and instead stick with what we actually thought.

Jo remained disconsolate. Can you remind me what I think again? I don't fucking know at this point.

We'd reached the Grande École. Through the second-story window I could see some of the others waiting for the session to begin. I looked firmly at Jo.

I think this petition is a no. We talked through it already; it's too big a risk. Obviously I can see the other side, and I have no idea if this is what Ivret wants to hear, so maybe I'll get cut today, but—that's what I'm going to say.

Her eyes seemed to clear a little. Okay. Seriously, thanks. At least if we get axed for this, we can stop feeling sick every Friday.

We lifted our foreheads from our desks. Jo and I walked over to where Ivret pointed. I saw the thread she had added to the wall map, red instead of white this time, connecting our valley to Ouest 1. The girl named Cadieux joined us, as did the girl named Brusson. The other five candidates, who had voted yes, stood across the empty desks. Everyone looked tense.

Mlle Tan, said Ivret.

The conseiller's daughter stepped forward. With her hands folded in front of her burgundy uniform, she spoke with solemn certainty about the imperative to permit visitation in cases of terrible suffering. Everything she said fit perfectly with Ivret's remark about the unfathomable nature of C.R.'s loss: approving C.R.'s request was the only moral path open to us. As Renée methodically eliminated all room for disagreement, I made myself look at Jo. She was keeping her face neutral but her arms were rigid at her sides.

Renée stepped back into the majority. Ivret turned to us.

Verdier.

Jo nodded and straightened her blazer, and somehow, in the space of that instant, I sensed that she would go wrong. I squeezed my fist and willed her to pull it off.

But hearing Renée conform to Ivret's comment was too much for her. Jo's delivery was weak. She began by conceding that no one could deny the suffering, the awful nature of the murder, it was truly, truly awful . . . But the safety of everyone needed to be considered as well, and if we put our-selves in his shoes, it would be hard to contain ourselves in Ouest 1, seeing the killer walking free, maybe already planning his crime . . .

Up to that point, I didn't think she had said anything wrong, only that she'd said it without conviction. Gone was the assuredness of the previous week. Still, as she reached the end, she seemed to remember something, and rallied. In a more assertive tone, she concluded:

The son's death was *preventable*. And in those cases, cases of preventable deaths, the interference risk is too great, and visitation should not be granted. That is a vital principle. Therefore I vote no.

Jo stepped back. She didn't glance at me or Ivret, just stared forward as she had before. My stomach sank on her behalf.

She had repeated something I'd said in the woods, but she had blundered. If the death in question could have been prevented, the interference risk would always be a greater consideration—that much was true. But never had I made the stronger claim that a petition should be denied *solely* on the grounds of a death's preventability. If that were the Conseil's position, we would surely see fewer visits than we did. No, the specific trouble with C.R.'s case was the particular vileness of his son's death and the person who was responsible for it, which all but guaranteed that C.R. would try to intervene. Jo had mentioned this, but used too broad a principle to back it up. Nervous, she didn't have a firm grasp on her reasoning.

The next candidate trod much the same ground as Renée Tan, but worked in a bit of obsequious praise for the gendarmerie's ability to stop visitors who tried to interfere. Then Ivret called my name.

I knew my verdict would be good from the first word, like knowing how a jump will land the moment your toe leaves the ground. I took everything that had been said about C.R.'s pain and I turned it around on him, bringing it all back to risk. The very things that made him sympathetic, the monstrosity of the murder and the enormity of his suffering, were precisely what made him impossible to trust. Every good argument for mercy was an even better argument for resolute denial. In fact, saying no to C.R. *was* an act of mercy, mercy for the rest of us: it was an act of preservation, keeping our lives as we know them. The voice delivering this judgment did not sound like an impersonation of a conseiller. It sounded like mine alone.

Ivret looked as impassive as ever, but the next speaker, Barreau, was visibly dismayed to follow me. I half absorbed his argument, a strained bit of logic about voting yes just to forestall a defiant escape attempt, but my thoughts were finished with the case. At the end of the verdicts, Ivret snapped her notebook shut and announced the day's dismissals: Brusson, Barreau, and Verdier.

I kept my eyes down, scared of the look on her face. Behind me was the deathly shuffle of desks being cleared. This time no one threw a tantrum. Only when I heard their departing footsteps did I gather the courage to send Jo a stricken glance, but she didn't see me, she was already at the top of the stairs. Far from disgraced, she looked haughty and disgusted.

The parlor now had six candidates and six empty chairs. I had no more neighbors at the back of the room. Ivret shared with us that C.R., like L.M., had been a real person, and his request had been denied in both valleys.

Did he try to escape? Cadieux asked. In the sparse new intimacy of the classroom, she did not first raise her hand.

Ivret nodded. Yes, he tried.


My mother waited near the fountain in the square. As soon as she saw me, she readied her arms in hesitant triumph, and when I hunched in embarrassment, she threw them in the air. Hugging me tightly, she told me that now I'd made it further than she had, and she'd always known I was meant for this. Swelling inside, I gave a shrug. For the first time I realized I agreed.

We went to the tea boat for a slice of pie before dinner, and when I got home, recalling that Edme was busy tonight, I changed into soft clothes and read on the couch until bed. The book was a collection of short stories that I'd read before. At the beginning of each one I couldn't quite recall if the ending was happy or sad, but I always seemed to remember right as it was unfolding. I leafed through a lot of the book. Between the stories, I would go back to feeling elated, then worrying about Jo.

In Cazelles even the door chime sounded expensive, like jewels jingling on a chain. The boutique's air was misted with rosewater. The shopkeeper was folding blouses. She gave me a short smile and returned to her work.

I found the bathing suits on a rack along the wall. It was the kind of store where there were only a few items to choose from, and all looked alarmingly minimal on their hangers. I held up a two-piece, opting for green so as not to copy Jo or Justine. When I got up the nerve to try it on, the shopkeeper apologized that it wasn't allowed. But she reached into my cardigan and touched my hips lightly, then eyed my chest and legs and said that I'd picked the right size, the suit would flatter my frame.

My mother had given me the money as a reward for vetting. She'd dropped me off while she did some errands, so I had another half hour to myself downtown. I walked from the boulevard to the park, feeling proud and self-conscious about the gold foil logo on my shopping bag.

It was Saturday, almost noon, and the lake breeze offered the last respite from the midday heat. I sat down on the grass under a maidenhair tree. It was still too early for most people to be at the beach, but there were dog walkers on the promenade, and the usual kites pulling against their strings. I lay on my back studying the fan-shaped leaves above.

I hadn't wanted to succeed in vetting until I'd started succeeding, and now I didn't want to stop. I wondered whether this change in me revealed a weakness: my own desires seemed dependent on external approval, on the permission of others. But maybe I wasn't so strange. Ambition might be like a living organism, reliant on nurture to grow. With some encouragement, mine had protruded from the dirt, a tiny shoot crawling toward the light.

In the car my mother asked if I'd bought anything, but before she could follow up on what, I distracted her with small talk about her errands, then led her further off topic by mentioning something I'd seen on the way to meet her: a man lying facedown in the pavilion, a bottle near his hand. As I'd gotten closer I started doubting whether he was alive, but he gave an abrupt phlegmy cough and I hurried away. My mother tsked her tongue and shook her head and muttered how shameful, he was probably on furlough from the western border, all the town miscreants ended up there. I acted like I was listening, the Cazelles bag hidden under my arm. I thought of asking to get dropped off at Jo's to see how she was doing, but I was also afraid she might not want to see me, so we continued driving up the hill.

I tucked the bathing suit deep in my dresser and helped my mother clean the house. I piled our books on the living room floor and dusted and wiped the emptied shelves. We left the sliding door open and flies blew in with the wind. A spartan guitar played from the kitchen radio, getting lost in thickets of static, picking its way out again.

The plan was to meet the others at eight. At seven-thirty I put on the bathing suit. I'd drank a glass of wine at dinner, but still only managed one glance in the mirror. To my relief, the sight looked normal, a girl you'd see at the beach, not the naked body I felt like. I wore a flowery sun dress over it and told my mother I was going to spend some time with Jo Verdier. As I expected, she said yes, adding that I was being a good friend.

Edme and Alain were at the end of the cul-de-sac under a streetlight. Hanging off the bus stop post with one arm, Alain gave a lazy wave. Edme had on his trunks and an unbuttoned plaid shirt. He was holding a bag of rolled towels.

Hi, I said. Did you escape okay?

Yeah, I have a couple hours before they get back.

We heard walking on the road, and Justine entered the streetlight's amber pool. She gave me a grim little look.

Where's Jo? I asked.

I'm not sure she's coming.

Why not? Alain stopped swinging from the post. She said she'd bring the wine.

You didn't tell them? Justine frowned.

Suddenly I felt like I'd been hiding something. I explained that I'd just arrived myself.

What's going on? asked Edme.

Jo was dismissed from vetting. She won't get a Conseil apprenticeship.

Alain and Edme said it was bad news, Justine and I nodded somberly, and then no one knew what to say. After a dutiful silence, Alain commented that the night wasn't getting any warmer, and at least Odile's got something to celebrate. He and Edme hopped onto the wooden steps that led down to the cove, and Justine and I followed, our feet clomping on the old boards. It was dark enough that you had to use the railing not to fall. I asked how Justine's application for the veterinary apprenticeship was going, and although she answered, she seemed a bit reluctant to talk to me.

Alain and Edme were waiting halfway down the steps, but when we reached them Alain jumped over the handrail and dashed into the forest. It was a narrow sidepath that led to the cliffs. We heard him trip on something and yelp. Edme shrugged and climbed the railing. I maneuvered my bare legs over it and did the same.

The north end cliffs were part of the same rocky promontory as the bluffs where Edme and I had been a few nights before. Near my house, the dropoff to the lake was fairly mild; near the cove, the cliffs rose above the water by sixty feet or more. It was risky to jump off them because of hidden boulders under the surface, but people still did it, taking running leaps. It was something of a neighborhood tradition each June when the senior students graduated and had a bonfire on the beach. According to rumor they blocked off the steps: you could get to the party only by braving the cliff, then swimming around the corner into the cove.

When the rest of us emerged onto the clifftop, arms and legs scraped by thorns, Alain was standing impatiently with his hand on his side. He had taken off his shirt.

I hope you're not thinking about jumping, Justine warned. Alain didn't answer, just grinned and slid into a luxurious stretch, extending his leg and grasping for his toe. The night felt cooler on the cliff; you could smell the height of the air. Mellow water washed against the rock face below.

We joined Alain near the edge. I could see the entire geological formation that ran beneath the neighborhood, craggy as exposed bone, shouldering the weight of the houses, holding up our childhoods. I tried to see the distant rocks where Edme had coaxed me into playing his violin, but I couldn't tell the outcrops apart. The bluffs shrank until they became hills, and finally vineyards.

Look, I think you can see Jo's gazebo, I said, pointing at a twinkling light. Farther off, near the downtown marina, the red dot of a houseboat was floating on the lake.

Truly splendid is the view, Alain proclaimed in a deep voice. Now, from his splendid perch, a hawk will unfurl his splendid wings. Alain raised both arms as if preparing to jump, but Justine swatted at him and tried to hold his arms down. Despite all manner of obstacles, Alain said as he struggled, the hawk is determined . . . to realize his splendor . . .

Justine gave up. Fine, she said warily, die if you want to.

With an injured look, Alain held his hand out to Edme. Will you remain loyal, fellow bird?

Edme stepped closer to the edge, and to my surprise, he lowered himself into the same pose that he'd struck on the bluff with me, bending his knee and raising his arm, only this time without his violin. Then, in a familiar falsetto, he crooned in my direction: *Bird.* I pushed down a smile.

Justine raised her eyebrows. Beautiful. Can we go to the beach now? On foot?

Glancing at each other, Edme and Alain answered by singing *Bird* again, loudly and in unison, drawing out the word, searching for harmony without success. I didn't know why it was funny, it was stupid, but things were just funny when they did them, and Justine and I cracked up. We all left the cliff and made our way back through the brambles to the steps.

Is Jo upset with me? I asked Justine softly.

You'd have to ask her.

I'm just worried if she blames me for what happened. I feel like there was a misunderstanding.

She didn't talk about it much. She was mostly saying she didn't want to be on the Conseil anyway, it's a bore, that type of thing.

Did she say anything about me?

Justine hesitated. She said the Conseil makes sense for you.

At the bottom of the steps was the cove. It was an unpopular beach, largely shadowed by the back-ends of the surrounding cliffs even when the sun was out. There was some scratchy grass and gnarled peach trees. The only sand was a strip of mealy grit along the shore, where a lone black spruce grew improbably close to the water. I had childhood memories of trying to arrange my towel in the spruce's shade while avoiding its braided roots and fallen pinecones.

Out in the lake, the small swimming area was roped off with desultory buoys. Justine dipped her toe in the water and shrugged. She pulled her dress up over her head and dropped it on her towel. She was wearing her periwinkle suit. When Edme took off his shirt, I realized that if I didn't strip now I'd have to do it alone, so I did it hastily and clasped my dress in front of my bare stomach, trying to recall something I'd never learned: how to stand naturally. I had chosen this, had felt excited to buy it, but now I hoped Edme wasn't looking at me, and wished for dimmer moonlight. The night felt brisk against my ribs.

I made myself keep up the conversation in spite of my anxiety, and my voice sounded almost normal. No one else could tell I was this nervous, I thought: perhaps this was all that self-possession ever was. Alain started talking about the sunken rowboat in the cove, ensnared in algae and harboring clouds of tiny fish. I said I'd always avoided swimming over the sunken boat, and Justine seemed to warm up for the first time that night, agreeing that the boat was creepy, she didn't like swimming over it either.

Edme was about to say something about it—When I was little, he began—when a whoop spilled down from the woods. A boy's voice yelled something inarticulate, and we turned toward the sound of people jumping down the last steps. The first one I saw was Henri, with Tom close behind him. Then a few downtown girls whose names I didn't know, and Marie from school, and Jo.

Hello there! she called. She raised a wine bottle over her head with careless flourish. Some of the others carried bottles too. Jo slung a bag off her shoulder and it clinked beside us on the sand.

You came fully stocked, Alain observed. He helped himself to a bottle from the bag.

Greetings Alain, greetings Edme, greetings best friend, said Jo. Then she glanced at me. Wow, look who went to Cazelles.

I kept quiet. Henri waved his hand in the air.

Everybody listen, he announced, his voice fuzzy. I'm supposed to say that—*occasionally*—I've been a bit of a fucker. Beside him, Tom broke into splurting laughter, but Henri slurred on, feeling out his words like stepping stones across a creek. Joelle Verdier wants me to apologize, on this very night, so here goes: Rosso. Pira. Guys. I'm sorry.

For what? said Alain.

For whatever. Henri's laugh was raspy and glazed; he threw his head back as though at a secret joke. I thought Edme might have glanced over at me, but I wouldn't take my eyes off Henri. Jo extracted the bottle from his fingers. Everyone, let's have a toast to Henri and his big heart.

Alain drank and passed the bottle to Edme, who had some and offered it my way. I gestured no thanks.

But then I did drink, because it was the only thing for me to do. I draped my dress over my lower half as I sat resting on my elbows. The group lolled around draining the wine, partly on the towels and partly in the sand. Most of the talk was between Jo and the downtown girls, with the others interrupting here and there: past parties I hadn't been to, future ones I hadn't known of. Their loud voices echoed in the cove, turning the night obnoxious and confining. Whenever a bottle came my way I took it.

I don't know if it was Jo's idea, swimming naked, but she was the first to take off her clothes, claiming to have forgotten her suit. Some of the other girls giggled weak dissents, but as Jo undid her bra she archly declared that everyone would be participating. Henri whistled and she retorted that it would never happen in a million years, which I noticed made Edme chuckle. He and Alain stood up and stripped without protest, and as I quickly cast my eyes away, the others joined in too. They ran into the lake with shrieks and shouts.

Justine was the last to go. She got up, took off her suit, and in a tipsy voice asked if I was coming. Maybe in a while, I mumbled at the sand. When she stayed standing in front of me, I darted an awkward look at her.

Nothing you haven't seen, Odile, she muttered.

Before I could reply, she left me, seeming a little embarrassed. My blush engulfed my entire body.

I hoped more wine might give me the courage, but it only made the night more rotten. I finished off a whole bottle. No one had beckoned to me. For minutes I mentally rehearsed putting my dress back on over my suit, and eventually I did it. The defeat stung my eyes and I wiped the tears away hatefully, trying not to look more foolish. Henri and Tom were hollering and splashing in the lake. Alain and Justine were swimming out by the buoys.

Apart from the rest, Edme was talking to Jo. They were standing in shallow water that went to their waists. She laughed at something he said. As she did, she spun away from him, almost losing her balance, and he reached out to steady her. With a bashful smile, she covered her breasts with her arm, and I thought Edme smiled back in the same way.

I watched them for only a second, but it felt like much too long. I fumbled for my sneakers and got up. When I still didn't hear my name, I climbed the wooden steps, crossed the cul-de-sac, and walked home as rapidly as I could.

I tore off my bathing suit and looked at myself in the mirror. My bedroom light was objective and unforgiving. There were rashy red pinch lines where the suit had been. I smacked my light switch and crawled into bed, shrinking myself against the whirling walls.

L ate the next morning my mother called through the door, telling me to start my chores because it might rain later. I rolled out of bed, put on my chore shirt, and shambled outside.

The day was cloudy. North of the valley was a line of deep blue rain, the first in weeks. Slowly I pushed the lawnmower up and down the backyard, fighting shivers of nausea, going inside once to be sick. I finished raking the grassy piles and sloughing them down the hill. The rest of the day I lay on the couch with a blanket, drinking balsamroot tea and poking through books, hardly retaining the sentences.

The living room floor contained a knothole, a rough-edged imperfec-tion the diameter of a coin. When I was bored as a child I used to squeeze things in and trot to the basement to collect them from the crawlspace where they'd fallen. Now, looking at the knothole, a drunken memory surfaced from the night before: I'd banished Edme's violin from my bed-room and shoved it in the crawlspace. His audition was in a matter of days.

At some point he would have noticed that I'd left the beach, and pos-sibly wondered why. There were reasons, then, to think that Edme might come to my window tonight, supposing that I even wanted him to. Yet there were no plans for him to come. And if he was sneaking out any-where, there was somewhere else he might go instead. Maybe he wouldn't even have to keep it secret: his parents might make an exception for the Verdiers, excited like my mother had been. I pictured him laughing with Jo's parents at their banquet table, and later walking to the gazebo, and later to her room.

Evening came without sunset. The daylight simply slid back into the earth. I let my room grow dark. Finally I retrieved the violin from the crawlspace to wait for him.

The rain began just after midnight. The first drop hit my window hard enough that I turned my head in hope. Then the sky caved in, pouring into the valley. The storm hurled water at the house.

Some humiliating voice argued that he would've come if not for this weather. I turned away in bed and watched the shadows coursing down my wall. The rain would have ruined his violin, it was true, but he had always come earlier than this, so that was not the reason.

*

It was so black that I needed the clock to tell me it was morning. I lay listening to the muddy patter outside. The bleakness felt welcome. At last I sat up and entered the ache of the day.

I wore a rain poncho big enough to fit the whole violin case underneath it. I was the only person walking to school. Halfway up the hill, Jo's car passed by. It strayed into the opposite lane to avoid spraying me with a puddle, but didn't stop to pick me up.

I hung the dripping poncho on my peg in the cloakroom. Although it was still before the bell, there were already several students camping indoors to keep dry. I turned in my damp homework on Pichegru's desk and left Edme's violin under his chair.

I heard him come in with Alain and Justine and Jo. I was scrutinizing my Conseil notebook, simply to keep occupied. I saw him notice the violin and glance back. I resolved to keep my head down, to look cold and unaffected, and was thankful when Pichegru arrived. The class stood for attention and sat down again.

I avoided them all day. At lunch I escaped into the hall, but I was too close on Pichegru's heels.

Where are you running to, Ozanne? he asked.

I picked a door at random. The library.

That's a reasonable idea on a day like this.

I agreed and tried to leave.

I've been told, Pichegru continued, that you've been acquitting yourself well in town. He looked at me directly for one of the first times since he'd nominated me. His eyes were still a bit grudging.

I guess we'll see, I replied.

Yes we will. I'm not sure if you're aware, but it's been a long time since a candidate from our school advanced past this stage—it would mean something to the north end.

I nodded, and Pichegru grunted at me to keep up the good work as he walked into the staff room.

I sat in the farthest corner of the library from the circulation desk, behind a row of shelves. My window faced the sodden playing field. A book was abandoned on my table, a guide to flora and fauna. It was for children but I flipped through it for the hour. After the bell I stayed seated for a stubborn minute, then another. The hallway outside the library fell silent as classes resumed. I sat staring at the grey field. The pond might flood.

When I came in late the classroom smelled dank with wet clothes. As soon as the day ended I hurried outside and crossed the road, not even putting on my poncho until I was at the bus stop. Edme might have tried to get my attention again on the way out, I couldn't be sure. But how could I explain why I'd fled the cove, why I'd returned his violin, without admitting how I'd felt about him; and how could I admit that without making myself wretched in front of both him and Jo. I was not ready to face them yet; distance was my only dignity. The bus entered the cul-de-sac, its tires descending into vast puddles, lights straining in the rain.

*

Vetting felt quiet without Jo. I had no one to talk to beforehand, but the other five candidates were more subdued as well, and didn't gather by the window. Separately, we waited at our desks.

With the room so bare, Ivret's voice sounded different, trebly echoes ringing off her sibilants. She distributed the beige cards for the final test, which was titled *Case of J.N. & P.N.*

At least it was not a violent scenario like C.R.'s, but to me it was sadder than L.M.'s. The petition was submitted jointly by a father and daughter, requesting to visit their wife/mother in Ouest 1. Unlike the other cases, this woman was not dead, and so on first pass the family's petition seemed ineligible. The woman's mind had crumbled early, a rare condition that left her senile by the age of forty-five. Her husband had effectively raised their daughter alone, and the daughter had few memories of her mother from when she was herself.

After a moment's thought I saw that their petition should be approved. The father and daughter were correct: I could easily construct an argument likening the woman's state to a living death. Perhaps it was worse, because she remained there, a constant emblem of loss. The family could go to her bedroom and sit beside her absence. She was a ghost whose body they cleaned.

Hardness had served me well in vetting, but I should not be unyielding. The objections to the family's request could be anticipated and disarmed in advance. I pushed the card to the end of my desk and folded my hands. The rest were still jotting their first impressions, which Ivret permitted for a moment. Our eyes met across the classroom. Right then, I lost any doubt that I would be chosen as one of the Conseil's apprentices. A small gratification shot through me, a flare in the night.

Now that we were an even slimmer group, certain to work in the Hôtel de Ville in some capacity, she introduced us to the cipher the Conseil used to code their letters between the valleys, so the gendarmes were never tempted to open the mail. Dutifully I wrote out the key, a series of letter combinations that were substituted twice over, transposing the grave correspondences into gibberish. After the lesson ended and the others filed out, Ivret asked me how I was.

Surprised, I answered that I was fine, but I heard my own falseness. I felt the need to say something else to make up for it, and since I was the last one in the room, I said:

Mme Ivret, I know you asked, but I don't think I can go over to his house. I mean the Piras' house. I'm sorry.

She regarded me calmly. All right. I appreciate you keeping me informed.

Thank you, I whispered.

For a strange second, I was sure she was about to step closer and lay her hand on my shoulder. I was relieved when the moment passed. She wished me good evening and turned to wipe the chalkboard.

How obvious must have been my dejection, that even Ivret pitied me. Downstairs I held out my hand and felt the moistness in the air, but the rain had stopped at last. The lamps came on around the square, one after the next, and the flagstones were shiny and wet in the light. In the basin of the fountain, excess water trembled at the rim.

My mother was late to meet me. She came over without her jacket or purse.

I'm sorry, I have to stay on, we got a dump of work at the last minute. It'll be a few hours, you should just take the bus.

She went back inside. I lingered in front of the Hôtel de Ville until I heard music from the conservatory, and left for the bus stop. The bus was dark and locked, so I walked to the beach promenade to kill time. The boardwalk was still slippery and crickets were trilling deep in the park. The last bands of daylight disappeared behind the western mountains. I was tempted to keep walking, to walk all the way home, but then I heard the bus's ignition and headed back.

My house passed by on the left. As the only passenger, I could have asked the driver to let me off between stops, but I felt an odd combination of resignation and restlessness, too weary to speak up, too agitated to face the loneliness of my room. When the bus pulled into the cul-de-sac, the driver said to take care.

I wandered across the road to the school and entered the darkened playground. Somehow the underside of the swing's seat was wet too. I dried the rain with my sleeve and kicked off, pumping my legs and pointing them straight, tilting back my neck. The rainclouds were gone and the moon was out. I lifted and fell through the undulating sky.

When I got home, my mother still wasn't there. I cut a thick wedge of bread with jam and butter for dinner and made a pot of tea. The steam's climbing smell made me feel a bit better. I ate at the table as I did my homework, logic and cipher, then went to bed early. It was Monday night, the sixteenth of September.

B efore the morning bell I reviewed my proofs, another excuse to keep my eyes down. But I noticed all the desks fill up except his. I glanced around. Jo and Justine were both in their seats. Behind them, Alain seemed to be doodling.

Pichegru was unusually late. As the room began sensing an anomaly the chatter grew boisterous. Amid the rising din I stared at Edme's chair. The seatback was feldspar pink, covered in looping pencil scrawls.

Pichegru appeared in profile in the front doorway, talking in low tones to someone out of view in the hall. He put his hand on the unseen person, a placating gesture, but his jaw looked clenched. The classroom leaned forward to hear.

Then our teacher came in and beckoned to M. Pira. Edme's father removed his hat and held it tightly. Pichegru pointed him to the lectern.

Thank you, he said, fighting to control his voice. I'm sorry to interrupt. I just need to know if anyone here has seen Edme. He wasn't at home this morning . . . we were hoping he'd be here.

His worried eyes searched the room. Jo and Justine exchanged frowns. People looked to Alain, who slowly raised his hand.

I haven't seen him since yesterday. He said he was going home after school.

Yes, he was home for dinner. We thought that he went to bed. Can you think of anywhere else he might have gone later?

Alain glanced at Jo, who mouthed: *I don't know.* Jo began turning to me, but I averted my eyes.

We'll certainly contact you if we hear anything, said Pichegru. Please keep us updated. No doubt he'll turn up soon.

Edme's father thanked him again and retreated from the room. Pichegru placed a book on the lectern and silenced the murmuring with a warning look. His eyes grazed mine for less than an instant, then he started on geometry. We heard a car peel away from the school and Pichegru raised his voice over the squealing tires.

I had a floating feeling, as if I were watching someone else acting in my place. This person sat with the others in the familiar arrangement of desks. Her pallid face concealed everything. She was below me on the earth and getting smaller. I was drifting into the upper quiet, far away, tethered to her by a long unspooling thread.

They came to the wall at lunch.

Odile, have you seen him?

More than anxious, Jo seemed annoyed. I shook my head. Alain peered up and down the rear walkway, as though Edme might come ambling around the corner.

None of us made plans to sneak out with him, Jo said. Did you?

I shook my head again.

After they left, I took my sandwich out of my bag and chewed it, watching the windy genuflections of the treetops across the lawn. I rested one foot against the wall, then switched to the other. I pressed the back of my head against the stucco, grinding my hair into it until I could feel chips break off into my curls.

*

Ivret spoke about cases of ambiguity in mourning. She gave the example of a missing person who was never found: an analogy, we were meant to see, for the family with the senile mother, someone who was gone without the closure of a burial. I copied down what she said. The sunset filled the parlor, its color suffusing the walls. The remaining students were shadow creatures in the deepening light. Bent with care in the room of golden grief.

The lesson was winding down when, in the front row, Renée Tan asked Ivret about the timing of visits. She was savvy enough to frame her question generally, avoiding direct reference to the week's case. Normally, Renée asked, visits were scheduled prior to a death, but what if a case did not involve the impending death of either the subject or the visitor—what factors determined favorable timing then?

A good question, Ivret replied. Even in the standard cases, timing is quite sensitive. As a rule, the Conseil aims to schedule visits somewhat before the occasioning event—an imprecise proximity helps mitigate speculation and panic alike. Circumstances can complicate that, however. For example, if the event will take place in the winter or early spring, the borders are closed, so the visit may need to be scheduled earlier than otherwise desirable, while the mountains can still be navigated.

Ivret kept talking, but I heard nothing else. I was aghast at my error. I had applied the wrong principle. I assumed I knew how long Edme had after his parents' visit, based on the fact that when Yvette Cressy's parents had visited her, it was the fall and she lived well into the new year. I had not realized that visits didn't happen over the winter. It was obvious as soon as Ivret said it. Yvette's parents' trip, so far ahead of her death, had simply been scheduled before the snow started. Ordinarily, a visit could be scheduled much closer to the actual event.

I must have looked stunned as I stood up at the end of the lesson, because Ivret gave me another sympathetic look. It hit me sharply: she had known yesterday. It was why I'd sensed a tenderness in her. Not because she'd gotten wind of my romantic disappointments—ridiculous to think in retrospect—but because of what was about to happen. Of course she knew. The date would have been part of approving the Piras' visit from Est 1. I wanted to yell: Why didn't you tell me there was so little time? She had listened and nodded when I said I'd try to get invited to his house a few months from now. I grabbed my bookbag from my desk and recoiled from Ivret's smile, nearly falling as I rushed down the stairs.


My mother noticed my sunken silence in the car. Cautiously, she mentioned that she'd heard the news of my friend's disappearance—the words she used.

For a long time I didn't reply. Then I said: What kept you so late at work last night?

It was her turn not to respond.

At home I shut myself in my room. My mother wouldn't have known his name in advance. Not from the visitation records she was allowed to handle. Yet even a vague allusion outside the Hôtel de Ville might have made me realize. There might still have been time to warn him. She had followed the protocol, though: she had kept it to herself.

*

Pichegru began the next day by saying a volunteer search party was meeting after school. Gendarmes would help comb the forest. I noticed that Alain was absent. Pichegru commenced teaching grammar, but I could see that people weren't concentrating, many were just staring at their desks.

I walked off the schoolgrounds at lunch and crossed the chemin des Pins. At the end of the cul-de-sac I went to the beach stairs, climbed over the handrail, and picked my way along the overgrown path. Soon the cliff-top became visible. It was the place where, a few days ago, I'd watched Edme strike his mock-heroic pose, just as he'd done when he was practicing his violin at night with me.

I stepped over a deformed tree trunk that dipped down like a ladle. My ribcage curdled with dread. A few feet from the cliff's edge, his leather case was propped open. The violin lay nearby on some lichens. It did not look like something that had been set there deliberately, but like something dropped. There was a crack in the lacquered wood. I put it back in the case and clasped it shut.

I don't know how long it took me to look over the edge. When I managed to do it, there was only the lake. Stunted pines, thistle branches, white-flowered weeds poked out from the drop and shivered in the breeze. At the bottom, the submerged boulders were spectral green.

Edme?

My voice was small, as though he might be near. The valley gave no answer. Just the hiss of beetles, and tranquil lapping far below.

Halfway back to the beach stairs I turned abruptly off the path, stumbling several yards down the steep brush and deadfall. I came to a stop in front of a shrub with reddish stems and almond-shaped leaves. I was shaded on all sides by glowering pines whose trunks were covered in jigsaw cracks. On my knees, I dug until my fingers scraped damp clay. Then I put the violin case into the hole and buried it, covering his stenciled name with dirt. My breathing was quick and shallow: the act was wild and strange. When it was finished I climbed back to the path and looked down. It was indistinguishable from an anthill, it was hardly there at all.

The rest of my class joined in the search, and many younger students did too. Parked cars lined the street and the crowd waited in the roundabout for the gendarmes. I walked past them to the bus stop. I thought I heard somebody, maybe Justine, call my name, but I ignored it. On the bus I slid the beige card under my fingernails to remove the last of the dirt. Before vetting started, I overheard Renée Tan and Cadieux talking about the searches. They haven't sent hunters out of the valley, Renée whispered from her desk, so they must think he's still here.

I removed the painting of the lake from my bedroom wall and hid it in my closet, but I dreamed of the lake anyway. I could see a long way beneath

the water, artificially far. The lakebed sank toward a black horizon, where
Edme was suspended at the cusp of the abyss. His head hung down, and
his hands and fingers too, dangling as if over piano keys in a silent audi-
torium. His skin was green like the water. Other people swam above us,
completely unaware, and I had to keep them from noticing.

I thrashed in my nightdress and lurched from my bed, groping at my
dresser to stop the dizziness. It was four-thirty. My sheets were soaked
through. The clifftop would have been slippery from the storm.

*

Thursday was the day of Edme's audition. His desk remained empty, as did
Alain's. It was clear he was skipping school to continue searching on his
own, and Pichegru didn't ask if we had seen him.

An even bigger group of volunteers met that afternoon. I saw Jo and
Justine with Henri and Tom. Again I walked straight to the bus stop. The
bounce of the bus lulled me half-asleep, my head drooping and jerking as
sunlight flashed through the trees.

The Place du Bâtisseur was lively that afternoon. The Hôtel de Ville's
steps were full of people. Coming from the other end of the square, I
saw a boy with an instrument case headed for the conservatory. He was
bespectacled and wan, not mistakable for Edme, but his case was the same,
a violin. He opened the conservatory door and went in.

I glanced back at the Hôtel de Ville. There was Ivret, walking briskly
along the colonnade toward the Grande École. At the sight of her and her
robe I experienced an acrid distaste, like biting on a coin.

The noise of flutes and reeds filled the conservatory lobby. The bespectacled boy had already vanished down the hall. The same woman was
behind the reception desk. She began asking if she could help me, then
remembered: Oh yes, you're with Edme. Is he here yet?

It shouldn't have surprised me that no one had updated her—he'd kept
the audition secret—but I must have stared.

What's wrong?

It took me a moment to answer. He hasn't been seen, I began. Actually, Edme's missing.

My voice struggled and I started to cry. The woman left her desk quickly and put her arms around me. I collapsed into her shoulder and sobbed.

She sat with me in the waiting area, her hand resting on mine. I watched the clock turn four. I hadn't intended to keep vigil during the time of his audition, but as the minutes passed I didn't leave. The woman, Gilberte, quietly said that she'd heard about the searches but not the boy's name. She told me that his compositions were strong, one of them quite original. She'd had a promising feeling when I'd dropped them off. I realized that I'd never even told Edme that the conservatory was expecting me to watch his audition; I'd never asked his permission.

When his time slot elapsed I didn't get up right away. A girl had come in with a wheeled instrument case, and Gilberte had gone to sign her in. The girl rolled her heavy case down the hall. Gilberte gave me another look of consolation from the desk. I nodded goodbye. I was glad that, the whole time, she never assured me that he'd turn up safe.

The empty swim dock hadn't been removed for the season yet. A dog prowled the far end of the beach, snout scanning the sand, no owner in sight. I sat down between the cottonwood trees where they sometimes brought visitors. The park was brighter now that the leaves were mostly fallen. I was an hour late for vetting and knew I wasn't going back.

The sunset filled the sky with blazing clouds. Walkers appeared in pairs on the promenade. A family in the pavilion was setting up a barbecue. I stayed in the park until twilight, then waited at the Hôtel de Ville for my mother. I watched the other candidates exiting the Grande École together. When my mother came, I stepped out of the shadows of the columns. For god's sake, you scared me, she said with a laugh. How was vetting?

I told her it was fine.

I woke on Friday from the same underwater dream, as I would for many months. Always he was unreachable, a shape made from the silty darkness.

It was just past noon when word started traveling around the schoolgrounds. The first sign was Marie running up to Lucien, whispering and gesticulating; together they went to Henri and Tom, who looked for someone else to tell. Jo and Justine were coming over from the field. I heard Henri say: They found something. He and the others jogged toward the chemin des Pins. I left the wall and followed.

There were teachers among the crowd streaming into the cul-de-sac. I saw the back of Pichegru's head disappear down the stairs to the cove. The only sound in the forest was feet trampling on wood. No one talked anymore. At the bottom, people were gathered at the shore. Two women had their arms around Mme Pira. Her hands were clutching at her clothes.

Knee-deep in the water, Alain was helping Edme's father into a grey rowboat. Another man climbed in too, and Alain pushed them toward the buoys. I couldn't see anything in the lake. They rowed to the south end of the cove near the cliffs. The man in the boat who wasn't M. Pira looked repeatedly up at the clifftop, and I realized someone was directing them from above.

The boat adjusted its angle and stopped at the last buoy. The men leaned over the far side.

Edme's father let out a single wail.

I remember Alain's enormous eyes as he wheeled around in the water looking back at us. He turned and took another helpless step into the lake. M. Pira and the other man were dragging something into the rowboat that looked like sopping laundry.

Then the women with Mme Pira were hurrying her to the grass; Pichegru and another teacher were herding people back from the beach, shouting and pointing at the steps. A gendarme came out of the brush and waded into the water in his boots. Pichegru appeared right in front of my face, saying something very low and firm, but I backed away and ran up the steps to the cul-de-sac again. I tore across the emptied schoolgrounds and into the backwoods. I abandoned the path and fled up the ridge past the fort, which shrank to nothing below. I was breathless but kept running. I stopped only when I saw the fence rise from the mountain ahead, silver wires glaring sharply in the sunlight, a sky made out of knives.

# Part II

Part II

I came down from the fence, and reported to the Place du Bâtisseur.

The inside of the Hôtel de Ville smelled of newly waxed marble. Muted daylight, mausoleum grey, filtered in from skylights concealed in the spandrels. Every now and then a clerk appeared on the helical stairs, ferrying files between the mezzanine and the basement offices. She gave a small nod whenever she passed me, gliding through the rotunda in soundless black slippers.

Soon the afternoon sitting would be over. I waited on the stone bench, slouching and gazing up at the ceiling. A mosaic filled the lofty dome. In the center, as always, was our valley, composed of ancient tiles whose original colors were fastidiously preserved. The other valleys surrounded it in figurative orbit, rendered in duskier shades, as if shadowed by the interceding mountains. Our own lake was vibrant cerulean.

The chamber door opened at the far end of the mezzanine. I stood and straightened my uniform. For a moment I thought I could hear the voices of the conseillers inside, but then the door closed with a soft thump. Jean-Savile and his second-in-command, Coltelli, led the aged petitioner down the stairs.

As they approached I looked for an indication of how the hearing had gone. The petitioner was not smiling, but that was typical; more telling was the absence of tears or anger. This man wore the stolid expression of someone whose plans were progressing.

You'll hear back in a week or so, Jean-Savile said as they crossed the rotunda floor. For now, Ozanne will drive you home.

The petitioner shook hands with Coltelli and Jean-Savile in turn. When he looked at me, I saw a glint of doubt as to whether he was supposed to shake my hand too.

This way, I told him.

His name was Quinton. He was tall with a careful gait, and his gaunt face was dominated by large black glasses. I guessed that he was about thirty years older than I was. Being in his mid-sixties would put him in the upper range for a mourning tour, but he looked like he could manage the hike: two days there, two days back. Still, though nothing was outwardly wrong with him, I knew he was likely unwell.

I drove him to a neighborhood on the south end of town. After a while, to break the silence in the truck, he coughed and told me that the Conseil had approved his petition.

He waited for my reaction, yet seemed unperturbed when I gave none. We were passing a parkette where a group of boys, not yet school aged, were chasing each other through the blond grass. The air smelled pleasantly burnt from a backyard fire. It had been another hot autumn, but the days were getting crisper, and at night you could see your breath.

Quinton pointed to his turnoff. As I pulled into the narrow alleé des Platanes, he asked whether, if his trip were approved by the neighboring valley, I would be the one to escort him there.

I replied that our duties rotated, and it was my turn next.

Quinton paused, then said: Do you think they'll say yes?

I gave off a silence, and he didn't pursue it. When I stopped at his house, he said that he hoped to see me soon. I answered that he'd be notified of the outcome either way.

It was the end of October, and the viewing season was winding down. By November there would be snow up the mountains, making the hike treacherous in either direction. The border across the lake had already seen their last scheduled visitor return, and after Quinton's request was sorted, the eastern border would close for the year as well. Petitions continued to be heard over the winter, but delivering the notices to the exchange posts would wait for the following spring.

With Quinton dropped off, I switched on the radio and opened the truck's window. This neighborhood was not far from where my grandparents had lived, and the deteriorating asphalt lined with weeping willows had the same shady hues of childhood. There were ramshackle flowerboxes and herb gardens planted along the lanes that didn't seem to belong to any particular house. I drove back to the border road slowly, reaching out the window to grasp a long willow strand in my hand, stripping the last leaves.

*

The mess hall was noisy during meal hours. The guards around me grew ever younger, recruits in their teens and twenties with outrageous capacities for border liquor. The taciturn older guards congregated at the far end by the window with the view of the fence. I sat with them. Soon Raimond arrived and set his tray down across from mine. I greeted him without standing up; a few years ago, he'd told me not to observe the formalities or call him sir.

As an officer, Raimond Raboulet's presence would have been unusual in the mess hall if not for the fact that he came several times a week. He chose to spend time among the lower ranks because he was not especially liked by the members of his own. He was frank with me about this and unembarrassed by it, shrugging it off as inconsequential. But he was nonetheless proud of the trim black uniform he wore, habitually brushing at the shoulders to remove the flakes that fell from his weedy yellow hair. Raimond's lips were perpetually dry and peeling, and they cracked open in a painful way when he smiled. He was a few years my senior, in his early forties, and the closest thing I had to a friend.

Over dinner we made conversation in our usual style. Raimond loved talking about work, so I could ask him one question and listen to him for the rest of the meal. Today, though, he had questions for me. He knew that I'd driven a petitioner, and asked how I thought the hearing had gone. When I told him the verdict, he nodded knowingly, chewing on a chicken leg.

What was your impression of the man? Raimond said through his food. I ask, because he was my schoolteacher back in the day—M. Quinton.

Really, I said. Did you like him?

No complaints on the whole. If you kept your nose clean you didn't get flogged, so I never had an issue. I was sure they'd approve him. I heard he wrote a model petition. Sad without overdoing it.

Well, I replied, if Est 1 goes for it, maybe I'll hear some gossip about you on the trip. The inside story of your formative years.

As Raimond sipped cherry juice, the scarlet stained his torn lips. I doubt he'll have much to say, but we'll see soon enough. Jean-Savile will probably send you the minute we hear back just to keep ahead of the weather.

He moved on to another subject, clucking at the latest guards to be disciplined for infractions. Raimond handled some staffing matters and was known as a stickler for regulations. Once or twice he had cautioned me about my patrol pace with a hasty, apologetic air, but he had never written me up.

After dinner I walked alone from the mess hall to the barracks. The walk ran parallel to the border. The fence was floodlit at night, a cold glare that blanched every shadow out of the surrounding dirt, and I kept to the far edge of the light, where my breath disintegrated in silvery wisps. It was chilly and I regretted my thin windbreaker.

My quarters were in the south barracks. The room had not always been mine—the assignments shuffled every couple of years—but all the quarters were the same for ordinary gendarmes: a folding cot, a desk, a wardrobe, a sink fixed to the wall. Standard pieces in different configurations, plagued by primeval grime. An unpainted radiator ticked and sputtered under the window.

I undressed and crossed the room quickly to minimize contact between my bare feet and the warped linoleum. The cot sagged as I lay down. The blue bedspread was made of itchy wool and had cigarette burns from the room's last occupant, or the one before that. My nightstand was my only piece of personal furniture, if it could be called that: an upended wine crate that I used to carry my belongings when my room was reassigned. A lamp and some books balanced on it, covering the winery logo.

I got under the blanket and turned off the light. I heard a guard cough in the adjacent room and spit into his sink. As I watched the darkness settle, the floodlights bled around the sides of my curtain, creating a suspended square, a frame without a picture.

M y patrol sector for the week started at the lakeshore. At dawn I left the barracks and boarded the transport bus. Although the bus was full, it was too early for talking. Drowsy guards sipped coffee from flasks. I watched daylight spread over the passing farms and orchards.

I was among the last to be let out. The road never went all the way to the fence, so I walked there along the shoreline. That far south of town, the beach was a wasteland of muddy inlets, eroding dirt ledges, and withered cattails. Scorched beer bottles littered infrequent fire rings. I could see the fence ahead.

The expanse of wires extended over the water, secured by pillars that stood across the lake. The wires continued deep below the surface. Every few summers an escapee's body would have to be retrieved from the float-ing fence; some gendarmes called the beach towers 'lifeguard duty.' The guard in the watchtower tapped his cigarette on the platform's railing as I approached. We acknowledged each other for the first of several times. Out of habit I touched the tips of my fingers to the base of the tower, pushed off, then headed up the border path.

The sector was three miles of mild grade. On my left, toward town, were the valley's main orchards, thin and brown this time of year, a thread-bare fringe on the scrubby plains. On my right, through the fencewires, more hay-colored treeless steppe stretched to the distant eastern moun-tains. The border was quiet unless you talked to yourself or hummed.

The sparse grasses rustled when the breeze picked up, and the alarm bells clinked gently on the wires.

All patrols overlapped, so other guards came walking toward me at regular intervals. Some liked to stop and talk, but most of the time we traded hellos and walked on. I knew the right places and times to take my allotted breaks without being interrupted, and that day I stopped halfway between the second and third towers, where there was a boulder to sit on while I ate.

It was, as usual, a hard-boiled egg, a piece of jerky, and fruit in a paper bag. Sometimes the jerky was switched for rubbery cheese that sweated in the hotter months. The patrol rations from the mess hall reminded me of school. I saved the day's fruit and drank some water. Then I wiped my hands on my pants and opened my satchel of carving tools.

In these short gaps, I worked on my engravings. My blocks were mostly landscapes, views of the valley. Today I decided to add some windy flowers to the foreground of the image. Holding the block firmly between my knees, I entered it carefully with my chisel, the wood curling away from the beveled edge.

I'd given myself a rule: to carve only in the field, from observation alone, never from memory or a pencil sketch. Thus, I would keep adding to this particular block while I was posted to this sector, then store it away until my schedule rotated me back here in a few months. It was impractical in every way, but it was my game for passing the days. Because of it, a single carving often took me a year to finish. In the final product, four seasons occupied the same landscape, like a distillation of time.

When my break was done I put away my things and resumed walking. A guard appeared—at first just another green uniform with a patrol bag, but closer up, I recognized Caron. He was one of the ones who liked talking, and he offered me an illicit drink from his canteen. I tasted warm vinegary wine as he chortled about a guard who'd been caught having an affair in town. I squinted as though listening. We were standing on a distinctive hillock where the fence rose up abruptly from the plain. It was the hill visible from my grandparents' orchard, where my father had lifted me onto the old stone wall and given me the feeling of looking off the world's edge.

All for that runt? Caron was laughing. If you're going to chance it, make it count!

I raised my eyebrows and nodded absently. When his laughter subsided he asked how long I had until my next downtown shift. I answered that I'd had one at the start of the fall, so not till the new year, and he grimaced with pity. Too bad, he said. His was next week, he was counting the days.

I thanked him for his bad wine and we parted. It was typical for gendarmes to live for their downtown patrols. The accommodations were better, the shifts ended earlier to allow for recreation, but more than anything, it interrupted the monotony. For a week you got to live more like a civilian, choosing where to dine, drinking on tavern row. But I was less enthused about my downtown shifts. Partly it was about sharing quarters with a single random partner, but the main reason was that the quarters were located behind the chapel in the Place du Bâtisseur, and whenever I stayed there, I risked running into Mme Ivret.

Although she was nearing retirement, she still ran the vetting program. After Mme Acroyant ascended to the chair of the Conseil, Ivret became the vice-chair, and I sometimes saw her walking between buildings in the square. She'd begun carrying a cane but still mounted stairs spryly, her long braid swinging behind her, now as white as paper.

We hadn't had much reason to speak since I quit vetting. For months afterward, I hardly set foot downtown at all, first staying home, then holing up in my grandparents' house when things with my mother became too much. More than a year passed before I saw Ivret again, by which time I was a cadet. Our encounter took place in front of the Hôtel de Ville. She was walking from the Grande École through the alternating sun and shade of the columns while I trailed Coltelli and the other new recruits up the main steps. I saw her coming but could do nothing about it; I reached the door just as she did, and as the others continued inside, Ivret recognized me and paused.

Our conversation was cordial and brief. She'd heard where I'd ended up. I knew that she would have, of course, but it was still hard standing before her in my stiff uniform and cap. She gave no hint of anger at the fact that I'd left the program, nor at how I'd done it—a reaction I had worried about, however improbable it was. Instead, she looked at me with a touch of pity, understanding in a glimpse that I was already aware of my mistake. I remember her commenting that the gendarmerie was an honorable profession, and, to my discomfort, she commended me again on my discretion the previous fall. I don't know what I replied, if anything, but I do remember holding the door open for her, and her curt nod of thanks. It seemed also like a nod of farewell, even though it was hardly the last time our paths would intersect. Once a season, when I was stationed downtown, I risked seeing her, and thus seeing myself as she did.

It was the same way when I saw my mother, only worse. In contrast to Ivret's indifference, her response to my quitting had been rage. Abandoning a career in the Conseil was a betrayal of all her hopes for me. During the initial fight I'd sat wordless at the kitchen table, my ears and neck tingling with heat, as she shouted how stupid I was, demanded explanations, and ranted over my weak attempts to answer. At first I lied that I didn't enjoy the work, and then that I was scared of being cut, but she retorted that in that case I should have let myself get cut in the normal way—at least then I would have been eligible for clerical jobs, whereas now what options were there? And, since a consolation apprenticeship had in fact been my original goal, I was unequipped to defend myself, and let her logic lash me. It didn't take her long to strike on the truth.

Don't tell me, she breathed, that this is because of the accident.

My mouth uglied and I began blubbering. My mother slapped the table.

Because of a boy? she shouted. Oh Odile, you idiot!

What followed were months of stony recrimination. She took no interest in my grades or what I was going to do with myself now that the other apprenticeship deadlines had come and gone. All that fall and winter, when I hardly left my bedroom, I heard her come home and cook dinner for one. Finally, in the spring, I asked my grandparents if I could stay with them. When they agreed, I asked my mother's permission. She looked me over, as if seeing me for the first time in years, and muttered that I'd always been my father's daughter.

There was another row when I told her I was enlisting, but already that fight lacked the spirit of the first; she signed the papers with a skyward sigh, her attitude hardened into scorn. Over time things had cooled further into the formal estrangement that marked our relationship now. We still saw each other in passing when I delivered things to the archives, and a few times a year we met at the tea boat. These meals were reproachful, and her expression when I mentioned my job left me very little to talk about. With her silences, she seemed always to say: You see, I'm right, you squandered your life. With my silence, I would concede the point. But I did not really believe it. If my life was ruined, I had at least forged a tolerable nest in its wreckage. In fact, the gendarmerie had lately come to resemble the quiet career to which I'd once aspired. It was more exhausting, certainly, but like my mother in the archives, I showed up for work each day to carry out the wishes of the Conseil, unburdened by ambitions, and mostly alone with my thoughts.

T he verdict on Quinton was collected from the exchange post and brought back to the border. At a short morning assembly after reveille, Jean-Savile announced that the year's final viewing party would depart for Est 1 tomorrow. The assembly dispersed and he called me over.

Jean-Savile had turned sixty recently. His beard was still black, with just a fissure of white along the side of his chin. The stark blue eyes that had seemed so cold when I was a cadet now struck me as melancholic. I didn't know if they had changed, or I had. He passed the envelope to me and I studied the files.

There was a tumor in Quinton's stomach that the doctor couldn't treat. His daughter was pregnant with his first grandchild, but he was not expected to live long enough to see the baby born. As there were no red flags, the two Conseils had consented to a visit before he was too sick for the journey.

I flipped to the designated location and identification materials. Quinton's grandchild would be a girl. By age twenty she would be a teacher at the downtown school. Since Quinton was a retired teacher himself, I was instructed to attempt the viewing not at the school where he might be recognized, but at a nearby café. Inspecting the sketch of the granddaughter, I tried to find any of Quinton's features, but either there was little family resemblance or the sketch was inaccurate. The round-faced woman in the picture had short straight bangs and a petite nose.

Any questions? asked Jean-Savile.

No, sir.

I'll bring him to the gate tomorrow morning.

He was headed into town to inform Quinton, so he drove me to the lakeshore for my patrol. We rode together with the windows closed and the radio off. He was not known as a talkative man. I said thank you when he pulled over, and I was glad to set out for the fence.

I crossed the muddy shallows with their slow, fat flies. The eroded dirt ledges, the miniature sand cliffs the color of spat chaw, the fire pits, the listless water. I nodded up the watchtower, touched the base, and started my rounds.

Half nine, I passed the second tower.

Half ten, I passed Caron. Small talk and a swig of wine.

At eleven, I reached the third tower and turned back, and at noon I stopped to eat and carve. Today I used my engraving needle to outline the sun. A perfect circle behind a linen of cloud: something you could look at directly only if it was concealed.


The empty weight room stank of oniony sweat. I passed the men's showers and entered the private bathroom with the locking door, where I tossed my dirty uniform in the corner. I noted the progress of my purplish veins, bouquets of time spreading up my legs. A broad scar on my thigh from my early days of carving. As the shower warmed up I looked in the mirror. My eyebrows were gritty from the day's patrol. Brown dust deepened the faint wrinkles on my forehead.

Folklore told of a young recluse who left the valley to live in the mountains. There his aging had ceased, which led some people to make wisecracks about decamping for the outlands themselves. But the tale, like the rest of them, was no recommendation; the recluse went mad in his immortality. The story didn't explain what exactly had deranged him. When the mirror's steam erased me from the glass, I stepped into the shower and flinched from the heat. There was no curtain, and water splattered on the tile floor.

I was on my way back to the barracks, my hair still damp in the evening air, when Raimond caught up with me. With a grin, he said he'd seen me out the window and wanted to wish me a safe trip.

He fell in beside me as we walked along the fence. At first we made conversation about tomorrow's hike: the state of the plateau cabin by this time of year, the coming winter cold. Raimond began reminiscing about his own days of escorting visitors to Est 1 before he received his commission. He said it was one of the few aspects he missed about being a regular gendarme: the feeling that fills you on the descent, when the eastern valley opens up ahead, and you see the town reappear. Still, he wouldn't trade an officer's life for anything—patrol duties aren't easy, he hadn't forgotten how grueling the hike is, it's important to resist nostalgia.

He glanced at me. Have you ever thought about putting in for a promotion to officer? This spring'll mark your twenty years, you'll be eligible.

I made a scoffing laugh and kicked a pebble toward the cleared strip, where it rolled under the fence. No thanks.

Really? Why not?

I don't know, it's not for me.

Raimond was uncharacteristically silent, and I realized he might think I was slighting his own achievement. It's just that I'd never get chosen, I added.

He brightened. You can't be sure of that. If you do end up talking about me, M. Quinton will tell you himself: I wasn't always on track for big things either.

No?

Are you kidding? Raimond stopped walking. Can you keep a secret?

We were standing in the floodlights, Raimond's body partly blocking the glare. He was almost exactly my height. He ran a hand through his thinning hair.

I suppose he might spill this to you anyway, so I may as well get ahead of it. In school, my first choice wasn't the gendarmerie. I applied at the bindery for my apprenticeship—that was the plan. I spent so much time in the bookstore, so, you know, but that didn't work out, and my backup plan fell through too. Here Raimond rolled his eyes, passing off his grudge as a joke that we shared.

When I first got here, he said, I was a lot like you. Maybe a little disappointed?

He paused expectantly. My short association with the Conseil wasn't widely known on the border, but Raimond had access to everyone's files. He knew that I'd left the program near the end, though not under what circumstances. I shrugged.

He continued that although it was a difficult adjustment for him, he had chosen to make the best of the gendarmerie. Soon he decided that failing at his first two apprenticeships had been a stroke of fortune. I was good at being a patroller, he recalled, but maybe part of me kept licking my wounds, because I still wasn't imagining anything better.

A guard approached from the direction of the barracks, dragging his heels toward the main gate for the night shift. When he saw Raimond he corrected his posture. Raimond exchanged niceties with him and lowered his voice when the guard left.

The reason I'm mentioning this is that I was actually in Est 1 when I got the idea of trying out for officer. This is the secret part. The viewing spot they approved was a guildhall. It was just me and the petitioner sitting in our masks staring out the window. Her husband was supposed to eat lunch by the fountain or something. It was the middle of summer, so, you know, sweltering up there. Anyway, we're waiting. Then I noticed some local guards going into the Hôtel de Ville. Hand to god, I didn't mean to, but I caught sight of them in my field glasses. One in particular.

Raimond's look invited me to guess what was next. I waited, and he leaned in confidentially.

I've never been sure, because he never turned around. But he was my size, my hair color, my walk, maybe a bit more strapping. And I got this feeling. Like when you're about to cross the street and you catch your reflection in a window: you can recognize yourself, even from a distance. Except the man I was looking at was an officer.

Raimond smiled at me, revealing his teeth. Wow, I replied, and he laughed with agreement.

Once or twice a year I escorted visitors to Est 1, but I'd never seen anyone who fit my description or produced any feeling of knowing. The thought of seeing her there was disconcerting, but sometimes, if I was being honest, so was not seeing her. There was a clear explanation for it, though: in twenty years, I would still be posted to their eastern border. It was somewhere I never had any reason to visit when I was in Est 1, since we entered through their western gate, and the viewing spots were mostly downtown.

I realized Raimond wanted more of a response from me. What happened then? Did you report it?

No, I wasn't positive, so it didn't trigger the disclosure rule, otherwise I would have. But between us, I was pretty sure, and it had a big impact on me anyway. Because whether or not it was really him, suddenly I could picture myself wearing that uniform. *This* uniform, he remarked, pinching at his black breast pocket, as if in happy disbelief even now. I guess it was kind of my wake-up moment. A reminder to aim high.

The wind picked up, shaking the alarms on the fencewires. I shivered and pulled my cap over my wet hair.

I didn't mean to turn this into such a bloody pep talk! Raimond laughed. You go warm up, get some sleep, have a great trip. Feel free to tell M. Quinton that I turned out decently. But, Ozanne, don't write off the promotion idea. Keep your options open. You got the last trip of the season—it's a chance to be fresh in his mind when he makes his decision in the spring.

Yeah, yeah, I said, waving him off. Amused, Raimond turned back toward the officers' wing. I watched him go. I wasn't sure if I'd call his walk strapping, but it was self-assured.

His story of illicit inspiration was not the first that I'd heard. People let their imaginations run away with them. On my thirtieth birthday, my mother drank too much at the tea boat and revealed why she'd been so confident that I'd end up on the Conseil when I was young. It turned out that the archives had processed a petition record from Est 1, and while the particulars were redacted as usual, she became convinced that a quote from one of their junior conseillers sounded exactly like me. That was it: nothing more than superstition, a parent's baseless hope. By now, she'd forgotten the turn of phrase that had so impressed her. When she told me this, I felt slightly wounded to learn it hadn't been about my special aptitude after all. Mostly, though, I was embarrassed for her, and did a poor job of hiding it at dinner. Well, she muttered into her wine glass, obviously I was wrong.

I brewed coffee in the kitchen, inhaling its rank steam. The shining fence out the window cut through the predawn black. I drank standing up, slowly stretching my legs.

As soon as I opened the mess hall door the wind blew hard off the steppe. Three figures were at the gate underneath the watchtower. Jean-Savile and the night guard were unraveling the chain; the tall man waiting beside them was Quinton. He wore a down jacket with a twice-wrapped scarf, and his bag sat at his boots.

I walked past him to help with the gate. Once it was open, I faced the fence and raised my arms for the search. I felt my rucksack being unfastened on my back, and I steadied my footing as the guard's hands rummaged to the bottom. Beside me, Jean-Savile searched Quinton's bag and talked him through the itinerary.

When we were cleared to leave, I opened my greatcoat to show Jean-Savile my service pistol. It was a display orchestrated for the petitioner. Quinton saw the gun but regarded it without expression. I nodded him toward the gap in the fence.

Quinton stepped gingerly into the cleared strip and through the opening. Jean-Savile said good luck, and I followed. The chain dragged as the gate was hauled shut behind us. As we started walking out into the darkness, I heard our footprints being raked from the dirt.

The border lights receded behind the crest of a hill, and from that point onward the path was marked by lanterns. The oil lamps hung from wooden posts all the way across the steppe. The wind knocked them around on their crossbeams, swinging restless light over the raw abraded earth.

I trailed Quinton by a few yards. Visitors were kept always in view. His speed was reasonable for a man his age, and after an hour we reached the beginning of the foothills. The sky had softened to a pale pink. The ground under our boots climbed steadily upwards.

Hemming the base of the mountains ahead was a small birch forest, the only concentration of trees on the eastern steppe. I always took a short break in these woods, so I told Quinton to stop and leaned my rucksack against the terminal lantern post. Unlike the others, this post had a heavy black bell with a rope hanging from its mouth.

We sat on the dirt catching our breath as the dawn lightened the air. From here, the border and the town were invisible behind the hills, and the opposite valley wall was nothing but a filmy blue haze. We ate a snack and drank some water. Quinton had unbuttoned his jacket, and as he raised his throat to the canteen, I watched his small belly lift under his sweater. The body carried death wherever it chose.

I refilled our water in the stony creek that ran through the woods, holding the containers down as bubbles fled their spouts. Insects hovered and swooped over the creekbed, the autumn morning sun shining through their wings. Quinton was inspecting a cluster of tree trunks set back from the path. The parchment bark with its inky discolorations had been ripped in places, and ancient names were hacked into the trees' exposed flesh. He gave me a curious look. I motioned for us to get going.

The birch woods ended and the real climb began. The trail became vague, vanishing at the bottom of chunky rock faces, reappearing as a meager line in the upper distance. The only plants that survived on the mountains were desiccated desert shrubs. During this part of the hike I enforced stops every half hour. We slogged from one scruffy lichen patch to the next, resting a minute on the bristly turf. I used a rag to wipe the sweat off my face and lower back. Quinton did the same with his scarf.

I liked looking back down at the valley: the unbroken border, bending at each end toward the winding lake; the quilted squares of orchards,
green in the summers and tawny in the fall; the Place du Bâtisseur and the
chapel spire, small as wooden replicas. I closed my eyes and listened to the
shifting sagebrush. Sunlight played on my eyelids. If I were on my own,
delivering the Conseil's mail, I would stay longer and continue my latest
carving of the vista. Instead I offered Quinton a hand up and we resumed
climbing east.


The sun was low by the time we ascended the last rocks and made it to the
outlands plateau.

It was a windswept pass exactly halfway between the valleys, a narrow plank of land dwarfed by the surrounding range, which gave it the
queer feeling of a drawbridge. Jean-Savile's office had a painting of the
plateau from this angle, in which the far peaks on either side were severed
from the earth by fog, so that the mountains seemed to hang in the air un-
moored. Sometimes when I reached the summit I felt like a tiny nameless
figure entering the painting's foreground.

In the center of the plateau was the exchange post, and next to it the
cabin. They were still almost an hour's walk away, but as we approached, I
began hearing the swallowtail pennant whipping from the top of the pole.
It was the same flag as above the Hôtel de Ville, and in the day's last light I
could make out the tattered icon of the Conseil.

The cabin was an alpine refuge with a sod roof, a leaning brick chimney, and outer walls so rainbeaten that they'd shed all semblance of color.
Visitors and gendarmes stayed the night here before continuing onward or
returning home. I unlocked the door and let us in. Inside, the wind was a
dampened moan.

I knew every foot of the cabin, though there was little to know. It was
one musty room with bunk beds pushed against opposite walls. Folded
wool blankets and limp pillows waited on each. Four chairs were tucked at
a laminate table that was stained with coffee rings. The previous gendarme

sometimes left a jar of liquor—generous or forgetful—but nothing today. I opened my bag and set my own jar on the table.

I checked the lantern's oil and lit it. As the flame grew, the cabin became more inviting. The wallpaper, loose in spots, had rows of faded lilies. On the stone hearth was a bottle with a sailboat wedged in sand.

Quinton rested while I prepared dinner. He sat on a bottom bunk as I slid out the boxes of wood. The last guard had been lazy: the kindling was low. Brushing away cobwebs, I stacked logs and a hatchet in the canvas carrier and went outside, locking the cabin door behind me. Some visitors got upset about this, but Quinton didn't complain.

The mountain peaks around the plateau had withdrawn into dusk and left hulking crags of starless sky behind. Methodically I split a log into kindling. I crouched at the fire pit and worked up a flame, then lowered the heavy cooking grate that was lumpy with charred food. When I went back for the rations, Quinton carried out two chairs. One of them had the wobbly leg but I didn't correct him. We sat next to each other in front of the fire, blankets draped on our laps, soup bubbling in the scorched pot.

Afterward I offered him the jar of whiskey. In the firelight he looked calm and serious, shadows pronouncing his brow. You did not ask if they were in pain, or afraid; the easiest thing was to leave them to themselves. With a drink in him, however, Quinton started to talk.

First he asked me what it was like in Est 1, what to expect there, how different it would feel. I told him it felt like nothing.

Yes, of course, I know, said Quinton. Sheepishly he adjusted his glasses. I never believed those stories—but the night before you go, you apparently start remembering every rumor you've ever heard in your life.

He laughed awkwardly, sipped some more whiskey, and returned the jar. So how about Ouest 1? he joked. Any truth to those legends, the smells and tastes and the rest of it?

I answered that I'd never been to Ouest 1; if you're posted to the eastern border you escort people east.

Oh, I see. Stands to reason, I suppose.

I sensed that he wanted to ask if I was ever curious about the west, but instead Quinton gestured shyly at my whiskey again. They say that drinking makes my tumor worse, but I don't see how it matters—I figure I might as well nurture it a bit, like watering a plant. He chuckled, and I saw the schoolteacher in him, admiring his own wit.

He told me that first he hadn't truly believed his prognosis: the doctor had informed him, he had repeated the news to his daughter and friends, but it wasn't until the Conseil approved his petition that he knew it was hopeless. He smiled into the fire. I never imagined myself doing one of these tours—didn't think I'd feel the need, emotionally speaking. Goes to show how much of life is certain. Look at me now! I'm going to see my grandchild tomorrow! It's incredible. I'm just so very grateful.

After a pause he tilted his head. I don't remember you from school. I know you weren't one of mine. Forgive me, did you attend in the north end?

Yes.

Who was your teacher there?

M. Pichegru.

Oh, Pichegru! I met him a few times, quite a reputation. I was sad to hear about him.

Quinton noticed my startled look. Had you not heard?

No.

I'm sorry.

When?

Was it this year, or last? I remember it was springtime because he was about to retire. Between you and me, almost the most tragic part.

I gave a reflective nod and drank from the jar, burning my throat. I had not thought of Pichegru in years.

Was he the one who advised you to join the gendarmerie? Quinton asked. It's unusual seeing woman guards.

He'd turned toward me in his chair, paying attention in a way that made me uncomfortable, but some visitors became forward like this. Perhaps it was the frankness of mortality, or the whiskey, or the sense that outside the valley they'd left all other taboos behind.

I wonder if it's hard on you, he mused.

What? Being the only woman?

Well, yes. I didn't realize you were literally the only one.

We get the odd cadet. Most don't last.

Why not?

I bent my neck to work out a pain in my shoulder. When you were teaching, I asked, do you remember a student named Raimond Raboulet?

Quinton hesitated, then pushed his glasses up the bridge of his nose.

Believe it or not I remember them all.

What was he like? I work with him now—he said to say hello.

That's nice. Well, he was an impeccable student. He was badly bullied. You see it happening but there's only so much in your control. I always felt sorry for him.

I found that I wasn't surprised. I sometimes thought that Raimond's tireless confidence was compensatory, and guessed it was part of why the other officers found him off-putting. I remarked that he was doing well these days, and that he loved being in the gendarmerie.

That's wonderful to hear, Quinton said. Such a long time. Please give him my best.

He grew quiet again, probably thinking about tomorrow. After a while he stood up and asked to turn in, so I locked him in the cabin and came back to the dwindling flames. Clouds had smudged the stars. I nudged a log with my boot and sparks sprayed out, wending upward into the dome of night.

Pichegru was dead. When was it that I'd last felt anything about the past? I waited to feel something now, not about him in specific, but about the rest. The grief and regrets had dried up years ago, shed like brittle skin. Sometimes what was necessary was also what was natural. I raised my jar in tribute: Farewell, Pichegru.


The few girls who entered the gendarmerie were typically let go in their probationary year. The cadets were sixteen, seventeen, and it was never long before they were targeted. The official prohibition on sex between guards offered no protection. Not all of them started out as frightened as I'd been; some arrived fierce and defiant, but sooner or later that changed.

I was fortunate. There was an older gendarme, a woman named Rosa, who for whatever reason took a liking to me when I enlisted. She had been around long enough that she was respected by the officers, and while the safety her mentorship afforded was not complete, it helped me avoid the worst things. The few men I had been with, all in my early years, were gruff encounters on night patrols that I had sought out or accepted.

When Rosa retired, it had been a long time since I'd felt endangered on the border. After she left, however, I began noticing her absence in the newly unbridled leers of another gendarme. He was a younger guard named Gagne with a sloping forehead and a wiry beard, a coyote-like presence who slunk between cliques. His staring became relentless, whether in the mess hall or on the fence when our sectors crossed. Glaring back made no difference, and when I started resting my hand on my holster as he approached, his eyes twinkled, and he took to doing it too.

It was around then that Raimond and I first became acquainted. He had just received his commission and began joining me for dinner, sometimes walking me to my quarters. I never directly told him what had been going on, but soon I noticed a change: Gagne avoided looking at me, even alone on patrol. Raimond was an officer, but more importantly, he was a snitch, with a zeal for reporting infractions to Jean-Savile or Coltelli. The collegiality he showed me in public was sufficient to shoo away a creature like Gagne, who was soon transferred to the western border anyway— something I suspected Raimond had a hand in, though he'd never taken credit for it.


I opened my eyes in the cabin to see Quinton awake in the other bunk. Denuded of his glasses his face was moony and frail. I hit the alarm clock and asked if he'd gotten any sleep.

A little. I need to go to the bathroom.

Cold air sucked into the cabin when I unlocked the door. You can go anywhere I can see you. I usually go over there.

I waited in the doorway. There was a thin layer of frost at my feet. When he came back I made coffee, spooning stale grounds into two chipped mugs. I found some hard sugar on the shelf above the washbasin. We sipped in silence, listening to the lamp oil burn.

We crossed the plateau and began the steep descent under a false dawn. The second day of the hike was twisty and precipitous, with abrupt drops to navigate. The smartest technique in the drastic sections was edging down sideways: your boots filled with pebbles, but it was better than falling. In places I guided Quinton with my arm. I had done the journey enough to remember where my feet went in the dark.

At last the sun crowned and spilled down the mountains. We came to a turn in the path, and in front of me, Quinton halted.

It was the lake again. The town, this time on the opposite shore, sparkled in the sunrise. It was too far away to distinguish many individual buildings, but there was the beach, and the park, and the terraced vineyards; the depleted autumn orchards, and the fine seam of the fence.

God, murmured Quinton.

He gaped at the foreign valley with a visitor's fear and wonder. I peered up at the sky. A few clouds were crawling northward, losing their pinkness. The morning was a thin silicate blue. High up, a hawk glided on motionless wings.


We reached the giant lodgepole pine, the first landmark where we were visible to Est 1's watchtowers. I removed the masks from my rucksack, tightened the twine at the back of Quinton's head, and examined his face.

He looked back through twin slits in the wood. The mask was carved with simple nostrils and closed lips that fashioned an empty gaze. The tall black forehead was covered in spidery cracks. He was already wearing his baggy visitor's tunic.

I can't see, he said in a muffled voice, and held up his spectacles morosely.

I'll help you. From now on, never lift your mask. When we're in place you can hold them in front of you like field glasses.

I pinned a piece of fabric over my uniform's name badge and put my own mask on. The wood inside was worn smooth. For now it had the odor of lemon soap.

Neither of us can speak in front of anyone, I said. If you have to say something, don't, but if you do, whisper in my ear.

The mask nodded back.

I went to the black bell hanging from the tree and gave the rope a tug. The iron greeting tumbled down the slope. In its decaying echo I heard the response: the first toll of acknowledgment, the second of admittance. They were ready for us.

O n that wilder side of the lake, the border ran close to the shore: there was only a slender belt of land between the fence and the beach beyond. Unlike the stark borderlands I was accustomed to, the western terrain was shaded by dour pines, and had the rugged atmosphere of a camp instead of an expansive complex. As Quinton and I came down the last hill, I saw their guards assembled in two lines.

They unlocked the gate, stealing looks at us as they handled the chains. They would not have been told much, but they knew that the visitor was almost certainly dead.

The gendarmes kept their hands on their weapons as we were let inside. Some of them had dogs, brown shepherds who regarded us with straight ears and unblinking eyes. The contents of our bags were emptied over the dirt and we were patted down in turn. As the guard's hands moved up my legs, I saw Manduca strolling from the dock.

The western border captain was a stout man, flush-faced with a bushy grey moustache. In this valley he was well into his sixties, but still energetic. Whereas Jean-Savile chose to wear an ordinary officer's uniform except at hearings, I'd never seen Manduca without insignia on his chest. He tapped a baton against his thigh as he walked.

A few steps behind was his aide-de-camp, my former harasser Gagne. This many years on, his beard was unpleasantly long and invaded with white, but beneath his receded hairline I recognized his squat forehead and canine eyes. I disliked seeing him on the way in and out of Est 1. Since I was always masked, I was never sure if he recognized me.

Manduca sized us up and aimed a welcoming smile at Quinton. Good afternoon! How was your trip?

I touched Quinton's back in caution. Manduca smirked at his men. It was a routine of his, trying to goad visitors into speaking, so he could threaten to send us back.

All right, let's get these two on their way.

The guards finished repacking our bags—they were mainly searching for paper and writing implements—and we hoisted them back on. Then we followed Manduca and Gagne to the beach through the gauntlet of guards. Quinton raised his spectacles in front of his mask to look around as we walked. The buildings of the western border were set haphazardly among the pines. There was a kitchen and an admin building in a central clearing, but no common barracks, just isolated shanties strewn in the woods along the fence.

The beach smelled stagnant. Lake gnats hovered over tubules coughed up on the shore. The skiff was tied to a splintery dock. Manduca wrote our return time and thrust the clipboard at me. I made the mark confirming that we'd be back the next morning, and helped Quinton into the boat. Gagne untied us and pushed the bow with his foot. The hull scraped on the rocky bottom.

Be good, called Manduca.

For a minute we sat drifting out. Facing forward, Quinton gripped the sides of the boat with two hands.

How are you holding up, I whispered.

He nodded without turning: he was staring at the town across the lake. I started the motor and we began to move, bouncing on the water as we picked up speed. Turning my face from the spray, I glanced over my shoulder at the shrinking western dock. A wake spread behind us like an aquamarine valley, white froth pouring over its walls.

I steered to the far end of the marina where there was a private dock for the gendarmerie. Through the bobbing spars, I could see the Conseil pennant flying from their Hôtel de Ville.

We deboarded and left the marina. No one was around. The truck had been parked in the usual stall. I started it with the skeleton key and began driving to the tour quarters.

It was a sunny day, but there was a lifeless quality to the light. I always found something tiring about Est 1's sameness. Invisible ash seemed to coat its surfaces. Quinton kept holding his glasses in front of his mask, gawking out the passenger window as though he might see anything truly new here. A family on the sidewalk noticed us, and the parents quickly pointed elsewhere to distract their children.

The tour quarters were in a derelict zone behind tavern row. Unlike the boulevard or the Place du Bâtisseur, there was little foot traffic during the day: with the exception of a depressed corner shop and a billiard hall, the main establishments were bars that didn't open until later. I drove past shuttered windows and dirty awnings, turned down a road of warehouses, and parked in an alley next to a nondescript walkup.

The door was on the ground level, partly obscured by a fire escape. Its location was something of an open secret—occasionally gendarmes had to paint over graffiti. I set to work on the series of locks while Quinton stood close enough that I could hear him breathing through his mask.

The apartment was dim and had poor air, a wet sourness like urine on sawdust that smelled strongest in the kitchenette. There was a cramped living room with a settee, a coffee table, and a heavy-shaded lamp that hoarded the light. The windows were bricked up.

I turned to Quinton, still standing uncertainly in the entrance, and pushed my mask up onto my hair.

Leave your bag and use the toilet. In ten minutes we'll head to the spot.


You were instructed to travel on the outskirts of town, ideally along the border or the ring road, but viewings were usually in populated areas, and today we had to pass through multiple residential blocks to get where we were going. There was an informal network of backroutes used by visiting gendarmes to minimize sightings by locals. As soon as I could, I turned off the road toward a pair of tire tracks that ran behind the houses. The alley followed a storm sewer that was overgrown with silken grass. I drove the truck slowly, cautious of children who might spring from an abutting backyard. Most of the yards were hidden by trees. I caught glimpses of a stone birdbath, a loveseat with flaking paint, towels hanging on a line, a stray ball forgotten in the weeds.

When I had to rejoin the road, I noticed Quinton's leg shaking. Again I asked how he was, and he managed a tight laugh.

Nervous!

Checking my mirrors, I told him it was normal.

I'm glad I'm not the only one, he said. I want this more than anything, I just can't believe what I'm seeing, I can't believe this is real.

The street we'd turned onto was steepled with high branches, their leaves spinning to the ground. Framed between the trees, I saw the elegant façade of the downtown school and the coffee-brown awning of the appointed café.

It was three o'clock. The café's outdoor patio was busy with people basking in the afternoon sunshine. I parked across the road under a tree and scanned for the granddaughter from the sketch. I couldn't identify her yet. I wished the Conseil wouldn't choose such crowded locations, but they must have judged that the less populated alternatives would make our target too obvious. So far, no one on the patio had noticed us waiting in the truck, but they would. I held my pistol in my lap pointing at Quinton. Under his mask, his breathing sounded more apprehensive than before. It was not about the gun, I knew, but the anticipation of seeing her.

Let me hold your glasses, I said. I'll give them back when she comes. It's better if you don't look too much before then.

Reluctantly he offered them up. They were slightly sticky.

As I watched the people on the patio, I subtracted twenty years. There was an old man in the prime of his life back home; there was a group of students still yet to be born. One woman caught my eye. Though she faced the other way, she had curly red hair and an age that seemed right. The hairs on my forearms began to rise. Then she turned her head. The stranger touched her companion on the arm and laughed.

Seconds later we were seen. From a startled pair of men who might have been teachers themselves, the awareness spread like a stain, anxiety hushing over the patio. People held their beverages midway to their mouths, all looking at the gendarmerie truck parked in the shade. I stared back through the mask, and they forced themselves to resume talking, rigid and self-conscious now, abducted from their afternoon into a morbid tableau vivant.

Each time someone else came onto the patio, the door gave a chime; each time he heard it, Quinton's breath weakened until I whispered no. Then the door opened and I recognized her. The sketch was accurate. The young teacher wore a mustard dress with square pockets sewn in front. She held a plate with a scone or croissant. I watched her register the discomfort on the patio and look for the source. Her eyes stopped on our truck. I was about to pass Quinton his glasses when the granddaughter's plate dropped to the ground. Flustered, she bent to retrieve the broken pieces, but as she stood back up, she risked a furtive wave in our direction. Her hand stayed very close to her body but it was unmissable. I cursed under my breath and raised the pistol at Quinton. He turned to me with alarm.

What, is she there? Give me my glasses!

Across the road the granddaughter was wiping her eyes. She made the small wave again, this time with a stifled look of excitement. Other people on the patio leaned forward whispering.

I turned the key and started the truck.

What are you doing? Is it her? Where are we going?

I lurched into reverse. I saw the granddaughter crane her neck in confusion. I turned sharply and drove away.


He slumped on the settee, his mask next to him. His skin was ashen in the gloomy light, and the front of his hair was matted with sweat.

My glasses, he said quietly.

I held them out. He took them with trembling hands.

I don't even know what happened, he mumbled, and as I finally described it, Quinton's face contorted.

She waved?

Yes. She knew it was you. She was expecting your visit, which is coordination—any communication, direct or indirect, before or after your viewing. You agreed to those terms. Tell me what you did.

After some equivocation, he admitted that when his petition was approved, he'd suggested to his daughter that his grandchild might like to know he was coming one day. Not in so many words, he insisted, not actual coordination—just enough to plant the possibility that, *if* she saw a mask, it *could* be her grandfather, rather than a stranger visiting someone else. I didn't want to come all this way for my sake alone, he explained. I wanted her to believe I loved her enough to come. What harm would it do if she saw me in my mask and came to that conclusion?

Quinton dried his face and cleared his throat. I should have told you there was a chance she'd suspect who I was. I'm sorry for that. I understand I've made a mess of the viewing you arranged. But they must give you more information, like her address? Or maybe she still lives with Gabby? We could drive there after dark. I could look in the window from farther away, she wouldn't know I was there. Or tomorrow when she's on her way to work, before we go back? Put yourself in my position. The conseillers said I deserve to see my granddaughter before I die.

I thought the simplest course that night would be letting him think there was hope. I was noncommittal as I got out the meals provided by the local Conseil, leaving his plea hanging in the apartment's confined air. He was careful not to prod me, and didn't protest when I said it was time for him to sleep. He sat obediently on his shabby bed, looking bereft as I closed the door and slid the bolt.

I opened the pantry and found the liquor allotment where it should be. Cherish the Conseil as you cherish your own, I sighed to the hoary tune of the hymn. Unscrewing the cap, I poured a full glass. In the morning I would have to issue the refusal and be prepared to restrain him until we reached the border.

I didn't feel like carving, but I'd gone to the trouble of packing my supplies, and I was rarely here. The living room was one of my few interiors, and thus one of my only wood blocks that didn't track the changing seasons: time in the tour quarters always looked the same. I ran my fingers over the progress I'd made last spring, when I'd attempted to capture the drabness of the walls. That trip had been uneventful, a similar petition to Quinton's, except the dying viewer was a woman and the subject was her own child. She'd had tumors as well, in her breasts, and her viewing had gone smoothly; she'd gotten to see her son. When it was over she gripped me in a long embrace. I stood stiffly as she pressed her chest into mine. Then, for the whole hike home, she'd relished everything we'd seen him do, reliving the moment and delighting in it, bursting into laughter as she connected his adult features to branches of her family tree.

I took a drink and chose a chisel. I set about carving the clock on the wall. Each number had to be rendered in reverse. Eventually, when they were printed to paper, the hours would read properly, their order restored.

H e argued again in the morning but soon realized it was futile, so I didn't need to use the restraints. He followed my orders bleakly and without theatrics. As the skiff approached the western dock I made out Manduca and Gagne and a couple of others waiting in the mist. Gagne held up a lantern. They were half-dressed, undershirts and suspenders showing beneath their open jackets. Manduca bit some coffee from a red enamel cup.

Success, failure, infraction?

I held up three fingers. Manduca snorted at Quinton.

Naughty naughty. He motioned to one of the guards to tie the cleat.

Gagne marched Quinton up the path to their interrogation room. The retired teacher's comportment was disembodied. I'd warned him that although he'd be tried in his home valley, both of us would have to write statements here before we were cleared to leave.

I followed Manduca. As we passed the guard huts, I could smell their morning fires. On the ridge above, loosely spun fog floated through the trees.

He took me to the small admin building where he kept his office. The lights were already on inside. The narrow hallway's floor was wet and stank of ammonia; I saw a bucket of soapy water. Manduca ushered me into the debriefing room. It had wood-paneled walls pocked with thumb-tack holes, and a window facing the fence. I had been here a few years ago for another infraction.

He closed the door and cranked fresh paper into the granite-grey typewriter. In the staccato silence I typed what had happened and handed him the page. He glanced over my account, making the occasional hmph. I slid a finger under my mask to scratch my cheek. He marked my account as witnessed and went to his metal filing cabinet.

We're done, he said over his shoulder, motioning at the door. Ladies first.

I flinched—I'd thought there was a chance he didn't know who I was. Quickly, I stepped past him into the hallway. I was about to leave when I sensed another person behind me. Without thinking, I turned.

She was at the far end of the hall, hunched low on the floor. My first thought was my mother: the fallen lines of the woman's mouth, her lips pursed in weary hatred. She was on her knees with a sponge, her spine curved like an animal's. But she could not be my mother. A gendarmerie uniform hung from her bones, her jaw was wrong, and her hair, though shorter and duller, had the same curls I knew from the mirror. As my eyes fought it, the woman's shape became my own.

She lifted her head to meet my masked stare. She stopped pushing the sponge and held her face at a patient slant, as if bidding me to see the rings under her eyes, the frightful recesses of her cheeks. Lying beside her was a single crutch padded with yellowed tape. Then Manduca joined me in the hall.

He followed my look, and chuckled. He seemed to consider something, then relaxed his hold on his red cup, swinging it loose on his thumb and splashing coffee on the floor. Bile flooded my throat. I fumbled for the handle and escaped out the rear doorway. In the bright dawn light, I raised my hands to my wooden face.

During the search at the gate I barely felt the guard touching me. Why's this one shaking so hard, he complained.

✳

Nothing more passed between Quinton and me on the hike. I was preoccupied with what I had seen, he with what he hadn't. He didn't ask what would happen to him, so I didn't have to tell him. Mutely I followed the standard procedures, locking him in the plateau cabin after dinner.

I had the rest of my whiskey alone at the fire. The alcohol added some temporary distance between me and that morning, but the memory of the woman's face still floated like jetsam, never fully leaving my view, threatening to wash in again. At last I had experienced the hallowed recognition. The fire died. I stayed outside and listened to the dark wind churn.

I was drunk when I remembered to check the exchange post. The safebox, as black and dense as a stove, was welded at eye level. I had nothing to deposit, but when I mashed the key in and yanked the door, a single envelope from the Est 1 Conseil was waiting for pickup. It was marked as a standard warning, not urgent, and the nub of wax that had chipped off its seal was minor enough to not raise suspicions of tampering. I stuffed it in my jacket pocket. Suddenly her haggard face returned. I bent over and retched on the frigid soil.

Quinton woke me up in the middle of the night. I chose not to stir. He was whispering to himself in the opposite bunk: The damage was done, so why not let me see her? What difference would it make to anyone? What did you preserve?


I rang the bell for readmittance at the edge of the birch woods, and far off I heard the confirmation. The first snow began as we crossed the steppe at dusk, large wet flakes falling through the golden lamplight. My mask long packed away, I blinked frozen water from my lashes. By the time we were near the border the sky was shedding white, and the guards opening the gate had snow sliding off the shoulders of their greatcoats.

Jean-Savile waited on the other side. While Quinton was being searched I explained what had happened. He pointed for Quinton to be detained and told me to come to admin. The last time I saw Quinton was under the floodlights, his glasses blind with snow as the guards rifled through his bag.

The eastern border's admin building was nothing like Manduca's lodge; it was large and well lit, with a gleaming mail tray next to each white door. Several men were outside of Jean-Savile's office, including Raimond, nodding at something Coltelli was telling an older officer named Oury. When he saw me, he sent me a quick private smile.

The book-lined office had the comforting smell of leather. Standing in front of Jean-Savile's desk in my dripping coat, I recounted the trip in detail, along with Quinton's version of what he'd said to his daughter beforehand. I presented his plight with neither judgment nor sympathy. Coltelli and Oury listened while Raimond transcribed notes. Periodically Jean-Savile stopped me to clarify a detail.

That's unfortunate, he said when I was done, but it is what it is. Any other sightings to report while you were there?

No, sir.

I had not decided until then if I would disclose it. The commandant's pale eyes examined me, but then he made a tired gesture—our cue to leave. Coltelli and Oury resumed their conversation in the hall, while Raimond tapped his notes into a neat pile and passed them across Jean-Savile's desk. It reminded me that I had something to deliver too. Glancing at the letter from the exchange post, Jean-Savile thanked me and set it aside.

I hesitated. Actually . . . if you have a moment, sir, there's something else.

He looked up from his chair. For your report?

No, sir. Unrelated.

My throat felt dry and I swallowed before going on.

My twenty years are coming up, and I was wondering if I could be considered for a commission. To become an officer.

I reddened, and in the corner of my eye I saw Raimond's keen attention, but I kept myself trained on Jean-Savile. He betrayed no reaction as he reached into his desk drawer.

Remind me of the month?

April, sir.

He passed me an application. April, just under the wire. Fill this out and I'll keep you in mind.

I took the form and thanked him. He leaned back in his chair.

Ozanne, I should say, a few others have already put in for it. Aubuchon is coming up on his twenty, and Page. Next year we have the budget and lodgings for one.

He said it with perfunctory regret. I folded the paper into my pocket and replied that I understood.

The outdoor air collided with my burning cheeks. *I was wondering if I could be considered.* In my hurry to outpace my embarrassment, I was almost to the barracks before Raimond caught up.

Congratulations! What changed your mind?

I shook my head.

Well now I'm glad we had that talk, this is great news!

I shrugged but felt despair rising in my chest. You heard him, it's pointless, I said.

Raimond laughed. I didn't hear *that*. You've got the exact same odds as the others, you just need to impress him.

How? Everybody likes Aubuchon and Page. My eyes watered in the blowing snow. The fence hacked the storm into panicked white sheets. But Raimond gave me an encouraging smile.

Chin up, Ozanne! I promise you this is a good thing.

The end of December was horribly cold. Holiday reveling carried across the border tundra: the guards were bellowing bawdy songs in the mess hall. I listened from the platform of the watchtower. The platform's surface was coated with thick rivulets of ice.

Below me at the main gate, Frederic paced back and forth in his greatcoat, stomping to keep warm. He was an older gendarme with more holes in his mouth than teeth. He grinned up at me, waved, then rattled his flask to free its last drops. If you drank on duty tonight, the officers looked the other way.

I shuffled around the platform the required number of times, tossing salt crystals over the ice. On the windy side of the tower my eyes immediately teared up, but there was nothing to see on the steppe anyway; the lantern path wasn't lit in the winter. I ducked back inside the hut, where somehow it felt colder—the lack of warmth where it was hoped for. I huddled with a blanket drawn into a cowl, my breath forming transient shapes in the paltry lamplight.

At night the watchtower was a forlorn place. The only things on the wall were a frayed isochrone map and a calendar. The tuneless singing forced its way through the poorly sealed door. The men had switched to the maudlin traditionals that were everywhere during the holidays. I pictured the scene in the mess hall: fogged windows, glazed eyes, guards burping with laughter, swaying and fighting and throwing up. I turned on the transistor radio to drown out the noise. It was late, so the only thing playing was static, but I dialed up its bushy hiss until the sound filled the hut. Among the guards there was a legend that if you adjusted the dial slowly enough, suspending the band between frequencies, you could catch traces from Est 1. I knew the mountains ruled this out, but in the daytime I sometimes poked the dial around like anyone else.

It was not a healthy habit for me. Beyond its futility, the idea of Est 1 inevitably made my stomach feel ulcerous. The horror of seeing myself had not worn off; instead, as the season darkened, the memory had compacted into a denser, harder dread. No day went by that I forgot what lay ahead, although how it would happen, I couldn't think.

I hadn't revealed my sighting to Raimond. He took it at face value that my changed attitude toward a promotion was the result of his advice, that he was the one to part the clouds of my ambivalence. He had started pressing me to improve my social standing, saying I needed to make myself noticed, but it was something I didn't know how to do. I focused on being punctual for roll call after reveille and submitting flawless reports after my patrols. Both ought to be appreciated by Jean-Savile, but I knew that Raimond thought I was only demonstrating my fitness for basic tasks, not strengthening my case for advancement. It was common knowledge that if you didn't become an officer in your first year of eligibility, your window of opportunity effectively closed: fresh candidates would always crowd you out. Raimond's initial enthusiasm had begun mutating into worried sympathy. When I mentioned a spiritless plan to volunteer for more mail runs once the border reopened, he'd given a pained nod.

So, before my night shift, I'd made an attempt to ingratiate myself to Jean-Savile at the holiday party. Chances to mix with the upper ranks were relatively limited, but Jean-Savile typically put in an appearance at the main social events, limiting himself to a single drink and a short toast. Through a dirty pall of cigarette smoke, I watched him from the corner and rehearsed my small talk. He was near the serving counter with Coltelli and a few other officers. Aubuchon and Page were standing nearby.

Raimond chatted with me for a while, monologuing about some staffing decisions, but when he excused himself to mingle with the new cadets in question, I went to the serving counter and ordered myself a second whiskey. I didn't have the nerve to approach Jean-Savile yet, so I drifted vaguely into the proximity of Aubuchon and Page. Page noticed me, but, confused about whether I was joining them or not, turned away and continued his anecdote. I wandered past, now marooned in the middle of various closed-off groups, and soon my whiskey was empty. Though the liquor had yet to impart any bravery, the pressure of standing alone made me take a definitive step into the officers' orbit.

Amid the festivities they were conferring about work. Chin tucked down, Jean-Savile absorbed some information from Coltelli. After a moment he saw me lurking and briefly raised his eyes, but did not interrupt. Nonetheless, I moved closer. Jean-Savile motioned Coltelli to stop, and when Coltelli saw me he frowned. I managed a salutation.

Good evening, said Jean-Savile. I hope you're enjoying the party.

Yes, sir. I'm in the main tower later.

Yes, that's right.

There was a pause. Up against their blankness, the conversation starters I'd thought of seemed bizarre. I was about to bow out and back away when Oury spoke up.

Maybe Ozanne can weigh in on this—she wants a commission, doesn't she?

I blushed my confirmation.

So, she should have an opinion, Oury continued. He was being generous, making an effort to include me, but Jean-Savile shook his head.

Another time. Have a good shift, Ozanne, and make sure to cap it at two. He indicated my glass of melting ice.

I retreated to where Raimond and I had been standing. He was still lecturing to the cadets. A minute later, I saw Coltelli welcome Aubuchon and Page into their circle.

The alcohol was kicking in, too late to be useful. I heard Aubuchon's laughter join with the others, and understood that I would never be promoted, never stop falling toward the fate that I'd seen. After Est 1, I'd flailed for the nearest saving branch, but I had missed. In reality the branch had never been within my reach. I left the party and stood against the cold outside wall that faced the fence. Breath fled my nostrils in short fast plumes.


With still more hours before daylight, I retrieved the chamber pot from the corner of the watchtower. The steam escaped around my legs. I carried the pot out to the platform. Frederic was far enough away that I could empty it discreetly over the railing. I watched the steam gasp in the snow. There was less noise from the mess hall now.

I went back in, where the radio's static still tremored and popped, and removed my boots. The space heater on the floor worked only if you were basically touching it, so I held my socks to its tepid orange coils. For a minute, I closed my eyes.

The brassy Conseil anthem burst from the static and I jerked in my chair. The radio sat in a shaft of new winter light, blaring its accusation. I found my boots and hastily went out to the platform. A primrose dawn glowed on the glacial foothills.

Morning!

I looked down and saw Aubuchon. The gate shift had changed over while I'd been dozing. My own replacement, likely still sluggish from the party, was due at the watchtower too. I returned the greeting and Aubuchon turned back to the sunrise, letting the light hit his face as he yawned. In the direction of the mess hall, a thin pipe of breakfast smoke climbed into the sky. I went back into the hut to gather my things.

The anthem on the radio was over, and the next piece was beginning. Lone piano chords introduced an unusually stately mood for the early hour. The piano sounded graceful and measured in spite of the crackling asperity of the old speaker. A cello and clarinet came in, a kind of languid chase, avian tones. The piece seemed faintly, curiously familiar. Then the violin entered, and I remembered.

It was Edme. One of his audition pieces—the slower one. To my surprise, I found that I could still anticipate some of the phrases, still picture the gentle movements of his bow. Someone at the conservatory must have discovered the sheet music and arranged it.

I listened without moving from the watchtower doorway. It did not sound like the work of a child. There were sections I had found sad when it was just his violin, but together with the other instruments, the piece acquired a wistfulness, sometimes even touches of sly humor. There was the rushing middle section he had struggled to perfect: this adult violinist did it effortlessly. The quickness crested and fell again, like flung leaves floating back to earth, and then it was over.

I was unprepared for the concentration of its beauty. Nothing was ever as good on the radio. After the last note I waited to hear if the announcer would name its composer, but something else started up, a shrill choral piece that they played all the time. At the base of the tower I heard the next guard mount the rungs.

I switched off the radio. On my way out the door, I saw the calendar hanging from a nail and flipped the page to the new year. It was strange being reminded of Edme, today of all days. It was the year I would turn thirty-six, and fifty-six, and sixteen.

B efore my next downtown post I was assigned the worst of the winter patrols, night shifts on the northeast fence. The sector was nothing but naked hills, and at the top of every rise you caught the full force of the steppe's weather. In my quarters I donned layer after layer under my uniform, then waddled outside to catch the transport at sundown.

Like the other guards, I ate dinner on the bus, dropping my empty bag in the bin as I got off near my starting point. From there, I trudged beside the fence for seven hours. In the winter the night had a different personality, an endless aching moan, and during the most isolated parts of the walk where the floodlights were the weakest, I sang into my scarf to keep the eerie sound at bay. At the watchtowers I made shivery small talk with the duty guards as I pressed my hands to their heaters.

By the time I got back to my quarters my face was flared raw. Broken capillaries pricked my cheekbones, as though my freckles had bled under my skin. I arranged my scarf and gloves on top of the radiator and the greatcoat on my chair, then pitched forward on the cot in my carapace of clothes. Despite the incontrovertible dawn in the window, the night shifts made the mornings feel like fictions.

Winter was the one time when I yearned for downtown duty, regardless of my misgivings about bumping into certain people; the lodgings behind the chapel provided a respite from the punishing patrols and interminable cold lookouts. Each night I tallied the nights that remained. When my alarm clock commenced its screams I cursed and pulled my clothes on and headed back into the dark.

The fence was a sharp white scar across the empty landscape. Because the only other landmarks were the faraway towers, it sometimes seemed like I was walking in place, not advancing through space at all, the crunch of my boots disconnected from motion, a static pulse. In this disorienting limbo, when I heard the first alarm bell, I wondered if it was a dream.

But the sound was distinct enough that I stopped and turned toward the closest tower. I saw the guard entering his hut. A moment later I heard his alarm join in, leaving no room for doubt.

I withdrew my pistol from my greatcoat. The bells' signal meant that a tower in my sector had sighted a possible incursion. Careful not to slip, I began a ragged jog over the ice, scanning for an escapee in the floodlights ahead.

Another gendarme came shambling out of the gloaming, gun in hand. As a precaution I saluted.

See anything? he panted when he reached me. Verdussen was his name. A string of mucous dangled loose in his moustache.

Nothing.

How the hell does someone make it over the mountains in January?

I don't know. Maybe it's a mistake, an animal or something.

He groaned and shuffled on. I resumed jogging too. With each shoulder check, Verdussen shrank more into the distance, until there was just the desolate border ravaged by metal clanging.

The halfway point of my sector was a short stretch of tundra where the watchtowers couldn't be seen in either direction due to a pair of hills. In the distance a truck's headlights traveled along the ring road and disappeared. Officers would be amassing at the second line; during incursions only they were allowed near potential interference sites. In practice it didn't matter, since most escape attempts ended at the fence.

Suddenly a clatter erupted from the fencewires. I couldn't see anyone, so I stumbled up the next hill hoping it was the right direction. A perilous human shape ahead was clutching the very top of the fence, trying not to fall.

My trigger resisted the finger of my glove. Using my teeth, I ripped the glove off and fired a warning shot into the sky.

The climber spun at the sound and tried to regain balance, but they flailed and toppled to the ground. I heard the unmistakable bright crack of bone, and after an awful beat, a cry of pain. The figure started crawling away dragging one leg behind them.

I rushed at them and leapt. Fighting, we slid together to the edge of the floodlights, but I bore down. In our struggle I saw it was a woman—nobody I recognized. She thrashed against my grip. I shouted at her to stop, and as I pressed my weight into her, I felt her go slack. I wrestled her onto her back and she let out a howl as her leg rotated. Pinioning her, I pointed my flashlight in her face.

She was in her fifties. There was bruising around her eyes and neck, and icy gravel stuck to her forehead. Her hair was lank with sweat and her fear smelled strong and ripe.

The woman squinted in the light. Then her mouth fell open. A smile spread over her face, revealing bloody gums. It was so disturbing that my hold on her loosened, but this time she didn't try throwing me off. Instead, the escapee gazed up from the ice with a shining expression, amazed, almost exultant.

I ignored her and started the script. Give me your name and intentions. Don't say anything more.

The woman's answer was pinched with pain. It's Lucie. Do you remember me?

There was the glimmer of a memory in her bruised face.

Lucie . . . Erro?

She tried nodding but convulsed. Yes, from the Grande École! You're Odile—it's you!

Her lips stretched into the unnerving smile again. I recalled the girl

with the crown of lace braids. Ivret had dismissed her in the first week. All
I knew about her was that she'd married young.

The alarm bells had modified their signal in response to my shot. A
new pattern passed from one tower to the next, directing guards to my
position, but there was nobody yet.

Lucie, I said. Your intentions. What were you going to do?

Grimacing, she spat blood into the snow and licked her lips.

I'm going to never meet my husband.

She seemed about to say more, but turned her head and coughed. Her
scarf had come undone, and I saw black bruises continuing under her shirt
collar. The collar itself startled me: it was gendarmerie wool. Lucie looked
at me again and I clicked off the flashlight.

We're going to stand on three. One, two.

I moved into a squat beside her and helped her turn over. Grunting
with effort, she dug her knees into the snow. I lifted her and she sucked in
her breath, tottering on one leg.

Good, you're doing well, I told her. I dug through my patrol bag with
one hand until I found the sackcloth. When she saw it she recoiled.

What's that?

Procedure.

I had to fight her again to get the bag over her head. She begged me
through the cloth.

Odile, no! What are you doing?

As I searched for the restraints, she breathed harder through the fabric,
her mouth a wet oval.

She promised that you'd help! Lucie cried.

In my surprise, I let go of her arm, but although she must have felt her
chance, she didn't try to run. I don't know what I would have done next. I heard
icy footsteps coming from the fence, and as I turned to look, Lucie heard too,
and started limping blindly. I was about to go after her when she buckled and
keeled into the snow. The shot echoed. Belatedly I raised my hands to my ears.

The black-clad officer ran past me and knelt, lifting the sackcloth to
check her face. In that second I saw Lucie's rolling eyes, the blood jet-

ting up her cheek. The bullet had struck her neck. Covering her again, Raimond holstered his pistol and hurried back.

Give me your gun.

He did something fast with the cylinder and returned it. He was looking toward the fence where several guards were now making their way down the hill, moving precariously on the ice. Raimond raised his hand in acknowledgment. There were three, Verdussen and Caron and Page, their complexions all seared with cold. They stopped when they reached us and regarded Lucie, collapsed on her side. Her spasms had slowed. There was a growing stain around her head.

Awkwardly, Page reached out and gave Raimond a clap on the shoulder. Nice one, sir.

Not me, Raimond said, gesturing at the cold pistol in my hand. Ozanne got her.

They fetched a toboggan from a truck on the ring road, and when they set to moving the body, I stood apart and looked the other way. I heard them strap her down with a pair of belts. Then we headed toward the road, our legs sinking into deepening snow, the toboggan gliding higher on the surface beside us, casting us as profane pallbearers. The headlights from the waiting truck blasted our shadows over the frozen dunes.


Jean-Savile was in full uniform, his hair slightly scruffed from sleep. The clock on his office desk read five in the morning.

Raimond repeated what he'd told the other gendarmes: on his way to the town perimeter, he'd come across me just as I was neutralizing the escapee, a superb shot in the conditions. I kept quiet as he spoke. Jean-Savile looked thoughtful.

If I remember, he said, you've brought in your others alive.

Raimond leaned forward. Sir, the escapee was moving fast—I have to admit, I didn't even see her in the dark. Ozanne's only option was to shoot.

Jean-Savile's eyes stayed on mine as he sipped his coffee. Did you get anything out of her before she died?

Yes, sir. She gave her name as Lucie Erro.

Intentions?

She wanted to prevent herself from meeting her husband. My voice sounded hoarse, and as I coughed I saw he was studying me, waiting for more.

This is conjecture, sir, but I think she was just passing through. Her age in this valley . . . she'd be married here too. She'd have to go farther west to stop it.

Jean-Savile considered this. Then he pulled an envelope of Conseil mail from his desk drawer.

Erro was her maiden name. Her name is Lucie Sanna—you're right, she is married here. We received a warning about her in the fall. Actually, you brought it back with M. Quinton. Est 1 assumed that if she was going to try anything it wouldn't be till spring. Fair enough. Did she say how she made it here in this weather?

No, sir.

No small feat.

No it isn't, Raimond agreed. She really caught us flat-footed, sir. Who knows how far she would've gotten if Ozanne hadn't been there.

Jean-Savile frowned, distracted. If she was trying to reach Ouest 1, why not detour around us? You'd think it would be worth bypassing our borders.

He looked to me again, more intrigued than anything, but his question sent a corrosive feeling through my guts and I squirmed against my will. Raimond cast a fretful glance.

If I may, sir, I think Ozanne's just a bit shaken up. It was messy in the aftermath—in the snow you see everything. This was her first, as you said.

Putting on a pair of reading glasses, Jean-Savile consulted his schedule. Every escapee was a fellow citizen once. How about this. Your downtown patrol was supposed to begin tomorrow, but I'll drop you at the manse this morning. Take a day off to collect yourself.

Before I could demur, something else occurred to him. He glanced back at his shelf and took down an olive-green folder, flipping through a sheaf of application forms until he extracted one and read it in silence, as if for the first time. I glimpsed my own timid handwriting. Then Jean-Savile gave me a nod.

Excellent work tonight, Ozanne.

He placed my application on the top of the pile with a pointed pat, then closed the folder and told Raimond to take care of the disposal. I remembered to thank him as we left the room.

It was still dark out. Silently Raimond and I walked to the parking lot. The potter's field for escapees' remains lay somewhere outside the eastern border; no one but officers knew where. Raimond jumped in the truck's cab but didn't close the door, speaking in an incredulous whisper.

What a piece of luck—that's exactly what you needed! You're as good as in!

Dazed, I mumbled that maybe he offered motivational hints to every applicant, but Raimond was shaking his head.

He's Jean-Savile, he doesn't play mind games. I've seen it before: if he puts you at the top of the pile, that's where you are. Now you just need to stay there till April! God, can you believe what *I* just did, telling him a story like that?

He looked astonished at himself, and although I wanted to object that I hadn't asked him to lie for me, in the moment I couldn't do it, he was too excited. Raimond wiped his brow as he started the truck. Have fun in town and make sure to celebrate, he said. I'm not kidding—this uniform is yours to lose! He gave his collar a tug under his coat, then shut the truck door and U-turned toward the main gate. From the flatbed came a sliding thud.

I thought he might say more about Lucie, but the only thing Jean-Savile asked me on the way to town was whether I would drop off his incursion report when the Hôtel de Ville opened. I said yes, and we drove the rest of the way without further talk. He seemed more collegial than on our previous drives, however, and even let me glimpse his mild amusement when the snow in the orchard was so slippery that the checkpoint guard had to give the truck a floundering push.

It was too early for people to be out on the boulevard, but it would be quiet all day: everyone would have heard the alarm bells, and many people stayed close to home afterward. The vacant streets gave off a sad feeling. The holiday lights along the boulevard had all been removed, along with the evergreen boughs on the doors. Jean-Savile parked the truck and we walked into the Place du Bâtisseur through a gulch of shoveled snow.

The square was subdued as well. The statue of the conseiller and the family was nothing but a pair of white humps crisscrossed with delicate bird tracks, and the fountain below was boarded up for winter. Sometimes they found dead animals under the boards in the spring.

The chapel was set back from the rest of the square by a wrought iron gate and a cobblestone lane. I followed Jean-Savile around to the back, salt cracking under our boots. Between the chapel and the cemetery sat the old manse where gendarmes stayed during their downtown assignments.

It was a humble flat-roofed building, one of the few structures rumored to date back to the days of folklore. Its stone walls were covered in winter hawthorns whose plump red berries clustered in the snow like fish eggs in foam. Jean-Savile unlocked the door and passed me the keys.

Inside it was an ordinary apartment with stuffy air and the furnace rumbling at full blast. I followed Jean-Savile to the kitchen, where the sink was piled with days of unrinsed dishes. Jugs of cider lay empty, which explained the whiff of fermentation. The living room was arranged not unlike the tour quarters, except here there were large windows sloped with hoarfrost and pearled with morning light. Jean-Savile opened both bedroom doors without knocking.

Two groggy guards appeared. One was Turgis, nearing retirement; the other was a lanky, knobby-boned boy named Malcher. Both had covered themselves with the pilled robes that came with the apartment. Malcher's robe was too short for his height and revealed the patchy black hair on his legs.

They listened as Jean-Savile explained the night's events. He praised me in high terms, emphasizing the improbability of a winter escape and how efficiently I'd put it down. As a reward, he continued, one of you will donate your room to her early. Who volunteers?

Each guard raised a reluctant hand. Jean-Savile nodded at Turgis and told him to report back to the border when his rounds were done. Turgis retreated without reaction, but Malcher glared at me as he plodded to the bathroom.

Once Jean-Savile was gone I sank into an armchair. The shower started running. I unfolded the report for the Hôtel de Ville, which, since I was party to the incident, Jean-Savile had asked me to sign and seal. At the top was the name Lucie Sanna, written in the commandant's spiky cursive. I now recognized the surname from a mailbox I'd seen south of town. The paper shook in my hands.

*She promised that you'd help.* In vain I searched for other interpretations, but there was only one. Lucie had implicated me in her escape. Who else could she have been talking about? She: the woman scrubbing the hallway floor.

It could not be true. Think what an escapee, any escapee, might say to disconcert their captor. The lie was clever—I had faltered when she told it. Yet when I let go of Lucie, she'd made no attempt to flee. I remembered her smile, the rapturous way she breathed my name, her betrayal when I brought out the sackcloth. As though she believed, against any rational expectation, that there was something else I might do.

Jean-Savile was right, her route was unaccountable. It made no sense to enter our town if her destination was Ouest 1, which Lucie would have called Ouest 2, but the point was, she should have gone around, not risked everything to come through. Even the sector where she'd chosen to enter was far from the lake, increasing her chances of being seen. No, the route was inexplicable, unless someone had told her to take it.

I knew what miserable people were capable of. A committed interferer's desire for change was so overwhelming that it became a kind of mania, outweighing the fear of self-destruction. Lucie was clearly one such case, but I had no grounds to think I would be any exception. I had seen it my-self. I had watched Manduca trickle coffee onto the freshly cleaned floor.

Could she have come upon Lucie, hypothermic on the western shore, at the beginning of her escape? Instead of sounding the alarm, could she have assisted her, given her dry clothes and directions to the plateau cabin, so that she might survive? She could have sworn there was more help in the next valley over: all Lucie had to do was cross at a precise place and time. But when she reached me, I was not there to help her. Overnight, my promotion prospects had revived.

I heard the shower pipes honk, and Malcher stomped loudly to his room. Soon Turgis came into the kitchen tucking in his shirt. He took a bowl of boiled eggs from the fridge. Uncomfortably, I said good morning, adding that it wasn't my idea to relieve him before his week was up. The old guard gave a resigned shrug, but when Malcher emerged with his hair slicked back, he wore an open sneer. He complained that the two of them had saved an outsized share of their stipends for their last night on the town, which I'd now gone and spoiled.

I already said sorry, I replied. Turgis nodded as he peeled his egg.

You couldn't have said no? Malcher retorted.

Kid, settle down, Turgis said. You can get your rocks off without a chaperone.

Their plan together, I knew, had not involved civilian women, which was banned for security reasons—off-duty guards tended to run their mouths in the bars, let alone in bed. Instead, despite the grumblings of some townspeople, there was a house at the end of tavern row where such relations were kept as impersonal as possible, and these excursions were tolerated by Jean-Savile. The brothel was the primary recipient of many guards' stipends, and sometimes the downtown patrollers went together.

Malcher didn't stop pouting as he ate his breakfast. Before they left, he muttered that I could clean the kitchen if I was going to be around anyway. The manse door slammed before I could expel my dry laugh.

I sat in the living room, watching the light change slowly in the window as the day filled the chapelyard. I got up for an egg myself. The kitchen did smell. Sighing, I rolled up my sleeves at the sink.

The parallel with my having seen the Piras, so long ago, was not lost on me. I knew how a run-in with an eastern visitor could be turned to one's advantage, as long as one saw it through. Maybe the very shape of her scheme was a message to me too. Yet the most convincing thing was not this sense of familiarity, or the shards of explananda that my theory could account for. Lucie's route, the gendarmerie shirt, her urgent insinuation: all were secondary corroboration for what now seemed more plain. I remembered the dismal future, the ruined spine, the way she'd held her head to make me see her. For months it had confused me, but now I understood. She wanted her life to be undone, and by redirecting Lucie's escape, she'd conspired to send me the means.

And it had worked. In a few months, if I could avoid a misstep, I would be an officer. The new reality hadn't sunken in, but now, in the comfort of the manse, it entered through my chest, a warm incredulity spreading under my skin. The officers' wing was bright and airy, with skylights in the corridor. My junior suite would have a proper bed, a private bathroom, and a small balcony just for me. I raised a hand to my clavicle. The dire image of the western border shrank for the first time, like pain ebbing from an analgesic.

But Lucie had sought a similar deliverance: not for herself, but for the girl with lace braids, my neighbor in the parlor classroom. As I signed my name to Jean-Savile's report, a slimy shame entered me and sullied my relief. I put on my greatcoat and left the manse. The chapelyard was brilliant with snow. I heard the friendly cheeps of winter finches in the cemetery, where a man sprinkled feed from his pockets. The birds hopped and pecked at his feet. The man gave me a wary look, as though I might reprimand him for being there, then threw more seeds over the shapeless white graves.

The only person in the rotunda was a young clerk carrying a familiar-looking banker's box. She was eyeing me, so I told her I had a report to give Mme Ozanne in the archives, and the two of us went downstairs together.

The basement of the Hôtel de Ville was a series of corridors with rib-vaulted ceilings, covered in tiles that were a medical shade of green. The staffer's slippers brushed the floor softly as I followed her to the room where my mother worked.

Mme Ozanne, look who it is!

From her desk at the back of the archives, my mother glanced over her glasses. I held up the report. She'd gotten a haircut, a shorter style that aged her. As she came to the counter I remarked that it looked nice.

She made a skeptical face and put the envelope in the inbox for the Conseil.

Thank you, Odile.

Who's the new girl? Claudette's replacement? I asked.

Carina? New to you, I suppose. I've had her a few months. My apprentice. But she's still in school for half the week, so I'm understaffed as usual.

She goes to school downtown?

No. The north end. She's bright, she reached the last round of vetting. She was actually in M. Pichegru's class when he passed.

Why didn't you tell me about that? I only found out by accident.

My mother shrugged. Don't you get the news out there? I didn't think you'd care, you barely finished school as it was.

I sighed. The apprentice was watching from the rear of the archives, perhaps thinking we were talking about her. I looked and she busied herself.

Anyway, I continued, I can't make our lunch this week, work's too busy. I'll cancel the reservation.

My mother replied that that was fine, maybe she'd see me around my birthday if both our schedules allowed. Then she excused herself and went back to Carina. I left my late holiday gift for my mother, a fountain pen in a black box, sitting on the counter.

Normally I would be asleep after patrolling all night. Exhaustion hovered in the corners of my vision, a dull and glassy ache, but my tiredness had its own twitchy vigor and sleep felt impossible. I walked to the boulevard and passed some hours in the bookstore instead. The store was run by the previous owner's son, who seemed too young to be tending the overstuffed shelves. I knew him to be gregarious but today he wasn't, asking if I needed assistance and vanishing before I could answer.

Other gendarmes had similar encounters in town. People's discomfort with our presence came out in different ways—sometimes avoidance, sometimes forced cheer—but my experience was not unique. Still, today there were more glances than usual.

In the secondhand section I opened a few novels and put them back. Then I spotted a hardback edition of folklore that I hadn't seen before, and took it to the chair by the window.

The book turned out to be a scholarly collation of the many different tellings, compared side by side and copiously annotated. Some of the stories didn't differ much from one version to the next, but others varied, both in their main details and in their apparent morals. The author, whom I was curious to see listed as a retired conseiller, had included the more oblique tales, fragments and apocrypha upon which various editors had tried to impose their idea of sense. I read a perplexing story called The Laundress that I'd never heard of: a woman undertook a journey, not east to ask herself if she'd ever find happiness, but west to ask if she'd ever been happy before. There were two opposing texts of The Nomads, in which the town either welcomed an exodus from another valley or refused them entry, ending in disaster either way. The volume even contained analyses of the different illustrations, how the woodcuts' style evolved over time. I looked at the notorious figures juxtaposed, some with intricately wrought emotions, others with expressions that were more inscrutable, and still others whose faces resembled black masks in their degree of abstraction. There were the sundry renderings of the murderer girl, from menacing to coolly demure. One engraving of the death scene caught my eye. The kitchen floor was bloody, the woman was crawling away from the child, but on her face, there was something beyond terror; I was tempted to think it was relief. What if all the tellings misunderstood the story, I wondered. What if, between the lines, the girl had simply done what was asked of her, and the woman wanted this.

I heard a little thump. The bookstore's tabby had jumped onto the windowsill. He took me in with his coppery eyes. I offered my knuckle and he rubbed it with his cheek. The cat's mouth snagged open as he purred, exposing a pink gum and a fang.

On my way to the bindery I received more sidelong looks. Everyone knew there'd been an incursion attempt, and feelings about them were typically conflicted, but an officer would never be gawked at like this. I kept my head in my collar. It was dusk by the time I carried my bag of new printmaking supplies back to the manse.

Turgis had gone, but Malcher was there. He glanced at me without interest and went back to whatever he was doing in the kitchen. I saw him pour liquor into a glass of milk and stir it with a fork until it was soupy brown.

Can I ask you something? I said.

He tasted his swill and wiped his mouth.

Did you hear anything today on your patrol about me and the escapee?

A smile crept under his adolescent moustache. I sharpened my voice.

Do people know it was me?

Oh that. Yeah, sure, I told a couple.

You *told* a couple?

His smile expanded as he dribbled more liquor into his drink.

Why would you do that? I demanded. Just so I'd have a shitty week?

He shrugged. If anyone gives you trouble, go whine for another day off.

I was glad when he left for the night. I changed into my civilian attire, a mottled cream sweater and jeans, and headed out for tavern row.

There was no sign over the door, but the place was called Val's. It occupied a corner lot, and it was an architectural relic from a time when this had been the town's commercial center, before business migrated to the boulevard. It looked imposing for a bar, with grand rusticated masonry that contrasted with the shabbier drinking holes up the road. The roofs above its bay windows were blanketed with snow. I heard a piano inside.

I stomped my boots and entered the bar's humid air, dense with smoke and music. A long row of booths stretched down the wall, but everything was taken, so I carried my greatcoat to the bar. I landed near the far end where wizened regulars perched on stools resenting the weekend crowd. As I hung my coat on one of the barhooks the man beside me stared without concealing it. What remained of his hair was white and wild, and he had liver spots on his crown. Ignoring him, I flagged the barkeep.

Val was a large man whose intense eyebrows made him seem perpetually alarmed. He maneuvered around his wife, also pulling drinks, and slid me a glass of whiskey I drank in a gulp. My head swam with comfort.

How's things? he called over the noise.

I made an encompassing shrug. Val gave a big nod back, as though he had to make louder gestures to be understood. He tipped the bottle into my glass again, and we shouted a bit of small talk before I ordered dinner.

The white-haired regular watched Val leave for the kitchen. Then he whispered something in his neighbor's ear. I read the bottles behind the bar. The old man appraised them with me. There was a lineup of nicer whiskies I'd never tried, as well as some homemade jars, flowers and bark lodged in umber murk.

I know who you are, the man said. He had the nasal drawl of a lifelong drinker. Hey, did you hear me, I know you. The lady guard. You think your coat gave you away? It's the hair. I see you around. My wife was a redhead, but she was pretty.

The man's neighbor sagged lower on his stool.

The bar's pianist finished a jaunty tune and began a sentimental ballad. Somebody booed, to general amusement. The white-haired man leaned in.

Let me put this to you. I got woken up last night. A real commotion, lots of bells. I heard you were the one who took care of it.

I finally looked at him squarely. He grinned and mimed a bullet with his index finger, traveling toward his own liver spots. When his finger collided with his forehead, he splayed his hand open and cackled. I scowled. I saw my plate of food waiting in the kitchen window.

Anyway, you can't talk business. But if it *was* you, then thanks, from the bottom of my heart. Not only from me—aren't we all grateful? He nudged his wary neighbor. If *I* ever wanted to visit somebody, and I did the whole song and dance at the Bâtisseur and the robes still said no, I'm glad you'd be at the fence to pick me off like a dog.

Just then Val brought my plate. He gave the man a hard look.

Isidore, shut it.

The old man puffed defiantly and tapped his thick fingernail on his glass. Val raised a bottle, but poured the fresh drink into my glass instead.

On the house, with apologies.

Oh, jokes, now I'm getting joked on, except did I say anything that's not true? She's a killer and I thanked her for her service.

He was getting louder. Isidore rotated his barstool to address the room.

And now this bitch drinks for free! She's a hero here!

Okay, Val said, moving around the bar. Thierry, give me his jacket.

Though the piano was still going, nobody in the room spoke as the man was marched to the exit, and I heard his ongoing fulminations fade into the night. Some people laughed, but others watched for my reaction. Wordlessly I turned to my dinner, feeling the attention on the back of my neck. The man's neighbor got up as well, leaving a second empty seat beside me at the crowded bar.

Val returned with snowflakes on his apron. He grabbed the whiskey from the well and set the bottle in front of me.

Again, very sorry. Have the rest on us.

Don't worry, Val, I won't report your place. I meant this in jest, but my voice was uneven.

Still, all yours.

I poured a bit more and jumbled it around the ice. A conifer scent rose from the glass. I shut my eyes to the room and drank.

Someone else hopped onto the stool that had been Isidore's.

Who'd have thought she'd still be blushing after all these years?

I turned and saw a rough-looking character smiling at me. Behind a pair of flimsy glasses his eyes were eager and unblinking. Grizzled stubble covered the lower half of his face. Although he wore a wool hat, strands of orangey hair stuck out from the sides. He laughed out loud, and more than anything, it was that sound that was familiar.

Alain?

Odile? he mimicked, inspecting me with pretend scrutiny. I knew it was you, I confess, I recognized you, but then you and Isidore started tangling and I thought, hmm, let's see where this goes. So, how do you feel about your little scuffle, on a scale of one to ten?

I gave a dismissive shrug. Alain smirked at Val with mischief that looked strange on a grown man. That's what I love about this place, he quipped, the bartender who governs with an iron fist.

Val sighed. Can you believe it's next year already?

Odile, Alain explained, it's possible that I, too, have suffered my share of temporary banishments. Exiled to lesser joints up the row, each one worse than the next. Can you imagine me as a regular at fucking Fisette's? No thanks! Luckily, that was then.

No tab, Val grumbled.

Alain gestured at the open whiskey bottle beside my plate of mashed potatoes. A classic pairing.

Here, you should have some. Val, can I get another glass?

Val produced a thimble for sipping sherry and set it in front of Alain. No brawling or running your mouth either.

Alas, I don't run my mouth, it runs me. Alain filled the dainty glass until whiskey jiggled at the brim. He raised it and looked right into my eyes, almost unsettlingly sincere.

Good to see you, Ozanne.

I felt myself smile. You too.

We toasted cautiously so as not to spill. I watched him throw his head back and pour another.

The tavern grew busier, and gradually this man who was Alain transformed into a semblance of himself, restored from memory drink by drink. The truth was that he looked quite different. I'd noticed him around town over the years, but always at a distance, never to speak to. I remembered that he had, or used to have, a dog with black fur. Now, with his hat tossed on the bar, I saw his hair had grown long but thin, beginning high up his temples and stuck behind his ears. His scrappy beard was white in spots. On the stool he was taller than I remembered, but he draped his surprising length into a slouch, an approximation of languidness disguising a deeper fatigue.

He talked oddly now. Listening to him, I tried to think whether he always had, but decided he had changed. He still had his old flipness, his impish impropriety, but something was missing from it—levity, or ease. His restless energy felt more tense, and he seemed distracted by every stranger passing by. His eyes would return to me just as quickly, with a sudden jarring clarity, as if probing the state of my soul. Tell me, what kind of life are you having? he asked. The question was genuine, even serious, but then he snorted and drummed his fingers on the bar.

The oddest thing for me, however, was having a conversation at all. As we put back more of the bottle and had to keep moving closer to hear each

other, I realized that instead of addressing me as a gendarme, Alain treated
me like I was still the person I'd been when he'd known me. It was startling
to be seen as anything other than my job, to be recalled back into being,
and I found I was enjoying myself.

He filled me in on Isidore. I was not shocked to learn that the old man
had had a petition rejected, and ever since then, he'd rant about it when
he drank. His wife had died in a car accident off the hairpin turn. Alain
said that Isidore was the one driving and he was drunk as usual, which was
probably why the Conseil said no.

You know, since we're on the topic, something occurs to me. What
the hell happened with you and the Conseil? It seemed like you were a
shoo-in.

He was looking at me oversincerely again, and I exhaled an awkward
laugh. Who cares, that feels like another lifetime.

Sure does, he agreed. I guess I always wondered if it was about Edme.
That's what happened with me, everything went to shit. But you and I
never really talked afterward.

I thought of replying that we'd never really talked beforehand either,
that this was possibly our first one-on-one conversation. Instead, I asked:

Do you remember the music he was practicing for his audition? There
was a fast piece and a sadder one, or not sad, kind of peaceful? I was listening to the radio over the holidays, and I heard it—I mean, they played
Edme, I'm positive. Isn't that weird?

Alain's smile had turned puckish.

What?

I've got a mole in the conservatory. Well, a friend. I asked her if they
keep their old submissions. She dug them out of storage and liked them,
so she got an ensemble to record one—apparently Pira had even started on
an arrangement himself. I requested it at the station to commemorate the
year. It's good you heard it too.

Then Alain hummed the melody, giving it a tipsy gusto. It was so off-
key that I had to laugh. He'd been terrible at music in school, but his sloppy
rendition nailed the point of elision, the part of the tune that sank away

and lifted at the same time, making it feel briefly eternal. He paddled his fingers on the bar some more, bastardizing the rhythm.

Air swept in from the door behind us, and Malcher entered the tavern. When I saw him I moved a few inches away from Alain and sat up straighter. Alain looked toward the door, saw Malcher's greatcoat, and understood.

Already shitfaced, Malcher hollered at Val's wife to pour him a drink. I thought he might not have seen me, but he steadied himself against the bar and pivoted and attempted a salute. My new partner, painting the town red! Come drink with me!

I replied that I was heading out. He responded with an obnoxious leer, but then seemed to forget I was there, staring down his drink and trying to focus his eyes. I gathered my coat. Alain pretended not to notice, but as I stood, he said loudly to no one: It's not even cold out tonight, I'm contemplating a stroll on the good old promenade.

I arrived at the beach alone. The promenade's archway, a shape I'd always privately likened to a large hand mirror, was lined with dormant bulbs. The beach and park were equally unlit. I passed through the dark mirror onto the icy boardwalk, humming Edme's song under my boozy breath until I noticed I was doing it.

Alain came from the direction of the boulevard. He had a loping walk, hunch-necked, his hands tucked into a short corduroy jacket. He made a face of exaggerated astonishment—Fancy meeting you here!—then gamboled the rest of the way on comically rigid legs. Watching his shoes slide on the snow, I was glad I'd stayed out a bit later.

We walked on opposite sides of the promenade, him talking some more about how he'd gotten banned from the tavern—nothing scandalous, more of a gag that caught Val in a bad mood, which, to be fair, Alain said he should have anticipated, since that was standard for Val. I remarked that Val was always nice to me, and Alain said that's different, he has to be, no offense. Speaking of grouches, what's the story with you and the kid? He's your partner for the week?

Malcher? I said. Not really. He goes back tomorrow, that's why he's going hard tonight.

Doesn't look old enough to be a gendarme. He looks like he should be pulling wings off of bugs.

He might still be a teenager, I can't tell anymore. I know he's not old enough for assignments outside the fence.

So how'd you end up on his bad side? Forget to change his diaper?

I shrugged. We'd reached the end of the promenade, where the beach buried the boardwalk. The empty lifeguard tower stood on its heronlike legs. Black waves swayed beyond the ice. Alain was still waiting to hear the source of Malcher's grudge, so I gave a late laugh and said it wasn't important.

Oh shit, does it have something to do with the alarm bells last night? Like what Isidore was saying? I shouldn't have brought it up then, sorry.

That's okay. It's more of a scheduling thing he's mad about.

Alain nodded without conviction. Sighing, I went on in a quieter voice.

You're right, though. It goes back to the escapee. Jean-Savile gave me an extra day of recreation, or recuperation—I guess he thought I was rattled. Malcher's upset that I replaced his partner in the manse tonight.

Were you rattled?

I answered that I was fine, all in a night's work. The facetious words lingered grimly in the air. I gazed past the lifeguard tower to the place where the swim dock was anchored in the summer. I remembered watching a boy kiss Lucie Erro's neck. He might have been the husband she wished she'd never met. Shivering, I tightened my coat.

So did you keep that bottle? asked Alain.

I passed it over. He took a long swig, gave it back, then stepped up onto a bench and sat on the backrest, his soaked shoes on the snowy seat. He commented that he hadn't been to the beach in ages: I kind of lost my taste for the lake, if you can imagine. Edme and I used to talk about swimming across it—do people ever do that?

Only if they want to get arrested on the other side.

That's what we thought, said Alain, looking at the western campfires.

We just wondered if we could swim that far. He was actually a really good swimmer. Ha.

His eyes seemed to glisten. Not knowing what to say, I offered the bottle again. I was fine with him having the rest. It felt strange speaking about Edme so openly. A door that I'd sealed shut, nonchalantly toed ajar.

As Alain drank I brushed snow off the engraved dedication plaque on the back of our bench. I read aloud: *Lelli Pavana, who loved this spot / Those who loved her, shall never forget.*

Charming, said Alain, all of ten words and they used 'loved' twenty times. And does it cost extra for a bench to rhyme? 'Spot,' 'for-*got*,' that's simple courtesy. Lelli, sweet angel, you deserved better.

I chuckled. What would you have said about Lelli Pavana?

Never heard of her. I'd say hire a better poet.

Yeah, okay. What would you want written about you?

Why—are you going to buy me my own memorial bench, on a gendarme's stipend?

It'd be my pleasure.

Wow, you're too kind. I'll have to consider this carefully. I suppose my bench should be outside Val's place, so he can pay his respects on a daily basis. Maybe the plaque should just be my name and balance owing. Ah, poor Val, I give him a rough time. Poor Val, poor Lelli Pavana, poor Alain Rosso, poor Odile. Alain gave me a sloshy pat on the shoulder. Look at us, hey? Remember how Pichegru used to stare me down when he talked about the gendarmerie? Who'd have thought you'd be the one humping along the fence? Odile on patrol!

His words had begun to slur. I sat beside him on the bench's backrest. We watched the cold wind change direction, disturbing the surface of the lake.

Well, I said softly, I might not be patrolling forever.

Yeah? I thought there's no quitting allowed.

I don't mean that. I applied for a commission.

Ah! Not a patroller, something loftier. What's that, an officer?

Yeah.

Think you'll get it?

I paused. For a long time I was sure I wouldn't. Now I'm the top prospect. After last night.

Alain reflected on this. I knew that if I looked at him, his expression would again be earnest and wide-eyed.

Huh, you feel guilty, he observed. Was it Isidore's fault? He's a crank, but I guess he's not completely full of shit.

What do you mean?

Just how he was saying it's sad. That's all. Obviously rules are rules, the job's the job, but I can see how it'd be hard doing that to another person. Do you even know what they wanted to do here? The escapee? It's okay if you can't talk about it, I guess you can't.

I drank from the nearly empty bottle. The liquor stung my eyes.

It doesn't feel great. Getting ahead because of what happened . . . it feels like I'm using her.

Her?

I stiffened. Shit. Don't tell anyone I said that.

Alain laughed. So it was a woman, who cares.

Still.

Never, future officer! he vowed. But hey, how about this: maybe it's not too late to help her out. She must have been trying to do *something* here. If you know what it was, what if you just went and did it for her? That can't be against the law, right? You're just a local, dum dee dum, going about your day . . .

No, they treat that stuff as coordination. It's serious.

Dang rules, always a step ahead.

His shrug reminded me of him as a boy. He drained the last of the whiskey and pitched the bottle across the sand. It gave a hollow bounce on the frost and skittered onto the wrinkly ice that covered the shallows. Somehow it made me remember the day he and Edme had hurled sticks at Henri Swain behind the school, and I changed the subject by thanking him, years overdue. Oh, I'm sure we were happy for the excuse, Alain replied.

We walked back toward the archway. He asked me more about life as a gendarme, and I answered despite suspecting that he already knew most of it from other off-duty guards. As we reached the Place du Bâtisseur the conversation began shifting again to school days, but he noticed me yawn into my hand and said, We can do memory lane another night.

I just haven't slept, I'm so tired, I apologized.

You're preaching to the choir, he said. How about that for my memorial bench: *So tired*. He coughed out something like a laugh.

I smiled and said I was glad we'd gotten a chance to reconnect.

Likewise, said Alain. He started to walk backward, returning to tavern row. Sweet dreams, Officer Ozanne, and may success soothe your conscience! He almost tripped and swore at his feet as he stumbled around.

I let myself into the manse. Malcher was still out. I turned up the thermostat. By the time I lay down on the quilted mattress, my thoughts had returned to the hopeful look on Lucie's floodlit face, and the dull stare of the woman in Est 1.

A few hours later I was back on patrol. The morning was overcast, a merciful blank sheet pulled over the world, but I still walked slit-eyed to reduce the light. My skull felt distended by the thrumming in my temples.

Malcher had left first thing, dropping me off at the town limit. He hadn't said two words to me, but several times looked like he was going to be sick. The truck pulled away and I started up the unplowed road that bordered the eastern orchards.

Almost as if she'd been waiting at my bedside, I'd begun thinking about Lucie again as soon as I woke up. I needed something else, so, looking over the dirt-spewed snowbanks, I thought about Alain.

The week Edme went missing he'd stopped coming to school. He searched all day with the volunteer groups, and continued searching with M. Pira when the volunteers gave up for the night. On Friday the search ended; on Sunday was the funeral, which he did not attend; and on Monday he came back to class.

I remember he kept his head low and spoke to no one. He looked like he hadn't bathed in days. Pichegru taught as usual, never alluding to Edme despite having given a speech from the chapel's pulpit the day before. He didn't acknowledge Alain's return until shortly before the lunch bell, when he ordered him to the front to punish him for truancy. Alain stood and went without objection.

At the start his face was empty. As though, despite being bent over Pichegru's desk, he had yet to notice the blows. But it was a long beating. Moisture appeared on Pichegru's forehead, and Alain's face grew blotchy, his knuckles digging into the desk. Then it all seemed very slow, Alain wheeling around and hitting Pichegru across the face; very slow, our teacher falling backward, blood blossoming around his teeth as he began to roar. Alain simply walked away and out the cloakroom door. Jo, with a white rose of mourning pinned in her hair, stared in amazement. I remember Justine looking terrified as she broke free to chase him.

Of course he was expelled. That day the class went on the field trip to the mill without him. Ineligible for apprenticeships, he became the Piras' helper for a while, sweeping leaves from the sidewalks with Edme's father while Edme's mother was bedridden. When she returned to work the following year, he was seen with them less often. I didn't know what happened between him and Justine. He was never around the neighborhood anymore, but neither was I, withdrawing to my grandparents' house that winter.

Their old property was on my patrol route that morning. After my grandparents passed away, the neighbors who'd already bought their orchard purchased their house as well. Soon they had it torn down, along with the freestanding garage. When I'd come here to live, I'd spent hours each day curled up in the garage's loft, reading and sleeping, gazing at the rough-hewn spots where my grandfather had removed a single rafter tie. The stone driveway that still existed under inches of ice now led nowhere. The orchard at the driveway's end was full of young skinny trees, branches topped with slender wrists of snow.

Before the house was sold and leveled, my mother sent word that she'd be clearing it out. I couldn't ask for unscheduled leave from the gendarmerie—in truth, I didn't want to—so she got Claudette's sons to help her, and a box arrived at the border addressed to me. It was uncharacteristic of my mother to care about mementos, but later she clarified that the contents weren't her responsibility to deal with, and the men hadn't wanted to keep anything for themselves.

I kept hardly anything either. There were a couple books worth saving, but I fed all my schoolwork into the mess hall incinerator. At the very bottom of the box, under a linty cloth purse, I found my leather Conseil notebook. Dismissed candidates relinquished their notes as a precaution, but I'd never been asked to give mine back. Only upon rediscovering the notebook did it seem curious that Ivret had not arranged for its return.

I reread the whole thing. For what was only a few weeks of my life, I was startled by the quantity of notes, scrawled in my dutiful hand. The margins were marked with case designations next to any lecture material I'd deemed relevant to the tests: the circled initials of that week's grieving pseudonyms, *L.M.*, *C.R.*, *J.N.* & *P.N.*, repeated down the page. In comparison, my preparation for each verdict was succinct and decisive. There was a cipher key copied out twice. In mid-September, the notes terminated with no preceding change in tone.

When I closed the notebook, I realized that the impression it gave, the personality it evinced, was one of unexpected fortitude. The voice was impersonal but authoritative, confident, even slightly imperious in its remarks. In daily life I had thought of myself as such a cowering thing. And while I felt some chagrin at the brashness of this girl, I also felt chastened by her presence. She was a witness to what had become of me: lying on this folding cot, under these sallow lights, sapped of her audacity. I kept the notebook for a week before burning it like the rest.

People watched from their front windows as I did my rounds. They retreated when I returned their looks, acting like they were responding to sudden summons from deeper in their houses.

Between me and the next residential neighborhood was the eastern farmland, where the properties were farther apart and the landscape rolled open. Even in the cold air, the barns exhaled earthy gusts. Through one red door came the grubby shuffling of hooves.

A windbreak of ash trees marked the next farm. Past the trees I saw a salt-white farmhouse, two stories high, at the top of a long lane. It was still a ways ahead, but I could spot the mailbox where the lane met the road, and I knew the surname painted there. The smoke from the house's chimney was almost the same grey as the sky. A polished black pickup was parked in front. Lucie Sanna was home this morning, or her husband was, or both.

I slowed my pace, deliberating whether to go back the way I'd come. A few miles from here, her blood still darkened the snowbank; I might have missed a drop on the sleeve of my greatcoat. But I had known which route I was taking. I could have gone another way. My heartbeat sped up with my footsteps.

The hill began rising on my left and the house rose with it, like a boat lifting on a coming wave. As I got closer I saw exhaust puttering from the pickup but nobody in the cab. Then a man came from behind the house.

He was tall and broad and moved with bearish purpose. His hair was cropped flat and severe. He jerked the driver's side door open before noticing me near the bottom of his driveway. He seemed to consider me for a moment, then got in his truck.

He drove down the hill at half speed so as not to fishtail on the ice. I could have walked past before he reached me. Instead, I stopped and waited in the middle of his driveway, facing his approach.

Through the windshield I saw him cock his head. His face had the cloudy complexion of the reflected sky. He put the truck in park and got out with the engine running.

Help you? he called.

Chest thudding, I went to him. Only the open truck door separated us. I felt heat radiating from the hood. Up close he had unshaven jowls and ill-tempered eyes, but kept his glare civil.

What brings you here?

We received a complaint, I said. It sounded uncertain, the lie too blatant, and I steadied my voice. Your name is Sanna?

That's right.

Your wife's name is Lucie?

He blinked in sour surprise. What'd she do?

Up the hill, in the farmhouse window, I saw a woman staring at us.

Her hair was wrapped in a towel and her hand was raised to her throat. I returned my look to Sanna.

Nothing, I answered. This is about you, what you do.

His eyes became slivers. What are you talking about?

I began opening my coat to reveal my pistol. But a second thought stopped me. Abruptly I closed my coat again.

Never mind. This is the wrong house.

Huh?

Sorry.

You had my name, he said testily. What's the complaint, more property line bullshit?

No, my mistake. I turned around and walked away, heat rushing up my back. I reached the end of the driveway and kept going, shocked at what I'd almost missed.

If I succeeded in helping Lucie now, then in twenty years' time, she would have no need to attempt her escape. Yet all the while, I would owe my improved circumstances to her doomed attempt. The moment that Lucie didn't break out of this valley and encounter me by the fence, my comfortable existence as an officer would end. A wave of new time would roll over me, just as Ivret had warned: I would be undone. And for twenty years leading up to it, I'd know it was coming, but be powerless to stop it.

I looked at the horizon in disbelief. The snow on the western mountaintops was as barren as the moon, but a faint blue thumbprint had begun opening in the sky. I wanted to improve Lucie's lot, but there was a prohibitive cost to clearing my conscience.

Was it prohibitive? Annihilation was not the only option. I could walk back to the farmhouse, do what I could for Lucie, then simply withdraw my name from contention next week. Jean-Savile would be puzzled, Raimond would be thunderstruck, but that would be it: with no promotion, no change in my life owing to Lucie, there was no undoing to fear.

As I reached the next homestead, however, my pace was unchanged. If anything I walked faster. I had seen what would happen with no promotion. A turn back now would be a turn, with certainty, toward the western border and Manduca. I thought of the bright officer's wing where Raimond lived, even the uniform of which he was so proud. I would be respected, heeded, instead of abused. No: having barely caught hold of the saving branch, I could not let it go.

The sun broke through the clouds at the end of the farmland. Men like Sanna didn't change. Threatening him could just as easily make things worse for her. It was folly to get involved, to sacrifice myself for a tenuous cause. Even the distasteful future errand I foresaw—having to seek Lucie out in her misery and arrange the details of her winter escape myself, given my absence from the western border—I could make myself do it when the time came. The calculation would be the same then as it was now, two wretched souls or one.

I stopped in front of the first houses on the rue des Cerises and drank all the water in my canteen. In place of a clean conscience I felt cleansed by conviction, the clarity of choosing. Icicles dripped from the carports, and there was a thaw in the air. At last my headache started to recede.

The small green buds among winter's ruins seemed, as always, to be from another world. Color returned to the earth like the first true breath after a long illness. The hills reawakened with grass and golden flowers that frenzied with each sigh of wind.

Early in April I was assigned to the floating fence. I piloted the skiff to one of the northern lake outposts, where the last guard disembarked and I hauled my provisions into the raccard-like cabin raised on stilts above the raft. Although I had to scan all day with my field glasses, the solitary lake weeks were my favorites. Each day I woke to the gulls' cries and poured a glass of unsweetened cherry juice instead of coffee. Then I set to work carving the sunrise, stippling the wood block with a burin to try to capture the dazzling patterns of light across the water. Blinding fractals scattered from my vision in all directions, like schools of fish fleeing an intruding limb.

I bathed at sunset, dropping feet-first into the water before there was time to rethink it. The cold hit my body like the blunt end of an axe, but after some gasps my skin turned numb and calm, and I stayed in for a long time. I swam far from the raft, farther than we were supposed to go. I floated and leaned back until my ears dipped under and filled me with the lake's dense silence.

Back at the outpost, wrapped in my towel, I watched the night rise from the blue-ridged mountains. Isolated trees bristled on the horizon like stray whiskers. Gradually the lights came on in town, and the promenade's lamps spilled pellucid trails over the water. The wind carried errant music from the pavilion in the park.

One day it rained so hard I didn't swim at all. I ate my food sitting at the cabin window watching the storm. I thought about the distance of the clouds, how each tiny droplet managed to stay intact as it hurtled through the air. The blackness roiled overhead, but down the valley it was already bright again, and the rain splashed the raft in torrents of liquid sunlight.

The other nights I lay outside. As my pupils dilated I found deeper and deeper stars. If I turned my head to the right, I could make out teenagers' fires on the north end bluffs. I smiled a little as I heard empty bottles sailing into the lake, sounds that blended with the pleasant glip-glop of fish under the raft and the groans of underwater cables in their sheaths. I had brought no liquor with me, and I slept soundly at the floating fence. It was one of the few posts I anticipated missing after the promotion, but for the first time in my memory, I had a positive feeling about the future.

I'd gone back to Val's the same day I nearly confronted Sanna. It was still early, the sky a dusky violet, and the bar was dead inside. Alain was there, though, lounging alone at a shadowy corner table. I went straight to him, borne on giddy nerves. He might have noticed my changed air, but he simply studied me, curious. At the bar I had Val's wife pour a round for all the regulars. A confused Isidore looked up when he received his pint, and I gave a sardonic nod. Then Alain and I passed another friendly hour together. Our conversation was lighter: he gave me town gossip and I told him about patrolling, about Raimond, about what Jean-Savile and Coltelli were like as opposed to their reputations, and the glacial boredom, the quarters with their cardboard walls, the dour unchanging food. This elevated my mood too, burnishing the objects of my complaints to an almost affectionate shine. I mentioned my hobby of carving and printmaking, and he exclaimed that I should bring my prints the next time I was posted in town, when would that be? After some wavering, I'd agreed to show him my work in the spring.

Again it felt good to commune with part of the past. As though a bind-
ing had been loosened, even just a bit, and something I'd forgotten was
being freed. When my week in town ended and I was back at the border, I
felt a slight pang resuming my dinners with Raimond in the mess hall. Pres-
ently enough this melancholy settled, which I told myself was just as well.

Aubuchon was the one to relieve me from the lake outpost. With my bag
on the deck I watched him cross the water. The small boat hugged the
shoreline, then made a sharp turn and sped toward me, motor roaring
along the north end promontory. Up to then, I hadn't had much interaction with my competitors beyond the occasional hello. From his stand-
offishness that morning, it was evident that Aubuchon was aware of how
things stood. I took the hint and left without making conversation, steering the boat back across the mellow waves. At the gendarmerie dock I tied
up and exited through the public marina, smiling at the families preparing
to go sailing with their thatched baskets and wine.

Jean-Savile's announcement was due by the end of the month. Raimond
said that the chosen candidate would be called to the admin building to
be given the news, and the anteroom talk was still in my favor. His regular
confidences were both exciting and embarrassing; they reminded me a bit
of Claudette whispering about my odds at the Grande École.

Prudently, Raimond and I had never spoken again about what happened on the fence that night. As soon as I'd returned from town in
January, he joined in with all the other guards calling me a sharpshooter,
laughing the loudest when they praised me for finally growing a pair. For
months the most he hinted at our secret was a glimmer in his eye.

It was a mid-April afternoon when Raimond asked me to go for a walk.
We'd just finished a late lunch in the mess hall, and the kitchen staff had
rolled down the metal curtain to close the serving counter until the evening. I had a split shift and Raimond had discretion over his hours, so he

said we had time. I said I wasn't planning on going back to the barracks, which was our usual walking route together. Not along the fence, he replied. There's something I want to show you.

He led me past admin and the assorted outbuildings to a dirt road. The road went down a hill and soon the fence dipped out of sight. Ahead, I saw the secluded enclave where only senior officers lived.

It was an unusual glen on the eastern border for having trees: a line of aspens set back from the road, clouds of pale catkins budding on the highest branches. Peach trees also grew in the yards. Their thick blossoms were still compact and pressed together like lips.

I love it down here, Raimond said.

The stucco houses were small, no bigger than cottages, more modest than even my childhood home. But they were detached and self-sufficient, roomier than either the barracks or the junior officers' suites. I agreed it was nice. Each cottage had terracotta trim. We paused in front of Jean-Savile's residence. Surreptitiously peeking through his window, I made out a bookshelf the length of a wall.

Raimond ran a hand through his hair and brushed at his shoulders. He gestured down the road. It's this way.

There were only a few more houses. I saw an officer, not yet dressed for work, hunched by a sprinkler under his peach tree. Raimond raised a hand. Yseult, he called with aggressive good cheer. The man glanced irritably over his shoulder.

Maybe not the friendliest neighbor, Raimond remarked. Anyway, we're here.

Beyond Yseult's cottage, where the dirt road was consumed by weeds, there was a house much like the others but in disrepair. Raimond made a significant smile as he approached the front window and beckoned. I looked through the dirt-streaked glass. The interior was unfurnished except for a rocking chair facing a sooty fireplace curtained with chains.

Nobody lives here?

Not at the moment. It's been empty since Bellizzi aged out. Come on.

I followed him to the back. The grass was patchy but more peach trees flourished, their branches preparing to unfurl. Yseult must be watering these, Raimond speculated. He tried opening the back door but the knob didn't turn, and he nodded approvingly. Then he spread his arms.

So, what do you think? Can you see me here?

You mean to live? It's beautiful, sure.

He looked satisfied. Good, I can see it too. I've always wanted to be here, it just feels right. You know these houses are nicer than some of the ones downtown? With a bit of cleanup this place'd be like new. I bet I could fix it up better than Yseult's, maybe even Coltelli's, but don't tell them that.

He joined me in the thin shade of the peach trees and fingered one of the nascent bulbs, prying open its tip.

Of course, other people have their eye on it too. I'm still a spring chicken by gendarmerie standards, not at the front of the queue.

He ran his hand through his hair again, and chuckled. He was stalling.

If you want it, what's your move? I asked.

That's why I wanted you to see it, he said. What would *you* think about living here?

Me?

Yes. Obviously it's for officers—it'd be after your commission goes through.

Raimond saw my bewilderment and inhaled.

More specifically, here's my idea. Neither of us stands a realistic chance at this place on our own. But what if you and I offered to live here together? Now there's an incentive on their end—it would free up two whole junior suites.

He cleared his throat. Cohabitation is kind of a policy grey area, Jean-Savile isn't exactly getting swamped with requests, but as far as I can tell there's no rule about it either way. Still, it's outside the norm. We'd have to present him with a convincing rationale.

Raimond looked off to one side and hurried through his next words.

Personal relationships aren't allowed between the lower ranks, or between lower ranks and officers, but there's actually nothing on the books about one officer and another officer. No language about that whatsoever.

He risked a darting glance at me. My first astonished impulse was to laugh, but he looked uncomfortable, he wasn't joking, so I stopped myself. Nervousness seeped into my stomach.

You're saying there's a loophole? I said.

Loophole, oversight, who knows. I think if rules are rules, then the same goes for their absence. And . . . well. You've probably been out here in the autumn. It's lovely when these leaves turn. It's nice that you can't see the fence, no glare at night. Idyllic.

I nodded, and his confidence started to rebound.

You don't have to decide now. But we shouldn't wait too long. It makes sense to broach the issue with Jean-Savile before you move out of the barracks, and he's set to announce the promotion any day. I really think we'd have a shot if we made the right case. I'd do the formal request, but you could help plan my phrasing—we could put your old Conseil skills to good use! Imagine going from being a patroller to Jean-Savile's neighbor overnight!

He checked his watch and made a face. Speaking of patrols, your transport leaves soon.

Raimond started to walk back the way we'd come. I stayed where I was, facing the back of the old cottage.

But I'm not sure what you're really asking me, I said.

He stopped. What do you mean?

If there's a loophole about relationships . . . are you saying that's what we'd actually be? Or is that just what we'd tell Jean-Savile, to be able to move in here?

Raimond blinked. In the sunshine his small eyes were berry blue.

If word got out that it was all for show, they wouldn't let us keep it. Not to mention I'd be a laughingstock.

He colored and continued more hoarsely. Besides, in case I wasn't being clear—I'd *like* for us to be that. We're good for each other. I think I've shown you, lately, how good I am for you.

It took me a moment to realize he was alluding to Lucie. Raimond gave a strained smile, almost apologetic, with a vulnerability I'd never seen in him before.

I guess I do need to head back, I said quietly. I promise I'll think about it.

Sure, he recovered, resolutely upbeat.

*

The guard in the beach watchtower was Caron, and, true to form, he poked his head out the trapdoor to chat. The creek by the park might flood over; a guard across the lake had been hurt in a patrol mishap; the plateau cabin needed restocking. I peered up the tower ladder, half listening as usual, but when I was about to say goodbye, Caron added: Hey, I'd never jinx it, but I hear you're looking shiny for a commission. He crossed his fingers at me. Distantly I remembered that he'd had some kind of falling-out with Aubuchon.

On my patrol I brooded about what Raimond had said. Recalling earlier signs, things I'd dismissed at the time. Was this the reason he'd encouraged me to apply for a commission in the first place? Was today's conversation the last move in a meticulous campaign? His advice last autumn, that I should aim higher for myself, took on a different fragrance in hindsight.

The possibility of his feelings had occurred to me before. Over the years, especially when he allowed himself a drink or two, his gaze sometimes grew sweeter. I'd learned to let my eyes drift away on cue, and nothing more had ever come of it. Now there was no dodging the issue. He'd declared his intentions, and, in a phrase of my grandmother's that came darkly to mind, he had a man's expectations. I thought of the furtive way he knuckled spittle from the corners of his mouth when he got excited. The physical prospect was unappealing, but worse was the fact that, for him, sex was clearly about more than affection or lust—social status played a part, perhaps the central one. His objection to a chaste living arrangement was that his reputation was at stake.

Quinton had told me of Raimond's hardships back in school, and I considered them now. I knew he'd been rejected from multiple apprenticeships, and although he'd risen in the gendarmerie, he still acted like the striving outsider. I could picture his overproud look, arm around my waist in the mess hall, the only man on the border who never had to pay for it. Alongside these suspicions, though, his tenderness toward me seemed genuine as well.

I stopped between two watchtowers and opened my carving bag. The landscape on the wood block struck me as done, but since I'd carried it here, I deepened a few idle details in the sky. The wind picked up, and the alarm bells clinked over the sound of the chisel. Tenderness. I wasn't a fool. Raimond had brought up Lucie, ostensibly as evidence of his devotion, but really as a reminder: if I made officer, it would be thanks to him. If he believed that, did I even have the option of saying no? And yet I could not say yes.

Mournfully I thought of the junior officers' suites. My distracted chisel pierced the wood too deeply, botching the horizon. I cursed and blew dust from the fresh gouge, but decided the error was subtle. Alain had asked to see my work the next time I was around. My downtown week was coming up again, and the thought of drinking with him, of speaking casually, was a relief. Tonight I would make some prints.

I removed stacks of wood blocks from under my cot. In the room's weak light, my bedside lamp illuminated raveled nests of hair and grit on the floor. I evaluated the carvings I'd finished in the last several months, including today's. Half dissatisfied me and half I tossed on the cot. From a blanket I unwrapped a windowpane I'd foraged from a vacant house on patrol. Its frame, once painted yellow, was now shaggy with splinters, but the glass itself was smooth and uncracked.

I applied cobalt-blue ink to the pane, then rolled the ink onto my first block. The carved ridges shone glossy and dark. I took a blank sheet of mulberry paper, which was fibrous and sturdy and had a good weight. Gently I lowered the white paper over the blue block, then methodically rubbed each section down with a spoon from the mess hall.

The prints hung on a clothesline to dry: a banner of metallic blue scenes running along my wall. Seeing them in a row, I was struck by their spareness.

There was the view from the lake outpost, water on all sides. There was the moonrise over the plateau. There was the bleak eastern borderland, a sea of dry grass, with the skeletal outline of a watchtower in the far distance. Involuntarily, I remembered my times in the towers with much older guards, their tongues thick with coffee in the middle of the night. Things I'd wanted done to me, or thought I had: in retrospect, still wandering grief's long fever. Another print showed the chapel cemetery framed in the window of the manse. Headstones were the closest things I'd carved to people.

Perhaps I was lonely. Perhaps the person you shared your life with was less important than simply sharing it, and one person was basically as good as the next. I tried to be objective about Raimond. Even if he'd planned this in advance, was that the most sinister thing? And even if his ego played a role in his desire, surely that was not uncommon, and should I let it determine what I myself wanted? Which was what?

If I accepted him, I would still be lonely, but maybe less so. We got along well as colleagues; he could make me laugh. Also, the arrangement might renew my appreciation for solitude. I imagined Raimond away on a shift and myself in a lawn chair, carving the peach trees, listening to the aspens and the laundry gusting on the line. That idea was more than acceptable. Compared to what I'd seen in Est 1, the safety of such a future could only count as a blessing.

In the morning my prints were dry. I sewed the best few into an oversized book with floppy oilskin covers, the pages heavy as cloth. I rolled it into my rucksack to bring downtown. On my way out the door, I scribbled a word on a mulberry scrap and walked to the officers' wing. The wide hallway smelled of musk and coffee. I saw sunlight in the crack under Raimond's door: he was awake. I slid the note into his quarters and went to catch the bus.

M alcher shook his head when he saw me. Our unplanned pairing had been thought a success in the winter, so this time Coltelli had scheduled us together on purpose, to neither of our joy. I sat at the front of the bus alone. Once I got out at the Place du Bâtisseur and crossed toward the chapel, Malcher caught up.

You again.

Same to you.

Wonderful, he replied, continuing to walk with me.

A maintenance man was crouched in front of the dry fountain, where a square compartment was open in the rock. The boards that covered it in the winter were stacked on the ground, exposing the fountain's leaf-stained bottom. I saw a crowd filtering into the chapel. It was, I remembered, the beginning of spring Cherishment.

People were dressed for the morning service. Patiently they shuffled toward the entrance, where two smiling Conseil apprentices distributed programs. I hung back near the steps of the Grande École to wait until the crowd thinned, and Malcher leaned against the wall beside me. Nice to skip this, he yawned.

I looked for familiar faces. Alain wasn't around, but he would never go to this kind of thing. I spotted my old neighbor Clare waiting with her family, and possibly Marie Valenti from school. If I knew anyone else here, they were already inside.

Eventually we took the side lane to the manse. In the cemetery, a family of three was visiting a grave. I admired the regular mourners, the ones who were content with this. As I unlocked the manse's door, the bolt squeaked and both children turned their heads. Malcher obliged them with a nasty wave.

This time the quarters had been properly cleaned and aired. The kitchen gleamed and the cushions were plumped in the living room. Malcher and I sat on the settee dividing the week's sectors: four north and three south for me, the inverse for him. We unpacked our things while the service started next door. Lachrymose hymns leaked from the chapel windows. We left for patrol on foot, Malcher toward the boulevard, me toward tavern row.

On the main drag no one was about. The storefronts were shuttered, and weeds grew from heaps of cigarette butts sloping up the edges of the walls. In the gaps between buildings, the muddy wasted fields gave me a shiver of springtime melancholy. Warm wind trembled in the puddles.

I patrolled the streets, then the perimeters of the vineyards. After work, I logged the day's rounds and went to the diner on the boulevard, where it was agreeably noisy. The men in overalls who'd snagged the last table changed their minds and moved to the bar, so I inherited a booth. My waiter splashed a bit of water on the laminated menu as he shakily filled my glass.

Having just reflected on the lack of people in my prints, I decided to try carving in the restaurant, however odd it might look to the other patrons. I christened a fresh block with the heads of two strangers who were sitting in the booth beside mine. Tomorrow I might continue, copying the backs of different strangers' heads, thus recording from observation a pair of people who'd never existed. I tapped tiny shavings out of the ovals I'd made in the wood.

Something happy was playing on the diner's radio, and after I'd eaten and packed my tools, I was in a fine mood. In the center of the Place du Bâtisseur, water burbled in the newly filled fountain and wavy colors lit up the statue. Across the square a girl's voice swung through fifths and octaves in the conservatory, reaching ever higher. I perched on the fountain's lip as the hesitant stars arrived.

Now that it was dark, I hoped to find Alain. I tried first at Val's but no one had seen him yet. These days he was living in the Raspail Rooms, he'd said in the winter, so if I didn't run into him in town, I should try him there.

I drove as far as the end of tavern row, passing the house where Malcher was no doubt already on a spree. I parked the truck where he wouldn't spot it and continued up the potholed road on foot. The pavement ended and the streetlights tapered off at the gloomy remains of the brickyard and some factories. There was no more need for them to operate, the Conseil said. The gravel road now led only to the Raspails. I carried my oilskin book under my arm.

The housing complex was an L-shaped structure on the far outskirts of town; you could spot the Raspails from parts of the eastern border. The long building had dozens of small square windows, many of them blocked with foil. In the dark, the gappy rows of glowing squares resembled a mouth missing half its teeth. It was the place you ended up if you hadn't qualified for the types of work the town considered respectable, or if you didn't work at all.

Despite the building's size, there was only one set of stairs, leading to a shared balcony that ran the length of the upper floor. At the top, wall lights buzzed inside metal cages above heaps of junk: waterlogged cardboard, nail-ridden boards, the remnants of scavenged furniture. There was a coin slot for access to the toilets and a defiant smell of urine outside the locked door. I read the names until I found *Rosso* and knocked on his window. For a second I heard nothing. Then there was a noise within, and the door opened, and Alain's eyes lit up.

Odile!

I had never been inside the Raspails. Alain's apartment was a bare-walled bachelor with the sharp odor of mildew. A countertop in the corner sported a rusty hotplate and two bags of cereal. There was a suitcase spilling over with clothes and an unmade single mattress on the floor, no sheet, just a penny-brown quilt. Cluttering the middle of the room was a collapsible card table and chair.

He had no closet, but insisted on taking my jacket and laying it neatly on the mattress. I'd worn my other civilian outfit, a pearl blouse with a ribbon at the collar that had belonged to my mother. He asked if I wanted something to drink. A bottle with a black-and-gold label sat behind the hotplate.

Verdier, is it?

Indeed it is, said Alain. I'm a bargain hunter and she can afford it. He mimed putting something up his sleeve. The sink sputtered as he washed out two glasses.

His beard had grown since the winter, with empty craters by his cheekbones where it seemingly refused to fill. His hair was cut much shorter, which drew attention to his sparser temples. His shoddy eyeglasses slid down his nose as he stooped over the sink.

He gave me my wine and sat at the table, drawing a bare foot up onto the seat. He looked like he'd only recently woken up, and might have slept in the same shirt and slacks he had on now. I sat on the edge of his mattress with my book of prints beside me. We sipped the delicate wine in silence.

After the unexpected pleasure of renewing our friendship that winter, I was disappointed by the awkwardness in the room. Alain rested his chin on his knee and fixed me with his searching look, as if inviting me to say something of particular significance, but when I didn't, he asked me my recreation plans for the week.

Nothing much, I shrugged. Tomorrow I'm going to the tea boat with my mother for my birthday.

The tea boat. Is that fun?

Never, I said, and my harrowed tone helped break the ice. He suggested that I discreetly shoot a hole in the hull to cut the evening short. Imagining the stuffy dining room listing to one side, all the monied patrons protesting as they slid overboard, I smiled and raised my wine: Happy birthday to me.

Alain clinked my glass. We talked about birthdays, which led him to ruefully recount a notable one of his—his day of first arrival. He still lived

at home when his twentieth came along, and things with his family had become so fraught that he didn't expect them to observe the custom, which
was mawkish anyway. But when the hour came and went without anyone
suggesting they look at the mountains to pay tribute to his birth on the
other side, he made a little swipe at his parents. He swore the joke was
intended mostly as self-deprecation, but it led to a scorching row. By the
end, his father was yelling and his mother was crying, both pleading with
him to get his life together, Alain glowering and demanding how. He left
with a suitcase of clothes and a bag of his parents' liquor, which he took to
the cove and proceeded to get blackout drunk.

Guess where I ended up staying the night? he asked me. The first place
I officially moved after abandoning the nest?

He didn't remember going to the fort, only waking up there. Some of
the wall of foliage was still standing, and the main log hadn't moved. So I
made this lousy lean-to, Alain continued, and then who knows how many
nights I got wasted in the backwoods. Mornings I'd wake up with my shirt
full of pine needles and our initials unblurring in front of my nose, the
girls with their maiden names, and you and me. Not Pira, though. Kind of
spooky in retrospect. Did you know his birthday's three days after mine? I
did the whole ritual up there for him, eyes to the west, hand on my heart.
Apparently I even tried adding his name to the log.

Alain held up a wormlike scar and dropped his hand. I had a quiet
drink as I thought of something to say, then asked what had happened
between him and Justine, back in those days.

She broke up with me. Alain shrugged, but then admitted to having
provoked it. He'd spurned her attempts to console him about Edme, and
although she kept trying in the face of his depression, he got lashing drunk
one night and blamed Justine for the accident. If I wasn't with *you*, he
quoted himself, I would've been with Edme that night. Which is probably
true, but whose fault is it, not hers. Years later, he'd brought his dog to the
veterinary clinic to be put down. He finally apologized to her for what he'd
said, and, whether Justine forgave him or whether it was more about the
dog, she held him as he cried.

With a sigh Alain smacked his thighs and fetched the bottle from the counter. I wasn't sure why, but I asked him if he knew about the time I'd accidentally spied on him and Justine at the fort. He scrunched his brow as he refilled our glasses, so I described how I'd gotten too close to retreat and tiptoed behind a tree, where I was helpless not to hear them doing it. Alain burst out laughing, which made me laugh too, and the easing of the mood was welcome, both of us dissolving in spite of the sadness in his room. Wiping his eyes, he said: Well, I'm glad you've witnessed me at my finest, but poor Justine. Ah, she's happy now. Her man's a bit of a blockhead, but he's a Nice Stable Fellow.

He leaned back in his chair. What about you, Ozanne? I mean, in that department. No hanky panky allowed on the border, that's what I hear.

You've heard right.

Sounds lonely. You never pay a visit to you-know-where with the others? Alain grinned.

I coughed and felt myself blush. Actually, did I ever mention my friend to you? Raimond Raboulet, he's an officer?

I think so. A little older than us, right? I know the guy you mean.

Yeah. I paused, then gave a laugh. Yesterday, he more or less proposed to me.

Alain didn't say anything, so I went on. Apparently there's no rule against two officers being, you know—so if I get promoted, he wants to try to move in together. I described the house with the peach trees, and the high wind grazing the aspens, and the hill that obscured the fencelight. As I spoke, I noticed Alain's expression growing displeased.

So what did you say to him? You said no, right?

I shook my head. I said yes.

His eyebrows shot up in dismay. You can't think you'll be happy like that.

I frowned, not sure why he seemed put out. I muttered something about happiness being relative, constrained by the options available. He looked skeptical, so, without really wanting to, I spoke in Raimond's defense, explaining that there weren't many gendarmes I got along with, that he'd been a good friend to me, not just someone to talk to, but also looking out for me, helping me, even transferring a guard because he'd been bothering me—yet as I recounted all this, Alain was impatient.

Sounds like your officer had an agenda from the start. You get a promotion, he gets in your pants. I bet he transferred that guard just to remove his competition. Cunning bastard. Sorry to break it to you, Ozanne, but I can always smell a schemer.

There was a smugness to his sympathy. I think you're wrong, I replied, and even if you're right, so what? If he's being calculating, what am I doing? I never said I felt that way about him. I weighed the factors and it's a better arrangement for me.

God no, it's fucking depressing, it sounds like a horrible life. Alain sighed upward, as though an audience on his dingy ceiling was nodding in agreement.

I didn't ask your opinion.

Look, I'm not trying to offend you, I just think you were meant for more than . . . that.

I glared. That's what people keep telling me. Raimond says aim higher. You say it's not high enough. Tomorrow my mother's going to explain for the hundredth time how I should've been a conseiller. All this great feedback—especially from you. I gestured cruelly at his room, but Alain glanced around unchastened.

You're welcome. Actually, I agree with your mother. You should've been a conseiller, I thought that was obvious.

I made an exasperated groan. There's no should've been, just what is. You adapt to it or you don't.

I didn't want to be dramatic and leave during a fight, but I didn't feel like visiting him anymore. I reached behind me on the mattress and found my jacket, holding it in warning. Alain, seated between me and the door, uncrossed his legs.

Please stay. I swear I'm not trying to be an asshole. You know it's my natural state.

He gave me a guilty smile, and suddenly it seemed like he was deliberating on something, tapping on his thighs more anxiously than before.

He leaned forward, looked me in the eye, and drew an almost exaggerated breath.

In fact, Odile, I've got a different pitch for you. Something I need your assistance with.

He was making an effort to keep smiling, but his nerves were showing, and with an acid feeling, I sensed what he was going to say.

Please don't let it be what I think.

He took his glasses off and set them on the table. I have to. You know I do. I'll just come out with it, okay? I need to get out of the valley.

I shut my eyes. Alain, don't.

I'm going west this September. You know why.

You can't say things like that to me.

He pulled his chair closer. That's why I'm asking you, Odile—*because* you're a guard. I don't know the best way to get over the fence, or where to hike between the valleys. All I know is when I need to be there. That's why I need your help. If you show me the way, I can do it. I can save him.

His eyes were wet and expectant. My intestines were clenched with barbed wire.

This is why you found me in January, isn't it?

No it's not. I promise it's not. But can't you see it's perfect if we do this together? It makes so much sense.

It doesn't make sense at all! You're talking about annihilation! Even if you could do it, you wouldn't just wake up in a new life where everything's better. None of us would.

Except Edme, he replied.

I fell silent and looked down. Burn marks were crusted into his industrial grey carpet. A wooden mousetrap was loaded without any bait.

Except Edme, Alain repeated. He'd be alive, like he should be. He didn't deserve what happened. He was the best fucking person I knew, and it was *my* fault. I told him to practice outdoors for his audition, even before his parents got strict. I kept harping on it. I know that's what he was doing when he fell.

They never found his violin, I said slowly.

It's the only explanation.

I looked at him. His eyes were no longer shining, but burning. Let's just talk, he said.


The day they found Edme he began drowning too, an inch at a time. Expelled from school, unwelcome at home, unable to work, yet able to drink. There were years he could scarcely remember. He was sure by now that he'd never leave the Raspail Rooms. In the guise of boozy cheek, he'd taken to asking guards if they'd ever spotted him older in Est 1, and although they blew him off, he watched for the recognition to flit across their faces, and it never did. To him this confirmed that he'd expire before his time, probably alone, probably in this shitty room, but in a way it didn't matter, because who could call this living. Alain's grief was alloyed with self-disgust. The specter of his lost friend, the good one, the brilliant one, in contrast with him, the wastrel. Why preserve this, he spat at his apartment in the same contemptuous way I had. It's hardly even a sacrifice.

So he wanted a map: Whatever I need to know, how long it takes to get there, which paths, what they look like, where to break through, how to escape here in the first place. I need to start by crossing the lake, that much is obvious. We could arrange a time to meet over there, maybe the beach at night, but you'd know better than me. All you have to do is get me out, and then that's it, I'll do the rest.

He paused at last. It was too ludicrous. I felt at a loss. Eventually I said that I'd never been to Ouest 1 myself, that I didn't even work on that side of the lake: You don't know what you're talking about, you don't know the first thing about it. My tone was so hard that he hesitated before pressing me again.

I get that there's obstacles, he allowed, and I don't even know all the obstacles, but that's why it's good we're talking. We've got this week to make plans while you're around. Do you have another downtown shift before September? No, okay, well a week should be enough—like I said, there are only a couple of decisions, the rest comes down to willingness.

I shook my head. Alain clasped and unclasped his hands, grimacing.

Sure, I get it, we need to talk more. And I guess I was just blabbing on about me. Typical. We should be talking about you.

No.

You're unhappy, I can see it. I promise I'm not trying to use you, I wasn't planning this when I ran into you at Val's. I'm glad you're back in my life and I get to know you again. But that's why I know this is the right thing for you too. This isn't how you were supposed to turn out, Odile. I drove my life into the ditch, but so did you, maybe even worse. You were smart! You were meant for the Hôtel de Ville, not the fucking border! You say you're making the best of it—the best of *what*? And now you're going to be somebody's kept woman? You know that Edme was in love with you, right?

Stop it.

It's true. You were meant to be with him.

Oh my god, I hardly knew him, it was twenty years ago! I've forgotten what he looked like!

Doesn't matter. Tell me you don't think about it.

I don't. I mean it, Alain, I could turn you in.

But you won't, he rejoined. You don't believe in that shit, I know you bend the rules. In the winter you did something to help that escapee, just like I said you should. Afterward you were practically the happiest I've ever seen you, buying drinks for the house. Am I wrong? I'm not going to bust you for it—that's how I knew I could *trust* you. You're not some hidebound guard, you see the greater good. You're not afraid to change things for the better. That's all this is! You can't name anyone who wouldn't be better off if we did this. Not me, definitely not you . . .

He cut himself short as a pair of footsteps approached on the balcony. The muffled laughter of a man and woman rose and fell. I took the opportunity to stand up and put my jacket on.

I've got to go, I said. I came to say hello, we had some wine, and that's it. If you want to visit Ouest 1, write a petition for the Conseil like everyone else, and don't bring this up again.

Alain stood to his full height, blocking my exit.

I'm not an idiot. Petitioning's pointless—I know about the kinship rule, otherwise I wouldn't be asking you.

Please, get out of my way!

He looked startled and let me pass. As I tugged on my boots, he sounded more contrite.

Odile, I'm sorry, I know this is scary, obviously I'm scared too. It makes sense you need some time. Let's meet again this week, okay? We can go for another walk, whatever you want. If you won't be back in town, we do kind of need to figure it out soon, but it doesn't have to be tonight.

He tried to smile at me as he opened the apartment door. I looked the other way and hurried for the stairs.

B irds sang in the cemetery. I was surprised to have slept. Vague dream memories were strewn about my mind as I got up, like isolated puddles proving it had rained.

Before I put on my robe and composed myself for Malcher I made myself come to some sort of resolution. A course of action, if one was required. The simplest thing would be to go to Jean-Savile. I was not the first gendarme to have been approached with a wild escape plan, and, to my knowledge, no one had ever gotten in trouble for coming forward. But it was still an association I was loath to make in the lead-up to the promotion decision—to say nothing of the fact that Alain suspected I'd acted improperly with the winter escapee. He might say something if I had him brought in. It didn't matter that I hadn't actually intervened on Lucie's behalf. I thought of Sanna being interviewed, furrowing his meaty forehead to recall my cryptic mention of a complaint, and shuddered at the consequences.

Moreover, as foolish as Alain's idea was, I did not want him to be punished. I could still remember how that regret felt; I imagined how it might have rotted inside me if I'd let it. It was terrible that he thought himself responsible. Edme had kept our night practices completely secret, as I had.

I swallowed and tried to think more impersonally. Voicing his desire was criminal, but merely possessing the desire was not. The temptation to escape was why the gendarmerie bothered patrolling within the town at all, instead of just the border: my presence near people's homes reminded them that their desires were known. Who could claim to be wholly free of fantasies? So then, I thought, if Alain's wish was banal, what difference did it make if he'd spoken it aloud? Was it any less banal? I shouldn't let a common weakness upset me just because I happened to know about it. Telling myself this, I tied my robe and had breakfast with Malcher as though nothing important had happened.

By coincidence, my day's first sector was the north end. I did an unthorough patrol of the area, skipping both the cul-de-sac and the lane where the Piras lived. I was driving past the school when the recess bell sounded, and at the familiar chime, children flowed from the cloakroom doors toward the field and playground, shouting in high voices, their bodies impossibly small. I pulled over for a minute and ate a snack as I watched them. All I saw were future griefs.

Sitting in the old neighborhood, I decided the safest response was to keep my distance and give Alain time to cool off. If he was smart enough to know he needed my help, then he was smart enough to give up if my help was withheld. It was possible that I'd see him again later in the week, or maybe it would be better to let it fully blow over, reconnecting in October or November when his request was moot and our disagreement past. The drinks at Val's would be on me. If it felt right, I could imagine suggesting we do something to commemorate Edme together, a small ceremony of our own.

The tea boat was busy by half six. Most people there were seniors, as my mother was herself, though this didn't stop her from grousing about them under her breath as the maître d' ushered us aboard. An elderly couple was slow-dancing in front of the dapper, frosty-haired pianist who was a fixture since my childhood. One or two groups braved the windy outer deck in preparation for the sunset. I followed my mother to our table by the window, overlooking the ornamental paddle wheel.

She talked about the archives and the scant chances of retiring in the absence of a proper successor. Her opinion of her apprentice had inevitably spoiled, Carina's work ethic was proving lackluster, and maybe that was why I found myself telling her that I was being considered for a commission on the border and had reasons to be optimistic. I might even be in line for accommodations with the senior officers, I added without mentioning Raimond, so she could visit me if she wanted to.

I anticipated a tart reply about the gendarmerie, but instead my mother offered me a smile. If you're happy about it, that's good, she said. I felt relieved, then, almost as quickly, peeved it had taken her this long to say something so simple. But it was not worth ruining dinner over. We ate and caught up, and the gaps in the conversation felt less stark than usual.

Moments after the waiter left our bill, a voice from behind me exclaimed: Well well, as I live and breathe!

My mother suddenly turned bashful. I glanced around in my seat. Jo stood grinning in the restaurant aisle. I hesitated, but she opened her arms, so I got up from the table and accepted a hard, jovial squeeze. I'd forgotten she was shorter than me, even with her heels on. Her voice had the same thrilled rush: Oh god, hasn't it been forever!

I agreed, shifting out of the hug. Her cheeks were flushed with delight; she looked genuinely charmed. I still felt dimmer standing in front of her.

Odile, she declared, you're exactly the same! Mme Ozanne, it's nice to see you too—sorry for interrupting cocktail hour.

Not at all, we've just finished our dinner. Today's Odile's birthday.

Jo widened her eyes at me. Really!

My mother rose, setting a small gift bag on the table. I hope it's the right kind, she said. I'm afraid I've got to get back to the office, I have a work situation—well, I'm sure you know Conseillère Tan and how she can get. She gave a good-natured eyeroll, which Jo returned gamely.

Odile, very nice to see you, my mother said, touching my arm. Mme Swain, have a lovely evening, and wish your family my best.

You too, said Jo. They're here, as a matter-of-fact, over yonder.

I looked to the far corner where there was a private booth on a riser. Behind the polished railing I recognized the Verdiers, sitting with Henri Swain and several children. Jo waved, so my mother and I raised our hands too. Her parents acknowledged us politely, and Henri delivered a cheerful salute.

So, Jo said after my mother left, are you back to work too, or do you have time for a toodle on the deck? I wanted to catch the sunset. She cajoled me with her brow.

She was wearing gold eyeshadow, fine mascara, and earrings of sharp black stone. Together we went to the coat check, where she retrieved a long white jacket and I took my standard-issue windbreaker. I was going to tuck it under my arm until we were outside, but Jo donned hers at the counter, saying, It's nippy out, you'll regret it. As we walked back through the crowded restaurant to the deck door, she slipped an elbow around mine and transmitted her parents a smile. So she had not lost her taste for provocation: it pleased her to be seen arm-in-arm with a uniformed guard.

But she was right, it was blustery on the deck. Jo went straight to the edge and exhaled as she arched her neck to the sky. It looked like a turbulent sunset, heavenly light igniting the clouds. Down the shoreline the lamps of the promenade had come on.

Thanks for joining me, she said. Do I love my kids? Yes, yes, and yes— she counted on her fingers—but they're nothing if not incessant. She flicked her fingers as if into the lake, and I gave a knowing nod that made her laugh. Just trust me, you dodged a bullet, or in my case, three.

She wore her hair in black ringlets now. I saw no traces of grey. She withdrew a cigarette from a petite purse and shielded the match expertly with her hand. I turned to look at the western ridge. For the first time, I wondered whether children were something else Raimond might expect. Surely there were rules against that.

What'd you get? Jo asked. She gestured at the gift bag in my hand.

I don't know, I said, reluctantly looking inside. To my surprise it was a new chisel, its handle made of red cherrywood. A size I already owned, but a thoughtful gift from my mother, conceding something to my interests.

That bad? Jo smirked.

No. It's a hobby. This might be the best thing she's gotten me, maybe ever.

Jo gave the chisel a dubious glance and took a drag from her cigarette. Happy birthday, mine's in July. Thirty-six, good god, it's practically forty. What is it with age, how sometimes a number seems normal, and other times it seems completely bizarre?

I ventured a laugh. I don't know. It feels normal to me. I guess we always have our whole lives to prepare for the age that we are.

Ha, clever. She tilted her chin and blew smoke at the purpling mountains. The smoke vanished instantly on the wind. Personally I can't believe it's been so long since school. And the vetting program—twenty years! Too bad neither of us could cut the mustard. My folks got over it, it turns out they get to schmooze with the conseillers regardless. Seems like your mom survived too.

I nodded, putting the chisel back in the bag.

Wait, Jo realized, that makes today your sweet sixteenth! Right? Is your party happening right now? I forget, was I invited? Are you and I together over there?

I don't think I had a party that year.

Not even with Rosso and Pira? They were your people.

I hadn't really met them yet.

What are you talking about? Everybody knew everybody. Although I suppose you had your solitary streak, Jo reflected. Those two were something, weren't they, always marching to the beat of their own whatever. They should've cut Alain some slack about school. Sometimes he digs irrigation for us in the vineyards, but I'm sure you've heard he's a drunk. It's depressing. But *Justine*! Talk about dodging bullets, imagine her with him nowadays! Richard makes so much more sense for her, I said that the day I introduced them. He's got a big mouth too, but the girl's got her type—it figures she went for Alain. Are you in touch at all?

Me and Justine?

No, Alain.

I made a noncommittal gesture.

It's just as well. You're not missing much.

There was a knock behind us. One of her kids, a boy around eight, waved through the glass door and motioned toward her table.

They've sent a hunter, she deadpanned, pulling a face at her son and raising her hands in faux surrender. The boy dawdled, fascinated by me, then retreated into the restaurant.

There you have it. Well, I've appreciated the reprieve. Too short! Next time you'll have to regale me with some of your border tales. We should have you over to the house, I know Henri and the kids would want to hear all about it. So would I!

She touched my arm goodbye like my mother had. I watched her walk toward the door.

Jo, do you mind if I ask you something?

She stopped, quizzical. I glanced down the deck. The nearest people were out of earshot.

This will sound strange, it's been forever. I guess you made me think of it because you mentioned Edme.

I saw her frown, but I pressed on ahead of my blush. Back then, before the accident. Were you two . . .

Jo's expression shifted. She looked at me strangely.

No. We weren't. Is that your question? Of course not. He liked you.

I was silent. She rolled her eyes and smiled: Come on, you knew.

I forced a limp laugh.

Odile! It was obvious!

How?

For starters, I have eyes, but also, didn't he tell me? Yeah! We were at the cove, you must've been there.

Do you remember what he said?

Oh, not word for word, I was probably teasing him—I think he used some formality, like he 'had feelings'? He was shy about telling you, I re-member that. But not in a butterflies way, more like he thought it was presumptuous of him or something. I don't know, it's been too long. God, wasn't he serious?

I never knew, I said. My voice was almost too quiet to be heard over the wind and waves.

She hesitated and looked pained. Maybe, with what happened, that was for the best? Or not—it's horrible either way. I'm sorry, Odile, that was always so sad.

I nodded and turned back toward the lake. I heard the door open and close, a brief draft of piano and merriment.

The sunset was over. The few others who'd been on the deck had gone back inside too. Alone in the twilight, I tightened my fingers around the cold railing. Though it was muffled, I heard Jo's rich laughter at the family table, feigning annoyance at her children.

On the other side of the mountains, I was sitting alone at our dining table. My mother sang in her timorous voice as she carried my birthday cake from the fridge. Soon, in just a few months, he and I would befriend one another; he would start coming to my window. A small lump rose in my throat. I left the tea boat and walked without a destination, first down the windy promenade and back, then up the boulevard. In the Place du Bâtisseur, sheltered from the lake, the night was gentler. Spotlights lit up the colonnade and spread shadows across the square. I sat for a bit on the steps of the Hôtel de Ville with my back against a column, watching kids lounge at the fountain. A girl shrieked and leapt up. A boy chased her around the statue. He caught her and wrestled her, threatening to push her into the water. She struggled, then admonished him with a kiss.

The gift bag from my mother sat beside me on the step. I rotated the new chisel in my hand. Only then did I realize I had forgotten my prints: in my haste to end our conversation, I'd left them at Alain's. I would have to see him again after all.

I left the manse at dawn. The day felt alive: the grass and leaves gave off a fine morning steam, and the chapelyard's air smelled of spearmint blooming. I got in the truck and drove north.

I turned at the empty schoolgrounds and parked in the cul-de-sac. At the bus stop I sat listening to the engine tick. I had just shy of an hour before patrol.

Halfway down the steps to the cove I sensed the nearness of the lake, a deep blue glinting through the pines, the sounds of a few early boats. Instead of continuing to the beach I climbed over the railing and walked left into the brush. Scores of tan moths fluttered from the tree trunks where they'd been camouflaged, pinging off my uniform in panic. The cliff path was mangier than I remembered, hardly an intimation in the brambly slope. Where the trail began snaking toward the clifftop, I stopped and peered down into the steep forest separating me from the beach.

I couldn't picture the exact place I was looking for. I thought a bush had been nearby. If there was anything more distinctive about the spot, it was forgotten, replaced by the memory of black rims under my fingernails. The path thickened with thorns but I decided to go all the way to the cliff. I didn't want to, but hoped it would be easier to remember if I was walking in the same direction as before. Where the forest broke open and the ground hardened to rock, I stepped out onto the high vista.

Far below me, the water was motionless. Giant rocks lolled under the glassy surface. I looked around the valley. The floating fence transected the lake, distant and needle-bright. The night's last fog departed up the western mountains.

I saw where I'd found the violin: a small depression at the cliff's edge filled with hispid moss and coral lichens. Quickly, I turned back down the path. I let my feet lead, trying to outpace my conscious memory. When it felt right I cut to the side and stumbled down into the brush, fighting my speed, fearing I was going too far. But as I caught hold of a tree trunk, disturbing more moths, I noticed a familiar-looking bush with crimson stems.

Again I dug with my hands. At first I found nothing, but in a second attempt my fingers touched something hard. I cleared clayish soil from the remains of a wooden case.

The lid had caved in. All the leather exterior was gone. There were still corroded clasps down one side, small fists of black rust. When I tried to undo them they were fused shut, but my efforts split the box open on the other side, so that was how I opened it.

It was an undifferentiated cavity of wreckage. The violin had rotted into its case. Most of the body was destroyed, leaving only a curve of blanched wood at the base of the split neck. Sifting cautiously, I unearthed the stick of the bow and a narrow chalice-shaped piece that I didn't recognize. The four tuning pegs, hard little spoons, had been preserved, as well as a rust-spotted tuning fork that I tapped against my knee. Its hum faded into the forest. Sliding brown roots crept through the bottom of the debris like hairless tails.

It was much more decomposed than I'd imagined. If memories were objects, I thought, this was how they would look. The damage reminded me of a fire that I'd once helped to clean. Several houses had burned on the edge of town, the cause never revealed, and Jean-Savile sent us as a good-will gesture. I entered my assigned house to gather anything salvageable. The stairs to the second story were partly collapsed, and once I'd made it, the floor had chasms that I had to navigate carefully. Many of the rooms were impossible to enter. I saw books on the shelves whose spines bulged hideously, titles scorched off. Stinking black spillage had erupted from the closets, and some kind of sandy substance had been purged from the attic and piled up everywhere, heavier than ash.

I knelt now in front of similar waste. I picked up one of the tuning pegs. Though it was discolored, it still had the smoothness of tumbled stone. Holding it like a talisman, I concentrated on remembering him: how he had really looked, how it had felt when he looked at me. He was sitting in the music room at school. I watched him pluck two strings, listen, and tighten a peg. The tone rose slightly, inquisitively, an astonished lifting *oh*. He raised a bemused eyebrow and smiled, inviting me in on the joke, whatever the joke was in that moment.

Sadly, I smiled back. The image was one that I'd thought of many times before. It was not a memory; it was a reenactment of a fact. The bemused face was not really his. For a long time, this gradual depletion had anguished me, but the absence was no longer acute. He was a child, and he belonged to childhood. I had come this morning with a restlessness I couldn't fully articulate, but now it settled. I could not feel him anymore, not even here. I rested my hand for a moment on the exhumed grave.

A long black centipede sped from the ruins of the violin, legs flowing like lake grass. I retracted my hand with a gasp, and there was a skittering snap behind me. It was only a bird or a squirrel, fleeing from my surprise, but I shoved the tuning peg in my pocket and reburied the case rapidly, patting it down and covering the mound. I wiped soil off my pants and picked clinging nettles from my socks. At the top of the steps I calmly reentered the cul-de-sac, back from patrolling the cove.


I put off going to the Raspail Rooms that night and the next, and avoided tavern row. I ate meals alone, carved in the diner, and spent evenings in the manse. On my last day in town, I intended to wait until late and then stop by Alain's to retrieve my book of prints. So I was taken aback when I returned from the diner at seven o'clock to see Malcher sitting with the oilskin book spread open on his lap.

He made a performance of turning an oversized mulberry page, and gave me a sly grin. He had some sort of meatloaf resting beside him on the settee.

You did all these yourself, Ozanne?

I tried to sound unperturbed, to react like a blanket tossed over a fire. Where'd you find that?

Ha, good one. Where do you think? You had a visitor—that tavern rat Rosso.

He eyed me as I bent into the fridge. Oh right, I said, I was showing him at the bar, I must've left it there. I was going to ask Val if he'd seen it lying around.

Weird. That's not what Rosso said. He said he was delivering it from the Raspails.

I focused on opening a bottle of beer. I'm sure that's true. He probably took it home, then brought it here. Nice of him to drop it off.

Malcher smiled. I went to the settee and he relinquished my book without objection. You're pretty good at these pictures, he said, but you're crap at telling stories.

I don't know what you're talking about.

Really. It looked like he'd been waiting to see you all day. He ran over from the graveyard and made me swear to give you this right away. He was very, what do I want to say? Passionate.

I scoffed and retired to my room, but I heard his self-satisfied laughter through the door, and I cursed Alain. It was beyond reckless to show up here, but I was sure that wasn't the worst of it. I hunted through the pages for a message. At first I found only a stray black hair that looked like one of Malcher's, but when I flipped to a print of the plateau cabin, a square of paper slipped out.

He'd folded it like a classroom note. I tore it open. The letterhead was a blue lithograph advertising Val's—stationery, apparently, from the bar's unseedy past. Next to the address Alain had written a meeting time for later tonight. Below that, he'd sketched a map, or an appeal for one. The landscape was rudimentary, but I recognized two valleys. A dotted line traveled out of one and continued toward the next, terminating in the blank expanse between them. In the mountains was a single question mark, bold and imploring.

Malcher would have discovered it if I hadn't come back when I did. I grabbed a pencil from the nightstand and slashed an angry X across the page. Looking at the result, I pictured myself thrusting it at Alain in front of all the rubberneckers at Val's. I ripped the note into strips and waited until I heard Malcher go out.

In a corner of the dark cemetery where there was no one I knew, I nested the strips of paper on a flat gravestone and dropped a match. Within seconds the nest had burned down to nothing. I blew its ashes over the moist grass.

Sleep that night was frayed by fear. What if Alain blundered back after last call? But he didn't, and by morning, it seemed my silence had been understood. A disheveled Malcher drove us back to the border under dreary skies. Before the orchard outpost, he stopped to vomit in a ditch filled with tiny white flowers. I put my head out the opposite window, trying to breathe the aroma of the ripening trees. Drizzle tapped on the truck's roof. This time I was glad to be going home. Malcher returned wiping his lips, and when he saw my distaste, he winked.

*

Raimond had already filled my breakfast tray. He'd used an upside-down saucer to keep my coffee warm, but it didn't fit and his hapless I-tried gesture made me smile. He said nothing about the answer I'd slipped under his door—the mess hall was busy, and other guards were at our table—but there was a noticeable change in his demeanor. He let his eyes linger on me undisguised, saying we should have dinner that night. He wasn't off duty until after serving hours, but he'd have the kitchen set something aside for us. I told him I was looking forward to it.

Good. Because on the subject of looking forward . . . it's possible there was a little development while you were in town.

Yeah?

A decision on the career front courtesy of Jean-Savile.

I stopped eating. Tell me.

It's not my news to share, Raimond hummed, failing to hide his pleasure.

I was distracted all day. I paced the watchtower platform more times than necessary, ignoring the steady rain. I searched the misty landscape in my field glasses, but could find nothing to take my mind off Raimond's news. I recalled him saying I would be summoned if I got the commission, and even though it would never happen in the middle of a shift, whenever I heard a patroller on the path below I tensed with anticipation.

Rationally I knew it was done: Raimond was privy to the information and his insinuation couldn't have been clearer. I had gotten it. Yet I also knew that I would not stop looking for reasons to doubt it until I heard Jean-Savile speak the words, so I remained on edge.

The rain dwindled at nightfall. I waited out my last hour under the watchtower's trickling eaves. A single seam appeared in the clouds, a vein of weak stars. When the night guard showed up I hurried to meet Raimond for dinner.

The cook was locking up the kitchen, but I assumed Raimond had a master key. I went to our usual table to wait. Across the mess hall two guards were playing cards. Out the window I saw someone coming from the main gate, but it was Page bringing back the mail from the exchange post. After half an hour I began considering scenarios that might have delayed Raimond. I stayed for another few minutes, glancing up at any footfall, but decided he could find me in my quarters.

My hair was still a bit wet from the rain so I toweled it off at the sink. I had let it get long, unspooling down my face like wisteria. I'd meant to go for a cut downtown but I was beginning to like it; maybe I'd keep growing it out.

There was a knock at my door. I opened it expecting Raimond. Instead it was Coltelli.

Jean-Savile wants a word.

My lungs tightened. I grabbed my keys and jacket. Coltelli walked swiftly down the floodlit path, and I followed.

His office door was ajar. I heard a chair creak inside. Come in, said Jean-Savile.

He motioned me into the worn leather chair and went to the shelf where he kept his teapot and cups. I sat down, thinking he was making us tea, but Jean-Savile reached directly for an olive-green folder and laid it on the desk.

It's been brought to my attention that you've become involved with a civilian.

My face went cold.

There are challenges here for women, Jean-Savile said. The men have their outlet in town, I'm aware of the disparity. But letting you off with a warning is impossible. Word is already going around. Not to mention that the policy is important and contravening it is serious, as you know.

My words came out airless. Sir, if I could . . . I'm not sure what Malcher said, but he's wrong. I thought he might have gotten the wrong impression. I should have come to you myself. I assume he's talking about Alain Rosso? He stopped by the manse to say hi—he didn't know any better—but he's just an acquaintance, a school friend. That's all. Malcher resents being partnered with me. He didn't give you any actual evidence, did he? He couldn't have, because there is none.

Jean-Savile's eyes hardened. Malcher verified the situation, but he wasn't the source. Your school friend came to the orchard checkpoint today and asked to speak to Raimond Raboulet. He unburdened his conscience of his own accord.

My mind flurried. Jean-Savile sighed and opened the folder.

As to where we go from here: your promotion application is denied. It's a pity. Normally we'd go through the process of trial and sentencing, but I've decided to spare you the embarrassment and simply apply the standard rank reduction. Also, Raimond reminded me of a staffing gap on the western border, so as of tonight I'm transferring you across the lake. The timing works well for them, not to mention that a bit of distance from town means fewer temptations for you.

He rotated a form to me. It was a transfer order bearing the signatures of Jean-Savile, Coltelli, and R. Raboulet, personnel officer. My name was typed below the remaining line. The *N* key had stuck repeatedly on my last name, blackening its center, a frenzy of *N*s.

Let me explain, I whispered.

No need. Jean-Savile passed me a pen. Aubuchon is downtown tonight. He'll meet you at the dock. If you don't cross within an hour they'll be too far gone to show you your new quarters, so pack your things and take a truck.

Even if he had not walked me out and watched my numb return to the barracks, even if I could have run to the officers' wing to hit my fists against Raimond's door, there was nothing I could say. If Alain was willing to do this much, he would not hesitate to see me convicted of coordination with Lucie too. In my room I stuffed clothes into my rucksack with whatever else would fit: my carving satchel, my rolled book of prints, each thing shoved more hatefully than the next.

The guard in the orchard passed the logbook through the window. I signed it and marked the time—now I had half an hour to be at the dock. As I pulled away I thought the guard was concealing laughter. He might have been on duty and overheard Alain's malicious, tawdry lie. I drove faster through the dense leaves, the truck bouncing violently on the orchard road. The lights of town grew visible at the end of the trees. At the first intersection the red light rocked on its lonely wire. Before it turned green, I cranked the wheel and sped toward tavern row.

He was easy to find. Alain was hunched outside Val's in a holey sweater, apart from the other smokers. As I slammed the truck door I heard a band playing, drums clattering through the bar's open windows.

He saw me and seemed to wither. The people on the sidewalk watched me grab his arm and drag him into the alley. It looked like I was arresting him, although I'd already surrendered my gun. I pushed Alain against the wall beside a trash bin.

What did you do?

He could hardly look at me straight. He was very drunk, his lips rubbery and mangled with guilt.

Ozanne, I fucked up.

How could you say that to *him*, of all people! You wanted to get revenge on me that badly?

No, no, not revenge—we were running out of time. I asked you for help, you weren't answering.

So what! How does it help you to destroy my career? They took away my commission, I lost my rank, everything!

Sorry. I was drinking, it was a bad idea. Alain drew a shaky breath and almost managed to meet my eyes. You said you worked on the wrong side of the lake to help me, but Officer Raimond transfers guards there to punish them, so I thought, what if he wanted to punish you . . . that's all. It was just, um, practical. But once I saw the look on his face, I thought, you know, maybe I shouldn't have.

I stared at him in disbelief.

He did transfer me.

What?

I've been transferred. I'm going to the western border now.

Alain's mouth underwent a strange contortion, amazement wriggling under his shame. You're kidding! What the hell! It's not too late then, we can still swing this!

You *wanted* me sent there? This is what you were hoping for? You don't know what it's like there, it's horrible!

Yeah, that's what everyone says . . . Isn't that more reason to help me?

I was dumbstruck. But you're the one who did this to me!

As abruptly as his hope had resurfaced, he fell back on begging. I don't know what else you want me to say, Odile, please just do this for me. I can't get there without you. I'm an asshole, fuck me, you're right—so don't do it for me then, do it for yourself, do it for him.

Oh my god. I turned around to leave, but felt a savage surge and turned back. You know I already could have, Alain? I could have saved him twenty years ago.

Don't blame yourself, he mumbled.

No. I'm saying that I *knew*. His parents came for a viewing and I recognized them. I knew something was going to happen to him. Pichegru knew, and the Conseil knew, and me. That's why we became friends in the first place—I was reporting on him to the Conseil. I could've warned him, I could have said something to him, but I did what I was supposed to do. I let him fall. All those days you spent searching for him, I already knew he was dead.

In the dark alley Alain's face drained white; his eyes brimmed with ruin. He took an uncertain step away from me. I had nothing more to say to him either. I left him, I got in the truck and rubbed my eyes with my fists, I reported to the dock on time.

S weat rolled out of my kerchief and dripped onto the floor. I was on my hands and knees, so my shirt was buttoned to the throat.

Manduca watched me from the end of the hall. In a lazy rhythm, he struck his baton against his leg, clicking whatever was in his pocket. I wrung my sponge into the pail and continued scrubbing as he approached. His boots squeaked. He said nothing as he passed, but his trousers grazed my shoulder. I smelled the starch of the fabric mingled with the pail's ammoniac swill.

The door swung shut behind him. I dropped my sponge on the last dry patch of floor. In the near distance, I could make out the sound of the skiff reaching the lakeshore. Its engine cut, a sudden silence echoing over the western woods. It was the first day of September. I knew who was scheduled to leave on their mourning tour.

Stonefaced guards would be standing by as the boat drifted in. Manduca would offer his hand to the passengers, who would take it with nervous gratitude. He would pull them onto the dock one at a time, a little too roughly considering their age, and his patronizing smile would never waver.

Their escort had been selected only the night before. Unlike the clockwork rotation of duties on the eastern border, Manduca made a show of hand-picking the guard himself, teasing the men with his decision. Since entering Ouest 1 was always risky, the task came with a significant bonus, and everyone wanted to be chosen. This self-advocacy was treacherous, as Manduca enjoyed toying with and quashing hopes in his fiefdom. The lucky guard was a broad-shouldered, shaggy-headed man named Cassar, who immediately set to gloating and soaking up the fraternal animus. As I watched him from the kitchen's serving window, I thought I remembered how the guard's hair had stuck out from behind his mask as he stood at the pond with the Piras.

There was never any question of my escorting them, or even coming into contact with them before they left. My rank had been reduced to that of a new recruit, the only difference being that I would stay that way forever. On this side of the lake I had not so much as patrolled the border, and never would. Manduca told the others I was barely competent for cadet work as it was.

I looked at my reflection in the bucket of rinsewater. I was not yet the woman I'd witnessed in Est 1, coldly raising her head from this floor—but I could feel myself coarsening. Each day my hands reddened and my knuckles protruded further from malnutrition because my rations had been cut with my rank. I wondered how soon I would acquire her crutch, and tried not to think about why. Yet I thought about her constantly. When I arrived at the kitchen at dawn to take orders from the surly cook. When I cleaned the common buildings in between meals. When I dug out the stinking latrines, and burned the camp's garbage, and scalded their soiled uniforms. I knew the verdict she had issued on her life: she'd sought to erase it from the earth. One day Lucie Erro would come again, desperate for her own salvation. Taking advantage of her was grotesque, but my winter reasoning still stood. What would come of her escape attempt without my intervention? She would still die, and nobody would benefit. Thus could rationalizations be polished down to facts; scruples could erode over time. Time, though, was the worst thing to contemplate. For no matter how hardened I became to Lucie's plight, that chance would not present itself for almost twenty years—and there was no reason to think it would succeed, having plainly failed already.

The hallway was clean. I propped the door open with a brick that was warm to the touch. The dampness inside would evaporate quickly. I checked the clock and saw it was time to begin preparing the men's lunch. I locked the mop in the utility closet and walked to the kitchen, which sat in a field of desiccated bunchgrass like a concession stand stranded from the beach.

In the days leading up to the Piras' departure, their trip had been the main topic around the fire ring where the guards took their meals. After ladling their runny stew I hung back in the shade with a bin for their dishes. They sat on rocks and stumps, slurping from tin bowls and tossing wadded-up bread at the dogs. From the shadows I overheard fragments of news.

Some cared only about who led the viewing party, but others talked about the case: the age of the visitors, their stamina, the interference risks. Most guards had dim recollections of the missing boy. He was a north end kid, one remembered through a mouthful of stew. But after Cassar and the Piras were on their way up to the plateau cabin, talk about them ceased. There was always tension in the valley during visits to Ouest 1. In town, extra chapel services were held for those seeking reassurance. The attending conseiller listened patiently to people's concerns, then repeated platitudes about safety and led them through their prayers.

The western guards transmuted whatever anxiety they felt into violence. On the night the Piras left I was cleaning dishes when I heard cheering. I went to the door and saw two gendarmes swinging loose punches. One shoved the other into the fire. He thrashed his way out in a gale of sparks, swatting at himself until Manduca called, Uh oh, your back. The guard craned his neck frantically and dashed for the lake. Everyone stifled themselves until the splash, then erupted, and Manduca raised a bottle to the victor. I watched Manduca grin in the flickering light. He didn't yet wear the bushy moustache I knew from my trips east; it had taken me a while to get used to his younger face. He smiled a lot for an angry man. He had fine control of his temper, so his anger sat still on the surface, like hot asphalt.

*

The start of September passed without outward event, but the hours felt slower on the day that my life's course was being reinscribed across the mountains. I was cleaning the shower room when the clock turned three. I imagined the school bell ringing, and my essay being rejected by Pichegru, and walking into the backwoods alone. Dozing off in the newfound fort until the sound of hushed voices roused me.

I checked and rechecked my memories as the minutes passed. It was a temptation undiminished by its futility; what else was there to think about? As the day turned to dusk, the story seemed unchanged. I still remembered the black masks, and running into Edme, and leaving the schoolgrounds with him.

That night the cook, Bellamy, waved a bowl at me with a long red hair stuck to the bottom, evidence presented by a pissed-off guard. As penance I had to clean all the dishes over again, and didn't get out of the kitchen till late. I moved carefully on the unlit trail, passing the men's cabins without snapping a twig.

My cabin on the beach was the last one before the fence pierced the lake. The inside had a sulfurous smell. The floor was so uneven that an apple would roll down its length, and the boards sagged into the sand wherever I stepped. The window's curtain was clearly fashioned from an old tablecloth, and a tatty red rug was spattered with hard candlewax. My rucksack slumped on a wooden chair, still half packed; I had not carved since coming here. I fetched dull scissors and a flask from beside my cot and went back out, leaving the door open to release the day's residual heat.

I sat on my driftwood bench and drank. The border liquor that had once scorched my throat now soothed it, as healing to my stomach as tea. By this time in Ouest 1, the girl would be into her mother's wine. Perhaps she was already scrawling her defiant rant, blustering about what she'd seen, disparaging the tradition of the viewing parties, identifying the visitors by name. I looked out at the quiet waves. Across the lake, the Hôtel de Ville stood over the sleeping town, its granite façade washed in pale spotlights.

Once the flask was empty I picked up the scissors and hacked my hair short. My curls fell on the moonlit sand. When I went back in I locked the door.

Gagne, whom Raimond had transferred before me, was at the dock the night I first arrived. When I saw him smirking with his hand outstretched, I could not make myself touch him. Everyone, this is Odile, he announced. His lips gave a lewd shape to my name.

I slept little in those early weeks, sitting up with my mother's chisel, the best weapon I now possessed. It would be a lie to say that, during those nights, my thoughts had never turned to escape. If I could get to Ouest 1, I could try to prevent Edme's death myself, and in that way put an end to this. No doubt Alain clung to this hope as well, despite how badly we'd parted. What do you have to lose, he'd demanded in the Raspail Rooms. When I told him, he listened, and made sure I lost all of it.

I was no different from any guard: I'd considered the various steps. It was a mental exercise to pass the time on patrol, and helped with anticipating escapees' moves. Along the eastern fence, I'd noticed where the ground was lowest under the fence's bottom wire, and where the floodlights were dimmest between the watchtowers, and when a patroller would be walking away instead of approaching, and when a shift change left a short gap at night. In nearly two decades on the border it would have been strange not to have observed such things. But on the west side of the lake, the only sections of the fence I'd been close to were the main gate and this beach. Both had towers that were permanently manned. If the fence had any vulnerability, it could take me up to twenty years to find it. One thing I knew was that the guard coverage here was denser, partly because of the higher stakes of western interference, and partly because of the border's compact length. So my thoughts of breaking out led me nowhere.

When the wind rose outside my cabin, the waves picked up. I would not hear anyone coming across the sand. But when the wind died down, there was never any sound. Gradually I lowered my guard.

The re-entry bells rang down the mountainside. Everyone left their dinners at the campfire and assembled at the gate. In the kitchen's entrance, Bellamy lit a cigarette and considered my shabby haircut for not the first time that day. He offered me his pack and I stood and smoked beside him.

It took some time for the viewing party to actually arrive at the fence. The guards stood in impatient silence. Finally pebbles rolled down the steep path accompanied by the crunch of boots. The dogs began barking. I couldn't help but look.

Cassar was first, his rucksack slung on his shoulder. He flashed two fingers at Manduca, the sign for a failed trip. I absorbed what it meant: the Piras had never gotten to see Edme after I'd interrupted their attempt at the pond. They had gone to Ouest 1 for nothing.

I watched them come down the trailhead. Though their tunics and masks were off, they moved the same way I remembered from long ago. It seemed as if Mme Pira was having trouble walking and M. Pira was keeping her upright with his arm linked around hers. Cassar, already at the fence, yawned.

The gate opened and the searches started. Now I could hear Mme Pira weeping, even at a distance. I tried to withdraw into the kitchen.

Look it, growled Bellamy. Crows.

Several birds were bouncing between plates at the campfire, snagging scraps in their beaks.

Go scare them off.

I picked up a handful of stones. They mostly hit the campfire itself, sending up a feeble spray of sparks. One crow fluttered and landed near a different plate. Bellamy gave me a shove.

Hurry up, we're not cooking twice tonight.

With a reluctant glance at the gate, I walked to the fire ring. The birds were undaunted, and I had to circle continuously to keep them away from the food. Each time my orbit took me closer to the Piras and the phalanx of guards, I angled my head the other way.

But the Piras weren't looking in my direction; there was some kind of conflict at the fence. It seemed that Mme Pira was resisting the search. M. Pira attempted to help, but a guard held him back. I heard her make an incoherent sob, and thought I understood: she was not willfully disobeying, she was just too upset to comply.

For fuck's sakes, yelled Gagne. Someone else deal with this. Odile!

I froze by the fire. The twin lines of guards turned toward me. I stood, exposed, in my kitchen apron.

If we're going to have women they can handle this shit. Come over here, now.

Bellamy shook his head and left the kitchen to fend off the crows himself. With no option, I went to the gate.

Mme Pira had her back to me. She cried in ragged shudders. M. Pira was still being restrained, but he'd stopped struggling. Instead, he was reasoning with Manduca. In a tight voice he explained that Cassar had been negligent, failing to try another viewing spot after nothing came of the first. From the pond, he'd taken them straight back to the tour quarters and locked them in their room.

I tried not to make eye contact with them. The contents of their bags had been dumped on the ground. The black masks that had so frightened me as a child lay in the raked dirt with vacant eyes.

Go ahead, Gagne ordered me, you've done this before.

Mme Pira was covered in dust from the hike. I reached out and touched her shoulder. She didn't react, so I eased my hands under her arms and patted her in a perfunctory search, feeling the frail limbs under her clothes. I looked over at Gagne, hoping to be done.

Great, now the front, he sneered. He rotated Mme Pira to face me. Her eyes were bleary and far away. Like this, Gagne continued, moving his hands down to her waist and letting them linger there.

You get the idea, he said. He stepped away to search M. Pira himself.

I stood in Gagne's footprints in front of Edme's mother. Tears streaked through the dirt on her cheeks. I whispered that I was sorry. Gently, I brushed the backs of my hands over her and knelt to feel her baggy trousers. But when I stood up again, confusion entered her eyes. She parted her cracked lips.

Was it you, on the playground?

I evaded her look, acting like I hadn't registered the question. M. Pira was now scrutinizing my features too, but Gagne and Manduca didn't notice.

Wrap it up, Manduca said. He told the Piras to come along. Edme's parents stooped for their bags and followed him haggardly. Mme Pira looked back, this time more hollowed out, a face like a wound. I felt a spasm of guilt, then anger: *No, you wounded me, look where I am because I saw you.* I took refuge in the kitchen and attacked the pots with the scrubbing brush while the guards finished their meal in the dusk.

The camp relaxed whenever a viewing party returned. As soon as the puttering of the skiff signaled the Piras' departure for the downtown marina, mocking hosannas broke out. Cassar loped back from the showers with wet hair and an open shirt, and drinks began flowing his way.

There were rumors of an impending visit by the brothel. Each season Manduca chartered a houseboat to cross the lake as compensation for the infrequency of downtown furloughs. From the kitchen window I heard Cassar boasting that he'd been saving up his bonuses, he'd always wanted to rent out the whole boat at once.

Bellamy had joined the rest of them at the campfire. In the kitchen there was only the dissonant buzz of the freezer and the flies. The sink had gone cold with a greasy sheen, but the bin of dirty dishes overflowed in the jaundiced light. I risked stealing a burnt dinner roll, hardly chewing in my hurry to swallow. I washed it down with some cooking sherry from a sticky bottle and started cleaning the plates.

*

Reveille thudded down the shoreline. My eyelids opened to distant drums, the weary sound of morning.

I sipped from my flask on my driftwood bench. The lake was dull and fishy smelling. A severed gull's wing with a marble of blood lay on the sand. Farther up the beach I saw the watchtower guard descend his ladder. He went to the bushes and urinated, leaning his head back the way that men did. My eyes drifted to the empty tower. I turned the violin's tuning peg in my pocket, digging its petrified tip into my thigh. The guard returned from the bushes buttoning his pants, this time throwing me a bored nod. A moment later his rifle barrel poked over the platform's handrail.

Each day, as I went about my work, I was aware of what was happening in the younger valley. Few memories were vivid. Many felt emblematic, portraits of types instead of particulars. If it was a school day I remembered the classroom: the satisfying smell of wood oil, Pichegru's block letters on the blackboard. I pictured the bus rolling into the cul-de-sac to take me to the Grande École. There was a mirage-like quality to these general memories, hovering just above the ground.

But as September advanced, the events became more distinct. Some of them were fond, some were bittersweet, and still others surprised me with their pain, like the sensitivity of old fractures. One night I left my cabin and walked into the bushes by myself. It was, I believed, one of the warm evenings when Edme and I had sneaked out to practice for his audition. His violin had been so deafening that it seemed to soar across the sky. I listened. There was nothing except the rustling nearness of the trees.

The Friday came when Jo was dismissed from the vetting program. It was also, of course, the day I progressed to the final round, but what I remembered was not my own excitement or my mother's exultation: it was Jo's face changing shades as she exited the parlor classroom, and the sound of her feet on the stairs.

On Saturday, Manduca announced the coming of the houseboat. The campfire whistled in anticipation, and those who were short on money began urgently grubbing for loans. It was due to dock at nightfall but the boat ended up being late. The gendarmes got restless, and when the boat finally announced itself with a toot of the horn, a crowd bustled to the dock. Their hoots were followed by teasing laughter through the trees. I found it oddly touching to hear the sound of women's voices, and stood for a minute before loading my wheelbarrow for the trash pit. The sullen guards Manduca had scheduled to work carried their guns up to the fence.

I woke up earlier than usual the next morning to go for a swim. Judging from the brothel visits in the spring and summer, the guards were allowed to sleep in, which reduced my chance of being seen. In my towel I stepped out under the predawn sky and locked my cabin. There was only a mild breeze. When I reached the ribbon of black sand at the lake's edge, my toes sank in, and I smiled.

I checked the watchtower. I'd walked far enough past the floodlights that the duty guard wouldn't notice me, so I left my towel on the beach and slipped into the water. The lake was gloriously cool. Days of grime lifted from my skin. Pushing off the soft lakebed, I swam beyond where I could stand. In slow strokes, I followed the moonlight pooling on the surface of the lake, a shining disc that receded from my approach.

I floated. The night's final stars swayed atop the world. My body, rib-white, drifted in the inky water. It had been hours now since the girl had fled from the cove, confused and jealous and scared to swim naked with the others.

Then I heard a sound on the shore. Instinctively I sank down to my chin. I blinked water from my eyes. Three men were outside my cabin.

I recognized the slope of Gagne's neck. He motioned to his companions. One knocked on my door. The guard waited, then knocked harder— a taunting rhythm. Gagne moved him aside and went to the door himself. A second later, my cabin door opened.

He had a key. Of course he did. As the men entered my quarters, I began swimming backward, keeping my limbs underwater so as not to splash. I saw flashlights swiping behind my curtain. There was magenta on the horizon now. If the sun came up they would surely see me.

Gagne reappeared in the doorway and took a few steps down the beach. I submerged myself even more, my feet entering colder water that it felt like the sun never touched. I willed his eyes away from my towel on the shore. Then I noticed what he must have heard: it was a distant outboard motor, the skiff departing the marina on the other side of the lake. Gagne said something to the others. They left my cabin for the trail to camp.

The skiff reached the western dock and turned around as soon as it had come. I was scared that the men would come back too, so I stayed out in the lake. The sun was almost showing over the mountains. I treaded water near the floating fence. It was possible to swim under it if you knew where. I could dive that deep, I thought. But then what? Crawling onto an unfamiliar outlands beach without clothes or supplies. Dying of exposure if I managed to outrun the hunters.

The sunrise broke and dazzled the lake, currents flashing on the surface. I felt my arms and legs go limp. For a moment I still floated, and then, as if with a shrug, the lake claimed me. My hair lifted gently as I sank with open eyes. I saw the fencewires shining under the ceiling of light and the murky greenness beneath. I sensed the lake's tugged offer, a safe return to the world, but I pushed my hands upward, propelling myself deeper into the cold, until my breath ran out and the fear came. I kicked hard and within seconds I was gulping air in the dawn sun. The guard stared from the beach tower as I swam in and covered myself with my towel.

My cabin door was wide open. Insects crawled on the inside of the window and sand littered the rug. My carving satchel lay under my chair, but nothing seemed missing at a glance, not even my whiskey. It was almost seven o'clock. I put on my uniform, locked the cabin out of habit, and headed to the kitchen.

All the guards were grumbling about Cassar: when his turn came, he'd really gone through with his threat to monopolize the whole houseboat, leaving a frustrated lineup on the dock. It might have been during that time that Gagne and his friends had broken off from the group. Gagne said nothing as I lumped porridge onto his plate, treating me as if I wasn't there.

Once people were seated around the breakfast fire, Manduca stood up on a stump and waved a Conseil envelope. The warning stamp was legible from the kitchen's serving window: the letter was destined for the exchange post on the plateau.

News from the Bâtisseur! They had an emergency petition. Same case as the last one. Different applicant.

Manduca described the petitioner as the dead boy's best friend, who clearly was not the sharpest tool in the shed; his request to visit Ouest 1 had arrived very late, even by emergency standards. The Conseil rejected him on kinship grounds and initially set his escape risk at low, but then, last night, a fracas on tavern row made them raise the risk a notch: not enough to confine him, but enough that the relevant borders had to be notified as a matter of course.

I kept staring at the warning letter in Manduca's hand.

The guards seemed pleased instead of irritated by the news of a potential escape attempt, and from another warning in the summer, I knew why.

Manduca pretended to be heavy-hearted as he reached down to produce a dented coffee tin. You know what time it is, he sighed, everyone ante up.

The tin passed from guard to guard, who set down their breakfasts to dig out their money. Fire the shot, win the pot, continued the captain. Maybe then you can follow in Cassar's lusty footsteps—yes, I heard, what a rascal. You can't help admiring a young man's stamina. Oh! In fact, on that steamy topic . . .

Manduca looked around until he spotted me in the serving window. A moment of your time, he said, and beckoned.

Some guards looked vaguely intrigued as I walked over to them, but most were still counting coins. I saw Gagne emptying out his pockets and my stomach dropped: in his lap was the chisel my mother had given me. He didn't bother concealing it as I passed.

Up up! Manduca pointed at the stump next to his. At first I stayed where I was. He glared down at me through his smile. Odile, I guarantee this will be fun.

The stump wobbled under my feet as I obeyed. I found my balance and stood on display in front of the fire.

I have a piece of trivia about our petitioner, Manduca announced with relish. Once upon a time—how should I put it? This same idiot was Odile's secret paramour.

I reddened but forced myself to look blank.

Is it true, asked Manduca, that you two were caught rutting in the Raspails? What a beautiful image. He tucked the warning letter into his armpit and mimed a couple thrusts with his fist and hand. Anyhow, that's all, just a bit of smut to brighten your morning. Our condolences to you in advance, I'm sure he's not all bad. Maybe someone will give you a buck from the pot as a widow's pension.

With a curt nod of the chin, the captain gestured me back to the kitchen. I stayed standing on the stump.

Something else? he asked.

Wiping my palms on my apron, I cleared my throat and raised my voice. I want to bet too.

Manduca looked amused. She speaks?

Yes. I want to enter the pot.

You do! How dramatic. Gentlemen, who wants to tell her what we're betting on?

You're betting on who's going to kill him if he tries to escape, I replied. I say it's going to be me.

Everyone was watching. Manduca grinned around the fire. Isn't that something. A woman scorned. Where do you plan to get him—in the kitchen? Using what, a potato peeler?

I pointed at Gagne's lap.

I'll use that. It's mine.

The guards leaned to see. Grudgingly, Gagne displayed the chisel and said it was his, but Manduca motioned and he tossed it at me. I reacted reflexively and caught it midair without falling off the stump. All of them laughed, even Gagne. I drew myself taller.

As long as we're doing trivia, I was the last patroller to kill an escapee on the eastern fence—in the middle of a snowstorm.

Ah, that was an old lady, Manduca chuckled. But you know what, pass her the tin. Ordinarily the bet's fifty, but why not make it a hundred? If you're such a distinguished hunter, a handicap's only fair to the rest of these slobs.

I shifted my apron aside to access my pocket. Some guards tapped their plates in sarcastic applause, while others resented any added competition. Once I'd put my money in, I had nothing left. I handed Manduca the tin.

Every last coin, what confidence, he marveled. Betting is now closed! If he tries anything, it'll be tonight, so I'm putting extra patrollers on the beach. Please, no gifts if you want that assignment, I couldn't possibly accept. And for god's sake, don't shoot each other—look at the last replacement they sent us. He clapped me on the back. You know, Odile, I have to ask. This lover of yours. What did he do to deserve revenge with a fucking chisel?

I paused so they would all hear.

Do you want the truth?

The captain beamed. Always.

I looked back indifferently. I didn't think you'd need it spelled out. You already said it yourself. Alain's the reason I got transferred here. Of course I hate him—I hate you.

I kept my disdain trained on Manduca despite the snorts around the fire. The bright smile stretching across his face didn't flag.

Well, we won't hold it against her, will we. Everyone's entitled to their opinion. Although, there is one piece of protocol you just reminded me of. Not to put a damper on things, but somebody needs to hike this up to the exchange post.

He fluttered the Conseil envelope in the air again, and then, with flourish, slapped it in my hand so hard that I almost fell.

All yours! Not strictly by the book, but you know the way there. Shame you'll miss your chance at the jackpot tonight—I don't give refunds on wagers. He rapped his fingers triumphantly on the coffee tin. It's for the best, Odile. Vengeance is unbecoming.

As he strutted away, everyone departed for their stations, relieved they hadn't drawn the disqualifying hike themselves. I remained standing on the stump as the guards dispersed, bearing my humiliation for all to see, then gave my apron to Bellamy. He narrowed his eyes, annoyed to be short-staffed. I acted equally indignant as I stalked off toward my cabin to collect my rucksack. Only when the trees had hidden me did I break into a run.

The duty guard wrote my return time for tomorrow. I penciled my initials nervously as the gate opened, but the guard simply took the clipboard and waved me through. I hitched up my bag and crossed the western border.

The steepening pines soon gave way to the bare slope. I came to the massive tree with the black bell. The iron tongue hung mute in its mouth. I turned and looked back at my valley.

Though it was early, boats drifted away from the marina at languid angles, white sails raised like cuspids. The Sunday sun was a distant grey smear. There was a storm gathering in the muggy clouds over the north end. I remembered the rain would not begin until dark.

\*

I opened the warning letter in the plateau cabin. The envelope was now limp with perspiration, but the seal held firm. I cut it with the chisel and blew the wax shavings off the table. The cabin was utterly like the one I knew on the way to Est 1—the ship in the bottle, the bad chair that wobbled—and briefly I wondered if it could be true, if time held still in the outlands, breathing in and out but never moving.

In all my years of delivering it, I'd never seen the inside of their mail. Two things shook out of the envelope: a folded letter and a small beige card covered in blue-grey type. The card was a format I hadn't seen since the Grande École.

I'd retained enough cipher to more or less read the message. It explained the situation to the Ouest 1 Conseil, naming the disaffected applicant and summarizing his goal in the event that he successfully breached their fence. The projected target of interference was Edme Pira, aged sixteen, to perish Monday night near the north end cove, presumed drowned, precise place and time undetermined. Sentries were recommended at the beach access steps as a precaution.

I read back the age, the approximate fate, the tragedy in point form. The Conseil's flag flapped loudly outside the cabin. I unfolded the accompanying letter, which was a likeness of Alain, the first identification sketch I'd seen of somebody I knew. The picture emphasized the bleakness of his adult features, his wide-open sorrow. It resembled the way he'd looked when I revealed that I'd been spying on Edme during our friendship. Ever since telling Alain that, however, something about Ivret's old request struck me as false. It was a suspicion that strengthened when I learned that Cassar hadn't taken the Piras to a second viewing location. What were the odds, then, of anyone else in town recognizing them during their tour? Ivret would not have been worried about Edme or his family hearing rumors from another source. At the time it was unthinkable to doubt or disobey her, but in retrospect, her real concern was that I would tell Edme myself. Most likely she devised my task to reinforce my silence and make it feel conscientious instead of complicit; reporting to her was supposed to distract me from saying something to him. I had been the threat.

In a sense, she'd been right. I walked out in the waning light and burned the security documents over the cooking pit. The beige card curled inward and the ashes of Alain's forlorn face dissipated over the plateau. Normally I would sleep at the cabin, but there was no time. The clouds had swollen into mountains of waiting rain. I took a wool blanket and some deserted liquor, possibly left by Cassar, and pushed on.

By the time I got to the far edge of the plateau it was too dark to see, but the ground was beginning to descend underfoot. My boots sought the squarish rocks that protruded from the earth, and I made a conscious effort to subdue the anxiousness now simmering in my blood. I managed to get down the steepest part of the climb before the first raindrops pelted the dirt. The clouds groaned and lightning ripped the night sky, leaving behind eerie afterimages of white wilderness. Then the real rain started and I was soaked within seconds. I opened my mouth and savored the angry impacts on my tongue.

The way to get to Ouest 1 should be identical to the way home from my eastern visits. First I would come to their birch woods, then their lantern path, then their eastern fence. But for hours the rain fell so heavily that I saw nothing ahead. Gradually I became aware of a growing haze, but it did not sharpen into any landmarks, and in my exhaustion I had a sudden fear that the western valleys were all lies, that there was nothing more this way but endless mountains. At last the slope eased into muddy foothills, and when I made out the familiar trunks of birch trees, I staggered into the woods with a cry of relief. The rain battered the leaves and splashed in the shallow brook.

I filled my canteen, finished my rations, and walked to the trees' end. Wet amber light huddled around the first lantern post, rainfall glazing the bell. I thought of cutting out the bell's tongue and hiding it, but it was needless. Manduca wouldn't notice my absence until Monday afternoon; their hunters wouldn't catch up in time. The risk of capture lay ahead, in the valley of my childhood.

I walked out from the cover of the birch woods. The lanterns stretched across the steppe surrounded by black rain. I knew where to make my attempt on the fence: between two towers north of the main gate, close to where Lucie had tried climbing over. The problem was getting there. I'd only ever crossed the steppe using the lantern path, where my approach might be spotted by a tower guard looking through his field glasses. That argued for cutting wide of the lanterns—where the same darkness that protected me from the towers would prevent me from seeing the ground. I pictured rolling my ankle on the unknown terrain, but I couldn't let myself be sighted. I left the lantern post and veered off the path, into the starless void of the wild steppe.

At first the walking was easier than I expected. My boot caught on a wiry shrub but I was able to kick through it without tripping. Otherwise the ground seemed clear, so I began to build up my pace. I needed to reach the fence before dawn, and somehow it hurt my feet less to jog. My boots splattered beneath me; my rucksack rattled up and down on my back. I was moving in the right direction, a northwesterly route toward the border, which ought to become visible in about a mile. I wondered if I could already detect a faint frost of light glowing under the sky, and I peered into the distance trying to tell if it was my imagination.

Something hard slammed into my boot and sent the light careening upwards.

I cursed into the mud. My left hip and leg pounded with pain. For a second I lay motionless, then tried wiggling my toes and ankles. The relief was overwhelmed by self-recrimination: even a minor sprain could have stranded me on the steppe. Swearing again, I righted myself. The earth was uneven where I'd landed, an abrupt dense mound. I poked with my boot to find what I'd tripped on.

At first I thought it was a rock, but when I crouched down, my fingers touched rough bricks. Slowly I felt around in the dark. The bricks continued in both directions under my hands. A rudimentary boundary line took shape in my mind's eye.

The potter's field for captured escapees appeared on no map; it was said to be north of the gate. I took another uneasy step forward. The mounds of earth were arranged in a row.

I was in a grid of unmarked graves. The bodies collected from the lake in the summer, Lucie in January: all ended up here. Hastily I fixed my footing, avoiding standing on the crude plots that were turning to sludge in the storm.

Lucie. Raimond had buried her the night she died, but couldn't have dug a fresh grave in frozen soil. The chapel's solution was to dig graves in advance—which meant there could be empty holes out here too, and who knew if they'd be boarded over. I couldn't wait for lightning to show me a safe path across. I would have to follow the perimeter to the other side.

I dragged one foot along the bricks to track the boundary line. In spite of this clumsy walk I expected to reach the first corner soon, so I was surprised by how far I went before I felt the bricks turn. I thought the next side had to be shorter, but as I continued, the bricks stretched on and on. When I finally reached the second corner of the field I was shaken by its size. How many escapees lay sprawled in this dirt? I mouthed thanks to the darkness for shrouding my chances, and chased the now-undeniable fencelight into the foothills.

At the round of the last hill I saw it. In the storm, the fence's gleaming wires had an antiseptic shine. The area between the two watchtowers was less dim than I'd hoped. There was the distant spot where Lucie had clambered over. A little closer was a subtle furrow in the ground that straddled both sides of the border. It contained a puddle whose surface writhed with rain.

I checked my watch and calculated the timing. A patroller was due in the next few minutes, and sure enough I saw him through the fence, head tucked to his chest, shrinking himself against the weather. I wondered if it could be Raimond, recently enlisted, but he passed by without raising his head.

Once he was out of view I started counting under my breath. I would count to sixty and make myself run for it. If I didn't do it on sixty I'd never find the courage. As I neared the end of my count the wind unsettled the bells on the fence, and tin whispers traveled up and down toward the near-est towers. Fifty-eight. Fifty-nine.

I clutched my rucksack in my arms and rushed at the fence.

The light was merciless. My bootprints sloshed into the cleared strip but there was no time to cover them—I had to trust that they'd ooze clean. At the furrow I lifted the lowest fencewire, then the next one, until I held both wires in a careful pinch. With my other hand, I slowly wedged my rucksack into the puddle and propped the wires higher. The bells didn't protest when I let them go.

I wriggled into the water on my back, straining my face from the barbs. As I'd hoped, the muddiness had loosened the ground and allowed me to fit underneath. I moved painstakingly, inching with my heels through the mire, eyes locked on the hillcrest where the patroller had gone, even though if he returned there was nothing I could do but flinch before the shot.

But then I was through. I extracted my rucksack and lowered the wires as delicately as I could. They released a light, offended twang, and the bells jiggled up and down the fence, but they stopped, leaving only a steady shower of rain.

I got up in the cleared strip and took my first unobstructed look at the western valley. Straight ahead were the streaky lights of town, begin-ning with the Raspails; to the right, isolated lights dotted the north end. Drenched in cold mud, I ran into the flooded fields.

I made it to the neighborhood bypassing the streets, and came out of the woods onto the chemin des Pins. It was still mostly dark and no one was awake yet. I limped up the road to the stretch where you could see the roofs of the lower homes. I stepped closer to the edge.

Below me slept my old house. In the front carport, firewood was stacked in neat piles, sheltered from the downpour. My mother had not made a fire in years. Our blue car, long dead, sat faithfully in the driveway.

I let myself gaze at the bedroom window. I recognized the curtains' bunchy folds: on the other side, the girl was twisting in her dreams. It was dangerous to get this close, I knew. My memories were connected to her. If I so much as kicked a stone down the driveway and accidentally woke her up, I might remember that awakening now and get disoriented in the ricochet. Just looking at the window gave me a spinning, bottomless sensation. I backed away.

The sky had surrendered some dismal light, the grey dawn beyond doubt. Too risky to press onward to the cliff—I would have to wait until nightfall tomorrow. I climbed up a gap between two houses on the other side of the road. In one of the yards, sodden paper lanterns drooped from the trees like deflated wasp nests. I entered a grove of firs that was hidden from the neighbors' windows. I had memories of this place: in the aftermath of my father I'd come here to read picture books and feel far from home. In reality I could still see the ridge of my roof below, and the streetlights in the laneway, but the rest of my view was totally erased by rain.

I wrapped myself in the blanket from the plateau cabin and lay down on my unbruised side. The backs of my eyes hammered. I'd hiked for more than twenty hours and barely stopped to rest. When my head touched the ground, my mind bled into the earth like water.

At first the world seemed the same. The forest debris glistened in the grim day, and the air had the freshness of wet loam. Then I remembered where I was. The piney moisture transformed and grew humid with memory. The smell of this place was achingly familiar. I blinked up at the western sky. The rumors weren't lies, then; this was really how it felt here.

I'd slept into the afternoon. I peeled off the soggy wool blanket. My limbs stabbed as I sat up, my neck rigid with discomfort. I turned my head slowly from side to side and picked fir nits from my hair.

A car hissed by on the chemin des Pins. All I caught was the runny reflection of trees in its windshield. The rain in the valley looked like it was falling upward, rising from the lake in a wall of mist.

I sloughed mud off my uniform but it was useless. I put on the rucksack, which seemed to have doubled in weight. When it was clear I slid down the muddy hill, crossed the road, and slid again to the lower laneway into the ditch across from my house. The blue car was gone. Quickly I went to the back and took the key from the broken flowerpot. With a glance over my shoulder, I unlocked the glass door.

The murmur of our fridge was the first thing: it sounded so much like itself. Like staying home sick from school, like a bracing midday sadness. I stood unbreathing in the rainlit kitchen. The feeling of childhood was suddenly insistent, swelling against my ribcage. Their two coffee cups sat on the table, one drained to a ring of tar, one milky and barely touched. I floated my palm over it. It was cold. I brought it closer. A waxy crescent was on the rim, and I remembered my honeysuckle lip balm. I took a hesitant sip. In spite of the faintly medicinal flavor, it tasted more like coffee to me than anything I'd drunk in years.

I stole bread and jam from the pantry, then noticed that I'd muddied the tiles. I put my boots and damp socks in my bag and wiped the floor clean. Barefoot, I walked through the living room. A book of short stories was tented on the coffee table—that's right, I realized, I'd been reading it. I turned down the carpeted hall.

I stopped in front of the framed family portrait my grandfather had painted. I was seven or eight and smiling toothily. My mother and I were on a picnic blanket in the cove, the lone spruce towering from the sand behind us. Her hand rested on my freckled shoulder. She had on her old sunglasses, and the hairstyle she'd worn, sculpted waves that I'd somehow forgotten, which now seemed like forgetting the texture of water.

The door to my mother's bedroom was partly open. The quilt on her bed was tucked in firmly, and her perfume hung in the stillness. I felt a strange yearning for what lay there in front of me. At the end of the hall, my bedroom was open too.

I breathed in its stuffy warmth, its pastness thick as vapor. The room was smaller and cozier despite being just the same. The curtains were drawn, and as my eyes adjusted to the ambience, I saw my father's old desk, and a heap of textbooks with tassled bookmarks, and the painting of the lake on the wall.

I sat down on the girl's unmade bed. It gave its squeaky sigh. I longed to pull the covers over me and sleep, but forced myself to go to the dresser instead. Lavender rose from her clothing. Sifting lightly, I pulled out a pair of underwear. With my rations lately they would fit. I saw the Cazelles bag, the swimsuit, crumpled at the back of her drawer.

The clock on the nightstand read quarter to three, but she wouldn't be back yet. She would go to vetting, then loiter on the wet swings and slouch home after dark. My mother, too, was staying late in the Hôtel de Ville. I had time for a shower.

The bathroom counter was cluttered with my mother's toiletries: hinged containers in the shapes of shells, tubes of ointment, a sliver of soap, a brush coiled with still-brown hair. Again the throb of memory. I looked at myself in the mirror and grimaced. Though my face was fairly clean from the rain, my clothes were stiff with filth. I was about to undress when I heard the bells.

They were far off, but within seconds the eastern incursion signal was taken up and amplified by the lake outposts and backwoods towers. The alarm bells swept across the valley, massing overhead like a cloud of starlings, a billow of fear lunging through the sky. I stared at the frosted bathroom window that obscured our backyard. Then I remembered how the bells had interrupted the end of Pichegru's lesson: how he'd paused midsentence to frown at the window, and pointedly finished his lecture over the noise.

They might have seen where I'd gone under the fence. They'd know from the footprints that the escapee had broken in, not out. They would not know who, and I'd destroyed the warning letter about Alain, but their minds would still go to the recent Piras case, because failed viewings sometimes presaged incursions. This would put Edme's parents on their list of suspects, but also anyone else the older Piras might have persuaded to interfere on their behalf. I imagined a younger Jean-Savile asking the local Conseil for the names of children who might someday have danger-ous feelings about the Piras' son. Being upstairs was no longer safe for me. I got my bag from the kitchen and went to the basement.

The window over the washing machine was open a crack, and through it I still heard the alarm. I parted the shanks of insulation that blocked the entrance to the crawlspace. In the grey dirt, I saw the sliding impression of Edme's violin case, as clearly defined as fresh paving. Only a few hours ago she'd returned it to him. When the bells had started, Edme had looked around curiously in his desk—first at Alain, then, tentatively, at me—but I was still being stubborn, self-pitying, resisting the temptation to meet his eyes.

I pushed my rucksack into the crawlspace and climbed in after it. The insulation fell shut behind me, hiding me from the laundry room. The ceiling was too low for me to crawl properly. I ducked under the floor joists with difficulty, my body sinking into the sandy floor. The crawlspace had a bonemeal smell that stuck to my throat. I pulled myself toward the rear wall, trying to smooth my tracks as I went. Silky cobwebs drifted over my neck. I reached the back and lay flat against the cool subterranean bricks, where I could no longer hear if the bells were ringing.

I studied the raw boards above. My eye was almost aligned with the little knothole in the living room floor: by squinting, I could trace the worn fringe of our couch. I remembered sitting there on weekends watching quails cross the yard; I remembered my mother after work, a glass of wine on the coffee table, making her scornful little laugh at whatever she was reading.

The floor shuddered as a heavy vehicle drove up the chemin des Pins. Gendarmerie transports were already searching the area. I had wondered why guards were on the cove trail as I waited for the bus after school that day, and now I knew: they were trying to intercept the escapee before nightfall, well in advance of when the accident would take place. But as the estimated time grew nearer, they would be forced to fall back from the cliff, or else risk affecting Edme's actions themselves. All I had to do was wait them out, then get close enough to him to whisper a simple warning. Be careful, it's slippery—any words ought to be enough. And how much could I even hope to say before being undone? Edme would look around but see no one, perhaps surprised to have imagined Odile's voice.

It was a matter of hours now. I could feel the threat of panic growing, like underwater pressure on my lungs. The only way forward was to not think far ahead. I remembered the stolen food in my rucksack. In my confined position it was hard to retrieve, but I got it and propped myself up so I could eat without choking. The bread was rye, the jam apricot. I chewed in the chalky silence.

The last daylight faded from the knothole. I was beginning to contemplate leaving the crawlspace and making my way along the bluffs. Then, as if my thoughts had been overheard, the front door of the house opened upstairs.

It was too early. A set of footsteps entered, solid but cautious. The intruder roamed the house, beginning with the bedrooms. I heard the bathroom door creak on its hinges and the light switch flick on. There must be something I'd left out, something I'd left behind. I pictured pine needles on the edge of the sink.

The steps thumped toward the living room, growing in impact until they were directly above me, and there they stopped. Through the knothole, I saw the hem of an officer's trousers. If he just glanced down. My fingers crept to my pocket. I inserted the violin's tuning peg into the knothole and held it tight.

In the new darkness I chanced only the smallest sips of air. I felt the gendarme deliberate, trading his weight back and forth, sprinkling my forehead with sawdust. Finally he walked away, faster than before, and the front door shut. Immediately I was overtaken by coughing. I dropped my hand, letting the tuning peg dangle from the knothole on its own, as I strangled the hacking sound in the crook of my arm.

I made myself stay but I was restless to leave; who knew how many officers were descending on the neighborhood. When I crawled back into the laundry room, my dirty uniform had acquired a new coating of grey. I stripped and bathed briskly at the cold sink, scrubbing my skin with my hands. A basket of clean laundry sat on the dryer. Most of it was my mother's slips and stockings, but there was a dress of mine, short-sleeved and black with a rounded white collar, my grandmother's gift. Years had passed since I'd worn a dress, but I pulled it on, grateful for its looseness, and donned a pair of my mother's stockings for warmth. I threw my balled-up uniform into the crawlspace where I'd left my rucksack and adjusted the insulation as before. Nobody would look there until after my personal effects were undone too. I climbed on top of the dryer and out the basement window.

The storm had ended, but rain dripped from the pine trees under the thinning clouds. I tiptoed along the perimeter of the backyard, heading for the trail that led to the bluffs. I had just about reached it when I saw him.

He was in our laneway, under the streetlamp. There was no doubt it was him. Decades younger, turned away, Jean-Savile had his same way of standing, alert as a lynx in the lantern's twitching glow. He had known to come here: he had been the one in my house.

I wanted to drop to the grass where I was, but I might get trapped in the yard. A bus drove past on the chemin des Pins, and in the disrupted quiet I stepped over the pine needle slag and dodged the raspberry thorns at the path's entrance. Jean-Savile disappeared from view.

Soon I came to the dirt amphitheater. I glanced for Edme's shoeprints, signs of his leaping and thrashing as he played, but there was nothing except mud. I perched on the retaining wall to retie a boot, then continued splashing through craters that were now flooded with starlight.

I reached the bluffs. Right away I saw a line of patrol boats positioned in the lake, all facing the land. They were doing spotlight sweeps in methodical succession, exposing the chunky lower bluffs, then the cliffs, then the cove. But the search would be cut off: like the foot sentries, the boats had to avoid attracting Edme's attention. I moved along the back of the bluffs staying out of the spotlights' reach, navigating fallen trees and wild rosebushes that were fragrant with rain.

Despite approaching from an unusual direction, I still recognized the clifftop ahead. A large gibbous moon had risen over the valley, illuminating the edge of the drop, sculpting the cliff in luminous white. I advanced slowly, wary of sentries lurking in the brush. Whenever the boats' spotlights cascaded up the plunging shoreline, I shrank and kept still. I only had to get close enough for my voice to carry. I stopped at a sprawling wolf-willow bush, a hiding place with a clear view of the clifftop.

I didn't know how long I'd have to wait. My bladder and guts ached; now that I was stationary I felt it badly. My teeth gave a chatter and I pressed my fingers into the softs of my cheeks to make it subside. The boats were still doggedly scanning the cliffs. I squatted behind the bush and urinated, listening to the heat hiss into the lichens. Of all the final acts, attending to such a simple need. But once my bladder was empty, the pressure inside me persisted, and I realized it was fear. It was the coming erasure, it was Ivret's warnings about interference, it was the hardness in her voice instilling the dread in me now. Helpless to escape her memory, I tried to rotate it, to focus anywhere else in the old parlor classroom, and so I visualized the giant wall map. Somehow the scale of it was calming. With closed eyes I counted the repeating lakes and towns. I pictured Ivret's pushpins and colored threads, and myself as one more taut line traveling between the valleys, one discrete choice among hundreds, the whole wall teeming with choices until tonight's could barely be discerned. Standing back it was redeemable; I knew the sacrifice and for whom. Several more seconds passed before I opened my eyes and noticed that the spotlights on the lake had gone black. I heard a rustle on the clifftop, and parted the wolf-willow leaves.

The guard, in silhouette, seemed to be aiming his rifle at the sky. Then he stepped into profile, and the moonlight fell on his poised violin. I saw a dark-haired boy, high cheekbones, eyes narrowed in concentration. He brought his bow down and a chord flared out over the lake. But he was standing much too close to the edge. My mouth opened, not in a whisper but in a scream. Before my throat caught the air his leg lurched out from under him.

Every other noise was extinguished from the world: just a single dying chord. He swung his arm once, then his violin cracked against the rocks and loud brush was tearing down the cliffside. I heard the lake crash open below. The patrol boats were hushed and dark.

I ran from the brambles. The shocked violin still hummed on the ground. The cliff's edge was slick with rain. I backed up, kicked off my boots, and leapt headlong at the valley.

I hit the water flailing. I opened my eyes but saw nothing. My dress billowed and I fought it away from my face. Then the surface of the lake lit up, and queasy emerald light rippled through the grains of rock that were falling everywhere like slow black hail. I saw a listless shape sinking into the abyss beyond the boulders. I hurled my hands and caught his elbow. His head lolled into view, lips open, hair drifting. I seized him and swam.

We surfaced in a mess of sticks bobbing at the base of the cliff. The huge spotlights were sliding down the lower bluffs. They'd heard a second splash but hadn't seen where I'd gone in. Holding his face above water, I kicked toward the mouth of the cove. I lifted the rope floating between the buoys, and soon my feet touched the slimy bottom.

I dragged him up the beach as far as the spruce tree, whose trunk blocked us from view. He was unconscious. A long gash on his forehead had begun seeping blood. Water leaked from his mouth—not nearly enough. Lifting his jaw, I pinched his nose and pressed my lips down, forcing breaths into his throat, then pumping his chest with all my weight. Water spurted from him like a broken fountain but he still wouldn't breathe. I knelt and gave more air, his mouth cold, his chest filling to unnatural heights. I pumped again and felt bone cave under my hands. But then his head turned and he started retching, water spilling through strings of spittle hanging down his chin. His eyes rolled white, sightless as he gasped.

I propped him against the tree and held my fingers to his neck. He had a pulse. The cut on his forehead would clot. I began shaking. The tears were uncontrollable, delirious. His breathing sounded clearer in his throat, and with it came the memory of his voice. I pushed wet hair out of his wound. He was so young, younger than I ever could have known. Without thinking I leaned in and kissed him, moving from his forehead to the edge of his mouth. I held still there, feeling Edme's breath on my cheek, my tears flowing between our faces, my last sensations.

But I waited. I felt him take another breath, and heard the steady lull of the waves. I opened my eyes. I looked around the cove.

The beach was as ever. I noticed the itchy wetness of my dress. Through my bewilderment came a surge of relief: he was alive, but so was I. Something impossible had happened. I struggled to my feet.

A spotlight blasted into the cove, throwing my shadow across the ground. A guard shouted from the lake and a gun boomed. Boat motors cranked and roared. I heard the pounding of boots on the wooden steps and saw flashlights splitting the pines.

I dashed to the side and scrambled uphill, climbing over deadfall in my stocking feet. Behind me the gendarmes splashed out of the boat, yelling to the others on their way down the stairs. The boat sounded the alarm.

At the top I came into an unlit backyard, one of the houses in the cul-de-sac, its lawn squishy with rain. I saw more officers hurrying toward the beach steps. On the other side of the chemin des Pins was the school and the empty playground. If I could make it to the backwoods path I could hide in the fort, long enough to think where to go.

When it seemed like all the gendarmes had passed I sprang across the road toward the schoolgrounds, but a bullet scorched by my ear. Covering my head, I sprinted past the cloakroom door and into the trees. I couldn't tell how close the guards were; I tried to hear them, but suddenly I was not thinking well, I felt like I'd done the same thing before, fleeing up the path from gunshots in the night. My feet slapped the muddy soil. My panting sounded hardly mine. Officers called out directions in the dark—they'd found the backwoods path. But the exposed hill was coming up ahead, where there were fewer trees and sharper stars. I ran off the path and up the slope, heading for the aberrant copse of brush at the end of the ridge.

I saw her first. She was on the ground, hugging her knees, her back to the fort's main log. Beside her lay a discarded rain poncho and a book-bag. My bookbag. I stopped, but it was too late. The girl turned her head toward me.

She got up quickly. Despite my own fear, I raised my hands to reassure her, but as I did, I remembered the same scene from long ago: the soaking-wet stranger, raising her hands, eyes gaping at me in the night.

I tried to speak, say don't be scared, but a chasm seemed to break open beneath me, and my voice tumbled in. I tried again, but each budding word on my tongue transformed instantly to memory, the memory of seeing this stranger try to say it. I forced my lips to make shapes, and in that halting croak managed to get something out, but the sensation of pastness bloomed around me like furious weeds, devouring every sound and gesture. Vertigo attacked in a rush of black gravity. I remembered seeing the woman falling sideways and grasping at the fort's wall for balance as I felt my hands thrash through the leaves. The girl took a step backward. She'd realized who I was. With her mouth open, she brought her hands to her face, and in my wild sickness I thought how unlike me she looked, how beautiful. I tried telling her it was okay now, I saved him, but my language fissured, instead I said *I saved you*. The girl seemed not to hear. She was looking past me, urgently out of the fort, and in that second I remembered taking the breath to scream, Up here, up here.

I flung myself down and buried my head from the shots. When they stopped, the silence was shrill.

A large hand shook my shoulder. A man asked my name.

I looked up. He repeated the words. Although it was dark, I recognized his face from the border field trip. Jean-Savile searched my eyes. Slowly I lowered my hands from my ears.

Odile Ozanne, I whispered.

He stared a second longer, then nodded.

Let's go.

He had already scooped up my bookbag, and held it in the same hand as his gun. He led me around the gendarmes crowding the fort. Through the cluster of uniforms I glimpsed her again, collapsed against the wall of foliage. Her head was tipping back, exposing her neck. A rounded collar speckled with blood. A guard began pulling her down.

Jean-Savile grabbed me by my chin and jerked my head away. You don't look at that.


The fountain in the Place du Bâtisseur was fully lit despite the hour. Aqueous shadows danced up the conseiller statue. Jean-Savile steered me straight to the Hôtel de Ville's steps. Another guard held the door, and I was led across the threshold.

It was a rotunda, bigger than I'd imagined, with a mosaic spanning the domed ceiling above the marble floor. People were milling about, both Conseil staff and gendarmerie, and they dropped their voices as we entered. I averted my eyes, but I saw my mother huddled on the far wall with Claudette and some others.

Jean-Savile ignored their looks and walked me up a set of curving stairs that led to a mezzanine lined with heavy doors. He pointed me into a narrow room and told me to wait. A lock clicked behind me.

On the wall was a framed painting of the Hôtel de Ville itself, stern under cloudy skies. The room had a table and two chairs. I sat and pulled my chair in tight. There were no windows, just a double-paned slit in the door. Afraid but exhausted, I rested my forehead on the table. I looked as if I were readying to raise my hand in the Grande École. I felt my heart beating in my brow.

The doorknob turned, and Ivret came into the room. I was struck by the disquiet in her eyes. But her first words to me were: You look upset.

I tried keeping my mouth from quivering. I'm okay.

Pursing her lips, she sat across from me with a paper and pen.

We have some questions about tonight. To start with, was the escapee familiar. Do you have any beliefs about who it was.

She stated this flatly: she knew that I knew. I could not meet her gaze.

You understand the importance of being candid, said Ivret.

I wanted to answer but couldn't form the words. I was looking hopelessly at the table when, to my astonishment, Ivret placed her bony hand on mine. I looked at her, moved, but her face showed only patience.

It was me, I said hoarsely. Older. Probably from Est 1.

Ivret withdrew her hand and wrote down a single word. And did you arrange to meet with her tonight?

My eyes widened. No.

How did she find you there, if not by coordination?

I don't know. I was on the playground. I didn't even plan to go to the woods. I saw transports coming, then I heard guns and I got scared and ran. It's just a place I go with my friends.

And then?

I shook my head. I guess she ran there too. They were chasing her.

Ivret scanned my face, the flakes in her irises dark as flint.

Did she speak to you?

No. Yes. I think she tried. I could hardly understand her. She opened her mouth but it didn't sound like words.

I realized that I was covering my throat and took my hand away. Ivret held her pen very still.

What did you understand?

What?

You said you hardly understood anything, implying there was something.

I'm sorry, I meant nothing. It was like . . . it was like she was choking on her own voice.

I see. And then?

I heard the guards and called them.

She studied me some more, but at last, uncharacteristically, she sighed, rubbing the bridge of her nose.

It's thought to be a type of mnemonic feedback that causes the distress. There are reports from other self-encounters. Her tone indicated that the aside was over, but she'd shifted, momentarily, from my interrogator to my teacher.

Regardless of the escapee's failure to communicate, Ivret went on, I wonder if you have any insights into her intentions here.

Somehow my voice grew meeker. To interfere?

That goes without saying. To what end?

I don't know. Maybe something was going to happen to me?

Ivret was silent. I could tell I was supposed to understand already, which confirmed the only thing it could be.

It was about the visitors, I whispered. At the pond. The same reason they came.

Yes, Ivret replied. It appears that her target was Edme Pira.

My eyes began swimming; my voice was a squeak. I told her I was sorry, that I couldn't imagine myself interfering, that so gross a violation wasn't in my character, that it was incomprehensible, and also, it didn't even make sense—why would she come here so early, if that's why she'd come?

Ivret inspected my teary face. Tonight there was an accident. Your friend was injured in the lake. Somebody brought him back to shore.

She saw that I wasn't breathing. The doctor is optimistic, she added.

For a moment I could only stare. Then I couldn't contain it, I made a pealing sob of joy. The weekend's jealous anger crumbled like a husk. Ivret did not react to my outburst. I tried regaining my composure but babbled at her: Are you sure he's all right? It was really supposed to be tonight?

Think before you speak, please. There is no 'supposed to.' One outcome has been supplanted by another. The outcome that remains to be decided is yours.

I nodded and swallowed. My tongue felt dry and tacky. Mme Ivret, *she* did something wrong, something unforgiveable—but *I* did the right thing. I kept my promise, I never told Edme anything. And I called the gendarmes, I helped them catch her. I swear I'm not an accomplice—

A thought snagged.

Did you say she pulled him out of the lake?

Ivret folded her hands on the table.

That's what happened? But after, she made it all the way to the back-woods? You just taught us about self-undoing—how did she reach me at all? Shouldn't she . . . ?

As I groped for the answer, Ivret's mouth curled into a thin expression, short of a smile.

You are a keen girl.

She picked up her notes. Without a word, she locked the door behind her, just like Jean-Savile.


There was no clock and my watch was in my confiscated bookbag. I paced without knowing how long I'd been there, then I sat some more. I thought of the woman bursting into the fort, her hair so severe, her face so angular, a wraithlike thinness, stockings shredded by thorns. I'd recognized the wet dress before I recognized her. Years later and I still owned it. I lay my head on the table again and tried thinking of Edme, not the bloody collar or the woman's emptied eyes.

When Ivret finally returned she had my bag in her hand. She told me I could go. The Conseil was persuaded of my loyalty by my record of collaboration and my call for help. They were impressed, too, by my geographical acumen, especially given the night's duress. Ivret seemed tired, but I dared to ask what she meant.

There are certain liberties we take when explaining the consequences of western interference, she allowed. Take the concept of self-undoing. The escapee you saw tonight was outside the borders of her home valley when it was swept away. As a consequence, she was not swept away with it. Call it safe distance from the storm.

Ivret let my eyes grow round.

Now consider the emboldening effect if this were common knowledge. It would remove a major disincentive. And at any rate, what we teach is not untrue. Interferers do not survive. All we elide is the means.


My mother was waiting alone in the rotunda when Ivret led me down the stairs. I gave a small wave, and she raised her hand in return, a constricted gesture that I knew hid convulsions of relief.

She expressed her gratitude to Ivret several times, which the conseillère accepted with weary courtesy before turning around to go. Tensely, my mother spoke after her. Please, one last thing—can she stay in vetting?

Ivret paused in the center of the rotunda floor, her robed figure dwarfed by the arching mosaic of the valleys. Her curt answer rang off the surrounding marble.

For what it's worth, your daughter remains our most promising candidate.

She walked away, and my mother gripped my hand.

✳

My room was filled with warm muslin light. A faded breeze came from the window. I stayed under my blanket watching the curtains tremble. I had slept, and the night felt clean of dreams.

Ivret had gone over everything I was forbidden to say. I agreed to all of it. My mother knew not to ask what I couldn't answer. She'd said she would stop by the school on her way to work to tell Pichegru I was sick. I looked at my alarm clock. That was hours ago.

I got up and went to my dresser. The middle drawer was slightly crooked. Inside, my underclothes seemed rumpled and fixed in haste. I nudged the drawer closed and padded down the hallway in my daisy nightdress, past my mother's room. Other small things were changed: mud caked on the carpet, a frame askew on the wall. Ivret said our house had been searched while I was being detained. My mother had closed the kitchen cupboards last night without a word.

I had no appetite, but I put on water for tea. The kitchen had the melancholy quiet of late morning, and as the kettle heated up, I sat on the living room couch. I picked up my mother's book of woodcuts from the coffee table and flipped to the map of the valleys, studying their tiny contours, and the unknown identical shape of the valley to the east.

It was while I was looking at that image, and the tea kettle launched into its plangent wail, that I heard a different sound, a soft but distinct impact below. I looked off the side of the couch at the knothole in the floor.


It was obvious the crawlspace had been disturbed. Parallel to the smooth impression of Edme's violin case was a muddled trail of dirt. When I aimed a flashlight at the back, I could see something hidden there.

I climbed in in my nightdress. What I discovered was a bundle of wet clothes, a tallish bag with metal frames, and the painful wooden nub that had dislodged from the knothole and now found its way under my knee.

On the laundry room floor, I unbunched the clothing and laid it out, pressing down the creases with the balls of my hands. It was a gendarmerie uniform, but the breast patch bore my surname. I touched the threadbare letters in incomprehension. A disguise, a ruse to cross the border? I bent closer and took in its smell. It had the same sourness of my gym clothes when I left them too long in the bag.

I moved from the damp uniform to the backpack, arranging its few contents on the floor.

An empty lunchbox with a dented canteen.

A jar with a dribble of brown liquid.

A wool blanket pileous with forest grit.

A chisel with a red handle.

I went down the row of artifacts until I came to a kind of portfolio held together by black covers. It had been rolled into a tube, and now its insides were curled and distended by moisture. I untied the twine and flattened the first wavy page.

It was a homemade book of prints sewn together with thread. The first picture, done in rich blue ink, showed an isolated cottage or hut. There was a flagpole with a swallowtail pennant like the one downtown, but this one was ragged and flew over a treeless expanse. Mountain peaks floated in the background, and more peaks beyond those. I had never seen such a place, either in person or in a book. A small fire produced a trickle of smoke. A tall bag just like hers leaned against the hut's outer wall.

Each page contained a different landscape, rendered in dense, scrupulous detail. All were by the same hand, a hand that could only be mine. I wasn't sure why I was so certain—I had never made a woodcut in my life—but I felt a kinship with the lines, their manner of diligence.

Many of the scenes were odd. An orchard, heaped in snow on one side, was full of fruit on the other. Ice chunks drifted past summery willow branches that hung over the lake like sleeping limbs. Nowhere, I noticed, was there another human being. It was as though she was the only person there, chronicling an eternity where the seasons glided into one.

The fence and its imposing watchtowers appeared in several of the engravings. Gently I closed the floppy covers and refastened the twine. The only people who could get that close to the fence, at least from so many vantage points, were the gendarmes. The uniform was really hers. Yet for the first time, the horror of her diminished. Her existence seemed baffling, pitiful. I had a feeling of overwhelming loneliness.

The last thing on the floor was the spoonlike piece of wood that had fallen from the knothole. It looked like an antique. A hole through its middle was filled with dry rot. As I turned it over in my hand, I noticed how my finger pads fit its curved planes: it was made to be held this way. Then I remembered Edme tuning his violin, rotating the pegs, willing his string not to snap.

Lightheaded, I shoved everything back in the bag. Later I would sneak the book of prints upstairs to pore over it nightly. For now, I hid it in the crawlspace again.

✳

My usual bus downtown wasn't due until after three, but I left the house at noon. Despite having skipped school I still wore my blazer, pinafore, and tie: no one at vetting had seen me wear anything else. With my bookbag under my arm, I walked up the hill.

Little kids were running and yelling on the playground. The swings flew into the blue unbounded sky. In a group of seniors at the edge of the field I saw Henri and Tom teasing the girls, but not Justine or Jo. Nobody paid attention to me passing on the far side of the road. The din of lunchtime was replaced by the insect hum of the pond. I turned off the chemin des Pins.

The lane where the Piras lived was short like mine, briefly splitting off the main road and rejoining it again. Behind waist-high fences the front yards were all paved with limestone tiles. Although I'd never been there, I knew the house was the last on the lane. I saw their station wagon parked outside in the middle of the day.

I knocked before my nerves got the better of me and immediately I heard footsteps inside. It wasn't one of Edme's parents who opened the door, but Alain. He was holding his school blazer in one hand and a shoe in the other.

There you are! I was wondering if you heard—I was going to bike over later. He's asleep though. Alain teetered as he tried to put on his other shoe.

Behind him, Jo and Justine were in the foyer gathering their things. I saw the Piras waiting politely. It was clear they were tired. They ushered us out onto the driveway, where I introduced myself to Edme's parents. M. Pira nodded kindly and said he knew.

I felt uncomfortable standing next to Justine and Jo; we hadn't spoken since the night at the cove. But their attitude seemed to have softened. Leaning over to me, Jo said, All we did was have tea with them, we haven't seen him yet either.

He's been sleeping most of the day, M. Pira apologized. He needs rest, it's a good thing.

Well sure, it's good for *him*, sighed Alain, but would it have killed him to put in an appearance for our sake?

Justine elbowed him. M. Pira gave an indulgent chuckle, and I saw his resemblance to his son.

Is he really going to be okay? I asked, unable to hide the quaver in my voice.

Tears slipped from Edme's mother's eyes, as if ready at the slightest prompting. They think so. He's got some broken ribs. They say he'll have a scar too. She pointed to her temple, and M. Pira murmured and pulled her closer.

Alain and Jo and Justine nodded soberly. I did too, trying not to cry myself. Justine made a small noise of sympathy and stepped forward to squeeze Mme Pira's arm, and then she turned and hesitantly hugged me.

We stayed a few more minutes, our voices low, as though we might disturb his recovery from the driveway. Edme's parents filled me in on what had happened in a way that made me think they'd been through it several times already. He had fallen from the cliff and hit his head, but must have kept conscious long enough to swim ashore, where some gendarmes found him during a day of training drills—the alarm bells we'd all heard.

Edme remembered very little. But when he admitted that he'd been practicing his violin outdoors in secret, his parents seemed remorseful instead
of angry. He could audition for the conservatory, they said, and they'd try
to keep an open mind.

The Piras took their leave, promising we could come back soon. Alain
proposed a group sleepover, and he and M. Pira exchanged parting jibes
about some snacks that were apparently infamous, maybe a good idea to
keep the doctor standing by. M. Pira made his Edme-like laugh again,
but the way he laid his hand on his wife's shoulder as they went inside
reminded me of how they'd looked in their masks a few weeks before.

The four of us lingered in the lane. Any minute the afternoon bell
would signal the end of lunch. Justine asked why I hadn't been in class that
morning, and I said it was a stomach thing. I started adding that since I'd
been excused from school, I was going to take the bus to vetting early—but
as the words left my mouth, I realized it was an awkward thing to mention,
and lapsed into silence. Jo just made a face.

You don't have to spare my feelings. Honestly, this isn't sour grapes, but
the Conseil is depressing, don't you find? The petitions are sad, rejecting
people is sad, and even when you give them what they ask for, it's not like
the viewings are a barrel of laughs either. She shuddered her shoulders and
smiled at me, sardonic and compassionate.

The bell rang in the distance. Groaning, the others started heading
back to Pichegru's classroom, but I stayed put. Alain noticed first. A look
crossed his face that was nearly earnest.

Ozanne, if you want to see him, just sneak around to his room. I use the
back window all the time. Then, with a sunny shrug, he took off running
for school.


Mindful not to be seen by his parents, I slipped behind the house. Unlike
the front's plainness, a vibrant ceiling of leaves spread over the Piras' backyard, vines weaving in and out of a pergola made from horizontal ladders
on poles. Grapes hung down from the wooden rungs. A hummingbird was

suspended in front of a homemade feeder, wings frantic and still. I stepped beneath the nectary shade.

The big back window was closed. At first all I saw in it was my own reflection. Cautiously, I cupped my hands to the glass and looked into Edme's room.

He was sleeping semi-upright in bed, leaning on pillows, his head relaxed and turned away. I saw a white bandage affixed to his temple, with a small stain shaped like a comma. His blanket had fallen down a bit, revealing the beginning of a bruise. I watched his narrow chest rise and fall. His violin case rested by his bedside.

In the coming days, as I transitioned out of vetting and into my apprenticeship, I would continue to recall Ivret's bearing toward me on the night Edme fell, and slowly realize what she had. Twenty years from now, the Piras would have no reason to go back and view their son. That afternoon, though, it was not yet on my mind, and neither was the question of how to tell Edme, this time, all that I knew, and what it might mean for us. Instead, gazing through the glass, I simply told myself I should leave, should catch the bus downtown, but I stalled, grateful to watch him breathe for just a minute more.

Then he stirred in bed. With a wince he adjusted his position, which made me feel ashamed to be there. I was about to back away when he looked out the window and saw me. There was nothing I could do. I offered a feeble wave.

He seemed surprised, but his expression cleared. He waved back, mimicking my sheepishness. I giggled aloud in the backyard. He glanced at his bedroom ceiling and pressed a finger to his lips.

It felt longer than a day since I'd seen him. I was relieved we weren't acting like strangers anymore. He gestured at his window. Really? I mimed. He nodded, so I tried to slide it open, but the window was unexpectedly noisy and I cringed. Edme almost burst into laughter—quickly his hand moved to his injured ribs and he caught himself in time. He gave me a ginger smile. Blushing, I started again, holding the window steady, trying to quell the rumble of the glass.

# Acknowledgments

Thank you:

To my incredible agent, Roz Foster. To the team at Frances Goldin, particularly Sulamita Garbuz, Tess Weitzner, Jade Wong-Baxter, and Caroline Eisenmann.

To my incisive editor, Loan Le. To everyone at Atria, especially Libby McGuire, Lindsay Sagnette, Stephanie Evans, Laywan Kwan, Jimmy Iacobelli, Jill Putorti, Paige Lytle, Shelby Pumphrey, Annette Pagliaro Sweeney, Elizabeth Hitti, Ali Hinchcliffe, Maudee Genao, and Sales and the Top Shelf Team. To Nita Pronovost, Janie Yoon, Sarah St. Pierre, Felicia Quon, and Adria Iwasutiak at Scribner Canada. To James Roxburgh at Atlantic.

To my invaluable early readers, Emily Bitting, Mike Chang, Tolmie Greaves, Joel Herman, Derek Howard, Haidee Kowal, Tara McDonald, Cass Picken, Ryan Van Huijstee, and Jan Zwicky.

To Chris Lupo, Sloan Whiteside-Munteanu, Michael Melgaard, and the staff of the Toronto and Vancouver public libraries.

To my parents, Gudrun and Mark Howard, and my parents-in-law, Russ and Deborah Greaves, for all of their encouragement.

To Alicia Merchant and Palmira Boutillier, in memory.

To Dara Greaves. Thank you for your brilliant advice and your love. This book is for you.

# About the Author

Scott Alexander Howard lives in Vancouver, British Columbia. He has a doctorate in philosophy from the University of Toronto and was a postdoctoral fellow at Harvard, where his work focused on the relationship between memory, emotion, and literature. This is his first novel.